END OF THE LINE

By ZOE MCGUIRE

Published by Aarluuk Press
Copyright © Zoe McGuire, 2017
This edition 2018

AARLUUK PRESS

Zoe McGuire has asserted her right under the Copyright, Designs and Patents Act 1988 to be identified as the author of this work.

This book is a work of fiction. The names, characters, places and incidents are products of the writer's imagination or have been used fictitiously and are not to be construed as real. Any resemblance to persons, living or dead, actual events or organisations is entirely coincidental.

All rights reserved. No part of this publication may be reproduced, stored in a retrieval system, or transmitted, in any form or by any means, without the prior permission in writing of the publisher, nor be otherwise circulated in any form of binding or cover other than that in which it is published and without a similar condition including this condition being imposed on the subsequent purchaser

ISBN: 978-1-980472-11-7

Original Cover Photo Mark Koellmann (Unsplash)

www.aarluuk.com

*The roaring of lions,
the howling of wolves,
the raging of the stormy sea,
and the destructive sword,
are portions of Eternity too great for the eye of
man.*

from
PROVERBS FROM HELL
by
WILLIAM BLAKE (1757-1827)

*For Graham Paton
— favorite uncle, firefighter, lost — not forgotten.*

1952-1991

END OF THE LINE

Friday

ANCHORAGE, ALASKA

Chapter 1

The 12" steel pick-head fire axe was not your classic gift for a girl, but at least the guys had made an effort; they had spray-painted the handle pink. The crew from the ALS Engine Company from the Anchorage Fire Department went quiet when Sandy presented me with the axe. Her eyes betrayed a mix of admiration and admonishment, and I knew what she was thinking: how could I leave when I was doing so well? By the end of the night, she would be the only female firefighter at the AFD, at least until they hired a new one. Alaska, I promised her on the day I quit, had the highest percentage of tough, professional, and cute women, in any state in America.

"Sure, I know," she said, "but they're not you."

"No, they're not. But I gotta move on, Sandy."

She didn't agree, and as I held that pick-head in front of me, doing my best to grimace at the pink handle, the words I had prepared for my thank you speech caught in my throat, and the best I could do was raise the axe above my head and yell, "Yeah."

It was enough. Short and to the point, and now we could get back to drinking.

"You'll call?" Sandy said as I rested the axe on the bar room floor and picked up my beer.

"I'll be working down the street, Sandy."

"Yeah, I know. But you'll call?" she said.

"I'll call, "I said and raised my beer. "To the AFD."

"AFD," the men and the last remaining female firefighter cheered.

Sandy shrank away as I swigged my beer from the bottle. I felt for her, really I did, but I just wasn't cut-out to be a firefighter. At least not forever. I thought about the last six years as I smiled and thanked the guys around me. We had seen our fair share of action, and they had done their best to shape my twenty-two-year-old enthusiasm into something close to professional firefighting. I would never forget that. But, after mom died, and when I started reading at night to boost my high school grades and get another education, I distanced myself from them. It was the beginning of the end. They knew it, I knew it, and when, at twenty-eight, I landed the Federal Emergency Management Agency job, the only consolation was that I hadn't completely sold out. I was still in the emergency business.

I took another swig of beer, grabbed my axe, and drifted to a quiet booth at the end of the bar. The soft cushion hissed as I sat down, resting the axe against the side of the booth. My aunt Maggie looked up as I set my beer on the table.

"That's a pretty axe for a young lady," she said.

"Isn't it."

"Every woman should have one."

"For a couple hundred bucks, every woman could."

"I'm guessing the paint is extra."

"Yep," I said and picked up my beer.

Maggie watched me lift the beer to my lips, and I drained it as she tutted and shook her head.

"I never did like you drinking."

"Neither did mom."

"Bless her," said Maggie. "She would be so proud of you today."

"And dad?" I said and pressed the cool bottle to my forehead.

"My brother is an idiot, Jaylen, but yeah, he would be proud. He wouldn't understand," she said. "He never understood much beyond guns and ammo…"

"Yeah, daddy's a real hick."

"No, not quite. He's a prepper. There's a difference."

"Sure," I said. "The difference is that mom had enough of that crap and drug me back to the city."

"She did," Maggie said and wrestled a nacho chip from beneath a blanket of cheese.

"Do you see him much?"

"I don't see him at all, honey. No-one does."

"No. I guess not."

That was the thing about dad, he didn't like to be seen. The last I heard of him, he had gone to ground somewhere around Fort Yukon, had built a fish wheel and was making a living off the land in Bush Alaska. The rumor was he had taken a wife, too – local native girl, not much older than me.

"Of course," Maggie said and nodded at the TV on the wall behind us. "Might be that your daddy was right after all."

"You believe that?" I said and glanced at the TV. They had been running the same story about a flu epidemic in the Lower 48 all day. I hadn't paid it much attention. "Crazy white folk, mom would say."

"She would know," Maggie said. "She married one."

"Yes, she did."

"She was the most beautiful girl I had ever seen. No-one knew what she saw in your daddy," Maggie said, and I remembered the gossip, as soon as I was old enough to understand it. No-one knew what it was that mom saw in him, but I figured it out, right about the time I started school.

"He was colorblind," I said. "That's what she saw in him."

"What are you talking about?"

"Mom came to Alaska from the South. Daddy was the first boy she ever met that was colorblind. Sure, he had a lot of faults, but the one thing he did right was fall in love with her. Not the color of her skin, the curly nature of her hair, the clothes she wore, and the accent she had. No, he fell in love with her, and she loved him back. Right up to the day she died. She just couldn't live with him anymore. That's what she told me."

"I never thought about it."

"Yes you did, Maggie. Everybody in the family did."

"Maybe." Maggie shrugged and took another nacho.

Truths can hurt both ways, and Alaska had a way of exposing them. Something about the rawness of it all. The wilds of Alaska stripped men and women to the bone. You learned fast who you could trust, who you could turn to for help. I considered myself African Alaskan, with my daddy's wild roots all bottled up inside my mom's ebony skin and gentle nature. Dad had got out once or twice in the past. The first time resulted in a suspension from school, and the second, on the worst night of my life, in a promotion with the AFD. The trick with my dad's nature was knowing when to let him out.

I tipped the bottle to my lips and licked the last few drops from the mouth before setting it down.

"That's one thing you got from your daddy."

"What's that?"

"Your love of beer."

"Love of beer? Seriously, Maggie, this is only my second tonight." I leaned back and waited for the story that I knew was coming. I had only heard it a hundred times already. Maggie's favorite. But then, it was about the only sweet story about my father and me that she knew.

"He would hold you to his chest and you'd be giggling and all that..."

I actually remembered. Maybe because I had heard it so many times. Dad always had a beer handy, and when he carried me in his arms, I would reach out for it, and he would let me take a sip. The smell of beer reminded me of him, the crazy old coot in the woods. The sad thing was, that was the only thing that reminded me of him, and when mom died in the fire, and the AFD pulled her out, beer was what stopped him coming to the funeral. And...

"I'm sorry, Jaylen," Maggie said.

"Sorry about what?" I rubbed my eyes before any tears began to well.

"Whenever I tell that story, it upsets you. Those big brown eyes of yours, they get even softer when you get sad."

"I'm not sad, I'm celebrating."

"That's right," she said, happy to change the subject. "Tell me all about it."

"Okay," I said, and then I paused, because that's when he came in to the bar.

Technically speaking, Nathaniel Canizales was a co-worker, he had an office right next to mine in the FEMA building, but I had seen him only twice before. The first time when I went to interview, and later the same day in the Walmart on A Street. I had noticed little about him beyond his tousled black hair that highlighted his dark chocolate eyes. Mexican born, he dressed like an Alaskan, denims and boots, topped with a check shirt and an outdoor jacket. He hadn't changed, I noticed, since the last time I saw him. He hadn't shaved either. He stopped at the door, scanned the room, and nodded when he saw me. His eyes lingered for a moment on the pink axe, and then he shook his head and walked to the bar. I watched him sit down and order a beer. He sat alone.

"Jaylen?"

"What? Sorry," I said and faced Maggie.

"Someone you know?"

"Kind of. His name is Nate. He's my co-worker. Sort of."

"Sort of? You're going to have to explain, honey."

I tried.

"The Anchorage FEMA office is a small one. It's more of a group of departments working together. Nate works for the city. He's an engineer and has the office next to mine, but he's never in it, or so the boss tells me."

"Your boss?"

"Yep," I said. "The Alaska Area Office Manager."

"Does he have a name?"

"Bob Andrews."

"So you're the Assistant Manager?"

"I am."

I could feel my cheeks flush as I said it. Of course, every time I got excited and proud about my new job, I worried about the responsibility. Bob had tried to reassure me when he told me that Alaskans can pretty much take care of themselves. And that most of what I would be doing is education, talking to schools about pre-disaster preparedness. In fact, he reminded me, paperwork was going to take up most of my time, and that was the only thing that concerned him about hiring me.

"Bob's worried that I am going to get bored."

"He is?"

"Sure," I said and hiked my thumb in the direction of my axe. "Too much paperwork and not enough action. Folk will need my help with flood insurance more than fighting fires, he said."

"But that's what you want. Isn't it, honey?"

It was. I had been a firefighter for three years when mom died in a fire in her apartment block. A laptop charging on a blanket started a fire in the apartment next to hers, and she died from smoke inhalation before we found her. That was the day I got my promotion. The day when I let dad out of the bottle. I pulled three people out of the fire before the guys had to drag me out. I was out of oxygen, out of energy, and out of luck. Mom died before I could get to her. But it was dad that made me keep going, his rage, best suited for the backwoods, was just what I needed to go back inside the building, and again, and again. I would have kept going, until I had used up every last drop of dad, and I would have died, too. But the guys pulled me out, saved my life, and the Fire Chief promoted me to the Advanced Life Support engine company. It was on the other side of town. I started night school a month later.

"Yes, it's what I want," I said, and I meant it.

Bob Andrews wasn't so sure, but he hired me

anyway. I told Maggie about the interview, and I mentioned the hours, and the pay, and the lousy vacation. She smiled and patted my hand.

"But you have weekends now. How about that?"

"Yep," I said. "And guess what? It's Friday. I don't start work before Monday."

"Your first weekend," Maggie said. She pushed the nachos across the table and I reached for them, my fingers poised to pull a chip from the cheese when my cell phone burred inside my pocket. "You going to take that?"

"I guess," I said and reached inside the cargo pocket of my pants.

It was a new cell, with only a few contacts added. The screen lit up when I swiped my finger across it, and my boss' name flashed in front of me.

"Bob," I said. "How's Seattle?"

"Are you in a bar?" he said. "Go outside, right now."

"Okay." I slid out of the booth and waved at Maggie on my way to the door. "I'm outside. What's up?"

I heard Bob take a deep breath, as I leaned against the hood of a Jeep; it was the smallest car in the lot. The Northern Lights drifted across the night sky, and I shivered for a second as the Fall air nipped at my skin.

"Jaylen," he said. "You've seen the news?"

"About the flu epidemic? Yeah, I've seen it."

"It's not the flu, and it is not an epidemic."

"What are you saying, Bob? I don't understand."

There was a pause, some static on the line, and I thought I heard Bob talking to someone, but his voice was muffled, as if he placed his hand on the receiver.

The line cleared and I heard a second voice, a female.
"Just tell her."
"But she doesn't have the authority…"
"Then give it to her."
"Bob," I said. "What's going on?"
"There's things you need to know, Jaylen, but you don't have the necessary clearance."
"What does that mean?"
"It means," he said, "I am promoting you, in the field. You are now Manager of the Alaska Office."
"You mean Anchorage?"
"No, I mean the whole state, for as long as it exists."

Chapter 2

As long as it exists. I was too wrapped up in my new responsibilities to think about what Bob meant about Alaska's future. The wind picked up and I tucked in between two trucks, sheltering from the wind and reducing the static on the line. I listened as Bob talked me through the things I had to do if I was going to coordinate Alaska's response to the pandemic.

"Hold up a minute, Bob," I said. "I still don't know what we're dealing with here."

"No," he said, and I could hear him sigh. "Okay, here's what we know."

Bob spent the next five minutes telling me everything the television companies hadn't. People weren't coming down with influenza, it was something much more sinister. It was also airborne, spreading from one person to ten more every minute. The FEMA office in New York had gone dark, with only a skeleton crew manning the phones for the entire city. Emergency service personnel, those that weren't already sick or dead, had been overwhelmed by distress calls, looting, and fires burning out of control. One city block, Bob said, had been burning for the better part of two days already.

"So the east coast in is a state of emergency?"

"Not just the east," he said. "This thing is spreading like wildfire, and there are no natural firebreaks. We're trying to shut the airports, but there's a bunch of pilots lifting off regardless."

"What about the highways?"

"They're practically closed through congestion. Everybody is trying to go west."

"West?"

"Canada closed its borders an hour ago. But that's not going to stop people from trying to get across. Even if they do get across, well… Canada is no better off." Bob paused. "Mexico, maybe. I don't know."

I noticed someone hovering by the door to the bar and I hunkered down, and lowered my voice. "What do you want me to do?"

"Homeland Security is holding the reins on this one, and that means us."

"Okay," I said.

"So, I need you to start coordinating with the Chief of Police, the Fire Chief, the Mayor…" Bob listed a bunch more people and titles. I lost count when I fumbled in my pocket for something to write with.

"Say again, Bob…"

"…everyone you think that might be important to get in a room together. Think basics: food, shelter, power, medical care…"

"Food, power… yeah, I got it."

"You have to close the borders, keep people in Alaska, keep others out."

"Bob," I said. The words caught in my mouth. "I'm not ready for this."

"No-one is. You're just going to have to deal with this one problem at a time."

"Yeah, okay, but…" But where to start? I had no idea.

"Hey, Lewis. You still there?"

"Yeah, I'm here."

"For what it's worth, I know this is going to be tough. My best advice is that you find someone you can trust. You can't do this alone." He paused.

"There's a guy out East…"

"East?"

"…Mark Erichsen – he's trained for this kind of thing. For when things get really ugly."

"Hey, Bob…" I took a breath to steady my voice. "East is no good to me. I need someone here."

"Sorry," he said. "I'm reaching just now. Find someone you can trust, someone reliable."

He said a couple more things, then the line went dead. I held the phone to my ear for about a minute before I realized he was gone.

"Damn." I stood up and stuffed my cell phone in my pocket. The wind caught the collar of my shirt and licked at my hair as I walked between the trucks and back to the bar. I needed to talk to someone. But the first person I met was the last person on my list.

"Interesting call?" said a woman; she stepped in front of me before I could open the door. She was familiar, but I couldn't place her. "I couldn't help but hear that you've been promoted."

"You heard that? Who are you?"

"Rachel Splint. I'm with the Daily News Miner."

"The press? I can't talk to you right now."

"No?" Rachel blocked the door. "From what I heard, there might not be a better time."

"What you heard?" I shook my head. "I need to get inside."

"First, just tell me what's really going on?"

I could feel my dad's genes unbottling, and I didn't want to let him out, not now. But the journalist was getting in my way and, well, I would have hit her if the door hadn't opened and two people walked out of the bar. I brushed past them and made my way to the bar.

I found Nate just as he was about to order another beer. He watched me as I sat down.

"Lewis," he said, with a dip of his head.

"You know my name," I said. "That's good. Uhm…"

"I was going to get another beer," he said. "You want one?"

"No, and you don't either."

"I don't?"

"No. We need to go."

I looked over at the booth to see if Maggie was still around. She was gone, but the journalist was on her way over. I slipped off the barstool and tugged Nate onto his feet. He frowned at me, and I mouthed the word *please*.

"Listen, Lewis…"

"Please, Nate, I need you to come with me." I gestured at the TV screen above the bar and said, "It's worse than people think."

"The epidemic?"

"Yes," I said.

Nate shrugged and pulled his jacket from the back of the stool. He tucked it under one arm and took out his car keys.

"We'll take my truck," he said. "Wherever we're going."

"Fine," I said and started to follow him.

"Hey, sweetie, wait a minute."

"I turned around to look at the barmaid. She held up one hand and then reached down below the bar. "You can't leave without this."

"Right," I said and took the fire axe from her hands.

"Your aunt said she had to go. She said she'll

call."

"Thanks." The weight of the axe felt good in my hand as I gripped it beneath the head. Whether it was the axe or the color of the handle, I'll never know, but it stopped Rachel Splint in her tracks, and I followed Nate to his truck without interruption.

I dumped the axe in the bed of the truck, behind the cab, opened the passenger door and climbed in. Nate pushed the key into the ignition, started the engine and then waited. I realized he was waiting for me.

"You gonna tell me where we're goin'?"

"I'm not sure. Just drive somewhere. Anywhere."

Nate pulled out of the parking lot and into traffic, slowing as we passed what looked like a panic at the drugstore. He nodded at the crowd of people spilling out of the storefront and the police doing their best to keep them calm.

"Is that what this is about?" he said and drove on.

"Maybe," I said. And then, "Pull in here."

"We're going to see a movie?" he said as he parked in a space in front of the Century 16 movie theater.

I waited until he switched off the engine, and for a police siren to wail into the distance. Nate scratched the stubble on his chin and, for a brief moment, our eyes locked, and then I looked away.

"Lewis?"

"Yeah, okay," I said and pulled the cell from my pocket. "I got a call from Bob Andrews when I was in the bar."

"I saw you go out," Nate said. "So?"

"So, I've been promoted. Area Manager for

Alaska. All of it."

Nate frowned. "You haven't started yet. What's going on?"

"Bob's in Seattle, and I don't think he is coming back. This flu epidemic, well, it's not influenza, and it's a pandemic now. It's global, at least I guess it is."

"So what we've seen on the news?"

"It's just the start of it. New York has shut down, declared a State of Emergency…"

"I saw that."

"And Homeland Security has given FEMA the lead on this one."

"So, bigger than Katrina?"

"This isn't a hurricane, Nate."

Two more police patrol cars wailed past, the emergency lights flashing through the cab as Nate tapped his fingers on the steering wheel. I imagined he was thinking about what to do next. I hoped so, because I was struggling to focus. Nate took out his cell and I watched him dial.

"I'll put the people in the room, but you're going to have to talk to them."

"What am I going to say?" I was going to say more but Nate raised his hand.

"Dave," he said. "Yes, I've seen the news. It's worse than that. Listen, I'm sitting here with the new FEMA rep for Alaska… No, it's Lewis…" he paused to look at me.

"Jaylen," I said.

"Did you get that? Jaylen Lewis. She's taking over from Bob Andrews. He's in Seattle. Not coming back. Yes, we need to meet. Can you get everyone together?" Nate tapped his fingers on the wheel as he pressed his cell phone to his ear. "Sure. See you there." He finished the call and tossed the cell phone into a well on the dashboard.

A cold hand clenched my gut and I forced myself to say, "It should be you talking to them. I don't know what to say."

"Neither do I, and don't let that fool you. Dave is a friend. He just happens to be the head nurse in the Emergency Room. He's on that list, just lower down, like me."

"And me," I said.

"No, you're at the top of that list now. Bob Andrews put you there. You'd better get used to it."

It was going to take some getting used to, but I didn't have much choice. I leaned back in the seat and closed my eyes. Nate was quiet, and I was grateful for the silence in which to think. If I was going to lead a meeting in response to a pandemic paralyzing the Lower 48, then I was going to need more information, details, and facts, so that we could prepare an adequate response. I opened my eyes and reached for the radio, pressing the button to turn it on. A preset rock channel burst through the speakers before Nate clicked through the buttons for a news channel. I nodded and we listened to the latest report about restricted traffic, huge crowds at the borders – all of them – and a request from the Governor of California for Orange County citizens, and people across the whole western seaboard, to remain calm.

"There's nothing new here," I said as the news anchor fielded reports from journalists and callers, trying his best to corral the different stories into some sort of order. I figured I had better start taking notes, as it would be my turn soon. I pulled out my cell and began tapping bullet points into a memo. "We're going to need more information before we can form a strategy," I said, as I recalled my course notes on emergency management.

"No," said Nate. "You don't have time to get bogged down in trying to figure out what this is."

"I don't? Then what should I do?" I said and let the cell rest in my lap.

"Lock the State down. We have emergency contingencies. Once we get them up and running, we can figure out the next step."

"There are contingencies?" I said and regretted it. Nate raised his eyebrow at me, and opened his mouth to speak. I cut him off. "Well, sure, okay, I know there are contingencies, but… give me a break, my job starts Monday."

"It's Monday," he said and shrugged. "Congratulations."

"Thanks," I said and managed to laugh.

"You're welcome."

"At least Alaska isn't affected yet."

"You don't know that."

"You mean the people at the drugstore? They're probably just reacting to the news." I thought about my father, and what he might have to say about it. "I mean, there haven't been any reports of crazy things happening in Alaska. You know, more than just Alaska-crazy."

The radio crackled as a local traffic warning cut into the news channel. Nate turned up the volume, his fingers frozen to the button as we listened to the reports of bush planes swarming into Fairbanks and approaching Anchorage as the skies filled up with nervous Alaskans.

Chapter 3

"There," I said and pointed at a gaggle of four bush planes heading for Ted Steven's Airport. Nate craned forward over the steering wheel and looked up.

"They're not waiting for permission to land," said Nate. "Just coming in one after the other."

"Three more to the east," I said as Nate drove into the parking lot at Providence Alaska Medical Center. He parked next to a bright red RAM Laramie Longhorn. It belonged to the new Fire Chief, newly arrived from Texas. Nate scanned the parking lot and said, "They're all here. You ready?"

"No," I said and opened the door. "But let's do it anyway." I looked up at the buzzing of three more bush planes flying low toward the airport.

"Better leave the axe," Nate said. "Pink may not be not so appropriate for your first briefing as FEMA Area Manager."

"You think?"

Nate locked his truck and I followed him through the main entrance. There was a bustle to the place that seemed to fit with Friday nights at the Emergency Room, except for the fact that we were in the administrative part of the building. The staff I saw running between wards and offices wore a strained look that suggested the need to hurry without really knowing why. I knew how they felt.

"There's Dave," said Nate. They shook hands and I waited to be introduced. I knew Dave Fob by name, but we had never actually met. He shook my hand and nodded for us to follow him.

"Everyone's here, and the coffee is on, and so is everyone's cell. It's like some crazy techno disco in there with all the different ringtones and message pips," he said and paused outside the door to one of Providence's conference rooms. "Everyone's a little on edge, and pretty much working through the playbook for emergency management. But no one knows what the emergency is." Dave faced me and said, "They're looking for answers. I hope to hell you have some." I nodded and he opened the door.

I walked in first and stood just inside the door and stared. The room was full of men. Half of them had a coffee in one hand and a cell in the other. The other half were bent over maps or stabbing fingers at manuals. The noise level peaked with barks and commands to assistants and subordinates, only to soften with calming words to loved ones. I dialed in on one in particular as the new Fire Chief, Mat Grolsch, talked to his daughter in Dallas.

"I know, baby, but you're going to have to be strong for momma. She's sick, I know, but you let your aunt go in there. I don't want you going in to see her, not until I get home." He paused and looked at me. "I have to go, baby. You put your mask back on now. I'll call you later." Mat ended the call. "Lewis," he said. "What can you tell us?"

The room stilled as the men realized someone new had arrived. They lowered their cells, straightened their backs, and turned as one to look at me. I heard Nate close the door and Dave move to one side. I felt very alone all of a sudden.

"Well?" said a man with a voice like metal being filed. It was Kent Wambaugh, Chief of Police. "This is your show, FEMA. What is this?"

"It's what it looks like," I said, surprised that my voice didn't falter. "It's a nationwide panic in response to a virus of some kind." The words began to flow as I pieced sentences together from the little Bob Andrews had told me. "Homeland Security has given this to FEMA to manage, but we're struggling." I waited as a few of the men nodded, while the others sipped their coffee and stared. "You all know Bob Andrews? He's in Seattle, and he's not coming back. He promoted me to Area Manager."

Wambaugh sighed and reached for his cell. He walked to the rear of the room and began to dial.

"Hey, Kent," Grolsch said. "You want to give her a moment?"

"Mat, I've got a mob at the drugstore, bush planes landing on the Interstate, and a line of people trying to start a run on the bank. It's closed, by the way," he said and shrugged. I heard Nate stifle a laugh behind me. "Fairbanks has been on the line since I got off shift, and the only good news is that the damned tourist season is just about over. When FEMA has a plan they can call me, until then…"

"FEMA's not going to call," I said, and then, louder, "We're on our own. Alaska is on its own."

"Then what do you suggest?"

The female voice startled me. I thought the room was full of men only. I turned to look at June Waverly, MD, Chief Medical Officer. She looked tired, and had a cell phone in each hand.

"We have to lock it down. The whole State. Close the borders…"

"That's not your call," said Wambaugh.

I looked at him and caught the steel glint in his eye. If there was a defining moment in my new career, this was it. I stared back and said, "It is now. Close the borders, Chief."

"That's up to the Customs and Border Protection…"

"Which falls under Homeland Security," said Grolsch. "For God's sake, Kent, you go drinking with Hayes every Saturday night. Call him."

"I like you, Mat," Wambaugh said. "But you're new here. Let me tell you how we do things in Alaska…"

"No," Grolsch said. "Let me tell you something. My wife is 4,000 miles away, and she's sick. My daughter is scared out of her skin, and my sister broke out in a sweat an hour ago. She's still caring for my wife because there is no-one else. The hospital is jammed, the streets are congested, and the paramedics have a backlog so long the city has started sending postal workers with first aid qualifications on house calls – anyone in a uniform. Now, if this thing is as bad as it looks, we're going to start getting sick people real soon, and then we're gonna have a manpower problem. No offense," he said with a glance to Waverly and me.

"What are your wife's symptoms, Mat?" Waverly asked.

"I don't know for sure," he said. He wiped his forehead. "She started with sweats, then headaches. She said her skin was burning up, and then she stopped texting. When my sister got there she said there was a lot of blood, and she was bleeding from her nose, her mouth." He paused. "She said there was blood coming out of her eyes, and from beneath her fingernails." Grolsch sat down. Waverly walked over to him and I heard them talking softly for about half a minute before Nate tapped my elbow.

"Keep it going."

Grolsch had created a vacuum within which everyone in the room seemed ready to listen. The men shared a mix of expressions ranging from pity for the Fire Chief's situation, to anything from mild concern to outright fear of how things might turn out, how they might affect them.

"We need to close the borders," I said. "Until we know what this is, we need to prioritize." I remembered Bob's words. "We need to secure food and shelter. We need to maintain power, clean water." I paused to catch Waverly's eye. "We're going to have to think about medical supplies, what we have, what we might need." She nodded. "And," I said and looked at Wambaugh, "we're going to have to think about a curfew."

"What?" he said. "And how are you going to enforce that?"

"National Guard?" I said. "I don't know, but we need to lock everything down. If people get sick, we need to know that they are contained, until we can get to them. If this is as bad as Chief Grolsch says…"

"It is," Waverly said. She stood up, one hand on Grolsch's shoulder as he steeled himself and looked around the room. "The symptoms Mat describes sound like a hemorrhagic pox. It's not good," she said and squeezed Grolsch's shoulder. "If it is some kind of pox, there may be other variations, different symptoms, but we need to get a message out. Something like this – and it seems to be an accelerated, aggressive pox to react so quickly – it could rip through a small community, and Alaska is one small community, with population pockets separated by geography. People are flying in to the city. We need to stop that, because if they're here to get supplies, when they fly back, they might take more than just groceries with them. And I don't have to tell you what will happen if they do."

Grolsch stood up and looked at me. "No offence, but we're going to need some bigger guns to make decisions at the local level. Where is the Mayor?"

"He's in Juneau," said Wambaugh. "We talked about an hour ago. His flight is grounded."

"What's the word from the capital?" Waverly said. "Have they been hit?"

"An hour ago it was a storm in a teacup," Wambaugh said. "They were pretty pissed that Canada had closed the border, and then even more so when the FAA closed the airports on the west coast."

"But he has the authority to enforce a curfew in the city," I said.

"Not without the Governor's approval," said Wambaugh. "You want to mobilize the National Guard? The Governor is the only one that can do that?"

"And where is she?"

"Polly Mitchell is in Washington."

"Has anyone called her," I said. I felt a rush of blood to my cheeks. "I'm sorry, I don't have any numbers on my cell."

Wambaugh grunted something about "next to useless" but Grolsch silenced him when he walked over to me and took my cell from my hand.

"I'll put in the numbers you need," he said.

"Thanks."

"This is your last day on the job?" he asked as he scrolled through a list of numbers on his cell.

"Yes."

"I heard about what you did in the fire that took

your mom." He looked at me. "That took guts. It took strength. Now," he said and gestured at the whiteboard at one end of the conference room. "Break this thing into boxes, start prioritizing, start giving orders. These guys," he said with a gesture that took in the entire room, "have the skills to get things done, and the authority to get people to do it. They just need someone to coordinate it all. That's you."

"Okay," I said.

"Remember your training, your studies, and break this thing down. You're new to FEMA, you lack experience, but it's not like you can't cope in an emergency. You've proved that."

I looked for the words, any words that might come close to thanking him for the confidence he was shoveling into me. He said I had strength, but what strength he had – knowing that his wife was probably going to die, that his sister might be infected, that his daughter was in danger, and yet, he was here, in Anchorage, doing his job. No matter what happened, I would remember Mat Grolsch's pep talk. It encouraged me to take the next step, and I could feel a little weight lift from my shoulders as I nodded and took my cell from his hand.

"Keep it charged," he said. "Always."

"Right," I said and took a step toward the whiteboard. He stopped me with a hand on my shoulder.

"What did they give you?"

"What?"

"Your farewell gift. I bet it was an axe."

"Yes," I said. "A pick-head with a pink handle."

"Pink," he said and laughed. "Well, an axe is an axe. Keep it close. You might need it."

"I will."

"And remember, you're still a firefighter, still one of us. Don't forget that."

How could I? With Fire Chief's like Mat Grolsch in the world, hell, everybody would want to be a firefighter. I stopped in the center of the room and coughed to clear my throat.

"Okay," I said. "I'm new at this, and I am going to need your help. I turned my head to slowly take in the room, sparing a precious second or two on each face, lingering for a second longer on Grolsch and Waverly's, a few more on Nate's. I stopped and focused on Wambaugh. "I won't tell you how to do your jobs, but let me be the one to try and coordinate the effort. We have a crisis, one that has nailed America, but we're Alaskans, and we're tough, so let's get this done," I said.

I didn't expect anyone to clap, so I wasn't disappointed, but by the time I reached the whiteboard, just eleven steps from the center of the room, I was impressed by the bustle of activity and low voices as the department heads began to clump in small groups of interrelated professions, before sending a representative to me to draw another box, write another heading, and add the name of the key people, in order of availability and expertise. I had bullet points prioritizing actions, and priorities needing people to action them.

Nate was one of the first to give me a box.

"Power," he said. "If people start to get sick, we're going to need it. It needs to be automated in the cities, the villages will have to keep those generators going as long as the fuel lasts. It'll be winter soon. We have to think long term."

"What do you mean?"

"Most of the villages use generators that run on oil. If they haven't had the tanks filled yet, we're going to have to get them filled before people start getting sick, and there's no-one to pilot the boats downriver."

"We could lose the villages."

"If people get sick, yes."

I sighed and made a note, the marker squeaked between my fingers.

"One more thing."

"Yes?"

"You're doing okay, Lewis. Just keep going."

I watched Nate walk away, chiding myself for the thoughts that ran through my mind as I looked at the cut of his jeans. "Keep it together, Lewis," I whispered. "We're in a crisis."

I looked away from Nate and caught a glimpse of Grolsch as he left the room, his cell phone pressed to his ear, as he wiped a tear from his cheek. I remembered his words and realized it was going to get ugly before the end.

Saturday

ANCHORAGE, ALASKA

Chapter 4

I'm a Dylan fan. I'm also a fan of the guy who pressed a coffee into my hand around three in the morning. I thought about the dawn, about what should have been my first real weekend off, with no shifts and no studies. I wasn't even officially employed yet. The coffee was stronger than I usually liked it, but I guess the guy thought I needed it. I sipped as I stared at the boxes on the whiteboard – it looked like a concept drawing of the Tetris game – and thought about Dylan's lyrics, how the darkest hour comes just before dawn. I was still thinking about that, tapping my foot to an imaginary beat, when the darkest hour came, and dawn was still a good few hours away.

"Chicago has gone dark," said the communications officer for the Mayor's office. "They won't respond, and any attempt to get through to any local government rep just gets forwarded to voicemail."

"You sure?" said Wambaugh. He dragged himself out of his chair, tossed his cell onto the table and walked over to the man.

"They just called it on CNN."

"Let me see." Wambaugh crouched beside the young man's laptop.

"There's something else. They're calling it the Fortune Cookie."

"Calling what?" I said.

"The virus. They say it was manufactured in Asia. There's more information being put up on CNN's Internet page."

The men and women in the room stirred from

the different tables they were sleeping at and I heard them murmur. Those with more energy than the others began to speculate, and I listened to a few theories being bounced around until I noticed Nate as he pushed aside a pile of manuals from the table by the whiteboard and leaned against the edge.

"You should sleep, Lewis," he said.

"No-one else is."

"Yeah they have. Maybe not much, but a little."

"I can't sleep now."

"Now is the only time you'll be able to."

"What do you mean?"

"In a few hours, folk will start waking up, turning on the TV. If they haven't spent the night watching the reports live, they'll be catching up, and they'll be scared. Wambaugh, over there," Nate said and pointed. "He's got a hell of a day ahead of him. He'll be catching five, maybe ten minutes shut-eye at a time on a couch in his office, if he is lucky. You and me…"

"What about us?"

"We have to be ready to pitch in and get our hands dirty – at street level."

"I'm supposed to be coordinating Alaska's response."

"Bob told you that, I know," Nate said and picked my cell up from the table. "When did you last speak to him? In the parking lot at the bar?"

"Yep," I said and sighed.

"You called since?"

"No."

Nate turned on the speaker and scrolled through my call list. When he found Bob's number, he pressed the screen to dial. I caught his eye as we listened to the busy signal as it beeped between us. Nate ended the call.

"My guess is it has been like that all night."

"Mine too."

"So. Time to catch an hour or two of sleep before we get to do this all over again. Come on," he said. "Waverly showed me a room where the medical staff crash out on couches."

"What about them?" I said, tugging Nate's sleeve as he started walking toward the door.

"They know how to reach you."

I followed Nate out of the conference room and along the hall to a large lounge with low lights. He guided me to a soft leather couch with a small coffee table beside it. There were three different cables taped to the table, and the head of the largest one fit my cell. It beeped once as Nate set it to charge.

"They think of everything," I said.

"It's not quite the sleeping quarters of Anchorage FD, but it'll do."

"You sure about this, Nate?"

"I'm sure. I'll wake you in two hours. Then we switch. Okay?"

"And if anything happens…"

"I know where to find you." He pointed at my cell. "And so does everyone else."

"All right," I said and lay down as Nate walked to the door. "Hey, Nate?"

"Yeah?"

"Mat Grolsch – I didn't notice him on the way out of the conference room. Did he leave?"

"His deputy came in about an hour ago. Grolsch is talking with his daughter."

"His wife?"

"She died, about two hours ago. His sister is unresponsive, and his daughter... well, she's got the sweats. It doesn't look good." Nate pressed his lips into a thin line. "Sleep while you can, Lewis." He left, closing the door softly behind him.

I lay down, closed my eyes, and ran through what we knew of the virus – the Fortune Cookie. It seemed to have a very short incubation period, during which time it was incredibly aggressive. I knew nothing about viruses, or their treatment, but I remembered reading about smallpox, and how it was eradicated in 1980. The method had been to draw rings around cases, isolating the virus by inoculating potential hosts with a vaccine – effectively starving the virus. That was going to be difficult with the Fortune Cookie. Especially if there was no-one left to vaccinate. Hell, we probably didn't even have a vaccination.

"It's not going to work," I whispered into the dark. My words burst against the ceiling and I caught the echoes in my mind.

Bob Andrews put me in charge of Alaska, population 750,000 give or take. Just under half that number lived in Anchorage. I started to do the math, and realized that, given the virile nature of the virus, and how quickly it was trashing the large cities in the Lower 48, it would take a couple of days, tops, to infect the city. The best thing going for Alaska was its geography, and the distances between pockets of people. Wambaugh closed the airport, but reports of bush planes landing on the interstate, even the roads downtown, were still coming in. Bush planes were one of the greatest communication links in the Last Frontier – they were vital to daily life. But if they couldn't be stopped, they might become the greatest threat to life in Alaska.

"We need to get people beyond the range of the bush plane," I said, casting my thoughts into the darkness. I spared a moment to think of my dad, smiling when I figured he was probably one of the few who saw this coming. But dad wasn't alone in preparing for any eventuality. Most of the serious homesteaders in bush Alaska were self-sufficient. "If they put a ring around their home, they might be able to hold out." I shook that thought out of my mind as I imagined just how people like my dad might protect themselves.

I looked at my cell, realized I was squandering my sleep on such thoughts. But Bob Andrews made me responsible for Alaska, and I figured it was the least I could do to try and save the State.

"But how?"

I rolled onto my side and stared at the opposite wall. Tacked between a thirsty cheese plant and a floor lamp, was a poster of the *MV Seward*, a mainline ferry sailing the Alaska Marine Highway System. I sat up and used my cell to search for more information. The *Seward* was 382 feet long, 85 feet wide, and had nine decks. It could hold 120 automobiles, sleep 320 people, and carry 500 passengers total.

"I bet it could squeeze a whole lot more inside," I said and yanked the charging lead out of my cell. I walked over to the poster and stared at it, tapping each of the decks with my finger. "What if the automobiles were Recreational Vehicles. Sure it could take less, but then we could have accommodation on the car deck." I traced my finger to the solarium deck, smiling as I saw the tents pitched right on the deck. "More accommodation."

I looked at my cell and scrolled through the information on the screen, stopping at the part where it described how the *Seward* was designed to serve as a command and logistics center in the event of a disaster.

"We've been going about this the wrong way," I said. "We're focused on stopping people from getting in, we haven't even considered getting people out."

"We going somewhere?" Nate said as he walked in. I looked at him and he gestured at the couch. "You didn't sleep?"

"Later," I said and slapped my hand on the poster. "I have a plan."

"You want to cruise the Inside Passage?"

"Maybe. I don't care where we go, I want to put about 1,000 people on every one of these ferries."

"That's a lot on a small ship."

"Sure, it can take half that number…"

"But you want to double that?"

"Yes."

"And so," he said and sat down on the couch. "Where are we going to go?"

"Where? Nate, that's not the point."

"So tell me."

"Okay," I said and crossed the room to the couch. The cushions sighed as I flopped down beside him. "I was thinking about smallpox, about how they put rings around it, vaccinating the people surrounding the virus. Starving it."

"There's been no talk of a vaccine, Lewis."

"I know, but hear me out. The problem we have is that people can come in to Alaska, by road, by air. They can get in and out of the populated areas, transmitting the virus. We're trying to curb that, to enforce a curfew, stop people's movements – at least, that's what we are going to try to do today. But it won't work. People will get around it. We can't stop them, they're Alaskans."

"There's a complement wrapped up in there somewhere."

"I know," I said and slapped Nate on the arm.

"Lewis?"

"Just listen, will you?"

Nate shrugged and leaned back. I scrolled through the information about the different ferries in operation, the different sizes and capacity. I could feel my enthusiasm cooling as I realized that few of them had the capacity of the *Seward*.

"You've gone quiet," Nate said.

"Yeah, there are some problems."

"Not least locating the ferries. It's not like they are all in harbor waiting for you to launch your grand plan."

"There's a ship tracker. Give me a second."

"Lewis," he said and pressed his hand on mine. "It's a nice idea, but, think about it. You're talking about an ark."

"No," I said and pulled free of his touch. "It's not an ark. And it's not just one. I'm talking about population pockets – putting people, Alaskans, out of the path of the virus. I'm talking about saving the State of Alaska."

"And I hear you, but who are you going to save?"

"Alaskans," I said. I could feel the frown pinching my forehead. Why didn't he understand? And then my brow softened as it dawned on me.

"You're getting it now, aren't you?"

"Yeah." I sighed. "How do we choose?"

"It's not like you can do a lottery."

"No," I said, and then I paused as I zoomed in on the live tracking – the *Seward* was in Whittier. "Maybe it's not about choosing who, but where."

"What do you mean?"

"Look, the *Seward*, it's right there, in Whittier."

"At the end of the line."

"What?"

"The railroad. It stops in Whittier. From Anchorage, you can't get any further."

"And there's a tunnel."

"That could be blocked." Nate stood up. "I can't say that I like this, Lewis. But if you're looking for somewhere to close off, Whittier is the place. Helicopters can get in, but not much else. Not if you close the tunnel."

"We could fill a train and send it straight to the ferry."

"In theory."

I imagined a scenario where Wambaugh would seal off the two and a half mile Anton Anderson Memorial Tunnel, creating a natural funnel through which we could screen people for signs of sickness, and… I stumbled on my next word: suitability. If this was the end, and if my purpose was, as Bob Andrews intimated, to save the State of Alaska then it was implied that I had to make some tough decisions. My pulse began to race as I remembered the time when I had made the toughest decision of my life – saving the people who could be saved, even when it meant losing my own mother. Perhaps, that lesson, that experience, if I could draw on it, would give me the necessary will to save the State, before it was too late.

"Maybe you should have slept," Nate said, as he

stood up. "Don't over think it. Put the pieces into play that you have. Let the chiefs follow their playbooks. Who knows, maybe we'll catch a break? Maybe the virus will stop at the border – like there's some kind of natural firebreak."

"No," I said and looked at Nate. "The only natural firebreak we've got is water, and following the playbook on this one isn't going to help. You heard the reports, they're saying the virus was engineered, that it's faster, more aggressive than anything natural. If we are going to beat it, we have to throw out the playbook, and change the rules of the game."

"But you can't choose who gets to live, who dies. You can't do that, Lewis." Nate drummed his fingers on the sides of his pants. "I don't think I can let you."

"You won't have to. We'll let geography and fate decide."

"Geography and fate?"

"Yeah," I said. I got up from the couch and walked to the door.

"Where are you going?"

"To save Alaska," I said. "You coming?"

Chapter 5

I was convinced, I could feel it from the tread of the soles of my boots through my body, with every step toward the conference room. I could also feel Nate, hesitant, just a couple steps behind me. The vibes he was giving out were strong, he was clearly not convinced and, I realized, he was unlikely to publicly give me the support I needed. But, if this was the end, and it certainly looked like it, then we had to act in a manner fitting that end. With or without Nate's support, I had to mobilize my plan.

The commotion we could hear inside the room as we approached the door worried me, made me pause with my hand on the door. And then the room fell silent and I walked in. The people inside wore the standard four-in-the-morning look, and yet, deeper than that, there was something else.

"Hi," I said, as I stepped into the room.

"Lewis," Grolsch said with a nod. "You'd better sit down."

"What's going on?"

"Latest updates," said Wambaugh. The forty minutes I had been away seemed to have aged him. I realized why when they brought me up to speed. "New York and Philadelphia have gone dark."

"The cities?"

"No," Grolsch said, "the States. They're gone."

"From what we know, what we can piece together from the different news reports, the virus has knocked out all the emergency and administrative services. The people on the sharp end of the stick, police, firefighters, paramedics, all hospital personnel... they can't adequately protect themselves from infection. They're showing symptoms within half a day of exposure, despite the protective measures they're taking." Grolsch sighed and tapped the screen of his cell. "Washington just released a statement. The White House has declared a state of martial law, and they have ringed New York with the military."

"And there's no telling how long they can hold out," said Wambaugh. "They are just as susceptible as everyone else. The only difference is 100 meters."

"100 meters?" I said.

"A perimeter." Wambaugh wiped a hand across the stubble on his chin and said, "Anyone stepping inside it gets shot."

The room went quiet again as the gravity of the situation sank in. I looked at Nate. Suddenly, my idea didn't seem so extreme, and the look he gave me suggested he was changing his mind too.

"What about you, Lewis?" said Wambaugh. "Any news from FEMA?"

"No," I said and looked at him. "I still can't get through to Bob Andrews."

"We're on our own," said Waverly.

"Yes," I said, "and I think we have to make some decisions."

"We're already making decisions," said Wambaugh. "Just without the Governor's approval." He shrugged and said, "We have a State to save, we can't wait for the approval of someone who may or may not be alive."

Grolsch nodded and said, "I agree with you, Kent." He took in a deep breath and then faced the room. "This thing is going to hit us hard when it breaks. It has already hit hard," he said and glanced at

Waverly. "I lost my wife a few hours ago. My sister is sick, and... so is my daughter. Even if I could get there, even if I could fly, I still wouldn't make it. So, I am going to take a few minutes in between, and each time I talk to my daughter, I am going to imagine it is the last time."

There were tears welling in the Fire Chief's eyes, and few dry eyes in the room. We all thought of loved ones, friends, anyone close. I wiped a couple tears from my cheeks and then, with a nod to Nate, I coughed to get everyone's attention.

"I have a plan," I said.

The room hushed for a third time and I almost staggered under the combined attention thrust in my direction. I hesitated when I considered they might be hoping I had a solution to the problem, some kind of miracle that would shut down the virus and save everybody, but a glance at the strain on Grolsch's face, and the grim look of determination that Wambaugh wore reminded me that a realistic, practical solution would be favorable to any kind of sentimental optimism.

"We can't save the whole State of Alaska," I said. "But the difference is, we know this is coming, and while that might be chaotic to manage..." I paused to nod at Wambaugh. "We can still manage it while putting a Hail Mary into place."

"Such as?" Wambaugh said.

"The *MV Seward*."

"The ferry?"

"Yes, as many ferries as possible. But the *Seward* is the only one at dock right now."

"In Whittier?"

"Yes."

Waverly tapped a finger on the table as she thought, and I waited for her to speak.

"What are suggesting, exactly? Are you going to use the ferries to transport people somewhere safe? An island in the Aleutians, maybe?"

"Kodiak could work," Grolsch said. "But," he frowned, "there's not so much room."

I tapped my leg and said, "I don't want to use the ferries to transport people to a safe place. My idea is to create a safe place on the ferry."

"Lewis," Wambaugh said, "do you even know how many people can fit on the *Seward*?"

"Maybe 500," I said. I waited as people reacted with a shaking of heads, a few exasperated laughs. "I think I can push that to 1,000. If we fill the hold with RVs, we can create apartments on the car deck."

"Apartments?"

"Yes." I looked around the room. The expressions they wore said it all. The young FEMA agent was out of her mind. So, I stepped up to the plate. "Listen, you're all thinking about the procedures we have in place, and you're relying on emergency and disaster plans that are greatly underpowered." I paused. "We're outgunned. When this virus breaks on Alaska's borders, when it spills over and starts burning through the population, we'll find out pretty fast just how unprepared we are. We have to stop playing by the book. We have to change the game, and," I said, and lowered my voice, "change the definition of a win."

"A win?" Wambaugh said.

"Yes," I said. "Bob Andrews put me in charge of the State. He promoted me and gave me the responsibility to save Alaska. You guys have spent the whole night trying to do that, and everything you did needed doing. But, and we have to understand this, the virus, this pandemic, is a species-ending event. We can see that. We can see where it is going, how far it will go, and how fast. We can't stop it."

"So your answer is to save a couple hundred people by putting them on a ferry and sailing them out to sea?" Waverly said.

"Yes."

"That's called running away," she said and shook her head.

"Are you going to be on that ship?" Wambaugh said.

"What?" I hadn't actually thought that far ahead.

"Because this is sounding more like a save-your-own-butt than a Hail Mary."

"Who gets to decide?" said the Mayor's assistant. "Is there going to be a lottery or something? What about my kids?" He stood up, pulled his cell phone from his pocket. "My wife is with her sister in Fairbanks. If they leave now…"

"Hey," I shouted as the room descended into chaos. "Let me explain." But no-one was listening. I looked at Nate and he shook his head. He knew how they would react, he practically told me as much back in the lounge. What stung most was the implication that I was going to try and save myself, along with a couple hundred people. I heard the words *frightened* and *FEMA* as they bounced around the room. I began to wonder if they were true, if I really was frightened, and had just packaged it up in a neat little plan that was less about Alaska than it was about me. It was Mat Grolsch, once again, who saved me.

"You're all frightened," he said in a low voice,

but as he stood up, everyone in the room stopped talking. "I heard about Lewis when I took the job. She's no coward." He paused to take a deep breath. "Lewis saved three people from a burning apartment building. She walked through the flames three times, in and out of the building, she was working her way toward her mother's apartment. She could have run straight to it, but she didn't. When she got there, three apartments later, her mother was dead," he said and looked at me. "The job came first. Today, more than any day, I understand that. Sure, she has a survival instinct, we all do, but that's not what this is about. I believe Lewis is working toward her mother's apartment, but she knows now what she knew then – it's not possible. We can't save the State, just like Lewis couldn't save her mother. But we can save people, as many as possible, but we have to act now. Is this a Hail Mary? Sure it is. It's all we've got. I say we do it, and I say we do it now."

"It's not going to be pretty," Wambaugh said. He rubbed his eyes. "Are you ready for that, Lewis?"

"Yes," I said.

"I'll block the road to the tunnel – personally – but I want you on the Whittier end putting people in the ferry."

"I'll do it."

"You can't do it alone."

"She won't have to," said Nate. I felt a rush of warmth through my body and I gave him a quick smile. "It's the least I can do," he said.

I looked at Wambaugh and said, "I thought about the train."

"Forget about it. You want RVs? You need the road. That's what I'll let through, enough to fill the car deck of the *Seward*."

"I'll fill an ambulance with medical supplies," said Waverly, "and crew it with paramedics. There's a couple I know, young, with two small kids." She paused to smile. "Alaska's future."

"Thanks," I said.

"Something else, I'll get hold of Christa Matthews. She works in pharmacology, here at the hospital. We can outfit a mobile laboratory and send it down with the ambulance. You'll need it if you're going to fight this thing."

"You'll need food too," said Grolsch.

"I'll arrange it," said a new face, at the back of the room, a woman the same age as my aunt.

"Sorry," I said. "Who are you?"

"Beth Kowalski. General Manager for *Fred Meyer* in Alaska. Waverly called me, suggested I come to the meeting."

"I'm glad you're here," I said. She smiled and then picked up her cell.

"There's just one thing," said Wambaugh.

"What's that?"

"You're going to need a Captain."

I could feel the heat in my cheeks as I realized my half-baked plan was just that – I hadn't stopped to think who would sail the *Seward*.

"There's two I can think of," said Wambaugh. "Both of them work for the Department of Transportation. They both know the *Seward*." He nodded at Waverly. "How's your brother-in-law doing?"

"Michael Berg. He's been on and off the wagon for three months," she said and looked at me. "He's a good Captain, he knows Alaska, but…"

"He's a drunk," said Wambaugh.

"Yes, he is."

"And the other one?"

"Neil Grace," said Nate. "My old boss."

"You worked on the ferries?" I said.

"He worked on the *Seward*," said Waverly. "Chief Engineer under Mike before Grace replaced him." She smiled at the look of surprise wrinkling my face.

"Grace is a real son-of-a-bitch, but he can sail," Nate said. "He's probably also the best navigator in Alaska."

"Where are they now?" I said.

"Whittier," said Waverly. "Within spitting distance of each other. But," she said, "if Mike's watching TV, my guess is he'll be too drunk to spit."

And those were our options. I knew I had to get to Whittier, and I would have to create some kind of funnel to screen people, before getting them onto the *Seward*, and to keep them off once the ferry was full. My stomach churned at the thought, and I realized I was going to have to dig deep to find the resolve to get this done. We all were.

I looked at Nate and he raised his eyebrows.

"You ready for this, Lewis?"

"No," I said, "but let's do it anyway."

Chapter 6

The sky was still dark when I walked out of the hospital. Nate pointed at his pickup and I waited for him to unlock it. My pink axe was still in the back. I waited until he was behind the wheel before getting in and shutting the door. It was quiet all of a sudden. Nate sat frozen in the driver's seat, his hands gripped the wheel, his eyes closed. I caught myself studying his thick black eyebrows, the lick of hair curling around his ear, the tiny white diamond scar on his chin. In the pre-dawn light, his face seemed to absorb the shadows, and a darkness descended upon him. I realized that I knew little to nothing about him, and his sudden silence encouraged me to find out.

"Nate."

"Yes."

"Are you all right?"

"Just thinking for a second," he said and opened his eyes. "We need some things."

He turned the key in the ignition and the engine erupted into life. Nate shifted into reverse and backed out of the parking space before pulling out onto the street.

"I was thinking…"

"Do you need anything from your car?"

I paused at the interruption and looked at Nate. His forehead was pinched in a frown as if he was working through a list.

"No."

"Your apartment?"

"Yes, I guess," I said and imagined the things I would need. But for how long? Packing for the apocalypse was not something I had anticipated.

"We'll pick up gas and then go to your apartment," he said. "Think about what you need – the basics, any medications, durable clothes, sanitary products."

"Sanitary products?"

"We don't know how long we are going to be gone."

Nate slowed at a line of vehicles at the tank station. It should have been empty at this time in the morning, but the driver of each vehicle had at least one jerry can beside the car. One driver, a Native Alaskan Elder, had four five gallon cans in the bed of his truck. He handed the fuel nozzle to his son after he was done filling the tank. I caught his eye as he leaned against the side of his truck.

"This could take a while," Nate said.

I looked over my shoulder and saw three more vehicles behind us; they were backed out onto the street. It was busier than usual. I wound the window down and listened to the hum of Anchorage in the early morning, and the distant wail of emergency sirens to the north and east of the gas station. There was a subtle beat beneath the buzz I usually experienced so early in the morning, like a dull thump of bass, but I couldn't put my finger on it.

"Breakfast is on me," I said and got out of the pickup.

"I'll be right here."

"What do you want? Anything special?"

"Coffee. Breakfast burritos if they have them."

"I'll see what I can get," I said and shut the door.

"Hey," Nate said, "give Bob Andrews a call."

"Right." I pulled out my cell, as I walked past the Elder. He waved me over and I stopped at the rear bumper just as his son started to fill the last of the five gallon cans.

"How much are you getting?" he said.

"Gas? Just a tankful."

"Get more."

"Why?"

"Something's coming. You should be prepared."

I studied the lines on his face, the wrinkles of his plaid shirt, and the buck knife clipped to the broad leather belt cinched around the waist of his jeans.

"You've seen the news?" he said.

"About the virus? Yeah, I've seen it."

"It's pretty bad. You're going to need more gas."

I nodded and looked at the man's pickup. It was in good shape, as was the man and his son. I caught myself mid-assessment and wondered if this was what I was going to be doing from now on – sizing people up, categorizing them as survivors, or people likely to perish. I could feel the blood pumping through my body as I experienced a surge of adrenalin, different to what I felt when putting out fires, more refined. I couldn't explain it, neither could I account for what I said next.

"You have a demountable cab for this?" I said and placed my hand on the tailgate of the man's truck.

"Yep."

"Okay." I glanced over at Nate as he pulled up next to the pump beside us. "Whittier," I said, as Nate opened his door.

"What about it?"

"Get your family and go there now."

"Why?" the man said and frowned. "What's in Whittier?"

"A ship, the *Seward*. It'll be sailing later today. Bring as many supplies as you can and head down to Whittier." The name caught in my throat as I saw Nate pause at the pump. He looked at me for a moment, and then pulled out the nozzle and started to tank.

"How do I know I can get my family on the boat?"

"I'll be there. I'll get you on."

"And who are you?"

"Jaylen Lewis," I said. "I'm with FEMA."

"Okay, Jaylen Lewis," the man said and took my hand. His grip was firm, his skin warm and dry. "I will bring my family to Whittier."

"I'll see you there." He let go of my hand and took the fuel nozzle from his son. He replaced the nozzle and waved as they got into the truck and pulled away from the pump. Nate called out as I stepped out of the way of the next vehicle.

"Careful, Lewis."

"Yeah, I know."

"You shouldn't play God."

"Maybe not, but perhaps someone has to." I dialed Bob's number and shrugged as I walked to the tank station. I could hear his cell ring and I pressed my cell to my ear. "Bob?" I said when I heard someone answer my call.

"No, this is Janine." The woman's voice was hoarse, as if she had been talking for too long.

"Are you with FEMA?"

"No, I'm with Seattle Smiles and Service."

"Who?"

"We clean the offices. I'm the cleaner."

"Is Bob there?"

"Who's Bob?"

"Andrews, he's with FEMA. You're using his phone."

"Honey, I've got so many cell phones, you wouldn't believe. They're just sitting here, on all the desks. I figured I better collect 'em, just in case someone wants to steal them."

"Have you answered them all?"

"Oh I was busy around two a.m., and then most of them stopped ringing. 'Cept this one. People been calling this phone all night."

"Who's been calling it?"

"They didn't always give their name, but I could see the caller ID on the screen, just below the battery bar – there ain't much left."

"Can you remember any of the names?"

"I can remember two of them. One was a Polly Mitchell…"

"The Governor," I said.

"I don't know who she was, but she didn't sound too good." Janine paused and I could hear her pushing a cart or something on wheels. I imagined her pushing it out of Bob's office and along a hall; her voice was louder when she spoke again. "There was another lady, a Mrs. Andrews. She was nice, said she was the man's wife – I guess the man that owns this phone."

"That's right," I said, as I walked through the automatic doors.

"She started crying, and it didn't matter what I said, I couldn't get her to stop. She asked me to give her husband a message…"

I held my phone to my chest as I ordered coffee, burritos, and donuts. When I put it to my ear again, I heard Janine cry out."

"What's going on?" I said and moved away from the counter.

"Oh my Lord," she said.

"Janine?"

"Oh my…"

"Tell me what's going on, Janine. Tell me what you've found."

I pressed my cell to my ear as Janine racked air in an out of her lungs, stuttering single words, as she described what she saw in front of her.

"There's a man, his face is covered in scabs, they're yellow, like huge cornflakes, and bloody, there's lots of blood."

"Janine, step away," I said. "Move away from that body." I lowered my voice as the employee behind the counter looked up.

"Oh my…"

I heard nothing more but the beep of a disconnected call. I swiped the screen to end the call and let my hand fall to my side. I imagined Bob's face, crusted with interconnecting lesions, and I thought of his wife, and what she might have said in her message to Bob – most likely her last.

"Lewis?"

I turned to see Nate as he walked along the aisle toward the counter. He glanced at his pickup parked out front and I heard someone shout as the lines to the pumps backed up.

"We have to go," he said.

"Bob's dead. I think."

"Who did you talk to?"

"A cleaner at the FEMA office."

"And he's dead?"

"Maybe."

The sound of more raised voices filtered through the automatic doors as another customer walked in. The woman walked straight to the cooler, opened the door and started loading her arms with bottled water.

"Your order's ready," said the young man behind the counter. I paid and Nate took the coffee and the paper bags with our breakfast. We walked to the door and stopped as an old man at the pump reached into his truck and pulled out a hunting rifle.

"Back away," he shouted, as he chambered a round.

"Lewis," Nate said as the doors opened.

"Yes?"

"Are you armed?"

"No."

Nate sucked at his lip and then nodded toward his pickup. "Come on," he said.

The man at the pump pointed his rifle with one hand at the first of eight cars in a line behind him. He pressed the fuel nozzle into what looked like a rubber reservoir in the bed of his truck. He started to pump.

"That's going to take a while," I whispered as we passed.

"Yep," said Nate as he opened the driver door and climbed behind the wheel. "People are getting too testy for five in the morning."

"It's nearly six," I said and closed my door. He handed me the coffee and started the engine. I fiddled the paper cups into the plastic beverage holders, spilling coffee as Nate slammed his foot on the gas pedal and accelerated into the street.

"What are you..." the words caught in my throat, as I saw the driver of the car behind the man with the rifle, step out and draw a pistol from his belt. He fired two shots into the old man's chest and then turned on his heel to point his gun at the next car in the line. "He just shot him."

"I know," Nate said, as he shifted gear.

"We're not stopping?"

"No. We're going to your apartment."

"But that man just killed someone…"

"That's right. He did. We're not stopping."

"But…"

"Lewis," Nate said, "we have to change gear, change our mindset. You said so. The rules are different now, and pretty soon there won't be any."

Nate's brow was pinched, like before, but this time his eyes were open, and when he looked at me, I saw a grim determination, a hardness to the surface of his brown eyes. It scared me for a moment, and I recoiled in my seat. The window was open, it caught my hair, and the fresh air triggered more senses. I looked out through the windshield, and to both sides.

"What are you doing?"

"There are no sirens," I said, and looked through the rear windshield. "Where are the cops? Shouldn't they have responded by now?"

Nate slowed for a stop light and said, "I need your address."

"What?"

"Where do you live, Lewis?"

"Folker Street," I said. "But Nate, the cops…"

"They're not coming. Like you said, they should have responded by now. So…"

"So?"

"So this is it. It's started."

"What has?"

"The beginning of the end."

Chapter 7

Nate turned onto Wright Street and stopped. The sound of gunfire rolled up the street from the gun shop and the flash of blue and red emergency lights licked at the windshield. I glanced at Nate and said, "Is this how it's going to be, from now on?"

"Maybe," he said and started to turn the pickup in an arc. "We'll go around."

He pulled onto East Tudor Road and then onto Folker Street, the red condominiums looked black in the low light of a late dawn. I thought of the park behind where I lived, where kids played and people walked their dogs. It was pretty, safe, and now there was a gun battle just down the block. Wambaugh's police officers had their hands full all across the city, and I began to wonder – when the panic really set in – if they would have the resources to block the road to Whittier. They were going to need help.

"How big is the police department in Whittier?" I said, as Nate parked outside the Campbell Condominiums.

"Not very. The Chief and two officers. Why?"

"Wambaugh is going to have his hands full." I gestured up the street in the direction of the gunfire, as I got out of the pickup. "We're going to need more help. If the Mayor's office mobilizes the Alaska National Guard..."

Nate shut the driver's door and leaned on the hood, drumming his fingers on the warm metal. He looked over his shoulder as the gunfire increased and then he said, "The Guard have families, too. Just like the police, all emergency services. I'm not sure what we can expect when the first person to get sick in

Alaska gets splashed across the media."

"You think people will abandon their posts?"

"Yes," he said. "What about you, Lewis? Any family?"

"Me?" I walked around the pickup, stopped beside Nate and stuffed my hands in my jacket pockets. "My dad went AWOL a long time ago. Mom's dead. Apart from my aunt Maggie, you're looking at it."

"Friends? Partner?"

"Single," I said. "A couple friends, not so close." I nodded in the direction of my condo, just to the right of where Nate had parked. "Let me get my things. It's this way."

I fished my keys out of my pocket and climbed the stairs. I could hear Nate behind me and the thought of how I had left my apartment flashed through my mind. I stopped at the door and looked at Nate.

"It's not pretty in here," I said.

"I can wait outside."

"I can just grab the things I need, and…"

"Just be quick, Lewis. We need to get moving. It's gonna take about an hour to the tunnel."

"Okay," I said and opened the door.

"I'll go wait by the car, see if I can get a hold of Whittier PD. Karl Stevens, the Police Chief… we know each other." He turned on the top step and then said, "Take only what you need. A backpack, no more."

"Got it."

Nate went down the stairs and I walked into my condo. It was just how I had l left it. The kitchen table was piled high with books, my laptop hidden between the peaks of required reading. I closed the lid and reached for the power cord, shook my head and grabbed two legal notepads and a couple pencils instead. I carried them into my bedroom, tossed them on my bed and yanked my backpack out of the cupboard. I stuffed my winter camping clothes inside, along with a sleeping bag, a pair of sneakers, and assorted bits that might come in handy – a headlamp, a pocket knife, and a compass. I kicked off my trail shoes, pulled off my jeans and grabbed my hiking pants – the ones with the deep cargo pockets. I had been on trips with one pair of pants before, but underwear was going to be a luxury – I stuffed four pairs of bras and panties into the space by the side of my sleeping bag. My buck knife – a high school graduation present from my dad – was on my bedside table. I clipped it onto my belt and pulled on my hiking boots, looking up as Nate honked the horn of his pickup.

"Time to go," I said and dragged my pack into the bathroom. I filled the top pocket with sanitary towels, painkillers and an old strip of leftover antibiotics. I stopped to look at myself in the mirror, smiled at the absurdity of it all, and grabbed my toothbrush.

Another blast of the horn forced me out of the bathroom and into the living room. I stuffed a duvet jacket – the pockets bulging with a beanie, gloves and a neck gaiter – into the top of the backpack and reached for the door.

I stopped in the doorway to look around the condo – my home since mom died. The thought of never seeing it again crossed my mind and I let the pack slip to the floor. The nights at the Fire Station had kept me away from my condo, but it was still home.

"Such as it is," I said, my voice startling me in the quiet room. I could hear the neighbors stirring through the walls. Someone turned on the TV and I caught the edge of panic in the newscaster's voice as he brought people up to speed on the latest developments. According to him, there had yet to be a reported case of sickness in Alaska, but...

"It's just a question of time."

Nate honked the horn and I made an impulsive grab for the two books on the coffee table in front of my battered couch. I stuffed Galway Kinnell's *The Book of Nightmares* and Jonathan Waterman's *In the Shadow of Denali* into my pack. Nate might wonder at my choice of reading for the apocalypse, but they were the last books I had read other than my studies, and I figured I might finish them before the end.

"The end." The words clung to my lips before tumbling to the floor. "How is this going to end?"

"Lewis," Nate called from the bottom of the stairs. "We have to go."

"Right," I said, as I grabbed my pack, locked my door and jogged down the stairs. I followed Nate to the pickup, threw my pack in the back. It landed on my pink-handled fire axe, and I felt a strange rush of warmth at the reassurance the sight of the axe gave me. "I might need that before the end."

"What might you need?" Nate said and I climbed inside the cab and shut the door. He backed out of the parking space and headed back to the main street.

"My axe. Grolsch said I might need it."

"Yep," he said. "I reckon you might."

Nate accelerated through a red light, ignoring the

blast of horns behind us. He glanced at me and tapped the clock mounted on the dash.

"I talked to Karl. He's going to put an officer at both ends of the tunnel. He'll meet us on the Whittier end. But we have to get going."

"How do you know him?"

The corner of Nate's mouth twitched, but if he was going to smile, he suppressed it. "We have some history. It's not important. Anyway, I told him about our plans for the *Seward*, and he said he'll make the necessary calls."

"He's going to contact the Department of Transportation?"

"No," Nate said. "He'll do it all locally, organize things that end. No sense in contacting the head office, when all the crew live in, or are staying in Whittier."

"And the Captain?"

"Captains – we still don't know if we're going with Berg or Grace." Nate paused to overtake a bus. "He said he'll find both of them."

I leaned back in my seat and thought about the next step to Whittier. If he had the means, Wambaugh should have set up the roadblock on Portage Glacier Road. I pulled my cell from my pocket and then looked up as Nate pulled to a stop in front of a house opposite Wickersham Park.

"I'll be a minute," he said, as he got out. He left the engine running.

I scrolled through the numbers Grolsch had put in my cell and called Wambaugh, the dial tone sounded slow, tired almost, as if the line had been in constant use, which I knew it had.

"Chief," I said, when he answered. "It's Lewis.

I'm about to leave for Whittier."

"You're still in the city?"

"Yeah, we've had to grab some things…"

"Damn it, Lewis, you have to get out, now."

"What's going on?" I said. I could feel the pinch of my brow as I strained to decipher background noise on the line. "Are you at the airport?"

"Watch that exit, keep it closed, damn it…"

"Wambaugh?"

"Yes, damn… yeah, I'm at the airport. We've got a Cessna Grand Caravan on the apron, just in from British Columbia."

"Okay," I said. I heard a car door open and the background noise receded. I imagined Wambaugh sitting inside a patrol car. There was an edge to his voice, different from his abrupt get-the-job-done voice. It sounded like fear.

"There's ten people stuffed into the plane," he said. We've got it ringed. I've got my men on the doors, they're taping it closed with duct tape – it's all we've got. We pulled out the masks from the medical kit in the patrol car, but… Hell, Lewis, I don't know if it is enough."

"Enough for what?"

"To stop the infection. I mean, if the doors are shut…"

"What's in the plane, Wambaugh?"

"The passengers are sick, Lewis. The virus is here, it's in Alaska."

I bit my lip. I didn't even realize until I could taste blood on my tongue. The pinch on my brow disappeared and I felt clammy, as cold sweat beaded on my skin. I looked through the windshield at Nate, barely registering the huge pack on his back, and the weapons case he carried in each hand. He frowned at me, mouthing the question *What?* as he dumped his gear in the bed of the pickup and got in.

"Lewis?"

"Is that Nate?" Wambaugh said.

"Yes," I said and pressed my cell into Nate's hand.

"Who's on the line?" he said, as he held my cell to his ear. I studied his face as he listened to Wambaugh describe the situation at the airport. Nate grunted a response and ended the call. He gave me my cell, shifted into reverse, and backed out of the drive.

Neither of us said a word as Nate drove west on East Tudor Road and took the on-ramp on the Seward Highway, heading south. The traffic was light but confused, as if the people didn't know just how fast, or in what direction they should drive. Wambaugh had the virus contained for the moment at the airport, and so long as his officers didn't call anyone, so long as no-one knew, there was no reason for people to leave Anchorage.

Nate pointed through the windshield. "Wambaugh has two patrol cars on the highway, just north of Rabbit Creek," he said and accelerated. "We have to get to the mouth of the tunnel before word breaks about the Cessna. Two guys won't stop a city on the run."

"No," I said. "But neither will one guy at the tunnel."

"We'll block it with something."

"What?"

"I have no idea, but we have an hour to figure it out."

I caught a yawn as Nate overtook a large pickup with a cab on the back. The passenger waved as we passed and I recognized the Native Alaskan from the tank station. I waved back and enjoyed a small but significant feeling of optimism. The plan, at least the beginnings of it, seemed to be working.

"Don't get too excited," Nate said. "That's one RV, one family..."

"On their way to Whittier, yes," I said. "That's what we want."

"I know, but..."

"But when there's a hundred RVs, and another two hundred vehicles, it won't be so easy." Nate glanced over his shoulder at the gear in the back. I followed his gaze and saw the weapons cases.

"What's in there?"

"An M4 assault rifle and a Vector ACP submachine gun." Nate caught my eye. "I'm not a gun freak," he said.

"No? An assault rifle and a submachine gun?"

"This is going to get ugly before the end, Lewis. You need to understand that."

"I do," I said, and turned away.

We pulled ahead of the RV and Nate reached for his coffee. "It's cold," he said and put the cup back in its holder. He reached for a breakfast burrito, peeling the wrapper away with his teeth and taking a large bite. I listened to him chew for a moment and then reached for a donut. We ate in silence, sipping cold coffee until Nate slowed at the flash of blue and red emergency lights.

"This is it then," he said. "The first hurdle."

"They're going to let us through, Nate, that's part of the plan."

"Sure they are…" Nate paused to look in the rear-view mirror.

"What is it?"

"The second hurdle." He tapped the mirror and I turned around and stared at the traffic crowding the highway behind the RV. "Someone talked," he said and shrugged. "The Cessna isn't a secret anymore."

"No. I guess not."

Nate slowed to a stop in front of the police patrol cars, the spike strip just visible on the asphalt between them. The police officers looked nervous, their knuckles white around the grip of their pump action shotguns. Nate wound down the window. The officer took a step toward us. Nate opened his mouth to speak, but the man looked away, raised the shotgun to his shoulder and squared his feet into a fighting stance. I looked behind us and discovered why.

Chapter 8

There are two lanes running in each direction on the Seward Highway, all four of them were in use, and all the traffic was heading south. As the first wave of vehicles approached the roadblock, smaller vehicles slipped out of the pack and bumped along the grass between the lanes, others swerved into the emergency lane. The policeman with the shotgun moved to lean against the side of his patrol car, while his partner dipped his chin and spoke into the radio clipped to his vest. I looked at Nate.

"We have to get to the tunnel," I said. "We have to be first."

He grunted something and shifted into reverse. Nate pulled away from the roadblock and braked to a stop after just ten feet. "Look for a friendly face," he said and bumped the pickup over the grass dividing the lanes and parked it across what should have been the northbound lane leading into the city.

"What are we doing?"

"Improvising," he said, and opened the driver's door. "Get your gear."

I followed Nate out of the pickup, grabbed my pack from behind the cab and shrugged it on to my shoulders. Nate did the same, pulling out the first and then the second of the weapons cases. He opened the longer of the two and removed the assault rifle. He nodded at the second case.

"Take that one, and don't forget your axe."

Nate's hands moved swiftly over the weapon, and I made a note to quiz him on his background when I had the chance. I leaned over the side panel of the pickup, curled my hand around the shaft of the axe, just below the pick head, and held it by my side. I walked around the vehicle and stood next to Nate. The policemen moved their patrol cars either side of Nate's pickup, and put out two spike strips to stretch the roadblock across the four lanes, leaving a gap where the grass grew. The policeman who had flagged us down approached us, gripping his shotgun in both hands.

"Wambaugh said I should ask for Lewis," he said, and looked at my axe.

"That's me," I said, and scanned his face. I didn't recognize him, or his partner. "Are you new to Anchorage?"

"Wambaugh pulled us in from Wasilla," he said and added, "away from our families."

"Okay." I looked at Nate, as he finished checking his M4. He nodded that he was ready and slipped past the police officer to take a position at the rear of the patrol car closest to the gap. "We need to slow them down," I said and pointed at the approaching wave of vehicles fleeing the city. "We need a head start, so we can get to the tunnel before them."

"You going to Whittier?"

"Yes."

"What's in Whittier?"

Nate caught my eye and I saw him shake his head. The officer changed his grip on his shotgun, ever so slightly, but enough to suggest he was uncomfortable, and likely thinking of his family less than an hour's drive to the north. Even if they didn't have a car, he could call ahead, have them pack while he drove to collect them. They could be at this spot and on the road to Whittier two hours later. That was what I imagined he was thinking; it's what I was thinking.

"You know what's going on?" I asked.

"I've heard the news," he said and glanced over his shoulder as the vehicles approached to within a quarter mile.

"Then you know we're in trouble."

"Yeah, I got the impression."

"We're mobilizing the National Guard."

"Who is?"

"FEMA, the Governor's office. We need to lock things down, and try to get a handle on what's happening."

"Can't lock down a virus," he said. "My wife's a nurse. She says nothing can stop what's coming."

"She's right," I said, "but we have to try."

He turned to stare at the people fleeing the city, and I saw what I imagined to be a range of emotions, as they stitched his face into worry, a conflict between duty and survival, between the good of the many, versus the good of the few – his own family. When he turned back, I knew he had made a decision.

"We won't be able to stop them," he said.

I held my breath for a moment as he chewed at his lip. The sound of a helicopter approaching from the city made us look up. The blue and white Eurocopter AS350 circled overhead and hovered on the south side of the roadblock. The pilot waved as he settled the aircraft onto the highway, a B3 variant suited to Alaska's mountainous terrain and operated by the Alaska State Troopers. Four troopers exited the helicopter and jogged over to join us.

"Mike Nicholls," said the tallest of the troopers. He thrust his hand out and I leaned the axe against my leg to greet him. "Wambaugh said I should look for a firefighter posing as a FEMA agent." He grinned and pointed at my axe. "That's gotta be you."

"Yep," I said and let go of his hand. "Talk about timing. We need to get to the tunnel. Can you take us?"

"That's the one thing I can't do," he said. "We're the quick response team. We need the chopper. But we're here to help with the roadblock. Wambaugh briefed my boss, and we're going to get you to the tunnel." He looked at Nate's pickup. "Of course, that's parked real nice. We'll be in a bind if we have to move it."

"The keys are in the ignition," Nate said as he walked over. "We'll find another ride. Won't we, Lewis?"

That friendly face, I had forgotten to look for it. I turned to study the approaching vehicles and saw a familiar pickup with a dismountable cab, there were fuel cans strapped to the sides, and an assortment of spades, picks, and hammers clamped between them. As the driver slowed, I saw his face and recognized the Native Alaskan from the gas station.

"That one," I said and pointed.

"Okay," Nate said. "We're moving. Grab the case, and let's go."

"We'll do what we can here," said Nicholls, as his men spread out along the roadblock. The rotor wash from the helicopter licked at their uniforms as they held their weapons in the ready position. The police officer with the shotgun walked between the vehicles and waved our ride to a stop. The vehicles behind it slowed apart from one small Volkswagen that accelerated out from behind the first rank and slipped onto the emergency lane, heading for a gap to the left of the patrol car furthest from where we stood. The second police officer and a State Trooper ran toward it as the pilot lifted the helicopter off the ground and flew an intercept course.

"How bad do we need to stop folk?" Nicholls shouted.

"We don't know if the occupants are infected," I said. I looked at Nate.

"Stop the car," he said. "Whatever it takes."

Nicholls grabbed the radio clipped onto his vest and yelled into it. My fingers turned white as I gripped the axe, my stomach turning at the order given, and the aggressive pitch of the helicopter as the pilot flew low over the highway. The driver of the Volkswagen accelerated, swerving to avoid the skids of the helicopter only to spin off the emergency lane and up onto the grass embankment to the side. The thin wheels of the small European vehicle spun as they skidded on the grass, the driver's side lifting as the gradient of the bank increased. I held my breath as the helicopter veered away and the Volkswagen rolled onto its roof, the crunch of metal lost in the roar of the helicopter.

"Lewis," Nate said and grabbed my arm. "We're leaving."

"Go," said Nicholls. "We'll take care of this."

I called out over my shoulder, as I stumbled after Nate, "We want RVs, families, anyone not sick."

"How will we know?" Nicholls shouted as Nate pushed me toward the rear of the cab.

"Lesions and sores, high temperature," I said, "and blood. They might be hemorrhaging."

I saw Nicholls nod before Nate pushed me up the two-step ladder at the back of the pickup and inside the cab. The smell of herbs tickled my nose and I looked up to see bunches of grasses and tiny-leafed plants tied and hanging from small hooks beneath shelves busting with foodstuffs. Nate pushed me further in and I bumped into a tiny girl with long black hair and huge brown eyes. She stared at the axe in my hand, reached out, and plucked it from my fingers. She dragged it across the patch of carpet in the entrance and leaned it in a corner next to a shotgun and a rifle. I heard Nate thank the police officer, wish him luck, and then close the door to the cab. We bumped each other with our packs, shrugged them off our shoulders and held them next to our legs as the pickup pulled away and through the roadblock. Nate unslung his rifle and held it by the barrel against his leg. The girl stared at us.

"Hi," I said. "Are you alone?"

She shook her head and pointed up. I followed her finger and saw three sets of eyes beneath thick black bangs of hair as the girl's siblings peeked at us over the lip of the sleeping area above the kitchen. They giggled as we swayed to the motion of the pickup.

"My name is Jaylen," I said, as I reached behind me. "This is Nate." He waved and we received another round of giggles in response. I looked at the girl again. "Can we talk to your daddy?" She nodded and scrambled up onto the sofa at the end of the cab. She gripped a hatch with tiny brown hands and slid it to one side. The morning light lit the interior and I recognized the face of the young man that had filled the gas cans earlier that morning. He smiled and pointed at the girl.

"Nukka," he said, and then pointed at each of the

children hanging over the side of the bed. "Panik." A girl. "Suluk," he pointed at the thin boy in the middle, "and Miki." Another boy, the smallest of the four children.

"And your name?"

"Innuk, or David. And this is Aatag."

"It means *dad*," said the driver, as he turned and waved through the hatch. "Nice to see you again."

"You took my advice," I said.

"I did. It's too late to go home. We will come with you."

"Where's home?" asked Nate.

"Koyukuk. A small village, a long way from here."

I remembered reading about it, back when dad was gathering books and trying to convince my mother to go with him into the bush. Koyukuk was thirty miles or so downriver of Galena, on the Yukon River, a very long way from Anchorage. I started to speak but stopped when Nate pressed his hand around my arm. I caught his eye and he lifted his head to look up at the children.

"Listen," he mouthed.

As the children settled and the men in the front of the pickup turned around, I heard a faint groan, as if someone was in pain or unwell. Nate tugged at my arm as I took a step forward.

"Careful."

I nodded and lifted my foot onto the first rung of the ladder leading up to the raised bed above my head. The children retreated to the side furthest from me as I peered over the lip of the ladder. A small woman – her face thin, her forehead sweaty – opened her eyes and looked at me, it took her a few moments to focus.

"Hi," I said.

The woman blinked once, and then rolled onto her back as I stepped off the ladder and bent down next to the hatch.

"Aatag," I said. "Is that your wife in the bed?"

"Yes," he said, as he caught my eye.

"Is she sick?"

Aatag gripped the wheel and looked away. He reached for the soda in the cup holder and took a sip through the straw. I waited as he put it back. The highway slipped beneath the hood of the pickup as he settled behind the steering wheel and took a long breath.

"Yes," he said, and exhaled. "Since yesterday."

Chapter 9

As a firefighter, I learned to face fear, The dangers were real and we all took chances, but it was always calculated, we knew who had our back, and that we could trust them. Rarely were we in a situation that was out of our depth, or beyond our control. We trained for it, planned for it, and implemented both regardless of whether we were fighting fires, pulling people out of car wrecks, or searching for victims beneath collapsed buildings. We were, more or less, protected with our gear; training and teamwork took care of the rest.

I wasn't trained for this.

I certainly didn't have the gear for it.

The only thing I had going for me was my partner – I realized Nate had not left my side since I hijacked him in the bar. He had steered me on this course with gentle nudges along the way, and now he was going to pay for it, with his life.

I felt his breath on my cheek as he leaned close and whispered, "We need to know how sick she is." He stepped around me.

"No," I said, "I'll look. It's my fault. I chose this vehicle."

"If this is the virus, we're already infected. All of us." Nate worked his lips into a flat smile. "I'll look."

I watched as Nate climbed the short ladder and squirmed onto the bed, his back hunched beneath the metal ceiling. I crawled around the couch and pressed my body close to the hatch into the driver's compartment. Aatag glanced at me and took another sip of soda.

"Is it just your wife who is sick?" I asked.

"Yes. Sierra complained of a headache yesterday."

"And today?"

"I have been busy," he said. "She was alone with the children all night, before I picked them up this morning."

I looked up as Nate wormed his way onto the couch beside me. Nukka retreated to the far end of the couch – not a long way by any stretch, but enough to put some distance between us. She cuddled her knees to her chest, her eyes fixed on Nate.

"I'm not a doctor," he said, "but I found this." Nate tapped his finger on the surface of the table and the remains of a bloated black insect slipped off his nail.

"What is that?"

"It's a tick. I found it on her chest. Reports of ticks have been increasing over the past few summers." He paused as I raised my eyebrow. "I hunt," he said. "I also read, and there have been a few articles about ticks recently." Nate leaned around me to speak through the hatch, I could smell the tang of his deodorant, mixed with a touch of sweat – adrenaline, I wondered, and pushed the thought from my mind as he spoke with Aatag and his son. "I think your wife has something like Rocky Mountain Spotted Fever. That explains the headaches, the sweating, and the rash. Do you have any antibiotics?"

"In the first aid kit," Aatag said, and I could hear the relief in his voice. "Nukka, show the man where we keep the medicine."

Nukka slipped beneath the table and crawled between our legs to the cupboard closest to the door of the cab. She returned with a small wooden medicine chest. Tucked between the tubes and bottles of prescription drugs were tiny cloth and leather bags, wooden tubes, and plastic pill boxes. Nukka reached inside the chest and began to sort the contents onto the table.

"Nukka is apprenticed to a shaman in Koyukuk," Aatag said. "She is going to be a medicine woman."

Nukka looked up and beamed a broad smile at her father. He winked and turned away to concentrate on the road. With tiny fingers, Nukka flicked her way between the medicines and tugged on a foil strip with enough tablets for ten days.

"That one?" I said, and took the strip from her fingers. She nodded and went back to the kitchen. Nukka poured a glass of water from a cooler and carried it to the ladder. Suluk reached down and took it from her. I read the name of the tablets on the foil and pressed a single tablet into Nukka's hand. She carried it up to her mother.

"Dodged a bullet," I said and leaned back.

"Maybe. But there are going to be more bullets," Nate said. "We can't dodge them all."

I closed my eyes and listened to the sound of the asphalt burring beneath the tires. We had an hour before we reached the entrance to the tunnel. I thought I could use it to catch up on a little sleep. The vibration and ring of my cell phone shook that thought from my head as I sat up and pulled the cell from my pocket.

"Waverly," I said as I read the caller ID, "how is it going?"

"Not good. You heard about the Cessna at the airport?"

"Yes."

"It's the virus, all right. We now, officially have a case of the Fortune Cookie in Alaska."

I looked at Nate to see if he had heard, his expression said it all.

"Is it contained?"

"Yes," she said, "but it wasn't pretty. Wambaugh authorized maximum force to keep the passengers inside the plane, but they opened the door anyway, and one of his men opened fire. The passengers retreated back inside, and another officer ran to close the door."

"But he would have been exposed," I said.

"He was. Wambaugh yelled for him to stop, but it was too late. Now he's in quarantine inside an ambulance parked on the apron. There's a cordon around both vehicles, but it's unlikely to contain the virus for long." Waverly paused. "It's pretty chaotic up here. My people are scared, several have called in sick."

"Already?"

"They're not actually sick, but they don't want to work in case they get infected. The media is really churning things up. That reporter…"

"Rachel Splint?"

"That's the one. She's seen her big chance, and she is going for it – the uglier the news the better. She has people hanging on her every word. The trouble is, I think she is right, there is no stopping this. It's just a matter of time."

"Waverly," I said, "I have to ask…"

"About the supplies? Sure, that's why I am calling. I am blue-lighting them to you. Matthews and her driver are right behind them in the mobile lab – another ambulance. They are on the way, with the family I told you about. If this is the end, and I have an idea it might be, well, I can't think of a nicer family to shape a new Alaska."

"Or a new world," I said, my voice faltering.

"If it comes to that... there's still little word from Europe, and nothing from Africa. Asia has been hit hard, and the Arab states. There's a suggestion that it might have been engineered that way, or at least deployed in the east."

Deployed. I chewed over the word and then, as Waverly said she had to go, I remembered to ask about Grolsch.

"He lost contact with his daughter about an hour ago. Since then, well, he's out on the street. He hasn't checked in."

I didn't hear much more of what Waverly said. We finished the call wishing each other luck, hoping there was enough to go around. I ended the call with a swipe of my thumb across the screen. I was still wrestling with the idea of a virus such as this being deployed, and wondering if it was bio-terrorism, and, if it was, was it released by a group or a State?

"What if it was a State?" I said and looked at Nate.

"What?"

"What if a State released the virus – deployed it. That would be an act of war."

"Yes, it would."

"Are we at war?"

"If we are," he said, "we don't have the luxury of worrying about it. We have to get on that ferry."

"You've come around to the idea," I said, and smiled, grateful of the opportunity to push the thoughts of war to one side. My smile faded when I realized that a pandemic was hardly any better.

"Given what is going on, however much I don't like the idea, it's the best one we've got."

I flicked at the dead tick on the table.

"Don't," Nate said and pulled a tissue paper from his pocket. He scooped up the tick and reached over to a small trashcan to deposit it. "It's full of blood. We might have got away with that one, but we still have to be careful."

"Sure," I said and looked at him. "You said you had an idea about getting people onto the ferry. How?"

"We need to sort them, identify any who are sick, who might have the virus."

"That won't be fun." I imagined a mass of terrified and angry people, shoving at fences, trying to force their way onboard the *Seward*. It was a disturbing image.

"There will be lots of containers in Whittier. If we get there fast enough, I want to create a funnel with them, to guide the people through a visual check before letting them on the ship."

"It's going to be tough to turn people away," I said, smiling as Nukka crawled down the ladder and onto the couch. Her mom was safe, her eyes said as much, and she cuddled into my side and I wrapped my arm around her. I could feel the warmth of her body through my jacket and I unzipped it to let out some heat.

"That's your job. You and the Whittier Chief of Police."

"Why? Where will you be?"

"Onboard the *Seward*, checking the engines. I need to know what condition they are in. We have no idea how long we need to keep them running."

I stroked Nukka's hair and listened as her breathing deepened and her body relaxed. The thought of keeping things running, managing and maintaining a ship, a community at sea – the thoughts were overwhelming, and I envied the little girl in my arms.

"I don't know how I am going to choose who gets to go onboard, who gets to live," I said and looked at Nate. "I'm not qualified to make that decision. It should be Waverly, or at least someone with medical training – a doctor, a nurse, not a firefighter."

"You're not a firefighter any longer, Lewis," he said. Nate stood up and walked over to our packs. He opened the top flap of his own and pulled out a book. I wondered if it was the bible. The cover intrigued me as he tossed it onto the table.

"Do you read poetry?"

"Yes," I said, happy for the diversion. "But I would never have imagined you for a reader of poets."

"I'm not," Nate said. "Most of the time I just pretend to like it."

"To impress girls." I laughed, stopping as Nukka stirred. Aatag laughed too, and I realized we were far from alone. If Nate was embarrassed or annoyed he hid it as he flicked through the well-thumbed pages of his book. The cover was black and blank save for the poet's name: William Blake.

Nate stopped on a wrinkled page and read aloud, "The roaring of lions, the howling of wolves, the raging of the stormy sea, and the destructive sword, are portions of Eternity too great for the eye of man."

Those words, together with the thick, dark brows framing Nate's Hispanic face, caught in my chest, and I stared at him until he closed the book, with a quiet, slow movement of his hands. One corner of Nate's mouth rose, dragging his lips into a crooked smile, and he shrugged his shoulders.

"The Proverbs of Hell," he said.

"Because that's where we're headed?" I said, and Nate's Mexican spell was spoiled. "That's encouraging. I was asking for your help. That," I pointed at the book, "is not helping."

"You are going to face both lions and wolves before you even get to the sea. I'm just saying – Blake is just saying – that some things are too great to contemplate. You can't plan for them. We could never have planned for this," he said and gestured at the interior of the cab, but I knew his reach was greater.

"That's your interpretation? Did you forget the word eternity in that gem of a quote you just read aloud?"

"No, but that's the point, Lewis. We'll never see the bigger picture, we'll be too busy dodging the pointy end of the sword."

"So what should I do?" I was conscious of the indifferent, slightly incredulous, and equal parts pissed look that I threw at him. "Do you have anything positive to contribute, or is poetry all you've got? Because," I said as I leaned forward and tapped the table with my knuckle, "while you're safe and sound checking on the *Seward*'s engines, I'll be topside, facing down the lions and wolves, not to mention that sword thing you think God is waving around."

"I never said it was God."

"No? What was it: Proverbs of Hell? Is it the devil then? That just makes it all so much better." The children shifted on the bed above my head, and Nukka's body stiffened, her eyes closed tight. I lowered my voice, softened the tone. "I get it. The destructive sword, it's the virus."

"I thought so," said Nate.

"I just don't like the whole never-gonna-get-a-handle-on-this aspect, the *eternity* thing."

Nate slid the book along the table toward me. I felt the pages bump my fingers, the binding leathery – much abused for a man that only pretended to read poetry.

"Eternity. That's the positive part," he said.

"How so?"

"It means it will go on, that we will go on." I am going to check on Sierra." Nate moved away from the table and climbed the ladder. Nukka saw her chance and slipped out from beneath my arm and followed him. I sighed and reached for the book, the cover warm within my fingers. Staring down lions and wolves – how hard could it be? I shook my head and searched for the quote, tracing my fingertips down the lines of small print until I found the eternity quote as I had decided to dub it. Aatag pulled me out of the pages and back into reality when slowed the vehicle to a stop.

"There's another roadblock ahead," he said. "We've reached the head of the tunnel."

Chapter 10

Cameron Smith of the Whittier Police Department had the same skin color as me, the same background, practically the same upbringing, but we were definitely not on the same wavelength. After ten minutes of bickering back and forth, we were nowhere near a common understanding, let alone an agreement on how we were going to process a horde of vehicles escaping the city. I could feel my dad's genes begging to take control. I walked away and let Nate continue to press upon Officer Smith the urgency of the situation. I balled my fists against my temples and stomped in the direction of our ride. Aatag leaned against the driver's door and smoked. He stubbed out his cigarette as I approached.

"Trouble?" he asked.

"As if we didn't have enough problems. This jerk," I said and stabbed my thumb in the direction of Whittier P.D.'s finest, "has no idea what's coming, no idea how to block off the tunnel, and no clue as to why he should. I mean…" I paused as Aatag scanned the area to either side of the tunnel before focusing on Smith. He studied the man for a long time before speaking.

"He's stalling, that's all. He understands plenty."

"What?"

Aatag pointed to either side of the tunnel. "See those CATs, the digger on the left, the dumper on the right?"

"Yes?"

"You think they were here all the time? There hasn't been construction on this side of the tunnel for over a year."

"So."

He took a step away from the pickup and gestured at Smith. "See the way he has his hands tucked into his belt? The way he nods, no words, just a nod."

"Infuriating," I said.

"Interruption, that's all. He knows as much as you do. His boss told him to keep you here for as long as possible. Long enough for him to do something back in Whittier."

"Do what?" I said and looked at Smith. Sure enough, his hands were tucked into his belt, as Nate, for the fourth time since I walked away, tried to convince Smith that he had talked with his boss, and that was the reason he was there at all. "He's not stupid, is he?"

"Nope."

"Just stalling?"

"Yep," said Aatag as I walked past him and walked to the rear of the cab. "Young lady," he called out. "What are you planning on doing?"

I didn't answer. I decided it was time for dad to take over, with some checks and balances of course. I opened the door and stepped inside, looking for Nukka.

"Hey there," I said when I saw her on the bed with her brothers and sister. "Do you still have my axe?" She draped her arm over the lip of the bed and pointed to the space between the couch and the cupboards. I grabbed the shaft below the pick head and climbed out of the cab.

"Whoa," Aatag said and lifted his hands. "That won't do no good. You wouldn't want to do anything reckless."

"No?" I said and gripped the shaft in both hands. "Watch me."

Nate was still arguing the urgency of the situation with Smith as I approached. Both men stopped talking and stared at me. I caught the excitement in my step, steadied my walk, and hefted the pick head up to shoulder height. Smith slipped his hands out of his belt and took a step backward.

"That your car?" I said and waved the head of the axe at the patrol car.

"What are you going to do?" he said and took another step backward.

I lifted the axe into the top of what would be a measured arc, one swing to lop off the driver's side mirror.

"Lewis," Nate said. "What are you doing?"

"I'm getting the ball rolling," I said and cleaved the mirror from the patrol car with a clean cut. The mirror tumbled onto the road.

"Hey," Smith shouted as I walked around the car. I raised the axe again. He shouted, but I heard nothing but the sweet metallic clang as I removed the passenger side mirror. I rested the pick head on the hood of the vehicle.

"I enjoyed that," I said and waited for Smith to say something. He gritted his teeth and stared at me as I dragged the axe across the paintwork. "I could keep going – carve this baby up like a real chop-shop pro – or…"

"Or?" Smith said. He looked at Nate for support.

"Don't look at me," he said. "You took her there, it's up to you to walk her back."

"What do you want?" Smith said.

"I want you to stop stalling. Stop pretending like

you don't get it. It might be you've got orders," I said and waved at Aatag and Nukka as they walked over. Nukka held her father's hand, tugging at his fingers so that he might walk faster. I turned to Smith. "Honestly, I don't care why you were told to keep us waiting. I'm sure we'll find out soon enough. But what I need is for you to drive those CATs into the road, stick your patrol car and a spike stick, or whatever surprises you have in the trunk, in the gap between, and secure this road, at the very least for the time it takes for us to get to Whittier. After that, you can lead people through the tunnel and help us get them onto the *Seward*. I'll be that grateful, I won't carve up the rest of your ride."

"My ride?"

"This," I said, and used the side of the pick head to bump a sizeable dent in the hood. Smith turned green, and I had to pull on the reins and wrangle dad's genes back inside the box, until next time.

"All right." Smith gestured with his hand at the digger. "If one of you will take that, I'll drive the dumpster."

"I've got it," Nate said. He jogged to the digger and climbed into the cab. Smith reached the dumper a couple seconds later.

"That's a pretty axe," Aatag said as Nukka led him over.

"It is. It was a gift."

"One you know how to use."

"Once you got me going, sure."

I watched as Nate and Smith blocked the tunnel entrance, leaving an RV-sized gap between them. The men climbed out of the cabs and walked toward us.

"Time to go," I said.

Aatag nodded and encouraged Nukka back to the pickup with a few gentle words – something about checking on momma. He paused to listen to the distant drone of traffic on the wind coming from the north, and then followed his youngest daughter. I waited for Nate to join me beside the earless patrol car.

"I think you'll handle the lions and wolves just fine," he said with a glance at my axe.

"Long enough for you to check the *Seward*'s engines, at least."

"We still have to find a Captain, although the Chief should have sorted that by now."

"Unless," I said, but my thoughts drifted. I tugged Nate away from the patrol car as Smith got in behind the steering wheel. "What do you think he is up to?"

"Who? The Chief?"

"Yes."

Smith drove the short distance to the tunnel entrance, parked in front of the digger and got out. He pulled a spike strip from the trunk, together with a reflective vest and flares. He positioned the spike strip on the road, pulled on the vest and popped flares in two short lines to create a lane between the CATs. The flares smoked and fizzed on the asphalt.

"I don't know. We'll find out when we get there. Come on." Nate pulled me away from Smith and into the back of the cab as Aatag idled past us. "Get in, Lewis. We have to go."

I let him guide me inside, dumping the axe by my pack, as I sat on the couch and peered through the hatch at Smith. The man was all business all of a sudden.

"You were right," I said to Aatag. "He was just stalling."

Aatag waved at the police officer as we drove through the gap, the teeth of the spike strip glinting in the morning sun as we passed. I leaned back as the natural light outside was replaced with strip lights hanging from the tunnel ceiling. Nukka curled her hand into mine and I closed my eyes.

"When we get to Whittier," Nate said, "we'll need to move pretty fast to get things set up, depending on what they've done already." I heard him rummage through his pack, and then the seat cushion see-sawed as he sat down beside me. "You listening?"

"Yes," I said. "But I refuse to open my eyes." I squeezed Nukka's fingers and she giggled.

"I'm listening," Aatag said. "But my eyes are on the road."

"Great."

I suppressed a smile as Nate sighed. Dad's genes, those of a belligerent prepper, were bubbling with excitement, and I realized they didn't have to be used in anger only, I might get some other use out of them yet.

"Like screening the last survivors of the Last Frontier."

"What's that?"

"Nothing," I said, as I thought about who was being saved. Alaska was a mixed bag of indigenous people and immigrants. I hoped I could strike a balance of both. I hoped I wouldn't need to. We were leaving a lot to chance and to individuals in decision-making positions. We had already discovered that some of those people were more reliable than others, and that Whittier's Chief of Police may have his own agenda.

"End of the line," Aatag said as he decelerated.

I opened my eyes and blinked in the red glow of flares as they flickered around the smooth tunnel walls. Aatag drove between them, along a narrow lane that ended with two police patrol cars and what looked like a sheriff and his posse. My stomach turned and I had the feeling I was about to be lynched.

"It was only a couple of mirrors," I whispered, as I looked through the hatch. David smiled at me from the passenger seat, but the look in his eyes suggested that his thoughts were similar to my own.

"This could get complicated," Nate said as he leaned around me to look. "Let me do the talking this time."

"You want me to stay in the cab?"

"No. I didn't say that." He flashed a smile. "Just don't bring your axe."

Nate brushed past me as he got off the couch and walked to the door. I moved to follow him, but Nukka gripped my hand and pulled me back.

"Hey," I said. "It's all right. I just need to go and talk to those men, and then we will get on a big ship, and go on an adventure." She shook her head and squeezed my fingers. "Nukka." I stroked the hair falling down her cheek with my free hand. She glanced at her daddy and then stared at me with her deep brown eyes. I could feel her energy, as if the spirit of her father, of her family, the raw power she had inside her – that power was seeping out. Similar to what I imagined were my dad's crazy genes controlling me, once in a while. This little Native Alaskan girl had a similar power within, and, from the look on Aatag's face, he knew it too.

"It's all right, Nukka," he said. "You must let her go. She will be protected." Nukka shook her head. "No? Then give her your talisman. Let her carry it for a while."

Nukka's eyes softened and she let go of my hand to reach inside her t-shirt. She pulled a small leather cord over her head. There was a raven claw bound in the middle of it. Nukka gestured for me to dip my head, and she tugged the talisman over my frizzy hair and let it hang around my neck. She smiled as I turned it within my fingers, feeling the tough skin of the raven's leg, and the sharp prick of its claws.

"Thank you," I said.

"Well done, child," Aatag said.

He looked at his son and they shared a raised eyebrow and a smile. It was clear to me that something significant had just happened. Time would perhaps reveal what exactly, but for the moment I had to join Nate to discuss how we would screen the arrivals from Anchorage. That was when the first shot was fired. The second clipped the side of the cab.

Chapter 11

The tunnel was thick with the tang of cordite when I stepped out of the cab. I saw Nate, his hands in the air, standing behind a small car - there were several of them, arranged in a zigzag to slow vehicles as they approached the checkpoint at the entrance to the tunnel. Whittier's Chief of Police was not taking any chances. I realized I was looking at the first point of defense, and, however menacing it looked, it was a perfect sluice to screen people before allowing them onto the *Seward*.

A nagging thought stopped me from raising my hands and walking over to Nate. It came each time I thought about how I would screen people, how I would choose. If we really did only have one ferry, at some point that ship was going to be filled to capacity, perhaps even beyond what it could comfortably hold. I just hadn't given much thought to what I was going to do when I had to turn people away, for good, abandoning them to the virus. Leaving them to die. Just how was I going to look a father or mother in the eye and say "No, you're on your own"? I buried the thought and stepped out from behind the cab.

"Stop right there." The voice bellowed through a loudhailer.

"My name is Jaylen Lewis. I'm with FEMA. We're together," I said and pointed at Nate.

"FEMA has no jurisdiction here," the man said. I guessed he was the Chief.

"I think you'll find it does."

"When the Governor calls me, I'll consider it."

"The Governor is never going to call." I took two

steps closer to Nate. "We're in a state of emergency, and we need your help. I thought Nate explained that?"

"He did. But I have had time to think about it since then."

"Yeah, we noticed." I thought of Smith at the other end of the tunnel.

"Listen, Karl, you know me," said Nate.

"I do."

"And you need me. Where are your engineers? Do you even have a crew for the *Seward*? As far as I remember, it's only the Captains that live in Whittier. How are you going to sail that boat?"

"I need you," the Chief said and pointed at Nate. "I don't need anyone else."

"It's a package deal." Nate lowered his hands. "We're trying to save what we can of Alaska. You understand that, don't you?"

"Send them deep into the bush. They'll be safe there."

"Sure they will," I said, "until the first plane full of pox lands on some grass strip carved out in the wilderness. Then they will die, just as fast as they will in the city. You have to let us through. You have to help us." I walked over to Nate. "You talk about jurisdiction? What about doing what's right?"

Nate leaned close and whispered, "I've known Karl a long time, but I've never seen him like this. He's frightened. Take it slow, Lewis."

The tunnel was quiet as the Chief's men waited for him to respond. There was a soft squeal of metal behind us and I turned as Nukka stepped out of the cab and walked into the middle of the tunnel. David opened the passenger door to bring her back, only to stop as one of the posse jacked a shell into his shotgun.

"No," I said and waved my arms. "She's just a little girl." I gestured for David to wait by the pickup.

"Is she sick?"

"She's not sick. She's with her family. Mom, dad... there are five children in all."

At a nod from the Chief, the man with the shotgun lowered his weapon and rested it in the crook of his arm.

"Listen, Chief," I said. "Pretty soon, Smith is going to have his hands full with a bunch of folk wanting to come through the tunnel."

"I'm going to send some more men to him."

"And that still won't be enough. We need to do this properly. You can't isolate Whittier forever, not without someone getting hurt, or killed."

"We're prepared for that."

"And are you prepared for food and medicine shortages? What happens when you run out? I have a truckload of food and an ambulance full of supplies heading this way. But they won't get through if you don't help us. Then it won't just be an engineer you're missing." I waited as the Chief lowered the loudhailer. The look on his face suggested I wasn't saying anything new – he had obviously thought about this, maybe even worried about it.

"Food and medicine," Nate said. "That's what we're bringing to the table. That and qualified personnel."

"We've got paramedics in the ambulance. Together with the EMTs from Whittier, maybe even a doctor or two somewhere in the mix."

"You have a doctor with you?"

"We're working on that," I said. "But if we combine the resources we have, we can make this work, get a ton of people to safety…"

"At sea," he said, "at the start of winter."

"I didn't say it would be easy." He had a point. I didn't relish the idea of being at sea through the fall and definitely not in the winter. We would need a sheltered bay – far enough from land to isolate us from the virus, close enough to protect us from the storms. Another voice reminded me that I was thinking as if I was going to be one of the people onboard the *Seward*, that I was going to survive. The Chief must have read my mind.

"You intending to be on the *Seward*?"

"She is," Nate said, before I could answer. "Another part of the package." I looked at him as the Chief talked with the men either side of him. "What?"

"You want me with you?"

"You dragged me into this, Lewis. You think I am going to let you leave me to manage this and people like the Chief all by myself? You're wrong," he said. "You're coming with me."

I looked down as I felt the familiar warmth of Nukka's fingers as she twisted them into mine. She smiled and I said, "He wants me with him." We both giggled.

"Hey, don't read too much into this."

"Wouldn't dream of it."

"Yes," he said and sighed, "I kind of think you would." Nate walked forward, closing the gap between him and the Chief. "C'mon, Karl. Decision time. Let us through and we can get things started. Every minute is another minute closer to the virus. You know it's in Anchorage?"

"I heard," he said. The Chief handed the loudhailer to one of his men. "Why do you think we went to all this trouble?"

"I understand, I do, but we have to get moving if we are going to stay ahead of this thing."

The Chief nodded for his men to make a hole in the roadblock. We waited as the driver of a truck started the engine and moved to one side. I waved for Aatag to drive through the gap and walked behind the pickup with Nukka and Nate. The truck driver backed up and sealed the roadblock once we were through. Nukka ran to her brother while Nate and I waited for the Chief to climb down from his position. He wore a huge sidearm in a leather holster at his hip, and a smaller pistol clipped to his belt behind his back. I wondered if I was going to have to start carrying a gun. I guessed Nate would say that I should. But what would I do when dad's genes took over? Nate dragged me out of my thoughts as he introduced me to Whittier's Chief of Police.

"It was Jaylen's idea to outfit the *Seward*."

I looked at Nate as I shook the Chief's hand – it was the first time I had heard him call me by my first name.

"More like an ark," said the Chief, as he let go of my hand. "But, from all we have heard in the media, an ark might be just what we need." He tucked his hands into his belt. "I'm sorry about before," he said and nodded at the roadblock. "People are scared. Hell, I'm scared."

"We all are, Chief," I said. He looked away and I wondered if he was hiding something. I looked around. It was quiet; the only people in sight were the men in the Chief's posse. "Where is everyone?"

Whittier was supposed to have a couple hundred people.

"I told them to stay indoors, just until I had more information."

"And they listened?" I looked at the Chief, tried to catch his eye, but he looked away.

"We don't have any troublemakers in Whittier," he said. "They pretty much do as they're told."

"Really?"

"I should get on the *Seward*," Nate said. "Any luck finding a Captain?"

The Chief focused on Nate, and my gut feeling that he was hiding something resurfaced, only to be buried again as he described the situation with the *Seward*'s Captain – both of them.

"Berg is already onboard. Drunk as a skunk. He's locked himself in the Captain's quarters." The Chief shrugged as Nate rolled his eyes. "You told me to find him."

"I did," Nate said. "What about Grace?"

"He swore he wouldn't sail with you again, even if it was the end of the world."

"Did you tell him it was?"

"I did."

"And he's going to stay in Whittier?"

"He is. Paton, my other officer, is parked outside his house, but he's not coming out."

I remembered what had been said about Grace back in Anchorage, that he was an excellent navigator, but his personality could be challenging. If the IT infrastructure began to fail through a lack of maintenance, then we would need someone who could find the perfect sheltered bay – without GPS – to get out of the storms, to hide from the virus. Now that I realized Nate wanted me onboard, I didn't like the idea of sailing with a drunk.

"What's the problem with you and Grace?"

"We had a difference of opinion."

"They had a fight," the Chief said. "Both of them had to cool off in my jail. One longer than the other," he said and nodded at Nate.

"So I hit him a few times…"

"You broke his jaw."

"He was being an ass."

"You fractured his collarbone too, if I recall."

"He shouldn't have come down to my engine room, telling me what to do, when he…"

"That's when you moved to Anchorage?" I butted in when Nate broke off, his dark eyes sparking at the memory.

"Yeah," he said. "I had to get off the boats for a while."

"Nate," I said, and smoothed my hand on his arm. "We can't sail with a drunk."

The Chief backed away as one of the posse approached him with news from Smith. It seemed that the first of the RVs was approaching the tunnel entrance. I waited for Nate to speak. It had to be his decision, but he had to make it quickly.

"I'll go talk to him," he said.

"If he's as good a navigator as they say…"

"I said I'll talk to him." He lowered his voice, "I'll sort it out, get him onboard."

I squeezed Nate's arm and then looked at the roadblock. The Chief had created a sluice, now we needed to extend it. There were shipping containers in the distance, and cranes to lift them. I just needed drivers to put them in place.

Nate followed my gaze and pointed at the driver of the truck as he smoked beside the cab. "He can drive a crane," he said. "So can the Chief. You want me to tell them?"

"No," I said, "I'm going to have to start ordering folk around soon enough."

"True."

"And there's nothing like the end of the world to make people listen."

Nate smiled that half smile I was beginning to enjoy and nodded at the RV. "You'll get my stuff onboard?"

"Sure."

"I don't think it's a good idea for me to take a gun when I go see the Captain."

"Probably not," I said and paused as I caught sight of a smokestack in the distance. "Is that her, the *Seward*?" The feminine prefix tickled in my throat as I wondered if the *Seward* and I were going to get along.

"The top part of her, yes. Wait 'til you see the rest."

"She's a good ship, isn't she, Nate? She'll do the job?"

"If we treat her right, yeah, she'll look after us."

I stared at the top of the ferry and hoped he was right.

Chapter 12

Nate was gone when I had my first real taste of how unpleasant life had become in Alaska, one of the Chief's men decided to inspect Aatag's pickup. I heard the children scream and turned to see a man with a shotgun hurling them to the ground through the cab door. I ran over just as he lifted the butt of his shotgun to strike Aatag in the head, the big Native Alaskan from Koyukuk crumpled to the floor. David raised his fists and managed to hit the man twice before he opened fire. I cried out as David was thrown backward into the side of the RV, his shirt ripped open to reveal a bloody mess of skin and guts. David slid down the side of the cab. He was dead as his heels hit the asphalt.

"What are you doing?" I yelled as I grabbed the barrel of the shotgun and pulled it free of the man's hands.

"There's a sick woman inside," the man said, his face ashen, his eyes drawn to David's body on the ground. "She's got the virus," he said as the Chief arrived with two more men with guns. "They brought it here."

"She's not sick with the virus," I said. The men beside the Chief raised their weapons and I looked at the shotgun in my hand. I tossed it to the ground and stepped in front of the children, arms raised. "She's reacting to a bite. We're treating her with antibiotics."

"There were lesions on her body," the man said. "She was sweating, just like they said infected people would on the TV."

"It's a rash. She's got a temperature. It's all under control."

The Chief pulled the massive pistol out of its holster. He held it at his side. "You brought a sick woman into Whittier?"

"She's not sick."

"Oh, God, I am infected," the man said and shook. "We all are."

Despite the horror of David's bloody body, despite the wailing of the children, some part of me appreciated the calm that the Chief mustered in the face of the panic and terror that had gripped one of his men - a local, a civilian, now a murderer. The virus, the very thought of it, could drive people to acts of madness. It didn't even have to be close.

"Listen," I said. "If she was sick with the virus, her children would be too. So would I. So would Nate. This virus, it's fast, and it's airborne. We would be sick, all of us. We're not."

The Chief whispered to his men to take the man away. One of them picked up the shotgun, the other took the man by the arm and led him in the direction of the Chief's patrol car. I looked at the Chief and waited. Aatag stirred on the ground. Nukka, the only child not sobbing, crawled over to him and stroked his brow.

"Let's take a look," the Chief said and waved his gun at the cab.

"Put that away first." I waited for him to holster his pistol and then led him to the cab. David was dead; I could see that from his wounds. His blood seeped into the pores and cracks in the surface of the road. I opened the door to the cab and led the Chief inside. "Up there," I said, "in the bunk."

If any credit was due, then the Chief deserved at least some recognition for approaching the bed and climbing the ladder to see Sierra. I couldn't forgive him for being partly responsible for David's death – he had chosen that man for his posse after all. But to take my word that Sierra was not infected took courage of a different sort, the kind that set the Chief apart from the rest. Whatever he was hiding, I decided I could trust him to do the right thing when it counted.

"How long has she been like this?"

"Since yesterday, I think. Nate removed a bloated tick from her chest."

"A tick?"

"Sure, one of those crab-like insects. He thinks she has spotted fever."

"Nate thinks that?"

"Yes."

"He would know, I guess," the Chief said and climbed down the ladder. "Nate has been around, seen some things." He shrugged. "I trust him." The Chief leaned against the counter. "I am sorry about the boy."

I said nothing, my mind swirling with conflicting thoughts about the situation, questions about Nate, concern about what to do next, and the fear that David's death was not going to be the last. I corralled my thoughts and prioritized.

"Can we trust your men not to open fire when the first vehicles arrive from Anchorage?"

"Yes."

"And if they find someone who's sick? What then?"

"That's your department. You said FEMA had jurisdiction? I'm going to leave that to you."

"You'll get those containers in place?"

"Yes."

"Then give me a few unarmed men and I'll take care of the screening and searches."

"They won't like that."

"They don't have to like it, Chief. They just need to do what I say." Dad's genes stirred, but I figured I could contain them, besides, a measured dose of rage added an edge to my words. I felt it gave me a little authority. Given that it was Saturday, I hadn't slept, and my new job didn't start before Monday morning, I could use all the help I could get. "Good," I said and led the way out of the cab.

The same men that had led David's killer away, lifted the young man's body onto a stretcher and slid him inside the Whittier Voluntary Fire Department's ambulance. I walked over to where Aatag was sitting, a bandage wrapped around his head, his children curled within his arms. He looked at me with sad eyes and my voice stalled in my throat.

"I'm sorry," I said.

"You didn't kill him," Aatag said and looked at the Chief. "The virus did."

The Chief nodded and I silently thanked Aatag. I promised myself I would look out for him and his family, pushing away the thought that there were going to be a lot more people to look after very soon. I followed the Chief to the roadblock and watched as his men created a funnel with the containers.

"We're going to need a list of people, their names. We need to know who and how many people are onboard."

"Yes," the Chief said. He turned away. I reached out to pull him back, curious as to why he was avoiding eye contact when my cell phone burred in my pocket. I pulled it out and answered the call.

"Lewis," Nate said. I felt a sudden surge of warmth in my cheeks, shook it off and focused. "I'm outside Grace's house. He's not coming out. This could take a while. How are you doing?"

I told him about David, and then moved away from the Chief, putting a little distance between us. "That's not all," I said. "He's hiding something. I can feel it."

"Maybe he is. I don't know."

"Where is everybody, Nate?"

"Inside their homes. That's what he said."

"I know but…"

"Lewis, you need to focus. You're going to have to work with Karl, you need him."

"What I need is a way to record the people we're putting on the *Seward*. I'll use my cell."

"No. Pen and paper. Keep it simple. At some point we might run out of power. We need to be practical from now on."

"Okay," I said and laughed.

"What's funny?"

"Nothing, I'm just…"

"You're doing fine. Now hold it together. Once I am done here, I'll get over to the *Seward*, put some people on the entrance, check the engines. I'll need a duplicate of that list to check the names once you send them to me."

"Got it."

"And, Lewis?"

"Yes?"

I heard Nate take a breath. His voice was clearer when he spoke again, as if he was making an effort to be explicit. He needn't have bothered, his words had the desired effect, they tore at my gut.

"You need to think carefully about how you are going to turn people away."

"I know."

"Grab the Vector from my gear."

"I won't carry a weapon…"

"You're going to have to, Lewis. Half the people coming through the tunnel are going to be armed. Once you start turning people away, they are going to riot, and they will try to get on the *Seward* no matter what it takes."

"You talk like you have tried this before," I said. "You're not just an engineer, are you?"

"Don't worry about that. Just get those people onto the boat as fast as possible. Once we have reached capacity, once you have let the last people through, you seal that tunnel and you run. Do you hear?"

"Yes."

"You run, Lewis, and you don't stop until you are onboard."

Nate ended the call and I walked back to the Chief. I flinched as the last container was dumped onto the road. Behind the roadblock was a funnel of six shipping containers, three on either side. More men with guns, two on top of each container, walked back and forth, waving at the men on the roadblock that they were ready. I looked over at Aatag's pickup as he collected his children and lifted them one after the other into the cab. I told the Chief to wait and jogged over.

"Aatag," I said. "Drive down to the boat, and go straight onboard. Nate will meet you there." He nodded, a grim smile on his face. I looked at Nukka, as she clung to his leg.

"What about you?" he said.

"I need to be here, for now. I'll join you as soon as I can."

"You need to be careful."

"I know."

Aatag whispered to Nukka and she disappeared inside the cab. He looked at me and said, "It will be difficult, you need to be strong, and to show people you are in command."

"I am not going to carry a gun," I said.

"There are many ways to be strong. Guns can be a sign of weakness. You don't need a gun, Jaylen Lewis, you just need to believe in yourself, to believe that you are strong. Like your momma, like your papa."

"Yeah, well, he is becoming useful these days, that's for sure." I frowned as Nukka dragged my axe along the floor of the cab and pressed the end of the shaft into my hand. "I thought you said no weapons?"

"I said no guns, this is not a weapon, but it might save your life. That and the talisman around your neck," he said. I pressed my hand to my breast and felt the prick of raven claws against my skin. I lifted the axe and slid the shaft through my grip until my knuckles grazed the pick-head. "This is not a weapon, it is a tool, a rescue axe, is it not?"

"Yes."

"And it has saved your life?"

"Well…"

"You have used it to save lives."

"Yes," I said, and realized that he was right.

"Then you must use it again, to save lives."

I started at the sound of a whistle. One of the men from the roadblock waved his arm and the Chief shouted for me to hurry up.

"I have to go," I said. "Get your family onboard, Aatag. I will meet you on the boat."

"Be safe," he said. "Trust your instincts, trust your talisman, and your axe."

"It's pink," I said, and grinned.

"Let's hope it stays that way." Aatag lifted Nukka onto the ground and closed the door to the cab. He called for her to follow him to the front of the pickup. She paused and reached up, wrapping her arms around my neck. I realized I had never heard her talk.

"Nukka," I said. "Go with your father." She shook her head, her long black hair catching in the tight curls of my own. "Go now. I will see you on the boat."

"Come, Nukka." Aatag peeled his daughter's fingers gently from my neck, and lifted her into his arms. "She has become fond of you."

"I know," I said and stroked Nukka's cheek. The Chief shouted again and I let my hand fall to Aatag's arm. "I have to go."

Nukka buried her face in her father's jacket as I turned toward the roadblock. The tunnel amplified the sound of the first vehicles, and I could see what looked like the white and cream roofs of recreational vehicles. The State Troopers had done their job. Now it was time for me to do mine.

Chapter 13

I leaned my axe against the side of the container and pulled the metal folding chair out from under the table, the feet dragged on the surface of the road, just like I was dragging out the beginning of the end. The Chief dumped a legal pad and a bunch of pencils onto the table, nodded once and stepped back to lean against the container. The message was clear; it was my show from now on. I reminded myself that I had yet to begin my new job, that this was still my first weekend off in a very long time. Apparently the virus didn't care; neither did the bio-engineers who had created it. They might even be dead, I realized, and so would we be if I didn't get started.

So this was it, my grand plan, a Hail Mary to save the State of Alaska – a portion of it at least – and I had no idea where to begin. The motors of the RVs at the front of the line chuttered. I turned away and slipped my hand into my pocket. My fingers closed around my cell phone and I thought about calling Nate. I pulled it out and dialed another number, someone I should have called earlier. I listened to the ringtone and did my best to ignore the Chief and his men.

"Maggie?" I said when the call connected. The line was clear, but the voice faint, strained, as if my aunt was talking through cheesecloth. "Are you there?"

"Jaylen? Oh, my," she said, and then she coughed, the wracking kind and I could picture her shaking back and forth, her hands flailing in the air. She must have dropped her cell phone as I heard it clatter on the floor.

"Maggie?"

There was a scrabbling sound, wheezing, and then a voice, rasped like sandpaper, "I'm sick, Jaylen. Real sick."

"Where are you?"

"I'm home."

"You can't get to the hospital?"

"No," she said, and then a second round of coughing began. If I had hoped for words of wisdom, I found only guilt – I should be with her, but then I would be sick too. I should have taken her with me, but that damned streak of professionalism consumed me. Not for the first time, probably not the last.

I looked up at the first RV, pushing back the chair as I stood up. I waved them forward and two of the Chief's posse blocked the gap between the containers, just a few feet from my table. The RV rolled to a stop next to me as one of the men raised his hand.

"Maggie, I'll call you back, soon. Rest now."

Maggie whispered a response and it trickled down the line until I ended the call, swallowing my guilt, and biting back a childhood fear that one of the few adults left in my family couldn't help me. I was on my own.

The driver of the RV rolled down his window, shifting his gaze from me to the Chief's men as they inspected the vehicle.

"Hi," I said, my voice stronger than I had expected. "Who and how many in the vehicle?"

"Just me and my wife," the driver said. "Two dogs in the back."

"Small dogs?" I asked as the Chief's men froze at a sudden barking from within the RV.

"I guess. Regular size, maybe."

"What kind?"

"Oh, I don't know." The driver looked at the woman sitting next to him. "What do you say, Martha? They're your dogs."

"Pekinese," Martha said. "Female."

"Okay," I said and made a note. The logistical part of my brain kicked in and I asked, "You have food for the dogs?"

"Yes."

"How much?"

"What do you mean?" Martha said.

"A week's food. A month? How much?"

"I don't know. Maybe three weeks. They don't eat very much. They're small, like I said."

The Chief walked over and beckoned for me to follow. We took a few steps away from the car while his men searched inside.

"What's taking so long?"

"They have two dogs," I said.

"And?"

"Well, in theory, that's two more mouths to feed."

I watched as the Chief chewed on the thought, his hand resting on the handle of the pistol holstered on his belt. He tapped his fingers on the leather holster. I bit at my bottom lip as he looked at me, eyebrows raised.

"We need to hurry this along."

"I know."

He looked at the driver. The dogs continued barking. The man checking the vehicle gave the thumbs up sign; the vehicle was clean, no sign of the virus or sickness of any kind.

"It's your call, Lewis, but you need to make it fast. We can't waste time on every vehicle like this."

"What do you suggest?"

"Give them a choice, but no dogs are getting on that boat."

I thought for a moment, and then walked back to the RV, stopping at the driver's window. I had made my decision, and now it was up to them to make theirs.

"So, there's no pets on the ferry."

"What do you mean?" said the driver.

"I mean they are not allowed."

"I'm not leaving my dogs behind," Martha said. She looked at her husband, her eyes wild, her face ashen.

"You can turn around," I said. "Find somewhere else to go."

"Are you crazy," he said. "We can't go back … the virus …"

"Alternatively, we can take care of your dogs," I paused, "or you can, of course."

"Mike," Martha said as her husband gripped the steering wheel. He looked at me and dipped his head once. Tear's streamed down Martha's face and she hid her face in her hands.

"Do you want us to…"

"No," Mike said, "I'll do it. Just tell me where to go."

I took down their names and pointed toward the end of the corridor of containers, explaining that he should wait at the dock before driving onboard the ferry. The dogs continued to bark as he pulled away. I could hear his wife sobbing even after he rolled up his window.

Two names on the list, and I felt buoyed by the thought that I had saved two Alaskans, a middle-aged couple from the city. I remembered Aatag and his family and added another seven names, only to cross out David's as the image of the young man's body lying on the stretcher burst into view.

"Eight," I whispered to myself. "Only another 742 to go." I planned on taking 250 people more than the Seward could accommodate. It was going to be crowded. "But so was the ark."

The Chief walked toward me as the next RV rolled up. He nodded for his men to search the vehicle as we talked.

"We need to speed it up," he said.

"I know." I looked up at the men on top of the containers. "If you sent them down the line, they could check for sick people, get rid of the pets..."

"Get rid of them?"

"Or give the owners the chance to do it themselves, "I paused at the sound of two gunshots from a small caliber pistol, "or turn around."

"I'll get it done." He waved at the men above us and gave them instructions. They scrambled down the sides of the containers and picked their way along the vehicles, leapfrogging each other as they worked their way down the line.

We got through twelve RVs, twenty-six people, ten of them children, in nine minutes, then a minibus with another thirty Alaskans. I figured the bus could be converted to accommodation and let them pass as soon as they had been checked for signs of sickness. We had over four hundred names when Nate called to check-in three hours later.

"How are the engines?"

"They're good. We're taking on fuel and water. I even got hold of the Captain."

"Grace?"

"No, Berg. I'm going to need more time with Grace. Berg's sobering up as we speak – we're going to need a lot of coffee."

The Chief waved two Fred Meyer trucks through the roadblock and around the container funnel as we talked.

"This is going to work," I said, my voice laced with optimism, my head giddy with the thought of a win when so much of North America was losing. "Have you checked the rest of the ship? The cabins and…"

"No. Haven't had time. We have a line of vehicles at the dock. As soon as you can get that list to me, we'll start loading."

"I'll send a photo of it to your cell."

"That'll work, but don't lose the original."

"I'll call you back," I said, as two ambulances flashed their way to the head of the line, the single bursts of sirens echoed along the walls of the tunnel. The driver of the first ambulance rolled down the window and stuck out her hand.

"Stacey Idaho," she said. "This is my husband, Mack. We've got two kids – Ramon and Andrea – somewhere in the back."

"We flat-packed them," Mack said, a huge grin on his face.

"You're our paramedics?"

"We are," said Stacey. "We've got Christa and her driver in the mobile lab behind us – she's been working on some early samples since we hit the road. Oh, and June Waverly says 'hi'."

My shoulders sagged and I sat on the table. I let the notepad rest on my thighs and smiled.

"You okay, honey?" said Stacey. "You look pooped."

"I'm okay." I nodded. "Everything is going to be okay."

"All right then. Where do you want us?"

I lifted my hand to point only to pause at the sound of some kind of disturbance inside the tunnel.

Stacey caught my eye and said, "Everything okay?"

"Maybe," I said. "I'll check it out. Just head on down to the…"

Three gunshots in rapid succession, the heavy kind – shotguns, rolled down the tunnel like thunder. The Chief ran toward me from his place in the line.

"Go," I said to Stacey and slapped my hand on the side of the ambulance. She pulled away with the mobile lab following, as the Chief stopped beside me. He drew his pistol from the holster and handed me his backup from his belt.

"Take this," he said. "There's trouble."

"I don't want it."

"You might need it." I shook my head and he reached behind his back to clip the pistol on his belt. "Suit yourself."

"What's going on?"

He opened his mouth to speak, pausing at the exchange of gunfire, and the sound of bullets striking metal and the sickening sound of a softer, wet impact, close by.

"One of the guys saw someone coughing at the back. He had them pull over to the side. That's when the driver got out and started shooting."

"Why?"

"To get past him? I don't know. Apparently there were more people inside the vehicle." He looked up at the sound of more gunfire. "You have to get these people through by yourself. I'm going inside."

"Wait," I said, but the Chief turned and ran between the containers and disappeared from sight. More gunfire followed and I could see the drivers and passengers of the vehicles in front of me fidgeting in their seats. Someone blasted their horn, and soon the air was filled with a rage of bullets, air horns, and screams. It was the screaming that spurred me into action. I leaned over the table and grabbed my axe, sliding it through my grip until my knuckles rammed the heavy metal pick-head. I used my free hand to call Nate, waving the closest vehicle, a Ford Bronco, toward me with the axe.

"What's going on?" Nate said as soon as he answered. "Is that gunfire?"

"Listen, there's a problem, I'm sending cars to you, but the passengers… they're not on the list. Just load them as soon as they arrive. Get them quartered as fast as you can." Nate's response was lost under a volley of automatic weapons fire. I pressed myself against the container, and waved four more vehicles through the funnel.

"About the quarters – there's something you should know."

"What? Say again," I said as more gunfire thundered up the tunnel.

"Something you should know," Nate said. "I know what Karl has been hiding." I heard a bullet snap through the air above my head. I ducked as a second hissed close by. "Did you hear me, Lewis?"

I dropped the cell phone as a third bullet grazed my shoulder. It clanged into the side of the container behind me, and I scrabbled on the road to pick up the phone. The pounding of footsteps along the road made me look up, and I forgot all about the phone. A man, bleeding from his scalp, slowed to within a few feet of me, the rifle in his hands shaking as he leveled it at my head.

"It's you," he said, his voice charged with rage. "You're the one."

I leaned on the axe and pushed myself onto my feet, my heart thudding in my chest, sweat beading under my arms. I fought the urge to run, forced myself to hold my ground, like dad said I should when a grizzly charged.

"My name is Jaylen Lewis," I said. The words tumbled from my lips.

"I don't care who you are," he screamed.

"I work for FEMA…"

"I don't care who you work for." He raised the gun. It wobbled in his grasp, the barrel less than two feet from my chest as he staggered toward me.

Two feet.

About the same length as my axe.

Chapter 14

I swung my axe as he fired, catching the barrel of his rifle with the pick-head. He dropped it and lunged at me, something I wasn't ready for. We fell to the ground and he gripped the shaft of my axe and pressed it into my chest.

"You're the one playing God," he shouted, spittle flaying about his lips and spattering upon my cheeks. "The one who won't let my wife onto the boat, just because she's sick."

That worried me more than the demonic look in his eyes. If she was sick, then he was too. That part of my brain, detached from my body, considered the implications until the pain in my chest was too great and I began to panic. There was little to no air coming into my lungs, I simply couldn't draw it in. The man wasn't big, but the pent-up energy in his body – the rage, threatened to flatten me as he gritted his teeth and focused on crushing my body. I wasn't going to get sick, I was going to die on the road to the ferry, squashed between the containers at the end of the line.

"If my wife has to die," he said, "then so will you."

He dipped his chin to wipe the saliva from his face on his shirt. It was spotted with blood, dark with sweat, and torn as if he had caught the sleeves and shirttails as he ducked between cars, gunfighting with the Chief and his posse. I wondered if I was close to death. Was that why everything was so clear, so detailed?

"This is for my wife…" As he pressed down harder upon my chest, his knuckles digging into my skin, his head whipped forward and he struck my nose with his forehead. I felt the bone break and blood spill onto my lips, but the pressure in my chest eased, and I rolled the man onto his side. The back of his head was gone, a flap of skin folded onto the back of his neck. I moved into a sitting position, my axe rolling into my lap, and caught my breath. The Chief crawled toward me, blood streaming from his scalp, and the large pistol in his hand. I scrambled onto my knees and hurried toward him.

"You all right?" he said, his voice hushed and wispy.

"I'm fine, but you're not." I knelt by his side, as he collapsed onto the ground.

"Told you you'd need a gun."

"I should have listened."

"Never mind." He reached a hand toward the closest container and I helped him crawl to it and lean his back against it. "Two men and one woman, with guns," he said. The Chief pointed at the man who had tried to crush me. "He was the last. Slipped through. Killed two of my men. Killed me too, I guess."

"Where are you hit?"

"Gut-shot, Lewis. There's nothing you can do."

"I'll get the paramedics," I said and stood up. He grabbed my ankle.

"Forget it, I lost most of my blood crawling to you."

I sank to my knees and moved to tug at his shirt. He caught my hand to stop me, curling his fingers within mine. "Who do I call?" I said.

"No-one. I live alone."

"No kids?"

He shook his head. A raven cawed above us, its

claws scratching along the metal roof of the container as it landed, strutting back and forth as the wind picked up. The Chief looked up and studied the clouds.

"Storm," he said. "Maybe later tonight. You'll need to find shelter."

"Nate's working on that. He has Berg sobering up and…"

"Berg's a good man. Just likes his drink is all."

"And Grace?"

"Pain in the ass. Better off without him." He shifted position and looked me in the eye. "Confession time," he said, "before I die." I waited as he licked his lips and then said, "You've been wondering why the town is so quiet?"

"Yes."

"It's because everyone is on the ferry." He held my gaze. "Sorry."

"You filled the cabins with Whittier folk?"

"Yes. When Nate called, it was the first thing I did. You would have done the same."

I probably would have, but now my calculations were off and the *Seward* was way over capacity. I couldn't imagine removing people – I glanced at the man who had tried to kill me – I couldn't play God. Not any more. We had to save who we had, and get out to sea before the virus… The last thought sideswiped me as I realized it was already here, and it was only a matter of time before I got sick.

I couldn't get on the boat.

"What is it?" the Chief said. He gripped my hand as I tried to pull free.

"I have to check his body," I said and stood up, pulling free of the Chief's fingers as I straightened my legs.

"What are you going to do?"

"He said his wife was sick," I said as I approached the man's body. "I have to look."

The Chief's bullet had made a mess of the back of the man's head, the exit wound was even worse. I felt my own blood drying on my cheeks as the wind picked up. I stopped to roll the man onto his back. His face was still intact, only his forehead was missing. I bent down and studied him, looking past his dead eyes for signs of skin irritation, a rash, or lesions. Beyond the blood spattered across his cheeks, his skin was clean. He was haggard but healthy. So, either his wife had only just gone down with a temperature and he was in the beginning stages of the sickness, or he was immune somehow. If it was the latter, then this was important. I should preserve his body. But I couldn't drag every body I found onto the ferry just because there were no visible symptoms. But if I was going to get onboard, if I was going to survive, then I had to be sure. I had to find the man's wife.

I walked back to the Chief, stopping for a moment to pick up my axe.

"Where are you going?"

"I have to check something out." I felt a trickle of blood from my nose and reached up to catch it with my finger. So long as I didn't pinch my nose, I figured I could live with the pain. It was nothing compared to what the Chief was going through.

"Okay," he said. "Of course, I might be dead by the time you get back." He grimaced. "Never thought I would ever say something like that."

I stopped by his side and knelt down. "I'm not

sure you should. Let me help you."

"No." He shook his head. "Help my people instead."

"If I can," I said and looked toward the mouth of the tunnel. "Are your men still inside?"

"No. Once the vehicles stampeded for the ferry, they followed. I can't imagine the chaos down at the docks."

"Nate's there," I said.

"He is?" The Chief leaned his head back on the container. "Then he'll have it under control."

"How do you know?" Nate was cagey with his past.

"He did a stint with the UN, fixing generators in remote villages. He's been up-close-and-personal with some pretty scary stuff. Ebola, I heard." The Chief disguised a groan of pain with a cough and a laugh.

"But the weapons? He's had training."

"People get ugly when they are scared," he said and nodded at the dead man a few feet away. "Nate's seen his fair share of ugly. But after today…"

"Sure," I said and tried to smile. "I have to go check on something. I'm going to have to leave you. You're sure you don't want any help?"

"Go," the Chief said with a nod of his head. "Just get on the ferry before more people come through that tunnel. I'm guessing the next batch will be sicker than dogs, and if the *Seward* is still in dock…"

"I understand," I said and stood up. "Thanks, Chief."

"I'm forgiven?"

"For stuffing the ferry? Yeah," I said and tried a smile. "I would have done the same." I looked at the Chief for another minute before quietly picking up my cell phone and making my way to the tunnel, the axe heavy in my grip, the thoughts in my head heavier still.

There was smoke in the entrance to the tunnel. It drifted over the roadblock in thick coils, tugged and teased by the wind. I climbed up and over the hood of one of the Chief's cars, using the bumper as a step. The remaining vehicles were peppered with buckshot, the windshields cracked and splintered from stray rounds, or shattered where men had crouched to take cover. Some vehicles had been abandoned, clothes and items of luggage trailing from the doors as if the passengers had been ejected onto the road. It seemed they had hit the ground running, there were no bodies. The entrance to the tunnel was empty.

I found the first body half-hidden beneath the rear wheels of an RV, the man's shoes clipped by bullets, his lower legs riddled with wounds. I leaned on my axe to take a look at his body, moving on when I realized he was dead. I found two more bodies before I reached a vehicle parked in the middle of the tunnel. The area surrounding the vehicle, a large Dodge RAM, was devoid of litter and luggage, as if all manner of debris was hesitant to step closer. There were shell casings on the asphalt, but they too had rolled away from the open doors, as if escaping something abhorrent. The plague, I thought, and the thought stuck.

That's exactly what this was – a species-ending sickness, just fifteen feet from where I stood.

I walked around the vehicle, stopping at various vantage points as I tried to find an angle that would allow me to see inside. The interior was dark, and, as the evening closed and the light outside the tunnel failed, whoever was inside the vehicle was lost to me.

"And the virus is airborne," I reminded myself. "If she had it, then he had it, and I have it." I took a sad step toward the vehicle. My time was running out, if I could do nothing else on this earth, I could at least satisfy my curiosity. I approached and hefted my axe in two hands.

I wasn't expecting a young woman wearing a UAF Nanooks hat over long red hair. The peak covered her eyes, but I could see the welts on her cheeks as she crawled out from the space in the beneath the dash on the passenger side of the vehicle. She looked young, maybe five years younger than me. The man who had attacked me had seemed much older, but maybe it was the crazed look that did it? Perhaps he was her father? I lowered my axe and peeked around the open driver's door.

"Hi," I said. "You okay?"

"Is it over?" she said. Her voice was shallow, as if breathing was difficult.

"The shooting? Yes. Will you come out?"

The woman looked at my axe and I lowered it. She slid onto the seat and then swung her legs slowly out of the door. I watched as she slipped off the chair, found her footing and leaned against the side panel of the Dodge. She took a long, deep breath and steadied herself with flat palms against the metal. She was dressed like a student, a sick student.

"Are you alone?"

"Yes." She paused to point a pale finger at the back seat. "Now I am."

I took a step to my right and found the man's wife, the blood from her body had stained the seat and pooled on the carpet beneath the driver's seat.

"Is that your mom?"
The woman nodded.
"She was sick. Was it the virus?"
"Yes. Mom worked at the airport. She was working when the Cessna came in."
"That was last night."
"She got sick real fast."
"And you? Are you sick?"
"Actually," she said and used the cuff of her sweater to wipe away a tear, "I'm feeling better than I was a few hours ago."
"Better?"
"No more fever. Just weak."
"And you got sick after your mom came home?"
"I know what you want to know," she said, "but I haven't got an answer. I got sick with the virus, and now I feel better. You don't have to believe me. You can leave me here and I'll go somewhere, take a truck or something. Maybe head back to the city."

"Or you can come with me," I said and walked around the hood of the Dodge. I stopped within a few feet of the woman and let the axe slide through my grip to rest on the asphalt.

She laughed. "You have a pink axe."
"Yes."
"I'm not sure it will save you from the virus."
"No," I said, "but maybe you can. Maybe you can save us all."

Chapter 15

I led the young woman away from the vehicle, away from her mother's body. When we reached the containers I stopped, rested on my axe and waited for a moment. It felt like October had passed, that we had raced through winter and spring, and that the heat of the Alaskan summer had descended upon us, on Whittier, right above me. I looked up at the clouds and watched as the woman wrapped her arms around her chest, the tips of her hair flickered in the wind.

"Are you all right?" she asked.

"Maybe." I straightened my back and walked over to the roadblock and leaned my back against the door of the vehicle I had crawled over just a little earlier. "What's your name?"

"Mary."

"And how long after your mom came home sick did your fever start?"

"A couple hours. Why? Are you getting warm?"

"Yes," I said and slid down onto the road. Mary crouched next to me. She nodded at the cargo pocket on my trousers when my cell phone started to ring.

"You going to take that?"

I handed Mary my axe and pulled my cell from my pocket. The vibration from the call shivered through my fingers. It took me two swipes with a sweaty thumb before I answered the call and held the phone to my ear.

"Hi Nate," I said, as I leaned my head back against the car door.

"Where have you been? I tried calling."

"I've had some problems?"

"Had? Are you okay? Where's the Chief?"

"He saved my life, Nate. And then he confessed."

"That's what I was trying to tell you earlier. All the townspeople are onboard."

"Yep, at least Whittier is safe," I said.

I looked up as Mary stood up and tried the axe on for size, lifting it with one and then two hands. Either I was getting better or she was getting stronger. Perhaps soon she would be strong enough to grieve. That's why I didn't want to go any further. Checking on the Chief would mean showing Mary the corpse that was her father. A shiver ran through my body and I clamped my teeth shut as I felt them begin to chatter. I was still sweating.

"Nate, I'm not well."

"You're sick?"

"Yeah, I guess. I don't know. But I may have been exposed." I paused, and then said, "There's a good chance I have been."

The line went quiet but for the sound of vehicles bumping over what I imagined was the ramp onto the car deck of the *Seward*. I imagined Nate thinking, I even pictured him in a similar position, in the jungle, waiting for colleagues to return from an infected village. I couldn't say if the image was an hallucination.

"Nate?"

"I'm here. I'm thinking."

"I thought so." I laughed for a second and Mary turned around to stare at me.

"I'm coming to you," Nate said. "I'll grab a hazmat suit from one of the fire trucks in town and…"

"Wait. Listen for a minute. There's a girl with me. Her mom was sick – she caught the virus at the airport."

"Then you need to get away from her…"

"No… maybe… but she's getting better. She has been with her mom all night, and all day. She got a fever, she's pulling through now."

Another pause, more metallic clangs from the ramp. I pictured a hold full of RVs, and, perhaps with a little organization – the automobile apartments. I smiled at my creative faculties, and assumed it was the first tickle of the fever. Nate's voice graveled along the line and I closed my ears, wishing myself closer, just for a moment. I wanted to be close, to lean in and forget about things as he ran his fingers through the tight curls of my hair, stroked my cheek and…

"Lewis," he shouted and I blinked my eyes open. "You need to keep talking to me. I need you to focus."

"I am focused. Maybe I'm just tired?" My words slurred in agreement. "It's not like we've slept much today… last night."

"Tell me about the girl."

"Mary?"

"Yes," Nate said and Mary turned at the sound of her name.

"She looks perky, or perkier."

"Really?" Nate's voice muffled as if he placed his hand over his cell phone. When his voice returned it was a few octaves higher.

"Jaylen, this is Stacey. We met earlier. I'm the paramedic."

"Sure, I know."

"Okay, well, you need to stay where you are. We're going to come and get you, but the girl needs to be with you. Christa has set up the lab on the ferry.

We need to take some of the girl's blood. See what we can find out."

"Okay," I said and beckoned Mary over with a weak wave. "We're at the roadblock."

"Stay there," Stacey said and ended the call. My cell phone beeped with a low battery warning and I slipped it into my pocket.

"Someone is going to pick us up."

Mary leaned the axe against the vehicle and slid onto the road beside me. She wrapped her arms around her legs and cuddled her knees to her chest. I grasped the talisman around my neck and tried to smile at her. She smiled back.

"They want my blood?"

"Yes," I said. "They think it might help."

"Just like in the movies."

"Yep." I closed my eyes and struggled with conflicting thoughts of thick soft blankets, and air conditioning. I imagined the cool waves blowing over me and washing over the roadblock and through the funnel, washing the body of Mary's father beyond her sight, washing the Chief's beyond mine. The raven scratched again at the container, cawing, squalling and croaking at its mates.

Mary said little while we waited, and I had nothing to say. I focused on the insides of my eyelids, playing with size of the shaft of light I would let in through my lashes. Thin, accentuated, like the mouth of a venus flytrap, and then large, open, and wider still as a man in an orange suit bent over my body and shone the beam from a penlight in my eyes. The beam stung and I closed my eyelids.

"Hey, Lewis," the man said. His voice was distant, hidden, but the gravelly undertones identified him as Nate, and my subconscious was glad. The rest of me was in no real shape to comment. I felt his arms slip under my armpits and I let him drag me to my feet, content to slump against his body until he lay me down on a gurney. There was a sharp prick of a needle, and then I felt a sheet of thick plastic beneath me, and heard the zip of a see-through body bag being zipped over my head. The zip was sealed with a second plastic zipper and a strip of surgical tape.

"There'll be a riot if people see us bringing her onboard in this," said a woman. I imagined it might be Stacey.

"I've seen riots," said Nate. I felt his gloved hand squeeze my fingers through the plastic. "You can park up on the dock. We'll come down to you when she's ready."

"And if she doesn't get better?" Stacey said. I felt a wave of air in my face as she opened the valve on the oxygen cylinder and door to the ambulance was slammed shut. Beyond Nate's helmeted face, I caught a glimpse of Mary sitting by the door of the ambulance. "We need you to keep the ship's engines running."

"I'll be onboard. We just need to give her time. See if she can fight it like the girl did."

"The chances of that are slim, Nate. You know that."

"Yeah, but…"

"But what?"

Nate squeezed my hand and I smiled at the comical way his mask dipped over his eyes and obscured his vision as he nodded for the driver to drive back to the ferry.

"Okay," said Stacey. "But we're not waiting for

ever."

"A couple hours."

"One hour," she said. "Any longer and the next wave of folks from Anchorage are going to turn up, and we have no idea what they are bringing with them."

The ambulance lurched around the roadblock and I closed my eyes as the driver settled into a steady speed. The lights inside were sharp, and I welcomed the return of the evening sky as we stopped at the AMHS terminal and I was wheeled inside.

"One hour," Stacey said and then she left us alone. I listened as the ambulance drove off and then gave up as sleep caught up with me.

I saw my dad as I cut my way through the Alaskan Bush. It felt more like the tropics, and more than once I reminded myself that *I* was the tropics, and the thick bush was just how my mind envisioned my fever. Dad waved a few times, and I tried to reach him. Each turn was thwarted by thick willow, thicker alder, and the thorns of a thousand vines that seemed out of place in Alaska, and yet completely at home. My hand was caught a few times, and I had to shake off the image of a snake, rubbery, with five short heads, only to realize it was a hand, and that hand was all that was anchoring me to the present and the terminal building by the side of the dock where the *Seward* was tethered and waiting.

During one of the brief moments when my father was hidden from sight, I heard myself say, "You should go. I'm sick. This is the virus. I am not going to make it."

The anchor went taut each time I said these words, I felt the squeeze of something human, not snakes at all, but a hand – his hand. Nate.

He didn't speak, not in words, but he was there, and every time I ventured too far into the bush in search of my father, he pulled me back, and tugged me into the terminal. When I finally opened my eyes and could see, he was there, his thick eyebrows pinched beneath furrowed brows, a plastic facemask framing his cheeks and Hispanic skin.

"My Mexican," I said, and caught myself as I realized it wasn't the fever talking.

Nate let go of my hand and reached up to unhook his mask. I protested as he began to pull it off, letting fly with a string of words that flew too fast for me to recognize them. They brushed against his hair, flicking at the curls on his forehead until I realized it was the air from his oxygen tank. He let the mask and helmet fall into his lap, as he reached forward to unzip me.

"Wait," I said. "You don't know if I'm…"

"Better? I think you are."

"How can you tell?"

Nate smiled as he opened the last of the zips and pushed the body bag either side of my shoulders. He took off his gloves and stood up to run his hand across the tight curls of my hair. His helmet fell to the floor with a soft thud. Nate let his hand linger on my forehead and then said, "Trust me. I can tell."

He stood there for another three minutes and I looked into his eyes as he searched my face for signs of sickness. I ran my fingers over my cheeks, testing for a rash, or old blood that might have trickled out of my nose as I tried to reach my dad, but there was nothing, just the shiny waxiness of old sweat.

"You're clean, Lewis," Nate said.

"And what does that mean?"

"One of two things," he said and moved his hand. I reached for it and smoothed my fingers between his. "Either that wasn't the virus – exhaustion, maybe – or you're immune."

"I don't believe I am immune," I said.

"Neither do I, unfortunately."

"Then it wasn't the virus."

"No."

"Then the Chief and his men died for what? A common cold?"

"I don't know. There must be an incubation period, before people become infectious. But the lesions on Mary's mom's body must have been hot with the virus. Did you see it?"

"No."

"Didn't get close?"

"Mary crawled out before I got the chance." I paused. "You don't think she can help?"

"I don't know. But we can help her," Nate said. I saw him frown as he looked at the door. It faced the road leading to the tunnel, and I heard the roar of engines and the crash of metal as something came tearing down the road toward the dock.

"We have to go," I said and swung my legs over the side of the gurney. The plastic caught around my feet and I fell over. It was dark outside and the headlights of one of several trucks powering toward us blinded me as Nate lifted my feet out of the plastic and set me straight.

"You okay?" he asked.

"A little woozy." I glanced at the approaching lights. "I can't run."

"You might have to."

I held onto Nate's shoulder as I tested my balance only to stumble as he twisted to face the doors at the back of the terminal, the ones leading to the *Seward*.

"I won't have you on my boat," roared a man as he charged into the waiting area.

"Wait a second, Grace," Nate said. He held up his palms, and gestured for the Captain to take it easy.

"No, Canizales, I don't think I will." Grace drew a pistol from his pocket and fired, just as the first truck crashed through the glass of the entrance to the terminal and slammed into the seats nearest the window.

Chapter 16

Nate moved fast, pulling me to the floor and behind the gurney as the vehicle's engine whined under the hood. The waiting room filled with a cloud of dust, as debris tumbled from the ceiling and the pillar buckled around the vehicle's bumper. My boots caught in the lip of the body bag and I fought to kick them free as the doors opened and two men jumped out. Both were armed with shotguns, and, using the doors as shields, they opened fire.

The shot shredded the mattress on the gurney in a hail of lead pellets. I heard Grace cry out as he ducked behind an overturned table and fired blindly from behind it. Nate grabbed the collar of my shirt and fleece jacket and pulled me across the floor to his side.

"Stay low," he said and pointed toward Grace. "Crawl toward him and get his gun."

"How?"

Nate pointed at the gurney as it buckled under another blast of shot. The shaft of my axe was just visible in the dust, and I thanked the AFD for teasing me with pink.

"Use that," Nate said. "Just wave it at him and he'll give up the gun."

"Where will you be?"

"Negotiating." He flicked his eyes toward the vehicle and the men taking turns to fire from behind it.

I hooked the head of the axe with the toe of my boot, pulled it into my hand and crawled toward Grace. My body was sluggish from the cocktail of sedative and antibiotics that Stacey had given me, but

I could still feel the sharp edges of the litter and debris from the ceiling as it pressed into my hands and knees. I paused as I heard Grace reload. The bullets tumbled to the floor and he cursed his trembling fingers. A quick glance at Nate confirmed that this was the time to push forward and to take him by surprise.

A third volley of shotgun blasts made me hug the floor, as I idly wondered why they were shooting, and to what end? The smoke cleared and I scurried around the table and slammed the flat head of my axe into Grace's chest. He crumpled to the floor and I gathered up the bullets at his feet and let go of the axe to pick up the pistol, it looked like something a private eye might have in an old TV show. I pressed the bullets into the cylinder as Nate called out to the men in the truck.

"We're not your enemy," he said. I peeked around the table and saw his raised hands.

"No?" the driver of the truck said. "So leaving us to die was an act of friendship?"

"We didn't leave anyone to die."

"Tell that to the State Troopers."

I ducked back behind the table and thought about the troopers from the helicopter back on the Seward Highway. They had done their bit, and made it possible to receive people in vehicles through the tunnel in a relatively orderly fashion. But what had become of them?

"What about them?" Nate said.

"They got in the way, and we got rid of them."

"Huh."

I took another peek and caught Nate's eye. He nodded at the pistol in my hands and gestured for me to throw it to him.

"Who's 'we'?"

"What do you care?" the driver said.

"I'd like to know who I'm negotiating with. That's all."

"Negotiating?"

"Yeah," Nate said. "You want something, don't you?"

"We want to get on the ferry."

"Of course, and we can help you," Nate said. "But, not if we're dead."

The driver talked in a low voice to the passenger and I nodded to Nate that I was ready to throw the pistol. I knew enough to check the safety and flicked it on, but I had never been happy around guns. I would let Nate do what he was obviously trained to do, reminding myself once again to ask him about his background when we had a chance.

I almost laughed. The thought of a quiet moment to chat with Nate seemed unlikely as I glanced at Grace clutching his chest by my side and at the two men intent on killing us, hiding behind the doors of their truck. Nate clicked his fingers; I took a breath and threw the gun.

The driver must have glimpsed the gun as it arced through the air toward Nate. He swore and jacked a shell into the barrel of his shotgun. His partner aimed and fired, but the firing pin clicked in an empty loading port. Nate stood as he caught the pistol and moved to grasp it in a two-handed grip. He flicked off the safety and fired, catching the driver in the chest and dropping him to the ground. The passenger dropped his shotgun and pulled the 9mm pistol from his belt. He fired and Nate staggered as the bullet clipped his shoulder and thwacked into the wall behind him. The passenger hid behind the door as Nate recovered and fired two more shots as he ran to the right. As the man popped up to fire, Nate dropped him with a bullet to the chest.

"Lewis," he called out and I pushed myself to my feet. I grabbed my axe and picked my way between the tables, chairs and plaster debris to stand next him. Nate lowered the pistol and pointed at the men. Plaster and dust from the ceiling stuck to the sweat on their foreheads, and their cheeks were swollen with blisters and lesions.

I lowered my axe to my side and reached for Nate's hand. His fingers were warm within mine, a trickle of blood from within his suit pooled at the cuff and felt damp around my wrist.

"Third time's a charm," he said, his voice flat and sad.

"That's why the troopers tried to stop them," I said. "That's why they died." I looked up at the blaze of lights from the vehicles lined up in front of the terminal building.

"We're infected now, Lewis. We've run out of luck."

I squeezed Nate's fingers tight and took a step back, pulling him with me. The drivers in the row of trucks, cars, and pickups revved their engines and inched forward for every step we backed away. We reached the table where Grace was hiding as the first vehicle nudged over the lip of the sidewalk, the glass of the entrance crunching beneath massive tires.

Grace massaged his chest and glared at me. I beckoned for him to come with us, but he shook his head and staggered to his feet.

"They'll kill you, Grace," Nate said. "Come with us."

"I'd rather die," he said and sneered.

Two women and a man, all wearing scarves to hide their faces, stepped out of the pickup at the entrance and walked inside the terminal, armed with a mix of pistols and hunting rifles.

"Grace," I whispered. "Don't…"

He ignored me and pushed a chair out of his way as he walked toward the infected refugees. He reached the bodies of the driver and his partner before they shot him. Nate pulled me close and whispered, "Get ready to run." I looked down as the blood at his wrist trickled from his hand onto my fingers.

"You can't run."

"He hit my shoulder, Lewis, not my legs."

"But you need help."

"Not yet. Not until we're safe."

"But we can't get on the boat, we're infected."

The soles of Nate's boots scuffed the floor as he tugged me toward the door. I looked over his shoulder and saw the crew of the *Seward* heaving at the ropes and slipping the ferry free of its moorings.

"The *Seward* needs an engineer. Once we're onboard they can lock me in the engine room for all I care."

I gripped the shaft of the axe in my hand as the two women stalked us along one side of the building, the man walked up the center. Maybe Grace knew what he was doing after all. As soon as he realized he was infected, he let them finish him, before the symptoms began, and the pain started. They certainly looked like they were in pain – the scarves were tied a little over their noses, their eyes were red and the skin around them was blistered. If we got on the ferry, then everyone onboard would be infected, and all this would be for nothing.

I gripped Nate's hand in mine and said, "We can't get on the ferry. I can't let us."

"Don't be stupid…"

"I'm not, and you know it."

I felt Nate's hand shake. I wondered if it was the wound in his shoulder, as if his body was going into shock. Then I remembered what the Chief had said, something about Ebola, and I realized he was scared, that he was reliving some previous nightmare, and despite the glare of the headlights making us squint, the darkness was very real, and the thought of infection suddenly made it that much darker.

"We have a few hours," he said. "Long enough to get onboard and quarantine ourselves before any symptoms begin to show, before we are infectious."

"You don't know that…"

"I know enough. I've seen it before. This virus, it might be fast, but it's still got to take root and grow before it can work its way out of our bodies and into another. People with Smallpox become infectious when the fever begins, not before. We have time."

"This isn't Smallpox," I said. "The incubation period is ridiculously fast – it was engineered that way."

"But it still has to take hold. Keep an eye on your temperature. If we start getting hot…"

"It'll be too late." I stopped moving and let go of Nate's hand. "We can't get onboard."

As the *Seward* blasted its foghorn, Nate looked over his shoulder. I looked too and saw the ferry pull away from the dock, white foam frothing at the stern. The ramp was lifting – they weren't even waiting for it to close before setting sail.

"Lewis…"

"No," I said and looked at the women. They moved past Grace's body and stopped to wait for the man as he raised his rifle to fire. "Better to die than risk a boat full of…"

I didn't finish. The wind was knocked out of my chest. I thought I had been shot, until I realized the blow had come from behind. There was a shot, also from behind me, it deafened my ear, the ringing loud and disorientating as the man searched for cover and Nate curled his arm beneath my arms and around my chest. "Sorry I hit you," he said as he dragged me out of the terminal building and down the loading ramp.

The women shouted and fired, the bullets snapping above our heads. Nate pinched my body to his as he tightened his grip. I struggled for breath, my lungs shocked by the blow to my back, restricted by Nate's arm clamping me to him. I turned my head, saw his knees rising and falling as he pounded down the loading ramp, the impact of each step jolting my body. I saw a flash of pink as Nate twisted the axe in his grip, before sliding his hand to the end of the shaft; the pick-head turned downward like a hook.

Another snap of a bullet above Nate's head splintered through the air. He ignored it, gripped me tighter than I thought possible. There was a crack, one of my ribs, and then Nate increased speed, raised the axe, and yelled as he leapt from the end of the concrete ramp and off the dock. There was a moment when we were flying, and then we crashed into the *Seward*'s loading ramp as the pick-head caught on the lip. I gasped as air raced into my lungs, and then I screamed as I realized the only reason I could breathe was because Nate had let go of me. I clawed at the smooth side of the ferry only to crash into the foam at the stern of the boat. My world turned white, and then black. I was enveloped in darkness, so cold that all the air left in my lungs was expelled. I panicked and breathed in a lungful of water, choking as I fought in the tumult of the waves between the dock and salvation – I was going to die: dead at the end of the line.

Chapter 17

There is a softness in the darkness, something unexpected, a peace of a kind that acts like a release. In that moment, when the cavitation of the Seward's propellers was lost in the darkness, when the vibration was masked in the waters, and there was no room in my lungs for air, and they were filled, I sank, conscious, if only for a moment longer, and at peace. We had taken a chance, a Hail Mary to save Alaska. When the lights in North America had begun to flicker and extinguish, one by one, when the Fire Chief talked with his daughter for the last time, when Whittier's savior had hidden the town onboard the ferry, when David had died because of fear, and Mary lived because of hope, when the actors had left the stage and the lights were dimmed, there was one candle that burned, a tiny flame against the dark, a glimmer of a new dawn, the chance for a new start. The flame grew until it was round, sharp, the light refracted by the water, but not enough; it hurt my eyes as I sank and I closed them, my boots heavy upon my feet. My lungs filled within my ribs. And then my ribs began to hurt. I remembered one was already cracked, another one splintered beneath a hammer, and another, tiny fractures that continued, on and on, one after another until my lungs began to empty and I spilled the water of the fjord onto the hard metal surface that pressed into my cheek, that zigzagged before my eyes until I closed them with the first wrack of air that I dragged into my lungs, coughing, spluttering, choking on one breath and then another, more ragged with the added pain of ribs unused to the violent act of breathing. I rolled onto my back and opened my eyes, tried to focus on the dark oval that twisted above me, a head, hair, wet, dripping. The face twisted and shouted, the words bubbling through the air.

"Stay back, get away. Don't come any closer."

A question cast back as the water leaked from my ears: Why?

No response, but an order, "Clear a path to the engine room. Keep everyone away. I'll take her myself."

Nate. It was his voice, his command, and then a female voice: Stacey.

"You're hurt. You're shot."

"I'll live," he said, and then, softer, "for the moment, at least."

I blinked the sea from my eyes and reached a wet hand to his wet cheek and stroked the hair from his eyes with a hand that trembled, out of control, but alive. "Thank you," I said.

He gripped my fingers in his hand and I felt the scratch of stubble upon my skin and his lips, cold, blue I thought, as they brushed my fingers.

"I almost lost you," he said.

"I'm here." I smiled as he kissed my fingers once more. "Because of you."

Nate pressed my fingers to his cheek, his eyes locked on mine, the water from his hair splashing upon my face. "We have to go," he said. "I'm taking you below decks."

I cried out as he lifted me from the deck, surprised by the pain in my ribs. He carried me until I protested and made him put me down. We used the stairs, descending through the decks until we reached the engine room and he led me to a chair in the engineer's office, a workspace welded between the pipes. Our new home.

Stacey followed, the visor of the biohazard suit masking the look in her eyes as she waited at the door. Nate looked at her and said, simply, "Close it."

"Not until you tell me what's going on," she said.

"The *Seward* needs an engineer. That's me."

"You're sick. Aren't you?"

"Close the door, Stacey. Make sure no one comes in here."

"The air conditioning…"

"Is on a closed system to prevent fumes leaking into the passenger areas. We're locked down. You'll be safe."

"Until we need to get in here, when you're dead."

Nate pulled off his thermal top. It slapped wet upon the deck as he threw it onto the floor of the office. Stacey waited at the door until he looked at her.

"You're still here."

"And staying."

"And every second is another second of exposure."

"Do you have a fever?"

"No."

"And you, Jaylen? What about you?"

"I'm cold," I said.

"You nearly drowned," said Nate. I felt his gaze as he looked at me. I stared back, happy to lose myself in his eyes, if only for a moment.

The door creaked as Stacey pulled on it. "I'll find your gear," she said. "You need warm clothes."

"Coffee would be nice." Nate examined his shoulder in the glass of the office window. "And food," he said. "Whatever you can find."

Stacey nodded and then shut the door. It clanged, and then the dogs turned as she sealed it. We were alone, and that moment I had imagined had come, finally, when Nate and I could talk.

I had nothing to say.

My lips trembled and I started to shiver. He looked at me. I tried to smile but my teeth chattered and I managed little more than a mumble before he lifted my arms and started tugging at my fleece.

I managed to say, "Zip," and he opened it and shook the fleece over my arms and dropped it on the floor. I cried out as my ribs protested, and then he started on my top. It clung to my skin. I cried out again and he gave up, reaching instead for the knife on my belt. Nate opened the blade with his thumb and sliced through my top until it hung from my neck. He paused at the sight of my cloud-colored bra before cutting away the remains of my thermal top and draping a coarse blanket from the chest of fire equipment around my upper body. He nodded at my pants and boots.

"We'll need to take them off too."

"We?" I said with a slur, my tongue thick and lumpy with cold.

"It can wait."

He turned away and I watched as he rifled through the small kitchen area — a hotplate and an electric kettle — in the far corner of the makeshift office. Energy thrummed through the hull of the *Seward* as we sailed further from the dock in Whittier. Nate opened the lid of the kettle, checked the level of the water, and set it to boil. He leaned against a counter and looked at me. I thought it was only fair to look at him too, to study his broad chest, the muscles ribbed across his stomach, his arms, the tightness of his biceps, and the blood smeared across his upper body.

"You've been shot," I said.

"So people say."

"Are you going to do something about it?"

Nate glanced at his shoulder and prodded the wound with this finger. There was a first aid kit mounted on the wall above the kettle. Nate opened it and cleaned the wound with a sterile dressing. He pressed a thick patch of gauze over the ragged groove in his skin and secured it with a large square plaster. The kettle reached boiling point and Nate found a mug on the hotplate. He wiped it with his hand and filled it with boiling water.

"To warm you up," he said and handed it to me.

"Coffee would be nice," I said and smiled.

"That's what I said."

I warmed my hands around the mug and sipped at the water. It was hot, but that was all it had going for it. I watched Nate over the rim of the mug as he pulled a second blanket from the chest and wrapped it around his body like a cape. The word superhero sprang to mind and I laughed. Nate raised an eyebrow and I saw my opportunity.

"Tell me about Africa," I said.

In the silence that followed, I wondered if I had touched a nerve, or opened a wound. Nate pulled a second chair out from under the desk and sat down. He wiped the last drops of sea from his forehead and cleared his throat.

"Her name was Nneka. She was from Liberia."

The name took me by surprise; I had expected a

different kind of story. I took another sip and waited.

"She died in the Ebola outbreak in November, 2014. I met her when I was working in West Africa. I was fixing generators, she was an aid worker." Nate paused for a moment. He tugged the blanket tight around his chest, gripping the edges in a fist. "Ebola took her," he said. "She was exposed every day, and then one time too many. There was nothing I could do. Nothing anyone could do." He looked up. His eyes, dark, sad, they bored into mine and he said, "You remind me of her."

I jumped at the sound of something metal clanging against the door. When I looked back at Nate, he was on his feet. He walked past me and I held out my hand. Our fingers brushed together and then he was gone. I heard the door open, heard Stacey's muffled voice, and the soft thud of our packs being dumped onto the deck followed by a dull heavy clang.

"My axe," I said and smiled.

Stacey shut the door and locked it as Nate brought our gear inside the office. He leaned my axe against the desk and I frowned at the blisters of paint peeling in the spots where Nate and I had gripped it. He followed my gaze and laughed.

"You can always repaint it," he said.

"Maybe I will."

It was unsaid, but we were both thinking the same thought, both thinking about the end. Nate opened a package and pulled out sandwiches and chocolate. There was root beer too, and I swapped it for the mug in my hand, popped the tab, and enjoyed the first few mouthfuls before reaching for a sandwich.

"Stacey said the storm is coming in from the east. You can feel it," he said, "through the hull."

"How bad?"

"Bad enough. We're overloaded. She said the crew – short-staffed – is still tying down the RVs. They have people helping them, but," he shrugged, "there's not much they can do."

"And what about us? Do they know we might be sick?"

"Some people saw us, but Stacey says no one has said anything. Not yet."

"They'll panic if it gets out."

Nate shook his head. "Not during the storm. That will keep people busy. Keep their minds occupied."

"And what do we do?" I said. "Ride the storm out down here?"

"That's the plan."

"And wait 'til we get sick."

"I didn't say it was a good plan," he said. "But it's what we have." He took another bite of his sandwich.

"And Mary's blood? Can we do anything with that?"

"It's a reach, but Stacey says they're looking into it." Nate dumped the remains of his sandwich in a paper bag. "I have to check the engines."

"I'll come with you.

"No. Change first. I'll be in there," he said and pointed to a gantry leading to a door. "You might think it's loud in here, but you'll need ear defenders inside the engine room." He unhooked a pair hanging from a bent wire screwed into a wooden shelf. "Bring these when you come."

Nate left me to change and I pulled off my pants,

dried myself with the blanket and changed my underwear. I dug around for my spare clothes and realized I had not anticipated swimming. I had everything but a dry set of pants. I looked around the office and found a boiler suit. I stepped into it, tied the arms around my waist like a belt, and slid my feet inside my sodden boots. I clumped around the office while I finished my soda, and then decided to find Nate.

I stopped at the ladder leading up to the gantry. My head spun for a second, and, as much as I wanted to believe it was the motion of the boat, as it got closer to the storm, I knew that it was my own body. My temperature was rising, and with every degree of heat and discomfort, so did my levels of infection. The storm was going to be the least of my worries.

Chapter 18

I could see the engine room from the gantry, and hear the massive diesel engines compensating for the heavy seas being whipped up the fjord by the storm. I used the handrails and staggered to the window to see Nate moving between the digital display at the workstation and the analogue gauges spread at intervals around the engines. I clasped the handle to unlock the door just as a huge crash thundered through the deck above me. The *Seward* listed to its port side for a moment and then righted itself with a second roll of thunder. However fast the virus was attacking my body I decided that death by sinking was more likely. I turned away from Nate and ran for the stairs, stopping to grab my axe from the engineer's office.

The car deck looked like a Demolition Derby, and I hesitated at the door before stepping onto the deck. The crew were working at a fevered pace to secure the various vehicles of different sizes as the ferry slammed into the waves. I heard a scream and a shout of warning as a pickup with a cab separated, the cab hurtling into the port bulkhead, the pickup crumpling against one of the Fred Meyer trucks. I spread my weight and tried to compensate for the movement of the deck. I had been at sea before, and didn't suffer from motion sickness. Others were not so lucky. I searched the deck and spotted Aatag and his family sheltering between the family pickup and an ambulance – I recognized it as the one containing David's body. I waited for a lull in the motion of the ferry and ran across the deck toward them. I stopped when Nukka saw me. She flashed a smile and crawled out of her daddy's arms as if she was going to run to me.

"No," I yelled and waved my hands. "Stop, Nukka. Stay there."

She stopped and stared, a deep frown pinched her forehead. A woman got up from where she was sitting beside Aatag and I wondered if it was Sierra, recovered from her infection, only to be thrust into grief and grave danger on the deck of a ferry in the opening salvo of a Fall storm. She walked around her husband and took Nukka's hand. Aatag pointed at the crew of the *Seward*.

"Help them," he shouted. "Before we all die."

"Right." I turned away from Nukka and ran to the crew trying to secure the vehicles to the floor of the car deck. I found the foreman with a length of chain in his hand and a huge gash on his forehead.

"Who are you?" he said. "Where'd you come from?"

"Doesn't matter," I said. "I'm with FEMA. What do you need?"

"We didn't get everything tied down before we pulled away from the dock. Now the storm's coming and we're taking a beating. I've lost two men already – crushed beneath cars. If we don't get these vehicles locked in... it only needs one wave and we're finished."

"How many crew?"

"Me and Heath, here. That's it for the lower decks. Oh, and there's some guy in engineering, but we're not supposed to go down there. Could be he's sick."

"Could be," I said and thought of Nate doing his best to keep the *Seward*'s heart pumping. "Can I help?"

"I don't know? Do you know trucks?"

"I was a firefighter in Anchorage…" I raised my axe and smiled as he looked at it.

"That'll do." The foreman slapped a tie-down hook and strop into my hands, shouting as the deck groaned and the loose vehicles began to slide, "One at a time. Let's get this done."

The crewman called Heath secured the last hook around the car in front of me and then pointed at an RV slipping along the deck, tearing the mirrors and side panels off a row of vehicles.

"That one's heavy. I saw the inside," the foreman said, as he jogged after the RV. "Full of stuff. I guess the owners looted a gas station before they got to Whittier." He pointed at the right side of the vehicle, as the foreman moved toward the back. "It'll stop when it hits that truck," he said and pointed at the second Fred Meyer truck. "We'll tie it down as best we can, move it when the storm dies."

I watched Heath grab the first rung of the ladder at the back of the RV and clamber onto the roof, a strap and hook draped around his shoulders.

"What's he doing?" I said.

"You don't want to go down the sides, that's how Jones and Petersen bought it – crushed when the boat shifted." He reached out and grabbed my arm as the RV began to slide to the right as the boat listed. It slipped left again as the *Seward* righted itself. Heath rode the top of the RV like a clumsy surfer, staggering for balance, falling to his knees to grab the roof rack as the RV crunched into the side of the truck. He cursed like a firefighter and I decided I liked him.

Heath staggered to his feet and looked down at

us. "Go now," he said and pointed to both sides of the RV. "It's gonna roll back any second." He disappeared from view and I heard him slide down the windshield as the foreman and I ran down each side. Heath was still cursing as I looped one of my strops around the back wheel and hooked it into the deck. The second wasn't so easy. The nearest anchor point was too far away for me to hook the RV to the deck. I spun around as the *Seward* shifted again, slammed by another wave. The RV started to slide toward the row of vehicles to my right. I held my axe above my head, the shaft running parallel to my shoulders, and saw a coil of rope hanging from the back of a pickup. It was as thick as my wrist. When the RV pressed against the head of the axe, and the end of the shaft began to bend the side panel of the pickup, I grabbed the rope, looped it around the RV's wheel and played it out in my hands before securing the end of the strop around it. I hooked the end into the deck as the foreman yelled that he was done. Heath leapt off the front of the RV and onto the deck. He raised his thumb in my direction only to lower it again, as the *Seward* began to list heavily to one side, the port side – always the same.

I heard metal scraping along the deck and then a motorcycle slid down the gap between two rows of vehicles, a stream of sparks from its gas tank. The angle of the deck increased and so did the speed at which the motorcycle was sliding. Heath and the foreman grabbed the side of the RV and I grabbed the rope. The motorcycle sped past us, beneath my axe and the Fred Meyer truck closest to the bulkhead. It burst into flames, as its gas tank ruptured on impact.

"I've got this," I yelled and scrambled over the rope and between the cars to the firefighting equipment closest to the motorcycle. I could feel the heat of the flames on my skin, and the heat of the virus inside my body as I pushed myself to grab the hose, and yank it free of the wall mounting. I cranked open the valve and doused the fire with seawater.

"Let Heath do it," said the foreman as he made his way toward me. Heath was younger and faster than his boss, he took the hose from my hand and worked his way toward the motorcycle. "You need to get topside and see what's going on."

"But the deck?" I said.

"Leave that to us. Get up to the bridge. Find out why we're listing so bad."

"All right," I said and grabbed his hand. "Name's Jaylen."

"Haycott," he said, and grinned. "Welcome aboard."

"Thanks." I let go of his hand, conscious of the sweat I left on his palm. I pushed the thought of infection from my mind, thinking instead of Mary's blood and the skills of the lab technician being spun around her mobile lab like she was in a spin cycle.

"You all right?" Haycott said, as I moved toward the door.

"Just tired," I said. "Good luck." I slapped my axe upward and free of the RV and then I moved, as fast as I could, up the stairs from one deck to the next.

The decks were crowded; I had to push my way between people. I could only hope I wasn't infectious yet, but my body knew what my brain was trying to deny – it was hopeless, I was at the edge of a cytokine storm. As I shoved and pressed my way between the people lining the decks and stairs, I was overwhelmed by the number of people, the sight and smell of the survivors in such close proximity, the fear etched on their faces, the retching and the crying, the babies, the teens, parents, and grandparents. These were the people from Whittier and the parts of Alaska that had made it out of the city and through the tunnel. I had made this happen, the Chief and I had put them on the boat, But now, I thought as I climbed the last staircase to the bridge, I had probably killed them all as the virus began to build inside my body. Soon, it would leak out of the pores of my skin, disperse into the air from the breath in my lungs.

The bridge was locked.

I thumped on the door with the side of the pickhead. There was a scuffle behind me, and an old man pushed forward. He looked at my axe and then at me. He said, "The Captain locked himself inside about an hour ago. The only way onto the bridge is through it."

"Through it?"

"The window," he said and pointed at a door that led onto the deck outside.

I moved without thinking, pushing through the passengers and barging my way onto the deck. The sky was a tumult of granite and obsidian as the storm whipped the clouds into an anvil, the tip of which pointed straight down a few miles or so in front of the *Seward*. I clawed my way along the wet rail, glad of the rain cooling my face, and the weight of the axe in my hand. There was a chain across a small ladder leading up to the bridge. I sliced it in half and carried on, climbing one-handed, one rung at a time, the axe heavy, the wind abrasive.

I stopped at the top of the ladder, one hand on the railing as my feet slid to one side in the direction of the *Seward*'s list. I spared a thought for Nate in engineering, Nukka, Aatag and the rest of the family, for Haycott and Heath securing the car deck, and for the passengers, infected – or not, frightened by the virus and weakened by their flight and the storm on each deck. I made my way onto the narrow walkway between the window of the bridge and the long drop to the observation deck below. The Captain was clinging to his chair, a bottle of something in his hand, as a crewman fought with the wheel and another yelled at the Captain to do something. I couldn't hear, but the message was clear, the panic on the crewman's face clearer still. I tapped the tip of the pick-head on the window, let it scratch across the surface of the glass to the small door on the starboard side, and then raised the axe in both hands. The glass in the door splintered with my first strike, shattered with my second. I reached inside, opened the door and entered the bridge.

"I'm with FEMA," I said, as I half walked, half slid across the deck to the Captain's chair. I slapped the bottle from his hand with the head of my axe and grabbed him by the lapel of his uniform shirt. "Captain Berg?"

Berg rolled his head and stared at me. There was spittle in his chin and his breath stank of bourbon. I let go of him and he slumped in the chair. I turned to the crewman whose lips I had read from the other side of the glass.

"What's your name?"

"Trent," he said. "That's Worthing at the helm."

I looked at the officer doing her best to steer the

stricken boat away from the northern shores of the fjord.

"What's going on, Trent?"

"We hit something. The last time we listed, we must have put a tear in the hull. It's either that or all the cars below deck have shifted to the port side."

"It's not the cars. Haycott has that under control."

"Then we've got a hole," Worthing said, "because I can't right this."

I used the instrument panels and chairs to slide my way to the port side of the bridge and looked through the window. It was too black to see, but we were definitely drifting toward the shore, the storm whipped the water into surges of white terror that crashed on the rocks.

"If we have a hole in the boat," Trent continued, "and if we hit the shore, we will sink."

"How will we know?" I asked, although I knew the answer already. My stomach knotted as I thought of Nate below.

"Visual inspection," said Trent. "Someone has to get below decks and see if we have water coming in." He paused. "I wanted to go, but the Captain…"

"Stay here," I said. "Keep the door locked until I come back." I scanned the bridge. "Do you have an intercom system?"

"Yes, the black boxes on the bulkheads. There will be one by each door."

"And a flashlight?"

Trent staggered across the bridge and opened a cabinet. He pulled out a Maglite, twisted the head to see if it worked and then handed it to me.

"I'll call you when I know more," I said and

made my way to the door I had used to force my way onto the bridge.

"If we have a hole, it will need to be prepared, the compartment sealed at the very least."

"How do I repair it?"

"There's welding gear and patches in engineering." Trent frowned then his face brightened. "There's a man down there. The Captain said so before he started drinking. He said his name was Nathan or something, and that if anyone could fix a breach, he could."

I smiled at the thought of Nate, and how much praise had been showered on him by all the people I had met since the first reports of the virus, before I was promoted, before my job had even begun. I thought of his dark hair, his dark creamy skin, and his fathomless eyes. The timing was inappropriate to say the least, but the thought made me smile, lifted my spirits, until Trent's voice cut through any strength such thoughts had given me, and pummeled my stomach.

"Of course, there's no telling if engineering isn't already flooding, and, if it is, he might already be drowned, and we're lost."

"No," I said to myself and curled my fingers around the shaft of my axe. "We're not lost. Not yet." I stepped through the door, gritted my teeth and stared into the storm as I made my way to the ladder, to the stairs, and below decks. I had come too far to give up without a fight, too far to give up on Nate, and too far to give in.

Chapter 19

The *Seward* groaned with steel bellows rumbling through the bulkheads as she listed. Passengers screamed and clustered, some falling, some gasping for air, and more rushing and fighting for the starboard deck. I raised my axe above my head, my hands gripping the shaft at both ends, and pressed my way through the crowd. I tried to ignore the flushes I felt crawling up my neck, the throbbing at my temples, and what I imagined to be spoonfuls of sweat cascading from my brow and slicking the tight curls of my hair to my scalp. The virus, I thought, was beginning to rage – it wanted out, and the sight, smell, and sound of the passengers I shoved and barged my way through must have been tantalizing.

"Just give me one more hour," I said through gritted teeth. "That's all I need."

Honestly, I didn't know exactly what I could achieve in an hour, but I figured that sixty minutes from now it would all be over, Nate drowned, and the *Seward* sinking. Everything I had fought for up to that point would have been for nothing. The only bright side would be that the virus would be deprived of more hosts – they would all be dead. And Nukka, I realized – she would be dead too. The thought lingered as I reached the door to the car deck, yanked it open, and walked through it.

I saw Haycott and Heath, walking uphill toward the starboard side of the ferry, carrying a dead crew member. They set her body down beside another and sat down on the deck. They seemed oblivious to the shrieks of steel – louder and amplified on the car deck – as the *Seward* keened at the beginning of her death roll. I turned away and caught a dart of movement as a little girl – Nukka – slipped away from her parents and ran toward me, arms outstretched like she was a raven soaring. I remembered the talisman and pressed it to my breast, the claws pricking my skin as she flew closer.

"Stop," I said, but she ignored me. She flew to within just a few feet, her tiny feet tickling the metal plates. Nukka lowered her arms to her sides and pointed at me, her finger straight, sharp, it pricked me in the chest.

"Fight it," she said. "Don't let it win."

Her voice was strong, commanding, older than her years. Her eyes pierced mine, sharp like the tip of her pointed finger that pricked me. I blinked, thinking that the virus had taken hold and that it had given Nukka wings. But she stood there, just in front of me, and insisted that I should fight it, fight the virus, ignore the heat and the fuzziness, that I should get on and get going.

"Fight it," she said again. "Save Nate."

"I will," I said and felt the axe grow lighter in my grip.

"He needs you, Jaylen." Nukka's words were those of an adult, wiser than my own. "We all do. Now go."

It could have been the virus – the rational part of my brain said so – but when Nukka lifted her arms and spun on the balls of her tiny feet to fly back to her family, I could feel the wind from the beat of her wings, and it lifted me, gave me strength. I waited until the last lick of it was gone, turned, and walked back to the stairs and down to engineering.

The *Seward*'s shrieks were distant now as I pushed

them to the back of my mind and focused on the hiss of water, like a persistent snake that would not be satisfied until it had gorged itself on humanity, until its body was stuffed, or flooded like the lower decks of the ferry.

I reached the first door, dogged tight and sealed. I pressed my nose against the glass and saw Nate, his clothes clinging to his body, as he pressed a plate of thin steel against the bulkhead. He jammed his foot against it and lit the acetylene torch. Nate adjusted the flame to a jet of brilliant blue that resisted the spit of water as it hissed around him. He worked his way around the corners of the sheet of metal, fixing it temporarily so that he could remove his boot and change position.

"Nate," I yelled and banged on the circle of thick glass in the door. He didn't turn. It was likely he couldn't hear me, so I stopped yelling and tried the door, cursing when I realized it wasn't just tight, it was tied, something was wrapped around the handles. I lifted myself up and looked down through the glass at an angle. There was a fire hose wrapped around the dogs on the inside of the door, and a crowbar threaded through them like a hairpin. I could twist and curse all I wanted, but Nate had made certain that no one was opening this door.

"Damn it, Nate," I said and kicked the door. I smarted at the pain in my toe, turned in the space in front of the door, saw the intercom and pushed the button to speak to the bridge.

"Trent? I can't get in. The door is locked."

"There's another way in," he said. "Near the bow of the ship. There should be a map by the door."

I found the plan of the ship mounted to the wall

and traced the route around the engine room to a door on the opposite side. It would mean going up to the car deck and opening a door to a small service deck by the rear ramp, and then gaining access through a small door in the hull. I smashed the glass of the frame securing the map to the wall with the butt of my axe. When I studied it closely, I realized that the door I wanted was on the port side of the *Seward*.

I bit my lip and cursed, tasted blood, and then turned as a breath of air tickled my nose and tugged at my eyelashes. Nukka was teasing me into action, and I could feel dad's genes responding. It was time to listen to my old man, and to be inspired by a tiny Native Alaskan girl, wise beyond her years.

"All right," I said and stuffed the map inside the boiler suit. I spared a quick glance through the window at Nate. If the girl and my father failed to motivate me, the water rising to Nate's hips were all the encouragement I needed. I slapped my hand on the window and pushed off in the direction of the stairs.

The cars, RVs and trucks strained at the anchors hooked into the deck as the ferry listed further and further to the port side. I clawed my way along the bulkhead toward the stern, hoping that Aatag had taken his family to the upper decks. There was no sign of Haycott and Heath, the bodies of their coworkers were gone too, and I paused for a second to admire the risks they had taken to take care of the dead. I imagined burials at sea, and wondered if we would ever get the chance to perform them. I shook the thought from my head and climbed up and over a pickup that was wedged against the bulkhead. When I looked up I could see the door, just to the left of the ramp. I leaped over the side of the pickup and moved faster, the axe growing heavier in my grip as my fever threatened to return. I let my dad's genes take on the virus as I reached the door, grabbed the handle, and yanked it open.

The lights from the decks above lit the sea below, the light shining at an angle as the waves splashed against the hull, the white froth mesmerizing and deadly. The hairs on my arm prickled and my lungs fought for a proper breath as the wind buffeted my body. I hooked the pick end of the axe around the door handle and leaned over the railing. If I let go gravity would assist me all the way to the black water crashing beneath me. If I hooked my arm in the rungs of the ladder, I might just be able to work my way down onto the service deck below and get back inside the ferry. The axe would be a pain, I realized as I let my grip slide down the shaft so that I could reach the ladder.

"But I need it," I said, my voice lost in the wind. I thought back to Sandy and the guys celebrating my last night at the AFD. The pink paint was flaking and fading, but it was no ornamental axe they had given me – it was the real deal. I couldn't remember using a fire axe for so many uninterrupted hours before, except maybe on the day my mom died. That was the day I decided to study to become something else. I had had enough of being on the frontline. The thought made me smile, and, suitably distracted, I fooled myself into thinking everything was going to be all right, reached out for the ladder, and hooked my free arm through the first railing. I let the axe head slide free of the door handle and made my way down the ladder.

It struck me, halfway down, that it must be Sunday, or it would be soon. My first weekend off in a long time had turned out to be my busiest, perhaps even my last. The distractions – all of them – helped, and I descended the ladder and used the axe to hook my way onto the service deck. I got to the door, spun the dogs to open it, and crawled inside. The wind, its fierce bite and constant roar, retreated and I was left alone with the shrieks and groans of the *Seward*.

I reached for the map and cursed; it was gone. It must have blown out of my pocket when I climbed down the ladder. The flashlight was gone too. The lights began to flicker and I squinted into the gloom. I walked along the small corridor, my feet angled on the deck and the bulkhead, sloshing through a trough of water. The list was more pronounced so deep in the ferry. The slosh of my boots through the water echoed as I moved in what I hoped was the right direction. I could hear knocking ahead, and, as the lights flickered again, I saw a blue flare through the glass in the door in front of me.

There was Nate, closer now, but the water was at his chest. The patch was beneath him, and I watched as he took a huge breath and then ducked under the water to weld another patch into place. I couldn't see how far he had got, how many patches he had fixed, only that he was not stopping or slowing, the rising water determined his pace, and his purpose. I banged on the window when he resurfaced and slipped my hands around the circular handle. Nate looked at me and then at the door as the sound of the handle turning made him drop the acetylene torch and force his way through the water toward me.

"No," he shouted, his voice muffled. He waved his arms, as I continued to turn the handle. It jammed as he pressed his face to the window and I realized he was holding it on the other side. "You'll sink the ship if you open it," he said.

"You'll die if I don't."

"I'll die anyway." He looked away for a moment, a silent curse on his lips: Carajo.

"No," I said, and I could feel the tears begin to trickle down my salt-streaked cheeks. "You don't have to. Stacey said there might be a way, that they might even have some kind of vaccine… maybe a transfusion from Mary."

"There's no vaccine, Lewis. You'd have to be the same blood type as the girl to even stand a chance of it fighting the virus. I'm dead already, let me save the ship."

"Don't say that. Don't…"

"You know it's true." Nate paused to look down at the water. As the ferry listed the water rose to a level just below his armpits. He frowned, the water was lapping his body from the other side, the *Seward* wasn't listing to port, it was rising to starboard. As the ferry began to right itself in slow increments, I realized the height to the ceiling of the compartment Nate was in was shorter than it was wide. As the boat righted itself, the air space above Nate's head shrank and the water covered his nose. Nate climbed up onto the lip of the door and slipped. He banged his head on the frame of the window and a trickle of blood dispersed in the water like ink.

"Nate," I shouted. I grabbed at the handle but he held on from the other side.

"You'll sink the ship," he said.

"No, you've saved it. the patches are holding, the *Seward* is righting itself. Let me open the door."

"I can't do that."

"You can, Nate." My voice cracked and I cried out, "Please."

Nate's head dipped from view and I shouted again, yanked at the handle and then used it to lift myself higher so I could look down at him. I looked into his eyes as he looked up, bubbles of air streamed from his nose and the corners of his mouth. The water was above his head. Either he was too weak from the infection to try and climb above it, or he was too spent to care.

"Don't you leave me," I shouted. "I won't let you."

Nate blinked once, the bubbles continued to stream around his face. His eyes, those black orbs that I had fallen in love with, paled as the light drifted from them, absorbed by the dark waters cooling his body to a temperature way below what the human body could tolerate. Add to that the physical exertion, the virus raging beneath his skin, I realized he was all out of energy – he wasn't giving up, he was dying.

"Nate," I shouted again. His eyes closed and his body began to drift, as the lights flickered out on both sides of the door. I grabbed the handle and tugged at it. It spun freely in my hands and I turned it until I began to feel the pressure of the water behind the door. I wondered if it truly was a good idea to open it, and then realized I didn't care. Nate was near-drowned, I could save him.

I turned the handle and the door exploded open, catching me full in the chest, but not before the edge of the door struck me in the center of my forehead.

Sunday

PRINCE WILLIAM SOUND, ALASKA

Chapter 20

I don't remember the actual day my father left, but I do remember the month. It was October. The winter dark had begun and the stores in Anchorage had turned that subtle shade of plastic orange and black in preparation for Halloween. Dad had taken me to Fred Meyer's to explain what he was trying to accomplish in the wilderness, and why he hoped, one day, I might come and live with him.

"If you could bring your mom," he said, "that would be even better."

"Mom thinks you're crazy." I sipped my coke and swung my legs beneath the chair. I was twelve and loving it, determined to enjoy every single month before I was officially a teenager. Not being a teen was the best excuse I had for doing some things and not doing a whole bunch of others. I used it a lot. Daily. Anytime someone wanted to land me with the you-should-know-better, or you're-too-old-for-that-now I would remind them that I was only twelve, and that it would be a whole year – I was flexible with the precise number of months – before I could be accountable in the way that teens were. It drove people nuts. People like my dad.

"I'm not crazy. I just know something is going to happen one day, and I want you and your mom to be safe, with me."

"In the bush, dad. You want us to be in the middle of nowhere, in the wilderness. That's what you said – the wilderness."

Dad sipped his coffee and tapped a packet of cigarettes on the table. "It's safe there," he said.

I hoped he was right. I hoped he was safe. Mom

might have struggled with his prepping obsessions, and his temper, but she never stopped loving him, and I know he never stopped loving us.

Love. I thought about it as something bright threatened to peel the lids from my eyes. It was like the sun was just there, right in front of my face. I actually felt sunlight on my cheeks, and there was fresh air brushing my face, tickling my nose. I shelved my memory of dad and opened one eye. It was bright, and the sun was right above me. I opened my other eye and slipped my hands to my sides, spreading my palms across the surface of whatever it was I was lying on. It was cold, knobbled with tiny diamonds. I was on a deck. I looked around me, blinked, recognized the railings and the windows. I tried to sit up but a hand pushed me gently down, back onto the deck.

"Easy now," Stacey said, as she knelt beside me. "Give yourself a moment. You've had quite the cocktail."

"Cocktail?" I turned my head and saw a needle and tube pressed into my skin and taped to my arm. I followed the tube and saw Mary waving at me just a few feet away.

"Yep. You and Mary share the same blood type. When they found you, I figured there was nothing to lose, and hooked you up to the human vaccine machine…"

"I still don't like the name," Mary said.

"But it's what you are," Stacey said. She looked at me. "We got you dried out, then brought you out here – it's a little crowded inside. Something for you to work out later."

"Me?"

"That was quite a blow you took to the head, you've obviously forgotten this little experiment of yours: *Seward's Ark*."

"I like that name better," said Mary.

"It's good isn't it? But, we're not out of the woods, and barely out of Whittier. If this is going to work, we are going to have to manage this, and that's a job for FEMA. Nathaniel says you start tomorrow."

"Nate," I said and grabbed Stacey's arm. "Where is he?"

"Alive. He's in quarantine, on the car deck. I put my husband in charge of that one."

"Can I see him?" I moved to sit up.

"Sure you can. Later. Rest up first, and then we'll suit you up and you can go see him."

"Are there many sick?"

"Just Nate."

"But he's going to make it?"

Stacey pointed at Mary. "The vaccine machine over there has pretty aggressive cells for a Nanooks Athletics fan. Christa has been holed-up in the mobile lab since we got here. It seems the virus has a vulnerability; its speed is both its greatest strength and biggest weakness. The faster it attacks the host, the weaker it becomes. When it leaps to a new host with an abnormally large number of white blood cells…"

"Like me," said Mary.

"…it is engulfed and can't cope. It is so busy replicating that it spreads itself too thin. It's possible it may even have been engineered to blow over as fast as it spread."

I lifted my head and looked at Mary. "Why do you have such a high white blood cell count?"

"I have leukemia," she said and shrugged. "Never

thought I would be pleased about that."

"So," Stacey said, "it makes me wonder if they – whoever they are – intended to release the virus when they did, or we just caught a lucky break. We've spread the news about Mary as far and wide as possible, although," she paused for a moment, "I think the damage has already been done."

I lay down and thought for a moment. While the revelation about the virus' weakness and the potential vaccine to beat it was exciting, I only had one real thought in my mind: Nate was alive. I needed to see him. My heart started to beat faster and I must have flushed a bunch of blood – my own and Mary's – into my cheeks. Stacey reacted and ordered to me to rest. All I wanted was to get up and go see Nate.

There was a pinch on my arm and I watched as Stacey pressed a small square of bandage over the needle in my skin, withdrew it, and then covered the bandage with a strip of tape. "Bend your arm," she said, "and rest. I have to go see some more patients. That was quite a storm. You weren't the only one to get knocked about." She squeezed my hand, stood up and walked away. Mary followed, her arm bent, teasing the bandage taped to her skin with her finger.

I waited until they were gone, and I couldn't hear their footsteps on the deck. I sat up and then wobbled to my feet, holding onto the railing for support. A slow scan of the deck showed that I was on the restaurant deck. I made my way inside and walked down the stairs.

There was a buzz around the people I brushed past. They were less agitated, grateful that the storm had passed, and that the *Seward* was sailing level again. I caught glimpses of families and fragments of conversation as I continued down to the car deck. Several groups talked about the Captain, and I realized I was going to have to face Berg, and soon. I needed him and his authority if I was going to create any sense of order aboard the ferry. I also needed him to stay off the booze. So I decided, as soon as I had seen Nate, I would go back up though the decks to the bridge.

I paused at the entrance to the car deck and looked for anything that might look like a quarantine area. I didn't have to search for long, the armed guards and the perimeter of white rope and orange cones surrounding a long Winnebago kind of gave it away. I took a step toward it and stopped at the sound of tiny feet skipping along the deck.

"Nukka," I said, as the little girl slowed to a stop and grabbed my hand. Her fingers were warm and she pulled me down and placed her hand on the talisman hanging from my neck. "It worked. Thank you." I let go of her hand to remove the raven's claw, but she stopped me with a brief shake of her head.

"Keep it," she said and took my hand. Nukka led me toward the Winnebago stopping only when the guards stiffened and waved for us to stop.

"Go back to your family," I said to Nukka, and she slipped her hand free and skipped away.

"I need to see Nate."

"This is a quarantine," said the man closest to me. His voice was muffled by the respirator covering his nose and mouth. His hand rested on the gun holstered at his hip.

"I know. But I need to see the man you have in there. It's important."

"Maybe, ma'am, but…"

I had never been called ma'am, and I might even have been bothered by it, but I saw a hand tug the curtain inside the RV and Nate waved his hand in a weak arc. I pressed my hand to my mouth and caught the choke in my throat. He was alive, and, according to Stacey, he was being treated with the vaccine – home-brewed in the mobile laboratory. I made a mental note to find Christa and to call Waverly and thank her. If, that is, she was still alive.

"I have to ask you to go ma'am."

"Yes," I said and looked at Nate. "I'll go. In just a moment."

"You have to go now, ma'am." The man took a step toward me and I backed off. Nate disappeared from the window and I peered around the guard, waiting for him to come back. When he did he had something in his hands, something pink.

"My axe," I said and laughed. It had been with me from the start, and so had Nate, I realized. From the quiet, taciturn man I knew sharing office space with FEMA, he had become the silent hero on the front line, and he had brought me this far, to the end of the line. It was up to me to take us even further. I lifted my hand and he smiled, putting the axe away out of sight and reaching for something I couldn't see. The guard tried to move me on, but I stalled, moving to one side for a better view of the legal pad that Nate pressed to the window. There was just one word written on it: Date?

"Yes," I breathed and ran my hand through the tight curls of my hair. I nodded, yes.

Nate lowered the pad and waved once more. I shouted the word: later, and then let the guard move me on, beyond the boundary and away from the quarantined area.

I was weak, my head hurt, and a reflection in a window suggested why – there was a huge lump in the center of my forehead – but I climbed the stairs as if I had woken from a perfect night's sleep, as if nothing could stop me. No challenge was too great for Jaylen Lewis. Nate had asked me on a date.

I must have smiled all the way to the bridge, comments chasing me as I walked past the passengers carving out a space for their families and friends anywhere they could. Accommodation was high on the list of priorities, I realized, and I added hygiene, food and water to the list before I knocked on the bridge door and waited for it to be unlocked. Trent let me in and I smiled at him before approaching the Captain in his chair.

"Captain Berg?"

"Yes," he said. There was an awkward moment when he realized who I was, and then he pointed toward a coffee machine tucked into the bulkhead beside the charts table. "I've switched drinks, perhaps you'd like a coffee?"

"Yes," I said and followed him to the table.

Berg was younger than I had imagined, and he had lost ten years since I last saw him, now that the horror of the storm, the threat of sinking, and the waves of liquor had receded. He handed me a mug of coffee, adding cream when I nodded.

"You saved the ship," he said.

"Not me. It was Nate, my friend." The word *friend* tasted good on my tongue, and I suppressed my smile with a sip of coffee.

"Ah, Nate. I know him. He dragged me onboard yesterday." Berg was silent for a moment, and I wondered if he thought Nate had made a mistake. I hoped not for the sake of the thousand or more Alaskans he was now responsible for. "But it was you that saved him, or am I mistaken?"

"I'd like to think I saved him," I said.

"And now we have to save everybody else." Berg glanced at Trent and said, "Isn't that right?"

"Yes, sir."

"I have some ideas about that," I said. Berg sipped his coffee and I realized we had not been formally introduced. I stuck out my hand. "I'm Jaylen Lewis."

"And who are you with?" he said, as he shook my hand.

"FEMA. Well, not quite yet."

"Sorry?" Berg let go of my hand and frowned. "I don't follow."

"I start tomorrow morning. This is actually my weekend off. The first in a long time."

"Hell of a weekend," he said. "Are all your weekends as wild as this?"

"No," I said and smiled. "This one is in a class all its own."

"Let's hope it remains so." Berg beckoned me closer to the charts spread on the table. Prince William Sound looked huge on the chart, bigger than I realized. "Seeing as you start tomorrow, I'll have the crew – what's left of them – open the restaurant this evening. We'll take care of meals, and tell our passengers, the survivors, they can expect more information regarding accommodation, food…"

"Water and hygiene…" I said.

"…on Monday. Your first day at work." Berg smiled and I decided that, once sober, the title of

Captain was fitting. He wore it well. "I intend to sail out into the sound, toward Yakutat, but," he said, as I opened my mouth, "we'll keep our distance. I just want to be close enough to take on fuel, water and supplies. While we decide what to do next."

"Right."

"That's where you come in."

"Deciding what's next?"

"Yes."

I nodded my head, took another sip of coffee, and listened as Berg pointed out several features of the Sound that I did not know. He stopped when Trent coughed and pointed out of the window.

"Pod of orcas, sir," he said.

I followed Berg to the window and spotted the tall dorsal fins off the port bow. As the orcas swam away from the *Seward* I noticed a group of people on the main deck. Three bodies were wrapped in white shrouds and I spotted Aatag and his family gathered beside one of them.

"Excuse me, Captain," I said. I thanked him for the coffee and smiled at Trent as I left the bridge. I made my way down to the deck and stepped out into a fresh breeze that goose-pimpled my skin. A woman wearing black and holding a bible in her hands called out the names of the dead as they were committed to the sea. I waited until Aatag and Sierra's son was buried in the black water of the Sound and then walked over to them.

"I am sorry for your loss," I said as Aatag took my hand. "I feel responsible."

Aatag nodded and said, "You are." His words struck me harder than the ship's door that had knocked me unconscious. I faltered and he gripped my hands tighter, as Nukka slipped away from her mother and wrapped her arms around my leg. "Without you," he continued, "we would all be dead. You are responsible for saving my family, and I thank you."

Aatag pressed his hand against my cheek. He smiled and stepped away, calling Nukka to his side, and slipping his arm around her tiny shoulders. Aatag led his daughter a few more paces before she slipped out from beneath his arm and ran back to me.

"Your talisman," I said and knelt in front of her. "It worked."

"I know," she said, a cheeky smile dimpling her cheeks.

I looked at the little girl in front of me, tried to fathom the wise-beyond-her-years light that flickered in her dark brown eyes. The wind twisted her long black hair, and she pressed herself to my body and wrapped her thin arms around me.

The flicker of movement behind me caught my eye. I hugged Nukka to my body and turned to look at the window of the lounge. It was packed with passengers. So was the deck in front of it. They stared out at me, and beyond, toward the mountains of the Sound and the open sea. Nukka slipped out of my embrace, wrapped her fingers around mine, and led me to the very front of the ferry.

The *Seward* was our new home, and the horizon was our new destination.

We couldn't go back. Forward was the only option.

I gripped the raven claw in one hand, and Nukka's fingers in the other.

"Forward," I whispered. "To the horizon." And

an uncertain future, I thought to myself. Nukka's hand was warm as the wind tickled our skin. I thought of Nate as I squinted at the sun. "We're going to be all right, Nukka," I said. "You'll see."

The wind teased her long hair and she caught it in her fingers, pulled it away from her face. "I know," she said, and squeezed my fingers.

THE END

ACKNOWLEDGMENTS

Thanks to Andrea Duarte Faurby for last minute help with Spanish.

Zoe McGuire
August 2017

ABOUT THE AUTHOR

Zoe McGuire lives in Scandinavia, where she feels relatively safe, imagining that the apocalypse, when it comes, will happen somewhere else, hopefully very far away. That doesn't stop her thinking about it – a lot.

Zoe McGuire is the author's pen name. She has several more books planned for the *End of the Line* series, including a Zombie Edition set in the same world and featuring many of the same characters introduced in *End of the Line*.

If you would like to know more about Zoe and her books, please feel free to contact her via Aarluuk Press.

www.aarluuk.com

Made in the USA
Lexington, KY
29 September 2018

WITHDRAWN

Kirtley Library
Columbia College
Columbia, Missouri 65216

A MANUAL OF
SCANDINAVIAN MYTHOLOGY

*This is a volume in the
Arno Press collection*

MYTHOLOGY

Advisory Editor
Kees W. Bolle

Editorial Board
Angelo Brelich
Joseph Campbell
Mircea Eliade

*See last pages of this volume
for a complete list of titles.*

A MANUAL OF
SCANDINAVIAN MYTHOLOGY

GRENVILLE PIGOTT

ARNO PRESS

A New York Times Company

New York / 1978

Editorial Supervision: LESLIE PARR

Reprint Edition 1978 by Arno Press Inc.

MYTHOLOGY
ISBN for complete set: 0-405-10529-0
See last pages of this volume for titles.

Manufactured in the United States of America

Library of Congress Cataloging in Publication Data

Pigott, Grenville, 1796-1865.
  A manual of Scandinavian mythology.

  (Mythology)
  "Illustrated by translations from A. G. Oehlenschläger's Danish poem The gods of the North."
  Reprint of the 1839 ed. published by W. Pickering, London.
  Includes index.
  1. Mythology, Norse. 2. Eddas. I. Edda Snorra Sturlusonar. II. Oehlenschläger, Adam Gottlob, 1779-1850. Nordens guder. III. Title. IV. Series.
BL860.P5   1978   291.1'3'0948   77-79152
ISBN 0-405-10561-4

291.13
PIG

A MANUAL

OF

SCANDINAVIAN MYTHOLOGY

4191

A tale well worth to hear,
In mystic Runics writ;
Come, lend a listening ear
To theme for Sages fit:
Of many a legend old,
Told down from sire to sire,
The pregnant sense t' unfold
I strike my golden lyre.

Of th' Aser and the Giants,
Their long and fatal strife,
Of true-love's firm reliance,
Of Loke, with treasons rife,
Of Odin and Valhalla
I sing—of Thor the strong:
No subject light nor shallow,
Come, listen to my song!
        OEHLENSCHLAGER'S NORDISKE GUDER.

A MANUAL OF SCANDINAVIAN MYTHOLOGY

CONTAINING A

Popular Account of the Two Eddas

AND OF

THE RELIGION OF ODIN

ILLUSTRATED BY TRANSLATIONS FROM OEHLENSCHLAGER'S
DANISH POEM THE GODS OF THE NORTH

BY GRENVILLE PIGOTT

LONDON
WILLIAM PICKERING
1839

WHITTINGHAM TOOKS COURT,
CHANCERY LANE.

TO RICHARD

DUKE OF BUCKINGHAM AND CHANDOS

K. G. ETC. ETC. ETC.

THIS WORK IS INSCRIBED IN TOKEN OF RESPECT

AND REGARD

BY THE AUTHOR

PREFACE.

The Mythology of the ancient Scandinavians, respecting which so much curious information has been brought to light, of late years, by the researches of many distinguished writers, in Germany, Denmark, and Sweden,[1] has hitherto excited but little attention in this country, although the subject is well calculated to awaken our interest, not only as the source of most of our popular superstitions, from whence the favourite authors of our early childhood and of our maturer age have drawn their witches, their fairies, their dwarfs, their giants, and their ghosts;[2] but in an historical point of view also,

---

[1] More especially Suhm, Schoning, Nyerup, Grundtvig, Thorlacius, Rafn, Finn Magnussen, Müller, Grater, Abrahamsen.

[2] This observation applies peculiarly to Shakspeare. The ghost in Hamlet, the witches and apparitions in Macbeth, the fairies in the Midsummer's Night's Dream and Tempest,

for a short retrospect will suffice to shew, that the religion of Odin must have exercised a great and lasting influence on the character and institutions of the inhabitants of Great Britain. The Jutes, Anglians and Saxons, who in the course of the fifth and sixth centuries, effected the conquest of the greatest part of this island, were worshippers, and their principal leaders reputed descendants of Odin. In process of time these heathen invaders were converted to Christianity, but the old worship died away by degrees and slowly, and not without leaving permanent traces on the manners and habits of their descendants. England had scarcely begun, under Egbert, to recover from the troubles of the Heptarchy, when her Christian inhabitants were once more engaged in a struggle for existence with their kinsmen, followers of Odin, and were compelled, despite the genius and courage of Alfred, to divide the land with them, and that for no brief period of

---

are closely painted after their Scandinavian originals. From whence Shakspeare derived his information is less certain, perhaps in part from Saxo Grammaticus, in whose history he might have found the tale of Hamlet.

PREFACE. ix

time. It is well known that this great king, notwithstanding his signal and repeated victories, deemed it politic to compound with the vanquished Danes, by leaving them in possession of the kingdom of East Anglia, of the whole of England, North of the Humber, and of the best part of Mercia, including the five cities of Derby, Leicester, Stamford, Lincoln, and Nottingham. These Danes or Northmen were fierce idolaters, and the ruthless destruction with which they visited whatever came within their power connected with the Christian worship, affords too good evidence of their zeal for Odin and for Thor. No king, before the Conquest, ever possessed more substantial power in England than Knudt or Canute the Dane. He, as his father Sweyn before him, was a Christian, his grandfather, Harald, of the blue tooth, a sanguinary tyrant, having found it convenient to embrace Christianity. It was through the exertions of Canute, indeed, that the Christian faith was first firmly established in Denmark. But, although hostile to the ancient superstitions of his countrymen, Canute was essentially a Dane, and during his vigorous reign of twenty-eight years, contributed not a little to implant amongst the higher classes in this country the manners and the feelings of the Northmen. The sway of the Danish kings in England ended in 1041. Twenty-five years later a new tide of Northern institutions and habits was poured in upon England, from a different quarter, it is true, and somewhat modified, but of the same character and from the same original source as those which preceded. Quaintly but truly saith old Robert of Glo'ster,

" Of Normans beth these high men that beth in this land,
And the low men of Saxons."
Robert of Glo'ster's Chronicle.

and both nations were, for centuries, the worshippers of Odin.

It would not be difficult to shew, although this is no place for the enquiry, that most of the still existing peculiarities in the institutions and manners of the nations of Gothic descent, which distinguish them from the Greeks and Romans in what may be assumed as a parallel state of civilization, can be traced directly to the influence of the religion of Odin. The trial by twelve, the deference paid to the female sex, and the point of honour maintained by the practice of duel, are prominent instances in support of this assertion.

It is the object of the present work to give a plain account of the ideas entertained by the inhabitants of North-Western Europe, during a period of long duration, respecting the nature and power of the various deities and good and evil spirits, in whose existence they believed, as preserved in the Eddas, and explained and elucidated by the writers alluded to above. Its form was suggested by a similar work, " *Die Nordiske Mythologie*," published in Germany in 1827, by E. L. Heiberg, whose example has been followed, more especially in the insertion, by way of illustration of frequent free translations from Oehlenschläger's poem, "*The Gods of the North.*" The introductory chapter and the supplementary essay in the appendix, the materials of which are drawn chiefly from the works of Professors Finn Magnussen and P. E. Müller, of Copenhagen, were intended to shew generally the state of society which prevailed in the three Scandinavian kingdoms contemporaneously with the religion of Odin. The first chapter contains a general view of the whole system of the Scandinavian Mythology, which, although essential to a clear understanding of the subject, is necessarily of a more abstract character than the ensuing chapters. These consist of a circumstantial description of the various deities of the Eddas, of their attributes and attendants, of the power which they were believed to exercise over man and the elements, and of the most characteristic adventures in which they are supposed to have been engaged. Much of the matter contained in these chapters may be found in Bishop Percy's translation of Mallet's Northern Antiquities, but since that work was written, the publication of numerous well authenticated Sagas, and the works of Suhm, Magnussen, Müller, &c. have given a new interest and importance to the subject, have brought to light many new facts, and have sufficiently confuted the arguments advanced by Huet, Ritson and others against the authenticity of the Eddas. The unfavourable account of the religion of Odin contained in a work of such authority as "The Book of the Church," might suffice alone to justify this publication; the more so as the distinguished writer alluded to has elsewhere so well borne witness to the lofty poetry of Scandinavian fiction:

> "Through wildest scenes of strange sublimity,
> Building the Runic rhyme, my fancy roves;
> Niffl-hil's nine worlds, and Surtur's fiery reign,
> And where, upon creation's utmost verge
> The weary dwarfs who bear the weight of Heaven
> Wait the long winter which no sun may cheer,
> And the last sound which from Heimdallur's trump
> Shall echo through all worlds, and sound the knell
> Of Earth and Heaven." *Southey.*

It has been the aim of the author of the present work to bring within a small compass information spread throughout many a costly volume, and shut up in languages not much studied in England. It can boast no merit of originality, consisting chiefly of extracts from the works of others, loosely put together, and not always with due acknowledgments; an omission arising from no desire to appropriate their labours, but from the fact that many of those extracts, having been originally made without any view to publication, were not noted with sufficient exactness, nor after a lapse of some years when the original works could no longer be referred to, always distinguishable from the author's own conclusions. It is intended chiefly for such as desire, without much research, to obtain some definite ideas of the wild and warlike religion of their ancestors, which, teaching that death in battle or by violence was the only road to their Paradise, Valhalla, rendered them for centuries the scourge of Europe, and by the martial habits which it engendered, enabled them to gain and to keep possession of the fairest portions of Ireland, England, Italy, and France.

CONTENTS.

INTRODUCTION.

Early History and Mythology of the Scandinavians, a field hitherto comparatively unexplored. Attempt to account for this fact. The ancient Scandinavians by no means inferior to their contemporaries in civilization. Their trade, flourishing cities, fisheries, and general enterprize. Circumstances which at first opposed the introduction of Christianity into the three Scandinavian kingdoms. View of their early political state. Discovery and colonization of Iceland: became the resort of all the turbulent characters of Denmark, Norway, and Sweden. View of the state of society which prevailed there long after a similar state had ceased to exist on the continent. Influence of the Scalds. Introduction of Christianity and classical learning into Iceland. Changes in its political state: union with Norway: consequent decline in prosperity. Ancient language of Scandinavia preserved pure in Iceland, when lost in Norway, Sweden, and Denmark. Snorro Sturleson's chronicle: Angrim Johnsen: Brigniulf Svendsen: Olaus Wormius: discovery of a parchment copy of the Prose Edda. The subject of Scandinavian Mythology subsequently taken up by many eminent writers in Sweden, Denmark, and Germany: very little attention directed to the subject in England. Description of the Prose and Poetic Edda.

CHAPTER I.

GENERAL VIEW OF SCANDINAVIAN MYTHOLOGY.

All ancient nations had their peculiar theories respecting the creation. The Scandinavian, Egyptian, Chaldæan, Phœnician, and Persian Cosmogonies. General view of the Scandinavian Mythology. Odin, Vile and Ve slay the giant Ymer. The creation of the first man and woman. The nine worlds. The Aser. Asa Loke and his children: Fenris the wolf: the great serpent: and Hela, the queen of death. The great Ash Ygdrasill. Ragnarokur, or the great battle of the Gods and Giants. The Dwarfs and Elves. The celestial dwellings, or solar houses. The Grimnersmaal, a tale about King Hrodung's sons. The Scandinavian Calendar.

CHAPTER II.

ODIN—THE ORIGIN OF POETRY—VALHALLA—THE EINHERIAR—THE VALKYRS—ODIN'S HORSE, SLEIPNER—FRIGGA —HERTHA.

Odin: establishment of his religion in Scandinavia: etymology of the word: contradictory attributes assigned to him. Odin, the title of the supreme deity amongst the Scythians three Odins mentioned in history. The Odin of the Edda: his ravens: his eloquence: his wives and children: his love of adventure. The origin of poetry, from the Prose Edda. The titles of Odin: though powerful he was not omnipotent. His palaces, Gladsheim, Valaskialf, and Valhalla. The Einheriar: the boar Schrimner: the Valkyrs. Belief of the Scandinavians respecting Valhalla. Account of Odin's horse, Sleipner. Frea, or Frigga: her attendants: confounded with the goddess Hertha.

CHAPTER III.

ASA-LOKE—HELA, THE QUEEN OF DEATH—THE GREAT SERPENT—TYR, AND FENRIS THE WOLF—IDUNA—BRAGI— THIAFFE.

Two divinities in the Scandinavian Mythology, who bore the name of Loke. Asa-Loke, a creation peculiar to the Scandinavian Mythology. His attributes, character, and punishment. His three children: 1. Jormungandur, or the great serpent which encircles the world: Hela, the queen of death: her palace: 3. Fenris, the wolf: method by which the gods got him into their power. Iduna's rape and recovery: her apples. Bragi, the god of eloquence.

CHAPTER IV.

THOR—SIF—THE GIANTS, ULLER, UTGARDELOK AND MIMER.

Thor: his hammer, belt, and gloves: his residence, Thrudvanger: palace, Bilskirner: his sons. Thor: a personification of thunder: the worship of Thor more ancient in Scandinavia than that of Odin. In Norway more reverenced than Odin. Thor's wife, Sif: her son, Uller. The Giants: their origin, attributes, and residence. Mimer: his will, his wisdom, his death. Thor's visit to the giant Geyruth. The story of Thor and the dwarf Alvis.

CHAPTER V.

THOR'S JOURNEY TO JOTUNHEIM, OR GIANT'S LAND.

The cause of Thor's expedition. He sets out in his car with Loke: descends to Midgard: His adventure at the peasant's hut: Tialf and Roska: He passes the ocean which separates Midgard from Utgard. Adventure on the heath: the giant Skrymner: his glove. They proceed to Utgard with Skrymner as guide: the adventure of the wallet. They arrive at Helheim. Thor's interview with Hela. They reach Jotunheim, or Utgard: Utgardelok: his palace: he seeks to intimidate Thor: invites him and his companions to a banquet: they are deceived and foiled by enchantment. Thor quits Utgard in anger: Utgardelok explains the enchantments. Thor returns home.

CHAPTER VI.

THOR'S VISIT TO THE GIANT HYMIR.

Ægir's feast to the Gods. Thor and Tyr set out to obtain Hymir's brewing copper. Their adventure with the Giant: (from the Hymisquida. Oehlenschläger's version of the story, from the Prose Edda. Thor's visit to Hymir: they go out to fish. Thor's combat with the great Serpent.

CHAPTER VII.

THE VANER.

The Vaner a different race from the Aser: their residence. Niord: his residence; his attributes; his marriage with Skada. Freyr: his residence; his attributes; his love for Gerda. Skirner's journey. Freya, the Goddess of Love: her palace: shares the spirits of the slain with Odin: her husband, Oddur. Oehlenschläger's poem of the Vaner Freya's daughters, Hnos and Gersime: her attendants. Heimdall, and the bridge Bifrost.

CHAPTER VIII.

THE ASH—THE THREE NORNIES—THE ELVES—THE DWARFS.

Description of the sacred Ash: Yggdrasill: Nyd-hoggur the serpent: Urda's well. The three Nornies: Urda, Verdandi, and Skulda: the inferior Nornies. The Elves. The Dwarfs: their skill in Smith's work: their malicious disposition: Loke's wager with the dwarf Brokkur. One of Loke's knavish tricks, and his punishment *(from Oehlenschläger)*.

CHAPTER IX.

ÆGIR—RAN—GEFIONE.

Ægir: his riches: his residence: his journey to Asgard: his wife Ran; her net. Ægir's feast to the Gods. Loke's cunning: a poem from Oehlenschläger. Thor recovers his hammer.

CHAPTER X.

BALDUR—NANNA—HERMODUR—HODUR—FORSETE— VALE—RAGNAROKKUR.

Baldur; his gentleness: his dream. Odin's forebodings: his descent to Helheim. Loke conspires to slay Baldur: the misletoe. Baldur's death: his funeral: his wife Nanna: her death. Frigga's grief: Hermodur's journey. Forsete: the God of justice, worshipped in Heligoland. Vale: his palace: Valaskialf; Ragnarokkur: the destruction of the Gods and Giants. A new world created.

APPENDIX.

SOME ACCOUNT OF THE SCALDS AND SAGAS, AND OF THE PRINCIPAL SUPERSTITIONS OF THE ANCIENT SCANDINAVIANS.

The Scalds of Scandinavia bore no resemblance to the British Druids: the nature of their profession. The Scalda, or poetical dictionary, contains the rules of their art: high esteem in which they were held: Harald Haarfager: story of his Scalds. Professor Müller's sketch of the History of the Scaldic Art. St. Olaf: battle of Stickelstadt: the Biarkermaal. Eyvind Skalda-spiller: Eigil Skalagrimsen: his Saga. Meaning of the word Saga: upwards of two hundred of them still extant. Professor Müller's " *Saga Bibliothek.*" Account of Endrid's wedding. History of Raudulf. Favourite pursuits and amusements of the Scandinavian Chiefs: astronomy: the art of cutting Runes: running upon skees, or snow-shoes: footracing: skating: leaping: wrestling: sword-dancers: bowls: hockey: shooting with the bow: throwing the spear: slinging: broadsword-play: and above all swimming, and skill in Smith's work. Extracts from Olaf Tryggessen's Saga. Velent, or Vaulund the Smith: his Saga. Belief of the Scandinavians in Magic and witchcraft: Superstition respecting Barrows: the nightmare: invocation of the dead: tutelary Spirits.

INTRODUCTION.

It is within a comparatively recent period only, that the early history of the North of Europe has begun to attract much attention in this country. Previous to the publication of Percy's Northern Antiquities, all that was known on the subject rested chiefly on meagre notices gleaned from Roman writers, whose authority on this subject, from deficiency of sources of accurate information, was, to say the least, doubtful; and on the exaggerated account of the Monkish Chroniclers, who had too good reason not to love the people whom they described. Hence the history of the Scandinavians or Northmen, as they were afterwards called, has been generally looked upon as a mere sanguinary chronicle of piracies, murders and gloomy superstitions, and but little inclination felt to explore a field so uninviting. To those, however, whose curiosity has led them to examine the copious sources of information respecting the early religion and history of Northern Europe, furnished by the Eddas and by the numerous Sagas which exist in the libraries of Copenhagen and Stockholm; it cannot fail to appear a curious anomaly that, whilst the Grecian Mythology in all its varied details is made familiar to us from our childhood, we have been so long content to remain in great measure ignorant of the religious superstitions of our immediate ancestors; superstitions inferior it may be to those of Greece in refinement, but scarcely so in wildness or sublimity; which contributed so much to form the peculiar character that still distinguishes the inhabitants of Northern Europe; which even yet linger in the traditions of our peasantry, and whose traces are enduringly marked in the names of some of our festivals, and especially of the days of our week.

The omission of any serious research into the religion of Odin, by men of such profound learning, as was possessed by many of our early antiquaries, may, not unnaturally, raise a doubt in the minds of some of the degree of advantage or interest likely to result from an enquiry of this nature; but a brief account of the circumstances which attended the overthrow of heathenism and the introduction of Christianity in those countries, where the Scandinavian deities were chiefly worshipped, may otherwise explain the cause of this silence on a subject so likely to have invited learned enquiry.

It was not until long after the nations of Southern and Western Europe had been converted to Christianity, that its light began to penetrate into the northern kingdoms of Denmark, Sweden, and Norway; but this fact is attributable not so much to the barbarism or ignorance of the inhabitants of those countries, as to their warlike and predatory habits, the natural result of their previous religion, of their position with respect to the rest of Europe and of other concurrent circumstances, too various to admit of consideration here. It would not be difficult to shew that the Scandinavians, from the eighth to the eleventh century, carried on a more active commerce, and could boast a more constant and extensive communication with distant countries than any other nation of Europe. During the greater part of this period, Russia, Sweden, and Denmark, were the only European nations which had any regular commerce with the East. The Northmen or Norwegians traded for furs, round the North Cape, to Permia: Russia, which, from the ninth century, was governed by Scandinavian princes, possessed several flourishing commercial cities, as Kiew, Cholmogorod, and Novogorod. In the North of Germany there were the Slavic trading towns, Vineta, Juliu or Wolliu, Rhethra, and Mecklenburg, and later Lubeck, Hamburgh, and Bremen. In Sweden there were Wisby, in the island of Gothland, and on the continent, Upsala, Sigtuna, and Birca. In Scania there was Halor: in Norway there were Tunsberg and Steinkar, and in Denmark were Sleswick, Ribe, Leira,

Roeskilde, Ringstedt, Odense, &c.[1] Nor were these inconsiderable towns, but places of great extent and opulence, whose grandeur was a favourite theme with contemporary writers.

The Norwegians and their descendants discovered and made settlements in Iceland, Greenland, the Orkneys, and, as has been maintained with great semblance of truth, even in America itself. Their Princes and Nobles visited every part of Europe as traders or pirates, and, for a considerable period, the body guard of the Greek Emperors was composed of Northmen under the designation of Baranger or Väringer. Their fisheries, particularly the herring-fishery in the Sound, were so considerable, that Arnold of Lubeck, bitterly lamented the sums of gold and silver thus abstracted from Mecklenburg into Scandinavia, and besides all this they had the monopoly of the Arctic whale-fishery.[2]

Of their piratical expeditions, their conquest of Neustria, England, Sicily, and the devastations which they inflicted on the coasts of Europe and Africa, it is not necessary here to speak: but it may be fairly concluded, that a people possessing so many sources of wealth, and with such continual communication with the most civilized portions of the world, could not have been so darkly

---

[1] Magnussen's Nordiske Archæologie.
[2] Ibid.

barbarous as the well-grounded detestation of the monkish chronicles has represented them.[3] If we consult the Icelandic Sagas, many of which are faithful and unpretending pictures of the manners of the times in which they were written, we shall find that the Scandinavians were by no means unacquainted with the comforts and even the luxuries of life; that they were skilful mechanics; held music and poetry in the highest esteem; have some claim to the invention of oil-painting, and, above all, in their relations with the weaker sex, shewed a degree of refinement and generosity which we may look for in vain amongst the Greeks and Romans in their highest civilization.

The detailed descriptions which exist of some of the chief places of religious worship in Sweden, indicate them as possessing much grandeur and indeed magnificence. The courts of the first Dukes of Normandy,[4] composed exclusively of the

---

[3] The monk Alberich in his Chronicle, written about the year 875, speaks thus of them: " Est gens Normannorum gratiosa, quocumque venerit, et affabilis," whilst on the other hand he describes the Anglo-Saxons in respect of their manners as " *feroces.*" The great traveller, Pythias, who lived about the time of Alexander the Great, and, later, Tacitus, described the Scandinavians as superior in civilization to the Celts and Germans. *Magnussen.*

[4] Wace, in his Metrical History of Normandy, speaking of Duke Richard in 1030, says,

" Richart ki volt son dreit tenir

descendants of the Scandinavian conquerors of Neustria, and continually recruited from their kinsmen in the north, were the most polished and chivalrous of the time; and it is notorious that the chiefs who accompanied William to the Conquest of England (within the period of which we are speaking), looked upon the uncouth manners of the Anglo-Saxon nobles with undisguised contempt.

The difficulties, therefore, which the first preachers of Christianity in Scandinavia had to encounter, may be attributed rather to the contempt in which these lawless warriors held a creed which threatened them with a life of peace and inactivity, than to barbarous ignorance or even to any bigoted adherence to their ancient religion.

When St. Olaf, to whose zeal is due the establishment of Christianity in Norway, proposed to Gauka Thor to be baptized: the chief answered: "That he and his comrade (*Stall-broder*) were neither Christians nor Heathens, but trusted to their own courage, strength, and fortune, with which until then they had had every reason to be satisfied. But if the king was very anxious they should believe on some god, they were as well con-

---

De Danemarche fist venir
Daneis e bons combatturs
Ki lui firent si grant meneurs."

tent to believe on the white Christ[5] as on any other."[6] In like manner Arnliot Gellina told the same king: " That he had always been wont to put his trust in nothing but his own strength, which had never failed him, and that he had now thought to trust in the king; but, since he, the king, was so desirous that he should be baptized, although he was not aware what the white Christ was capable of performing, for the king's sake he would believe on him."[7] It was also said of Hrolf Krake and his warriors, at a much earlier period, that they never offered to the gods, but relied on their own strength. Some, although uninstructed in the doctrines of Christianity, rejected the superstitions of their countrymen, from more exalted motives. " When Thorkel Maane was on the point of death, he directed that he should be taken out into the broad sunshine, and there commending his spirit to the God who created the sun, breathed his last.[8] We are told also that Thorkel Krafla and Ingemund the old, worshipped the God who created the sun. The death of the latter was truly heroic. Having received treacherously a mortal wound from one on whom he had

---

[5] So called because those to be baptized were clothed in white.
[6] St. Olaf's Saga.
[7] Ibid.
[8] Landmanna Saga.

previously conferred benefits, he resolutely sought to conceal it in order to enable his murderer to escape from the vengeance of his sons.

The most learned of the enquirers into the early history of the north,[9] seem to be agreed that the three kingdoms of Sweden, Denmark, and Norway, after having long continued separately hereditary under the descendants of Odin, who appear, in Sweden especially, to have exercised at once the functions of king and priest; split by degrees into numerous petty sovereignties, the chiefs of which under the titles of kings, jarls, &c. enjoyed an almost absolute power.

Their subjects were divided into *Herses* (the great land-holders), free peasants, and slaves. The elder son of the Herse inherited his father's estate, and the others sought to make their fortunes either by piracy (*Vikingskab*), or by entering into the service of some foreign prince, but chiefly by the former.[10]

During this state of society the *Scald*,[11] or Bard, formed an important part, not only of the court of each petty prince, but also of the establishment of the more powerful nobles, always ac-

---

[9] Suhm, Schöning, Finn Magnussen, &c.

[10] Magnussen.

[11] The word *Scald* or *Scaled*, means, literally, a smoother of language, from *skaldre* to polish; in like manner the Saxon name for a poet was *scop* or *sceop*, from *sceoppan* to shape.

Henry.

companying them to war; undertaking difficult or delicate negociations; and often acting at the same time as bard, counsellor, and warrior. No idea of effeminacy was coupled with this calling, but on the contrary, the best Scald was usually the boldest warrior, and, indeed, it was considered as essential to an accomplished chief to be able to make verses. At table, the Scalds usually occupied the seats of honour, and their songs abounded with allusions to the feats and attributes of the gods of the Edda: so much so, that without an intimate acquaintance with the Scandinavian Mythology, it is impossible thoroughly to understand them.

Towards the latter end of the ninth century, ambitious and able princes succeeded, in each of the three kingdoms, in uniting the various petty sovereignties into one; a revolution, however, which, especially in Norway, was not effected without a long and bloody struggle, and the destruction of most of the families of the ancient chiefs. About the same time Christianity began to obtain a firm footing in the north. Bishops and Priests arrived from England and from Rome, introducing, with the religion of Christ, the language and literature of Roman Paganism. The occupation of the Scald was now rapidly departing, and the change of religion, the new form of government, the wars, which arose from civil dissensions, from foreign conquests, from alliances, and from religious disputes, at length effected a complete revolution in the habits of the people.[12] Their fables and legends were by degrees forgotten, and the zealous promoters of Christianity omitted nothing to destroy all reliques of the ancient superstition. The language itself, particularly in Denmark, underwent such a change, that the old Danish[13] was no longer intelligible.

After Harald *Haarfager* (or the fair-haired) had completed the subjection of the petty sovereignties in Norway, most of the chiefs who had opposed him fled the country, either from fear of his resentment, or from love of independence, and sought for establishments elsewhere. Iceland had been discovered by a Norwegian a short time previously; and, as its climate had little to terrify men accustomed to the bleak mountains of Norway, or to a life spent chiefly upon the ocean, Ingulf and Hiorlef, about the year 847, found no difficulty in conducting thither a colony, composed, for the most part, of men of the principal families of Norway.

The island, although equal in extent to Ireland, possesses but little fertile land, consisting chiefly of vast mountain ridges, the narrow dells between which, however, afford good pasture for cattle; and according to ancient documents, which there

---

[12] P. E. Müller.

[13] The language spoken originally by the whole Scandinavian family was called, generally, the Danish.

is no reason to doubt, it was at this time well wooded. Each chief took possession of the tract which best suited him, and a republican form of government of the most simple kind, was now established. The colonists of this new republic, in changing their country, did not abandon their ancient habits and pursuits. The summer was spent chiefly in piratical expeditions, and, during the long, dreary winter, the principal amusement consisted in festive meetings in the spacious drinking-houses of the wealthy, where, whilst the mead and ale went round, the Scald excited the emulation of his hearers by reciting the feats of their ancestors, or the most renowned events of the passing day, an accurate knowledge of which was considered an essential part of his art.[14]

Hither repaired many of the most turbulent and celebrated characters of the three northern kingdoms, often from necessity. As might have been expected, they were in perpetual feuds with each other; and, it being considered infamous to suffer bloodshed to pass unavenged, a quarrel between two individuals was invariably taken up by all their relatives and adherents, and was often productive of the most fatal results. It was, however, permitted, and indeed usual, to accept of a pecuniary compensation for the life of a kinsman or follower.[15]

---

[14] P. E. Müller.

[15] The same practice and a very similar state of society

Public meetings were frequent in the new republic. Beside marriage and burial feasts, which often lasted whole weeks, there were festivities peculiar to each bailiwick, consisting chiefly in dancing and wrestling; Horse-meetings (*Heste-thing*), where the amusement was to irritate horses to fight; quarterly meetings; and, above all, one great annual meeting, called *All-thing*, to be absent from which was considered a serious reproach.[16]

At these meetings the influence of each individual was in proportion to the number of his adherents, or *Thing-men*, which, in turn depended on his reputation for courage, strength, or talent; in short, on his power to protect the interests of his followers. Hence the art, to turn a rival into ridicule by means of satirical verses, became a talent highly esteemed, and we find in the Icelandic Sagas, that the most distinguished warriors had often recourse to this weapon, and that the deadly *Holmgang*[17] was not unfrequently preceded by a war of verse.

---

continues amongst the Arab tribes to this day, vid. *Wellsted's Arabia*.

[16] P. E. Müller.

[17] *Holm* signifies an island, or any isolated spot. In the *Holm-gang* the two combatants were placed within a circle of stones, and he who quitted it alive, without taking the life of his adversary, was looked on as a *Nidding*,—a term of contempt which none in our language will adequately con-

The improved administration in those parts of Europe which had long afforded a rich plunder to the northern Sea-kings, had encreased the dangers and diminished the profits of piracy, and the progress of Christianity tended gradually to abolish it altogether, but, in other respects, the state of society in Iceland remained unchanged.

The manner of life of the islanders was calculated to cherish a spirit of poetry when once it had been awakened. They had scarcely any corn, and their pastoral occupations gave them but little employment, excepting during the hay harvest, when all quarrels were by law suspended. Their warlike operations were also, necessarily, upon a limited scale. A contest in which ten men fell was considered bloody, and their expeditions were rarely prolonged beyond a few weeks at a time. For security's sake, however, they lived assembled together in large farm-houses; and spent the winter-evenings in story-telling or in talking over their feuds. To be skilled in the art of narrating adventures was therefore the most esteemed talent, and the surest method of securing everywhere a warm reception.[18]

---

vey. The *Kniv-gang* was still more murderous: the combatants were tied together with a girdle, and with the short knives still worn by the Norwegian peasants, stabbed each other to death. Instances of this latter kind of duel have taken place at no distant period.

[18] P. E. Müller.

P. Erasmus Müller from whose interesting work this brief review of the state of society in Iceland, from the ninth to the thirteenth century, is almost literally taken, gives, amongst others, the following extracts, in illustration of the simplicity of those manners, and of the powerful influence of the Scalds.

"As Bolle Bollesen, a bold Icelander, was on a journey through the land, a peasant by the way mocked him, and afterwards fell upon him. But Bolle overcame him, and from this feat and journey a new Saga arose, which soon spread through the Bailiwick, and greatly augmented Bolle's reputation."[19] In Gisle Sursson's Saga a stranger is introduced, who says to his neighbour in the public assembly, "Shew me the men of celebrity about whom Sagas have been written."

In fact, almost all the Sagas are composed of narratives of the feuds of individuals or families, or of descriptions of particular places. They are often, however, of high interest, not merely because they furnish original pictures of a singular state of society, but also because of the very ancient and curious accounts which they contain of the distant countries visited by their heroes; the high importance, frequently, of the events in which they took part; and the light which is thrown on the contemporary manners and history of various nations

---

[19] Laxdala Saga.

of the period, and, particularly, of those of Great Britain and Ireland.

In the words of Müller: "The Scalds belong to the heroic age of the north, which existed in Iceland long after it was extinct everywhere else." And in another place: "The importance attached by the Scandinavians to the delineation of character is evident from the language itself, which is much richer than any other of Europe in all terms expressive of characteristic qualities, whether of mind or body, so as to be able to convey the strength, weakness, obstinacy, quarrelsome or peaceable disposition of every individual in its finest shades." It was not, therefore, until sometime after the race of Scalds was extinct in the three great Scandinavian kingdoms, that those of Iceland attained their highest perfection. Their fame spread abroad, and the successful examples of Eigil Skalagrimson and of some others, encouraged them to perfect themselves, and to travel from court to court in search of fame and profit. We accordingly hear of them in the courts of England, Ireland, Scotland, Norway, Sweden, Denmark, the courts of the Orkneys, and in various other places. In the year 1000, Christianity was established by law in Iceland. Fifty years afterwards the first school was founded there, and Latin books introduced. The preceding cultivation of mind, and the circumstances of the climate, were the causes, probably, why more attention was paid to literature there than in the busy, turbulent kingdoms of Sweden, Denmark, and Norway. The *Kristnis-Saga* informs us that towards the end of the eleventh century, many Icelanders were learned enough to have been made priests; and, in fact, several were so; and in the twelfth century, Iceland possessed several considerable collections of books.[20]

The new learning which accompanied the introduction of Christianity, did not stand in the same opposition to the old as it did in the other parts of the north. Christianity had not been imposed on Iceland by force, but was introduced partly through the influence of the principal persons of the island, and partly by the example of the mother-country; nor did the influence of the bishops depend upon their power over the mind of a superstitious king, but rather on their personal qualities or on their kindred. So early even as the commencement of the thirteenth century an Interdict was but little regarded; and in 1213, the Archbishop of Drontheim was obliged to use the utmost caution in proceeding against the chiefs of the republic, who had cruelly maltreated one of their bishops.[21] During several centuries the Icelandic bishops were selected from the principal families of the island. Their temporary residence in a foreign country

---

[20] P. E. Müller.
[21] Ibid.

had not entirely extinguished their nationality; and they were content to encourage the new literature without seeking to eradicate the old. As the Roman letters and the art of writing came into general use, it was natural that the more enlightened should be desirous to secure their ancient traditions from oblivion. We find, accordingly, that Are Frode, who lived about this time, and somewhat later, Sæmund Frode,[22] are considered the earliest Icelandic historians; and, in the ensuing century, Snorro Sturleson, and the monks Gunnlang and Oddur, composed their histories chiefly from oral traditions.

It has thus been attempted to show how the peculiar situation and state of society of Iceland, may explain the seemingly improbable fact, that the traditions of the ancient religion and history of the great Scandinavian family should have been preserved and cherished amongst these its least favoured children, when they were altogether forgotten by those of the more flourishing branches.

But revolutions found their way hither also. By means of intermarriages, most of the estates in Iceland fell at length into the hands of a few families; and towards the beginning of the twelfth century, there were chiefs in the island so powerful, that two, at feud, rode to the *Thing*, the one

---

[22] *Frode* signifies *the wise*

with 700, and the other with 1200 followers.[23] In this altered state of things a solitary individual could possess but little weight, and the influence of public opinion rapidly diminished. From the middle of the twelfth century the three sons of the turbulent Sturle; namely, Snorro, the historian, Thord, and Sieghvart, were the leading men of the island; and the history of the republic ends with the parricidical contests of this family, which caused their own destruction and that of their country. In the year 1262, Iceland was united to the crown of Norway. By this revolution it was indeed freed from the miseries brought upon it by its turbulent chiefs; but all interest in public affairs thenceforth died away, and no Sagas were written, because there was nothing to write about. They were replaced by dry chronicles, which also ceased with the great plague in 1350, and were not resumed until so late as the seventeenth century.[24] During the latter troubles of the republic, the prosperity of the island had much suffered; the wealth of individuals disappeared; large estates fell to the crown and were neglected; commerce died away under monopolies and injudicious regulations; travels abroad ceased; and, lastly, fire and water, the sea and volcanoes combined to sink this devoted land to that state of poverty and misery in which it now languishes.

---

[23] P. E. Müller.   [24] Ibid.

INTRODUCTION. xxxix

Thus, gradually, and by a natural course of events, all memory of the ancient manners, history, and religion of the north, was lost to the world. The old Scandinavian language, however, was still preserved pure in Iceland; and the poor, but not wholly illiterate, peasant, treasured up in his cabin the smoky parchments in which were preserved the events of the olden times, and often excited the wonder of his family by reading to them the wild relations of the Scalds, or the more precious relics of the Northern Mythology. Until the latter end of the sixteenth century all knowledge of the religion of heathen Scandinavia, possessed by other nations, was confined to what could be gleaned from the works of Paulus Diaconus, Adam of Bremen, and Saxo Grammaticus. The first was a Lombard of the latter end of the eighth century; the second a Canon of Bremen, who wrote in the eleventh; and the last the secretary of Bishop Absalom in the twelfth, more celebrated for the elegance of his Latin and for his classical attainments, than for historical correctness; and whose information respecting the Northern Mythology is obscured and disfigured by his practice of decorating its deities with the inappropriate names of the gods of Rome.

In 1594 appeared a Danish translation of Snorro Sturleson's Chronicle of the Kings of Norway, written in the thirteenth century in Icelandic, which threw an entirely new light on this hitherto obscure subject, and excited the further researches of the learned in the north. One of the most ardent in this pursuit was Arngrim Johnsen, who died in 1648, and who, by his writings and industry in procuring and decyphering old Icelandic manuscripts, obtained a great mass of information on the subject. Contemporary with him, and his worthy coadjutor, was Bryniulf Svendsen, Bishop of Iceland, who died in 1675. The former discovered and sent to Olaus Wormius, in 1628, a parchment copy of the Prose Edda, now in the library of the University at Copenhagen, and scarcely ten years afterwards, Bryniulf discovered copies on parchment both of the Prose and Poetic Eddas, and sent both to the Royal Library at Copenhagen. The curiosity of the learned was now greatly excited, and the cabin of every peasant in Iceland was ransacked in search of parchments. The result was the discovery of a vast number of Sagas; some consisting of biographical relations of persons who existed between the ninth and thirteenth centuries; others extravagant fictions; and others again a compound of both: nearly all of which have found their way into the libraries of Copenhagen, Upsala, and Stockholm; and the most valuable are now in course of publication.[25]

Men of profound learning in Denmark and

---

[25] P. E. Müller.

Sweden undertook the illustration of these relics of antiquity, and the names of Stephanius, Olaus Wormius, Resenius, Th. Bartholin, Thormod Torfæus, Arnas Magnæus, Gudmund Andersen, Verelius, Scheffer, Rudbeck, Keysler, Dalin, and Goranson, are familiar to those who have ever turned their attention to the subject. A Frenchman, Monsieur Mallet, however, was the first author who gave to this subject a popular dress, and his coadjutor, Erichsen, contributed not a little to the correctness and learning of his work,[26] which was translated into English by Dr. Percy.

In 1771, Suhm published his work "*on the Heathen Religion and Worship in the North,*" the most clear and comprehensive which had appeared on the subject, and by his ingenious deductions drew the attention of the learned, particularly in Denmark and Germany, still more strongly to the subject, which now seems to have been exhausted, by a long list of writers of eminence.[27]

In England, however, it appears hitherto to have awakened but little interest. Mr. Cottle translated into English the Edda of Sæmund. The

---

[26] *Monumens de la Mythologie et de la Poesie des Celtes*, &c. 1756.

[27] Schlözer, Herder, Thorlacius, Finn Johnsen, Thorkelin, Sandtvig, Gräter, Abrahamsen, Bastholm, Nyerup, Grundtvig, Finn Magnussen, Rafn, Mohne, Möller, Müller, Ling, Henneberg, Vonder Hagen, &c.

xlii INTRODUCTION.

Honourable William Herbert, in the second volume of his Miscellaneous Poetry, has given, in elegant verse, translations of detached pieces of Icelandic poetry, with illustrative notes, and Dr. Henderson has appended to his " *Journey through Iceland*" a treatise on Icelandic poetry; but beside these, Sir W. Scott's account of the Eyrbiggia Saga, Weber's N. Romances, and the translation of Mallet's Northern Antiquities, the writer is not aware of any work in English tending to throw material light on this interesting subject.[28]

It may not be out of place here to give a concise account of the two Eddas.

There are two works which bear the title of Edda;[29] the one in verse, and the other in prose. The first may be considered a symbolical work on the Scandinavian Mythology: the latter a kind of commentary on the former. The Elder, or Poetical Edda, was long attributed to the Icelander Sæmund, surnamed Frode or the learned, who was a priest in Iceland towards the latter end of

---

[28] To this list should be added the short account of the religion of Odin, in Mr. S. Turner's Hist. of Anglo-Saxons, and the still more concise summary in this book of the church, also some articles which appeared in the early numbers of the Foreign Quarterly Review.

[29] Various interpretations have been given of the meaning of the word " *Edda*," which in Icelandic signifies simply " *the Great-Grandmother.*"

the eleventh century, and from his great love for the heathen traditions, and the songs of the old Scalds, acquired amongst his countrymen the reputation of a magician, which he still retains. There is every reason to believe, however, that the greater part if not the whole of the poems of the Elder Edda are of a very much earlier date, and that Sæmund had the merit of collecting them from oral traditions, or possibly from Runic manuscripts, and of thus preserving them from oblivion. Of these anonymous poems or songs there are extant about forty, the meaning of many passages in which is very obscure, but not so much so but that those, well versed in the Icelandic language, render them nearly in the same manner. Some of these songs treat of Theogony and Cosmogony; some of the adventures of the gods; one is composed of riddles; others treat of magic, sorcery, enchantments; a part of the Havamal, of Ethics; the remainder, of the feats of heroes.

The Prose, or, as it is more usually entitled, the Younger Edda, is, undoubtedly, of much later date, but it does not appear that Snorro Sturlesen was more than the compiler and continuer of it; and it may be attributed with more probability to the same Sæmund who was wrongly esteemed the author of the Poetic Edda. It is composed of First—Mythological Fables or, as they have been termed, Parables, containing (a) *"Gylfa-Ginning,"* or " *the manner in which Gylfe was deceived,"* which Dr. Percy has translated into English from Mallet's French translation, (b) *Braga-rœdur*, or the conversation of Bragi with Ægir.

Second—The Kenningar, a collection of epithets and metaphors employed by the Scalds, illustrated by fragments from their compositions and from the Elder Edda.

Third—The Scalda, or Poet's book, containing three treatises: (a) On the Icelandic characters and alphabet; (b) on grammatical, rhetorical, and poetical figures; (c) on prosody.[30]

---

[30] The above account of the two Eddas is taken from Professor Finn Magnussen's translation of the Poetic Edda.

SCANDINAVIAN MYTHOLOGY.

CHAPTER I.

GENERAL VIEW OF THE SCANDINAVIAN MYTHOLOGY.

ANCIENT Mythology has been considered by some as a mere collection of extravagant and, now, unmeaning fables, and as such unworthy of serious attention: on the other hand, it has been described, as the medium by which the history and philosophy of mighty nations, long since passed away, the opinions held by the earliest heathen legislators, respecting God, Providence, and the Universe, have been handed down, allegorically, to later generations.[1] Lord Bacon has compared the fabulous portion of history " to a veil interposed between the present and the first ages of the world;"[2] and that curiosity can scarcely merit the

---

[1] Heyne.   [2] De Sapientiâ veterûm.

reproach of idleness, or tend otherwise than to enlarge and elevate the mind, which leads us to inquire concerning the nature of doctrines, which, however erroneous, have exercised a powerful and enduring influence on the destinies of mankind. But such inquiry assumes a far higher importance when we reflect on the striking resemblance that, amid the variety of extravagant fictions in which the undirected imagination of these primitive philosophers indulged, has been found to pervade the Mythologies of all the great heathen nations: a resemblance, remarks Sir W. Jones, " too strong to be accidental," and which extends to the religions of Greece, Italy, India, Egypt, Persia, China, Phrygia, Phœnicia, Syria, the gothic nations of Northern Europe, and even to those of the American continent. " The conclusion to be drawn from this unquestionable fact," adds the same gifted writer, " is inevitable, viz. that a general affinity must have existed between the most distinguished inhabitants of the primitive world, when they first deviated from the worship of the only true God."[3] Some writers, indeed, have laboured with mistaken zeal, to prove that whatever is to be found good or elevated in the religious doctrines of the heathen nations, has been

---

[3] Anniversary Discourse on the Hindus.

derived from the Jewish or Christian religions: thereby falling into the precise error of the Jews themselves, who presumptuously conclude that the miraculous dispensation by which they were so long separated from the rest of mankind was in consequence " of a peculiar fondness of the Almighty" (to use the words of Bishop Warburton[4]) for their race, and not to preserve the memory of the one God in the midst of an idolatrous world. That all divine truth was not limited to the revelations vouchsafed to the Jewish people has been sufficiently shewn by Bishops Warburton,[5] Horsley,[6] and others, and the prophecies of Job and of Balaam afford alone sufficient proof, that God's warning voice was not at all times confined to the children of Israel.

Thus much is certain, that hitherto no community of men has been discovered, in any age, or however uncivilized, entirely devoid of traditions, more or less obscure, respecting the origin of the world; and of a belief, more or less distinct, in a state of existence after death. History teaches us, moreover, that all the principal nations of anti-

---

[4] Divine Leg. of Moses, book v. sec. 2.
[5] Div. Leg. book ii.
[6] Dissertation on the prophecies of the Messiah dispersed among the heathen.

quity had their peculiar theories respecting the creation, which formed the principal subject of their mysteries,[7] and were the foundation of their popular worship. The cosmogonies of many of these nations have been preserved to the present time, some in obscure fragments, some nearly entire, and afford an interesting subject of comparison. The following is an abridged account of the Cosmogony of the Scandinavians, as contained in the Eddas:

"In the beginning there existed nothing save one vast abyss, called Ginnungagap, (chaotic pit), which was wholly void. One side of this abyss, called Muspell, faced towards the south, and was warm; the other, Niffl-heim, faced northwards, and was cold. Out of Niffl-heim there rose a spring, Hvergelmer, which existed before anything else was created. It was full of poisons, and its waters flowed by means of several great rivers into the abyss. The largest of these rivers was called Elivagar (the cold stormy waters), which penetrated farther than the others, but in proportion as it receded from its source flowed with a weaker current, until on reaching the centre its waters became so sluggish, that they could no longer resist the cold, and thus became ice. Still,

---

[7] Div. Leg. Book ii. sec. 4.

as the rivers flowed on the ice accumulated, so that at length the whole abyss was filled up with ice and rime. But in the process of time also the heat from Muspell began to act on that portion of the ice the nearest to it, until the whole by degrees was thawed, and from the thaw was produced the giant Ymer, whose immeasurable bulk filled up a portion of the abyss. Ymer fell into a deep sleep, during which a man and a woman were generated under his left arm, and one foot begat a son upon the other. From these are descended the race of the Hrymthussar, or giants of the frost. At the same time that Ymer, or the evil principle (for the Edda tells us that he and all his race were evil), was produced from the contending elements, Alfadur, or the father of all things, created the cow, Audumbla, from whose udders flowed four streams of milk, by which Ymer was nourished. She herself procured sustenance by licking some stones on which the hoar frost still lay, and which were salt. By this process, within three days, they were moulded into a man who was called Bure. He had a son Bur or Börr, who married a maid of giant race named Beyzla, or Belsta, by whom he had three sons, Odin, Vile, and Ve. These three, shortly after their birth, slew the giant Ymer, the blood from whose wounds drowned the whole of the frost-giants, with the exception of *Bergelmer* (the old man of the mountain), who escaped with his wife in a boat, and continued the race. After this, Börr's sons took Ymer's body and set it in the midst of the gulf Ginnungagap. Of his flesh they formed the earth, of his blood seas and waters, of his bones mountains, of his teeth rocks and stones, of his hair all manner of plants. They made the heavens out of his skull, and set four dwarfs, whose names were East, West, North, and South, at the four corners, to support it. They took also fires from Muspelheim and fixed them in heaven, above and below, to light up the heaven and the earth. And they determined the course of all meteors and heavenly bodies, some in the heavens, some under the heavens. Moreover, they threw up Ymer's brains into the air, where they became clouds, and formed Midgard of his eyebrows."

Such is the account of the creation of the universe given in the Prose Edda, the author of which has put in the shape of a continuous narrative details collected from several of the Mythological Poems or Songs, which compose what is called the Elder or Poetic Edda. In the Voluspa, or the Song of the Prophetess, the most interesting of them all, as well on account of the evident marks which it bears of remote antiquity, as of the loftiness of its language, and the poetry of its conception, a Vala or Prophetess, probably Urda, the Norny of the past, from a high seat, informs the gods and the numerous race of lesser deities, assembled in intent silence around her, of the mystery of their creation, and of the destruction which must one day overtake them. She begins as follows:—

1.

Listen to my tale,
Ye holy beings,
High and low,
Of the race of Heimdall!
I will narrate the deeds
Of the sire of the slain,
With old traditions,
   The oldest I remember.

2.

I bring to mind the giants,
Born betimes:
They who, of yore,
Fostered my childhood,
I can tell of nine worlds,
And nine heavens,
Of the lordly central tree,
   Beneath the earth.

3.

It was the morn of time,
When nothing was,
Nor sand nor sea,
Nor cold billows,
Nowhere could earth be found,

> Nor the high heaven,
> There was a boundless gulph
> > Without thing that groweth.
>
> 4.
>
> Until the sons of Börr
> Gave life to clay,
> They who constructed
> The lordly Midgard.
> Soel from the south
> Shone on its walls,
> When earth was decked
> > With verdant plants.

In like manner, in another of these songs, the Grimnersmaal, to which we shall have occasion to refer presently, we are told by Odin himself:—

> From Ymer's corpse
> Earth was created:
> From his blood the sea;
> Plants from his hair;
> The heavens from his front;
> From his brows
> The wild gods formed
> Midgard, for the sons of men;
> Whilst from his brains
> The hard blowing clouds
> > Came into being.

Notwithstanding the extravagant wildness of the preceding fiction, thus much at least may be elicited from it; that its inventors believed in one supreme, eternal, and omnipotent being (Alfadur), to whom they assigned no origin, and respecting whose nature and attributes they presumed not to conjecture.[8] They intended also plainly to inculcate that matter was eternal, and in its nature evil, whilst good could proceed only from the allwise Alfadur.[9]

Finn Magnussen views the Scandinavian Cosmogony as an allegory, which he thus interprets:— The giant Ymer represents the chaotic state of the earth, produced by the combined effects of heat and cold upon water, which according to the belief of all nations, and to the account of the Holy Scriptures themselves, was the first existing

---

[8] Mysterious allusions to the supreme being occur from time to time in the poems of the Elder Edda. Thus in Hyndla's song,

> Yet there shall come
> Another mightier,
> Altho' him
> I dare not name.
> Further onward
> Few can see,
> Than when Odin
> Meets the wolf.

[9] The eternity of the world, remarks Bastholm, is an invention of modern philosophers; but the ancients, whilst they steered clear of this absurdity, believed in the eternity of *matter*, because they could not comprehend how the world could have been produced out of nothing. (Bastholm over de œldste Folkes-lægters rel. og philos. Meiningen).

matter. The cow Andumbla, he thinks not an inapt symbol of the atmosphere, which surrounded the chaotic earth, and might be said to nourish it. The production of a nobler being, Bure, from the salt stones might denote the emersion of the earth from the ocean. His son Börr, the heavenly mountain Caucasus, called by the Persians Borz, and which plays so prominent a part in the earliest mythologies almost of all nations. From his union with Bestla, or Belsta, were produced three powerful beings, Odin, Vile, and Ve. Air Light, and Fire, which put an end to the chaos, or, in the words of the allegory, slew the giant Ymer.[10]

But whatever may be concluded as to the real meaning of the Scandinavian Cosmogony, we should be careful lest the extravagance of its details lead us to too hasty conclusions with respect to the ignorance or barbarousness of the people by whom it was received, for upon examination we shall find that the notions entertained on this subject, by the most enlightened nations of antiquity, were scarcely more intelligible.

The doctrine of the Egyptians did not differ widely from that of the Scandinavians. According to Diodorus, they taught that there was an original

---

[10] Magnussen Edda Lære, vol. i. p. 29.

chaos, from which the world was formed by motion, and the action of the sun, or of fire, which was worshipped by the ancient Egyptians, as the supreme deity, under the title of Phthas. The earth, when separated from the waters, began to ferment, and through this fermentation all animals came into existence.[11]

The ancient Chaldeans also taught that the world was produced from a chaos, composed of water and darkness, but inhabited by various monsters, who were destroyed by Bel, the sun. In like manner as Odin and his brethren destroy Ymer, and from his body form the universe; Bel cuts in twain the giantess Omorca, and converts the two halves of her body into heaven and earth. In other respects the Chaldean allegory, whilst it strongly resembles, may be said to surpass in extravagance, the Scandinavian.[12]

The Cosmogony of the Phœnicians, that active and intelligent people to whom probably Greece, and the whole of Europe chiefly owe their early civilization and religious worship, as far as we can judge from the fragments handed down to us, was still more extravagant than those we have cited.[13]

---

[11] Diod. Bibl. Hist.
[12] Berosi Chaldæi fragmenta in fab. Bibl. Græc. v. 14.
[13] Sanconiatho in frag. Philonis.

According to the ancient Greek Cosmogony, as contained in the fragments of the songs of Orpheus, preserved by Athenagoras, water was the principle of all things. From water was produced a slough or mud, and from this again a monster with three heads, of which one was like that of a god, one of a lion, and one of an ox. This monster however was a god, and produced an egg, of the top of which was formed heaven (Uranos), of the bottom, earth (Ge). From the union of these two were produced, first, the three fates, Klotho, Lachesis, and Atropos, and then the giants and cyclops, who rebelling against heaven, were cast down to Tartarus. The Titans, also, were the offspring of the earth, and from them descended the gods.

It would lead us too far from our subject to detail the cosmogonic theories of the Persians, Chinese, and the different Indian sects, all of which are easily accessible to the curious reader. Each of these nations, as has been already stated, had a peculiar theory, all in their most important particulars strongly resembling each other, all evidently distorted copies of one divine original. Striking indeed, as Magnussen remarks, is the contrast between the sublime simplicity of the account of the creation as given in the book of Genesis, and the laboured and monstrous allegories which compose the heathen cosmogonies. And yet if we duly consider these venerable traditions, we shall find that the light of truth, which through especial revelation was preserved in all its purity to the descendants of Israel, although greatly dimmed, was not altogether extinguished amongst the heathens. This may be said more especially of the Persians and Hindoos. The Zend-Avesta (living word) of the former, and the Vedas of the latter, have been deemed by wise and good men [14] to contain the remnants of divine revelation. The religious doctrines of the other ancient nations have been almost entirely lost, but the resemblance of their cosmogonies to each other, and to the Mosaic account, afford a striking corroboration of the truth of the divine mission of the Hebrew legislator, and of his account of the derivation of all the nations of the earth from one original stock. Almost all the heathen nations, as Magnussen remarks, recognised one supreme God, eternal, almighty, creator of the universe, enthroned in the highest heavens; but whilst the Jews, taught by inspired prophets, worshipped the one God in

---

[14] Amongst those of our own countrymen who held this opinion, may be cited the distinguished names of Bryant, Hyde, Holwell, Bishop Horsley, and Sir William Jones.

Spirit and in truth; and rightly viewed the angels of heaven, the cherubim and seraphim, and Elohim as the mere servants of his will; the heathens gradually lost sight of this great truth,[15] and deified in proportion to their ignorance and to the artifices of their priests, men, the elements, brutes, and at length, even stocks and stones.[16] But to return to the doctrines of the Scandinavians, we have already shewn how Odin and his two brothers formed the world out of the body of the giant Ymer. We shall now give a description of that event in the words of the poet Oehlenschläger. Thor, the god of thunder, and the sworn foe of the giants, is engaged in a discussion with Utgardelok, their king, on the nobility of their respective descents, in the course of which, the dæmon-monarch addresses his adversary as follows:—

> In being's earliest dawn,
> All was one dark abyss,
> Nor heaven, nor earth was known,
> Chill noxious fogs and ice,
> North from murk Niffl-heim's hole,
> Piled up in mountains lay;

---

[15] A considerable portion of Bryant's learned work, the Analysis of Ancient Mythology, is devoted to the proof, that the earliest defection to idolatry consisted in the adoration of the sun, and the worship of dæmons, styled Baalim.

[16] Magnussen Edda Lære, vol. i.

From Muspell's radiant pole,
South-wards fire held the sway.

Thus after ages past,
Mid in the chaos, met
A warm breath, Niffl-heim's blast:
Cold with prolific heat:
Hence pregnant drops were formed,
Which, by the parent air,
From Muspell's region, warmed
Produced great Aurgelmer. [17]

He was the mighty root
Of all our ancient race,
Which now, from light shut out,
In caves their days must pass;
High as thou hold'st thine head,
Say where was then thy car?
[18] The hammer-swinger said
Now lend to me an ear:

" Thy vaunt, how little worth,
My plain tale soon shall show!
The hour brought Ymer forth,
Saw, too, the mystic cow;
She shaped the cold salt stone,
Whence Bure our parent stood:

---

[17] The giants and the gods had each their peculiar language, Aurgelmer was the name which the giants gave to Ymer.

[18] A favorite epithet of Thor, from his celebrated hammer. He always, in his expeditions, used a car drawn by two goats, no horse being sufficiently strong to carry him.

No vapourous root, we own,
But breathing flesh and blood.

" With beauty, strength and power,
Him, great Alfader bless'd;
His son was mighty Börr
Who the tall Bestla press'd.
The maid was good and fair,
Though of a giant race;
Their birth, hence spirits of air,
Elves, Aser, Vaner, trace.

" Need was the primal powers
Should ripen and unite,
Ere that, such race as ours,
Could fitly come to light;
The oak, the forest's sire,
Long in the earth must grow,
Ere empyreal fire
From its gross limbs can flow."

After bringing to his memory the destruction of Ymer by the three sons of Bore, Thor proceeds:—

I' the gulf his body hurled
Odin and Vile and Ve;
Thereout to form the world:
His blood, the boundless sea,
His flesh they turn to earth,
His bones to mountains high,
His teeth as rocks spring forth,
His brains, clouds upwards fly.

They take his shaggy brows
And build fair Midgard's towers

> Which with a fence they close
> 'Gainst Utgard's demon powers;
> His spacious vaulted front
> Aloft the brethren threw,
> It formed the firmament,
> And Freya [19] tinged it blue.
>
> *Oehlenschläger.*

We next come to the creation of man, which is thus described in the prose Edda. " Gangler asked, whence came men, who dwell upon earth? Har answered, as Bör's sons went out to the seashore, they found two trees; out of which they created man. Odin gave spirit and life; Vile, understanding and vigour; Ve, form, speech, hearing and sight." In the Voluspa we are told that it was Odin who gave the spirit (soul); Hœner, understanding; and Loder, blood and a fair complexion.

> Askur and Embla hight,
> The first of human kind;
> Their home the spirits of light
> In Midgard's realms assigned;
> The countless human race,
> Their praise on earth who sing,
> From these their lineage trace;
> All from one couple spring.
>
> *Oehlenschläger.*

---

[19] Freya, the goddess of Love and Beauty, the Scandinavian Venus.

The word Askur signifies an Ash; Embla has been said also to mean Elm, but this is not so certain. The Greeks had a similar belief; Hesiod tells us[20] that Zeus created men from ash-trees, and the nymphs of the ash-tree (Meliæ) were said to be sprung from the blood of Saturn, and to have been the mothers of the human race. The gods took for their own habitation the celestial city, Asgard; Utgard, or the outermost abode, was allotted to the Giants. The Aser, the Giants, and the Human race, however, were not the only inhabitants of the universe. There existed various other beings, and nine distinct worlds for their abode. In the Voluspa the prophetess says,

> I call to mind nine worlds
> And nine heavens.

The Giant Vafthrudner also boasts of having seen the nine worlds, and the dwarf Alvis tells Thor,

> All the nine worlds
> Have I travelled through,
> And every being known.

The prose Edda says: "Bad men go to Hela, and from her to Nifl-hel, that is down to the ninth world."

---

[20] Ergai kai Emerai.

Magnussen classes these nine worlds as follows:—

I. Gimle, the residence of the supreme being, with its world, from whence the light Elves first had their origin; Gimle is to be the abode of the good after the destruction of the universe.

II. Muspel, or Muspelheim, the region of the genii of fire.

III. Godheim, or Asgard, the residence of the Gods, or Aser; the starry firmament.

IV. Vanaheim, the home of the Vaner, or spirits of air; also called Vindheim, or the home of the winds; the atmosphere.

V. Man-heim, or Midgard, the residence of man, the middle residence, being equally removed from Gimle and from Nifl-heim.

VI. Jotunheim, the home of the Jotuns, or Giants; also called Utgard, or the outer residence, as being placed outside the great sea which surrounded the earth, in which lay Jormungandur the serpent.

VII. The world of the Black Elves, or evil demons, spirits of Darkness and of the Dwarfs.

VIII. Helheim, the home of Hela the goddess of death; the abode of those who die ingloriously of sickness.

IX. Nifl-heim, the lowest of all the worlds, in

which is the river Elivaga, and the poisonous well Hvergelmer, which, after the destruction of the world, is to serve as a place of punishment for evil men. Nastroud, which was to serve the same purpose, was also here.

Of the worlds above enumerated and their inhabitants, seven were transitory and to be destroyed at the great catastrophe of Ragnarockur, the twilight of the Gods; two only, Gimle and Nifl-heim were to endure for ever; the former as a place of happiness for the virtuous, the latter of punishment for evil doers. We shall have occasion to describe all these regions more particularly in the course of the following chapters, and in the mean time, with a view to a more distinct understanding of their order and relation, the reader is referred to the annexed engraving, borrowed from Finn Magnussen's elaborate work on the Doctrine of the Eddas, where he will find the position of each of the nine worlds clearly marked out.

As it is the object of the present chapter to present a general outline of the whole system of the northern Mythology, previously to examining in detail its respective parts, we shall proceed, in imitation of Heiberg, to touch briefly on its principal points, and to enumerate the various beings of which it is composed. And first it will be necessary to explain the meaning of the term Aser, by which the northern gods are usually designated. The word As or Asa (pl. Aser) amongst the ancient Scandinavians, appears to have been nearly synonymous with Lord,[21] and to have been a title applied to persons of an elevated rank, whether deities or mortals.

According to Snorro Sturleseu, the celebrated Icelandic historian, and reputed author of the prose Edda, the Aser were a tribe settled on the Tanais, whose capital was called As-gaard, or As-hof, (Azov) which two words are synonymous, and signify merely the " residence of the Aser." A number of these Aser, under their prince or chief priest, Odin, left their country, and penetrated through Russia into Scandinavia, which they conquered, dispossessing the ancient inhabitants, probably Celts, and introducing their own language, manners, and religion.

In the Edda, however, the title of Aser is given only to the principal deities, of whom, besides

---

[21] According to Bryant the word As, Ees, or Is, was a title of the sun. In like manner in Phœnician, Ad signified Lord, and often occurs compounded, as Ad-On, the Lord Sun; whence Adonis, Ad-Or, &c. &c. It was sometimes compounded with itself, as Ad-ad, Lord of lords. Ham, the son of Noah, was sometimes styled Ad-Ham, which appellation has given rise to much mistake.—*Analysis of Ancient Mythol.*

Odin, there were twelve; viz. Thor, Baldur, Niord, Freyr, Bragi, Heimdall, Hoeder, Vidar, Ali or Vali, Uller, Forsete, and Loke or Loptur. There were likewise Asynier, or goddesses, who enjoyed equal power with the Aser. The Aser were benevolent spirits, the friends of man, emanating from the good principle, but not immortal. Their sovereignty over the world was to cease at Ragnarokkur, or the great battle, the twilight of the gods, when they and their eternal enemies, the Giants, were mutually to destroy each other, and the whole earth was to be consumed. They dwelt in the celestial Asgard, which was placed in the centre of the universe, and which will be more particularly described hereafter.

Odin's wife was Frea or Frigga, by whom he had his first born, Thor, the strongest and most formidable of the Aser, and the mortal foe of the Giants. Their second son was Balder, the fair, the wise, the merciful, the lover of peace. His death is the principal event in the Mythological drama of the Scandinavians, being foredoomed to serve as the prognostic of the approaching destruction of the universe, and of the gods themselves. The next to Balder in rank was Niord, by birth one of the Vaner, and lord of the winds. The Vaner seem to have been a people with whom the Aser, at a remote period of their history, before their migration northwards, had much intercourse. The Edda tells us of a war between them, at the conclusion of which Niord remained a hostage with the Aser. After this he married Skada, a daughter of the giant Thiasse, but had had previously by his sister, whom he had espoused according to the law of the Vaner, two children, Freyr and Freya. Freyr was high-minded and benevolent, fair to look on, lord of the sun and summer rains, and of the fruits of the earth. His sister, Freya, was the goddess of beauty and of love, the Scandinavian Venus. Besides these there were Tyr, the god of battles, another son of Odin, as would appear from the Eddas, by a giant woman; Bragi, the god of poetry and song, whose wife Iduna plays a conspicuous part, from the circumstance that she possessed certain apples of such virtue, that by eating of them the gods were exempted from the consequences of old age, and retained unimpaired the freshness of youth. Heimdall, the warder of Asgard, whose post was on the summit of Bifrost, the rainbow, the bridge which connects earth and heaven; Hodur and Vidar, the one blind, the other dumb. Lastly, there were Forsete, the son of Balder and the god of justice, and Ægir, the god of the sea, whose wife Ran, was hideous and cruel, the chief cause of shipwrecks and the terror of sailors. Ægir was of giant race, but received amongst the Aser. Last, although not the least important, comes Asa-Loke, the most busy and prominent actor of the Scandinavian Mythology. Descended from the giants he was, notwithstanding, received amongst the spirits of light. He retained, however, all the vices of his race; though eloquent and fair of form, he was cowardly, treacherous, and cruel, ever plotting against his benefactors, of whose destruction he at length proves the cause. He is called Asa-Loke, to distinguish him from Utgard's-Loke, a giant or evil demon, and king of the lower world, Utgard (or the outer residence) being, as already remarked, the abode of the infernal deities of the Scandinavians. As son of a giant, Asa-Loke claimed the advantages of his connexion, and had frequent intercourse with his infernal relatives. Both giants and gods, however, distrusted him, and he, not unfrequently, received punishment at the hands of both. The Edda describes his laughter as terrible, making the hearer shudder. By his wife, Signi, he had a son, Narfe, and by an amour with a giant woman, Augerbode, the three monsters; Fenris, the wolf; the great serpent, Jormungandur; and Hela, the queen of death, the constant source of terror to the gods, as destined to prove the chief engines of their destruction.

Besides the Aser and the Giants, the Scandinavian Mythology included various subordinate intelligencies, the most important of which were the dwarfs, sprung from the decaying body of Ymer, who form a connecting link between the Aser and the Giants, in their nature partaking of evil and good, but most inclined to evil. They lived beneath the earth, and could not endure the light of the sun.

Akin to these, but devoid of their evil qualities, were the Alfs or Elves, fair and well proportioned, cherished by the Aser and friends of man.

The Valkyrs were the especial messengers of Odin, in his character of god of battles. Their province, as their name denotes, was, before the commencement of a battle, to select the warriors who were to fall during the contest. Such a death was considered an especial favour, as it secured to the slain an immediate passage to Valhalla, where these warlike maids served them as cupbearers. The translated warriors were called Einheriar, and were to compose the army of Odin at the last combat.

The great Ash Ygg-drasill, which Magnussen conjectures to be a symbol of the earth in its organized state, in like manner as the giant Ymer represents the earth, in a state of chaos, forms an important feature in the Scandinavian Mythology.

In this also we find the same contest betwixt good and evil, which pervades the whole Mythology. Two of its roots spring from the infernal regions, the third from the abode of the gods. Various beings are incessantly employed in its destruction, whilst the three Nornies or fates, Urda, Verdandi, and Skulda, (the past the present and the future), prolong its existence by watering it continually from Urda's well. Its branches extend over earth and heaven. Four stags who nip off the young buds have been explained by Gräter and Finn Magnussen, as symbolical of the four winds, by Grundtvig more poetically, if not more justly, of time.

Night was the daughter of a Giant; she married an Aser, Delling, (the dawn), and by him had a son, the Day. Odin placed both mother and son in Asgard, gave to each a horse and car, and directed them to traverse the heavens unceasingly. Night's horse was called Hrymfaxe, or the dewy-mane, for by the shaking of his mane dew-drops were scattered over the face of the earth. The horse of Day was called Skin-faxe, or the shining mane, because from his mane rays of light were emanated throughout the universe. Besides these, Soel and Maane, the sun and moon, travelled daily in cars the same route; the former was daughter, the latter son of Mundilfaxe. Their course was hurried, for they were in continual fear of two wolves who followed seeking to devour them.

The winter was ruled by a giant in the shape of an eagle, who sat at the north pole, surrounded by ice and snow, and the waving of whose wings produced the bleak north wind. He is thus described in the Elder Edda:—

> The giant Hrsuelgur,
> At the end of heaven,
> Sits in an eagle's form;
> 'Tis said that from his wings
> The cold winds sweep
> Over all nations. [22]
>
> *Vafthrudvers maal.*

The title Hrsuelgur signifies the devourer of carrion, a title equally applicable to the eagle, and as Heiberg suggests to the bleak north wind, of which he is the personification, which dissipates noisome unwholesome vapours. The lord of summer was called Svosödur, the sweet and pleasant, but is not particularly described.

The remainder of the Mythology consists in

---

[22] "The Chippewyan Indians believe that originally the globe was one vast ocean inhabited by no creature except a mighty bird, whose eyes were fire and whose glances lightning and the clapping of whose wings were thunder. On his descent to the ocean and on his approaching it, the earth instantly rose up and remained on the surface."

Mackenzie's Travels, p. 126.

narrations of the various feats of the gods, and particularly of their adventures with the giants. The chief event in the drama, as has been already said, is the death of Baldur, brought about through the agency of Loke. The gods, after taking a fearful vengeance on the traitor, consult anxiously together how to avert the fate, of which his death was to be the forerunner. Odin descends to the tomb of a deceased vala or prophetess, to seek to extract from her the secrets of the dead; but his journey is profitless, and he returns convinced of the necessity of submitting to the decrees of destiny, and that Ragnarokkur must at length arrive, when the wolf Fenris will break his chain, the huge serpent awakening from his stupor escape from his ocean prison, Surtur, the god of fire, leading on the Giants and the children of Muspell, storm Asgard, and gods, giants and the universe perish in one common ruin.

By the decree, however, of the eternal Alfadur, who, during this terrific struggle remains on high, a tranquil spectator, a new earth will arise from the sea, fairer and more verdant than the old, the gods will be recalled to life, and the human race be renewed from one couple, miraculously preserved.

Of the old universe, two portions only will remain, one turned towards the south, the other to the north, Gimle and Nastroud. The former composed of pure gold and destined to be the place of abode for good and just men. The latter constructed of poisonous serpents and to be the place of punishment for perjurers, murderers, and the seducers of other men's wives.

> Men forsworn,
> And wolf-like murderers,
> And they who beguile
> The wives of others.   *Voluspa.*

It remains, lastly, to speak of the dwellings of the gods.

Their abode, Asgard, in the centre of the universe, has already been alluded to. In this great city, as the Edda calls it, each of the principal deities had a residence, apart from the rest, and all these residences are enumerated and particularly described in one of the poems of the Elder Edda. They were twelve in number, and denominated as follows:—

1. Ydale, the residence of the god . Uller
2. Alfheim, ... Freyr
3. Valaskialf, ... Vale
4. Soequabeck, ... Saga
5. Gladsheim, ... Odin
6. Thrymheim, ... Skada
7. Breidablik, ... Baldur
8. Himmelbjeig, ... Heimdale
9. Folkvangur, ... Freya

10. Glitner, the residence of	. .	Forsete
11. Noatun,	. . . . .	Njord
12. Landvide, .	. . . .	Vidar

Besides these twelve, there was Thrudheim, the residence of Thor, the Thunder god; but these celestial residences have a claim to our attention, beyond that which they could have derived from the simple fact that they were the dwelling-places of the deities enumerated, for it has been shewn by Finn Magnussen,[23] that they were invented for astronomical purposes, and that they hold the place of the zodiac in the astronomy of the ancient Scandinavians. In the introduction, we have endeavoured to shew that this people were far removed from being so rude and barbarous as they have usually been considered.

We know that the worship of the stars prevailed throughout the East, and especially amongst those nations from whom the Scandinavians more immediately derived their origin. To the latter, from their maritime position and habits an accurate observation of the heavenly bodies became almost indispensable. According to Herodotus, the Egyptians, who worshipped the twelve great gods, were the first who divided their year into twelve equal parts or months, consecrating one part to each of their gods, and marking the divisions by certain

---

[23] Den Ældse Edda, vol. i. p. 134.

groups of stars, in or near the sun's course through the heavens, to which they affixed names.

Whether the honour of this invention be due to them, or to the Chaldeans, it is certain that the practice was adopted either in imitation, or by original discovery, by almost every considerable nation upon earth, for example, by the Persians, Hebrews, Syrians, Hindoos, Chinese, Arabians, Japanese, Siamese, Goths, and by the inhabitants of Java, of Mexico, and of Peru. The Scandinavians also divided their year into twelve parts or months, and had twelve principal deities, to each of whom a month was consecrated, and each of whom had a celestial palace in Asgard. In like manner as the Romans, who, we know, borrowed the practice from the Egyptians, and that at a late period of their history under the emperors, the Scandinavians divided also their time into weeks of seven days, and consecrated the days of their week to the sun, moon, and five of their principal deities. It is not improbable therefore, that having retained so much of the eastern worship, they should not have been altogether ignorant of the division of the ecliptic into twelve parts. We shall not however pause to discuss this question, but proceed without further preface to give an account of the Grimnersmaal, the poem in which these palaces are described together with the commentary of Finn Magnussen, in illustration thereof. This poem, which forms a part of the Elder Edda, is preceded by a prose introduction, entitled

A TALE ABOUT KING HRODUNG'S SONS.

"Hrodung, king of the Goths, had two sons, Agnar and Geirrod, the one ten, the other eight years of age. One day that they were alone fishing, their boat was driven out to sea, and, after tossing about for some time, was wrecked on an island. Having got to shore, they were hospitably received by a poor peasant and his wife, who proved to be Odin and Frigga in disguise. Odin adopted Geirrod, and Frigga, Agnar, as their foster children, and took care of them for a whole winter, during which time Odin instructed Geirrod in many things; and when the spring came, gave the two lads a vessel in which to return home. As he and Frigga were accompanying them to the shore, he talked apart with Geirrod for an hour. With a favourable wind the youths reached their father's kingdom. Geirrod, who was in the bow, leaped at once on shore, and kicking the boat from him cried, "Float away into the power of the evil spirits." The skiff drifted out to sea with the elder brother, and Geirrod hastened to the town, where, his father being dead, he was well received by the people, who made him their king, and he came to be much considered.

Odin and Frigga sat in Hlidskialf and looked out over the whole world. Odin said, behold now Agnar, your foster son, how he is poor and a wanderer, whilst my foster son, Geirrod, though his younger brother, is a king, and rules over his father's realm. Frigga replied, that Geirrod was a pitiful niggard, who starved his guests when he thought they were too numerous. Odin refused to credit the fact, and they made a wager upon it. Frigga despatched her confidential hand-maiden, Fulla, to Geirrod, to warn him to be on his guard, for that his life was in danger from a wise man, who was at that time in his kingdom. She gave him as a sign by which the stranger might be discovered, that no dog, however fierce, would venture to attack him.

Although it was not true that Geirrod was inhospitable, he now issued orders to seize the man whom no dog would attack. One was brought to him clad in a blue Peltz, who said that his name was Grimner (the disguised), but however questioned he would give no further account of himself. With a view to force him to confess, king Geirrod ordered him to be placed between two huge fires, and to receive no food. In this state he continued eight nights, when the king's son, a boy of ten years old, called Agnar after his uncle, reached him a full horn to drink, saying, that his father did ill to punish one who was innocent. Grimner drank out the horn, but by this time the heat of the fire had so increased that his fur cloak began to burn, when he thus sang,

> Hot art thou grasping flame!
> And all too powerful,
> Let me go from the fire!
> The fur is singed,
> Though I gather it up
> The Peltz burns upon me.
>
> Eight nights have I sat
> Here, between the fires,
> And no man
> Hath offered me food:
> Save Agnar alone,
> Who shall rule the land of the Goths,
> The son of Geirrod.
>
> Hail to thee, Agnar!
> Good fortune bids thee now
> Be the ruler of heroes!
> For a drink
> Never shalt thou
> Enjoy richer reward.

After this prophetic rhapsody, Odin proceeds with his celestial song as follows:

> Holy is the land
> Which I see before me,
> Near to the Aser and the Elves.

> But in Thrudheim,
> Shall Thor abide,
> Until the gods are no more.

Thrudheim is the atmosphere between the heavenly Asgard and the earth, the proper residence of Thor, the god of thunder. The twelve celestial residences are next described; the first is Ydale, the abode of the god Üller, to whom the first month of the Scandinavian year was dedicated, commencing with the entrance of the sun into Sagittarius, and including the period from November 22 to December 21. Of Uller the prose Edda tells us, that he is the best of archers, that snow flakes and hail are his arrows, that he runs so swift on snow shoes or skees, that no one can cope with him. He was said to be of a fair and warlike appearance, and was lord of the snows and of the chase, which in the north usually begins with the first snow.

The second celestial habitation was called Alfheim, the land of the Light Elves. It was the abode of Freyr, and given to him by the Aser, in the morning of time, when he received his first teeth. Freyr was the god of the sun, and to him was consecrated the second month, commencing at the winter solstice, when the days begin to lengthen and the sun may be said to be born again. In the same manner the Egyptians celebrated the birth of their sun-god, Horus; and the Romans called the winter solstice " natalitia invicti Solis." Freyr and Freya were twin children of Njord, the god of the sea and air. The Edda tells us, that " Njord begat in Noatun two children, Freyr and Freya. They were fair and noble, and Freyr rules over rain and sunshine, and the fruits of the earth. He is to be prayed to for a good year and for peace, and it is he who dispenses blessings to mankind." In like manner the Greeks pretended that Apollo and Diana were the children of Latona, who, like Njord, was the personification of the lower atmosphere, or of the ocean. In the third month the sun entered Valaskialf, which the Edda tells us the god Vale acquired for himself in the morning of time. Vale was a son of Odin and Rinde (Rind), a personification of the frozen, unfruitful earth, and was brave and a good archer. The name of this month was Liosberi, or the light-bringer, and it extended from January 21 to February 19. The Christian Anglo-Saxons called it the sun month, and formerly in the north it was the custom to celebrate at this period the mid-winter festival, by lighting up the houses with torches, and making bonfires on the heights. In place of this feast the Catholics instituted Candlemas, or the feast of torches, and Candlemas is still denoted on the Swedish and Norwegian Primstaves, or

Rimestocks, the wooden almanacks in use amongst the peasants, by a lighted torch, in like manner as the winter solstice by a bale-fire. In place of the rejoicings of the great mid-winter festival, were substituted the merrymakings of the Carnival. A similar festival (Ambarvalia) was held at this time by the Romans.

The Catholic priests seem to have dexterously substituted St. Paul, whose festival is held on the 25th of January, for Vale. It is marked on the primstaves by a bow, and the peasants who call the saint, Paul the archer, or Paul with the bow, believe him to have been a warrior, who fought in the morning and prayed in the afternoon. St. Valentine also, whose feast is early in February, puts us in mind of the deposed Vale. Valaskialf was said to be white, and roofed with silver; a poetical and not inapt representation of the effect of the reflection of the snow-covered earth on a clear frosty sky.

In the fourth month, from February 19 to March 19, the sun was in Socquaboek (the deep brook), where Odin and Saga drink every day out of golden cups. Magnussen remarks that Saga here is put for Urda, and with great propriety, Saga being the goddess of history and tradition, Urda the norny of the past. In this month the sun begins to thaw the snows, and to fill the brooks and rivers, and in some parts of England it is still called Fillbrook. Urda's well is the source of all fertilizing waters, and answers to the sign of the fishes in the Greek Zodiac.

In the fifth month the sun was in Gladsheim, the abode of Odin, and the entrance to the radiant Valhalla, the general place of assembly for all the gods, whose roof is composed of shields and spears.

> Easily can they
> Who come to Odin,
> Perceive and know Valhalla.
> The roof is decked with spears,
> The hall covered with shields,
> The benches strewed with helmets.

> West before the gate
> Hangs a wolf,
> An eagle soars above it.

The wolf and the eagle were probably constellations, as it appears that these two animals, as well as the raven, were attributes of Odin. Gladsheim, answers to the sign of the ram, in which falls the vernal equinox, designated by various eastern nations, and by the Greeks also, the gates of heaven.

In the sixth month, from April 21 to May 20, the sun was in Thrymheim, which answers to the sign of the bull.

> Thrymheim the sixth is called,
> Where Thiasse dwelt of yore,
> The powerful giant:
> But Skada now inhabits,
> (The chaste Aser's bride)
> Her father's ancient halls.

The giant Thiasse here spoken of was slain by Thor, and the gods gave his residence to Skada, on her marriage with Njord. As the new married couple could not agree about their place of abode, it was settled that Skada should remain with her husband, at Noatun, for three successive days, and then return for nine, to her paternal mountains. Magnussen thus explains this fable: " The summer of the ancients began with this month, and Thiasse, the genius of winter, is represented as slain by Thor, the god of thunder, which in mountainous regions, such as Caucasus, where this fiction probably originated, or at least in Sweden and Norway, begins once again to be heard. Skada is a personification of the clear, penetrating wind of spring, which loves the mountains, and partakes of the nature of winter and of summer. Thor, having slain Thiasse, is said to have thrown his eyes up to heaven, where they became stars.

The seventh solar house is called Breidablik (the wide shining), and is the dwelling place of the fair and gentle Baldur. This fairest of months, including the period from the 21st of May to the summer solstice, was fitly consecrated to him who was beloved of gods and men, and for whose untimely fate everything in nature wept. From the end of this month the days get shorter, and night slowly resumes her reign, which is figured by the death of Baldur, through the agency of the blind god, Hodur, the symbol of night, who in his turn is slain by the young Vale.

The eighth month begins at the solstice. The sun being now at its highest, its house is called " the celestial mount." Here dwells Heimdall, the heavenly watchman, who stands on the summit of the rainbow. His golden teeth and golden maned horse, and the declaration " that he is the whitest or brightest of the Aser," are evident allusions to the splendour and brilliancy of the sun at this season. He is also called Hallinskeide (the declining), for the sun now begins to decline in the heavens. As at midsummer, in the northern latitudes, night can scarcely be said to exist; the Edda informs us that Heimdall requires less sleep than a bird, and that his sight is equally penetrating by day and by night. His exquisite hearing, which can detect the wool growing on the sheep's back, may be intended to denote the stillness which pervades all nature during the great heats prevalent at this season.[24]

In the ninth month the sun is in Folk-vangur, the residence of the goddess Freya. The word Folk-vangur signifies a meadow or field, filled with people. This month ending on the 23rd of August, and including the dog-days, is the month of harvest, and appropriately consecrated to the goddess of love and fruitfulness. She is also the queen of the night, the goddess of the moon; and the planet Venus in the north bore her name.

The tenth solar house was called Glitner, and belonged to Forsete, the son of Baldur.

> Glitner is the tenth.
> On golden columns rests
> The silver dome of its hall:
> There dwells Forsete.

Forsete is the god of justice; he holds a Thing at Urda's well, and from his tribunal gods and men depart reconciled and satisfied. In this month falls the autumnal equinox, assumed as the symbol of equality and justice. In the north it was the custom to suspend all feuds during the harvest,

---

[24] Magnussen remarks after Rudbeek (Atlantica 11. 30.) on the resemblance between Heimdall and the Greek Hermes, who presided over the same month.

and a solemn Thing was held yearly at this season. The word Forsete signifies " president."

The eleventh month was consecrated to Njord, who lives in Noatun. Njord controls the course of the winds, and checks the raging of the sea and of fire; he is the beneficent deity of the sea, in opposition to Ægir and Ran. Noatun is said to be by the sea side, probably because the sun, now in northern latitudes, fast lessening his diurnal arches, appears to approach nearer and nearer to the sea.

At length in the twelfth month, from November 21 to December 22, the sun enters Landvide, the abode of the sullen, dumb god, Vidar.

> With osiers and with
> High grass is overgrown
> Landvide, the house of Vidar:
> Thence the son descends
> Quick from his horse's back
> To avenge his sire.

The leaves have now fallen from the trees, dense fogs obscure the heavens, and all nature seems depressed. In mournful silence this month outlives its elder and more cheerful brethren, as Vidar himself survives the other gods, and avenges the death of his father, Odin, on the wolf Fenris.

Besides these twelve heavenly palaces on which we have dwelt at such length, Odin enumerates the sacred rivers, and the various mystic animals, the ravens, the wolves, the goats, the stags; describes also the Ash Yggdrasill, the Valkyrs, and lastly gives fifty-five of his own names. All this divine instruction may have been intended as a part of the reward of the young Agnar, and the enumeration of his names probably as an indication to Geirrod of his real character. Geirrod, however, overcome by the pleasures of the table, gives no heed to his discourse, and Odin, at length, losing patience, pronounces his death doom in these words:

> Geirrod! thou hast thy reward—
> Thou art overcome with drink—
> The mead hath stupified thee:
> Great was thy loss
> When my support went from thee:
>   The favour of Odin and the Einheriar.
>
> Much have I laid open to thee;
> Little hast thou heeded:
> Thy friends disappear,
> I, of my friend,
> Behold the blade
>   Dripping with blood.
>
> Sword-enfeebled spectre
> Now shall Ygg[25] receive:
> I know thy life has passed away,

---

[25] Ygg, a title of Odin.

> The Nornies are wroth with thee:
> Now mayest thou see Odin;
> Approach me if thou canst.

King Geirrod was sitting with his sword lying upon his knees, half drawn from the scabbard. When he heard that it was Odin who addressed him, he rose up suddenly from his seat to release the god from between the fires. In the act of rising, his sword slipped from his hand, and fell on the hilt to the ground. The king stumbled and fell forward, and the point of the sword entering his breast gave him his death wound. Odin disappeared, and Agnar long reigned over the land.

This story bears internal marks of great antiquity, and was probably composed soon after the introduction of the religion of Odin into the north. Geirrod is said to have been a king of Reid-gothland, (which includes the district between the Vistula and the Gulf of Finland,) who was slain by Odin, and his son, Agnar, made king in his place. With respect to some of its details, Magnussen remarks that it was a very general superstition amongst heathen nations, that immortal spirits, good or evil, although possessing the power of assuming various forms, yet could not divest their eyes of a preternatural expression; a superstition which gave rise to that of the evil eye so prevalent still in the east, and not wholly extinct in the north. In explanation of the torture to which Odin was subjected, he tells us also that the heathen inhabitants of Caucasus believed that this was the most effectual mode of rendering harmless the machinations of sorcerers. The blue mantle in which Odin was enveloped was an indication of his celestial character.

In conclusion, for a fuller understanding of the northern zodiac, as explained by Magnussen, we refer the reader to the annexed calendar, taken together with the preceding explanation, from that learned writer's annotations on the Elder Edda. In addition to the heavenly palaces already described, the Eddas mention Vingolf the place of assemblage for the goddesses, as Valhalla for the gods, and Fensale, Frigga's favourite seat.[26]

---

[26] In the east also the divisions of the Zodiac are called the twelve houses of the sun, represented by the twelve palaces in the celebrated Egyptian Labyrinth.

Calendar of the ancient Scandinavians, as explained by Professor Finn Magnussen.

Signs.	Sun enters.		Northern Solar House.	Deity.	Remarks.
♐ Sagittarius	Nov. 22	I.	Ydale	Uller	The old name of this month was Yler, Uller considered the deity of winter.
♑ Capricornus	Dec. 21	II.	Alfheim	Freyr	The birth of Freyr or the sun-god, the real feast of Juul or Jule, the mother night, the winter solstice.
♒ Aquarius	Jan. 21	III.	Valaskialf	Vale	In this month, termed the light-bringer, was celebrated the feast of torches, and in the northernmost countries that of Juul itself, the sun now first becoming visible.
♓ Pisces	Feb. 19	IV.	Socquabeck	Saga	In this month, now called Goa, in Sweden Goja, a solemn feast was held at Upsala, where the chief amusements were drinking and poetical recitations.
♈ Aries	Mar. 19	V.	Gladsheim	Hropt, or Odin	The vernal equinox.
♉ Taurus	April 21	VI.	Thrynheim	Skade	This month was called Harpa or Harpeu, and was considered as the commencement of summer.
♊ Gemini	May 21	VII.	Breidablik	Balder	The finest month of the year, called of old the sun's month, Balder, a symbol of the summer sun.
♋ Cancer	June 23	VIII.	Himmelbjerg	Heimdall	The summer solstice, formerly the festival of Balder and Heimdall, now St. John's day.
♌ Leo	July 23	IX.	Folkvang	Freya	The warmest month, harvest.
♍ Virgo	Aug. 23	X.	Glitner	Forsete	Autumnal equinox.
♎ Libra	Sept. 23	XI.	Noatun	Njord	The great autumnal feast, now Michaelmas.
♏ Scorpio	Oct. 23	XII.	Landvide	Vidar	The fall of the leaf, the mournful month which survives the rest.

CHAPTER II.

ODIN—THE ORIGIN OF POETRY—VALHALLA—THE EIN-HERIAR—THE VALKYRS—ODIN'S HORSE, SLEIPNER—FRIGGA—HERTHA.

MUCH learning and research have been employed in the attempt to ascertain who was the individual who bore the name of Odin, and how and when that religion, of which he was the supreme deity, was first established in Scandinavia. Until comparatively a late period, so little communication existed between those parts of Europe in which his religion prevailed, and the more civilized portions of the world, that a question of this nature must necessarily be involved in much obscurity.

As it is the object of the present work to give only a general view of the superstitions of Pagan Scandinavia, it will be sufficient here to state briefly those points on which the most learned of the northern antiquarians are of accord.

It is generally agreed that there must have been more than one individual who bore the name of Odin.[1] Under any other supposition it would be

---

[1] Antiquarians have widely differed respecting the etymo-

impossible to reconcile the contradictions of the Edda.

At one time he is represented as the primal cause of all things, creator of the universe: at

---

logy of the word Odin, some pretending that it was originally Wodan, others Guodan or Guode, whence Gode, Gud, God, the title of the supreme being in Danish, German, and English. Others, again, that God was the original title from which the others were derived. There can be but little doubt, as Suhm remarks, that Odin, Guodan, Godan, Wodan, are but different ways of pronouncing the same word, although it is not easy to determine which was the original. It has been asserted that the Goths derived their name from Godan, (by them pronounced Gothan) which would go far in favour of that version; but we find that in Daghestan, Auden is still a man's name, and as Odin no doubt came from that neighbourhood, Suhm gives that name the preference. Auden is also used as a man's name in Norway, and the Swedes, Danes, and Norwegians, the three principal people of the north, called the supreme deity Odin.

The Sclavonian word Wodan or Woidan, signifies a leader, but it is by no means clear that Odin or Wodan was ever worshipped by a people of Sclavonic origin and language. Odin signifies, in Russian, one; and Russia, we know at an early period, was inhabited by a people nearly allied to the old Scandinavians, and the received tradition also is that Odin came into Scandinavia through Russia. It is not impossible, therefore, that the name may have been derived from Odin (one), thus indicating the belief of the ancient Scandinavians, in the unity of the supreme being. Wodan has been derived from the Anglo-Saxon word Wod, "raging," so called as being the god of war. (Suhm on Odin.)

another the conflicting elements of cold and heat are the original cause, and Odin is the grandson of the first being or god, and is to perish, and another heaven and other gods are to replace him and Valhalla. Sometimes he is represented as an evil being, as outwitted, as near to perish by the power of mere men.

The learned Bryant has observed that, in disquisitions of this nature, great confusion has arisen from not considering that, in many cases, deity and priest were named alike, and this remark seems peculiarly applicable in the case of Odin.

It has been assumed, however, that there were three Odins, whose feats and adventures, like those of the Grecian Hercules, have been confounded.

According to Suhm and Schöning, the first Odin or Othin, (Authun) was never in Scandinavia, but lived, in times very remote, on the shores of the Black sea, and was worshipped as the supreme god of the Scythians.[2]

The second, a descendant or priest of the former, is supposed to have lived in the time of Darius Hystaspes, about 520 years before the birth of our

---

[2] In a memoir read before l'Académie des Inscriptions, in 1823, M. Abel Remusat mentioned that inscriptions in Runic characters, similar to those of the Scandinavians, had been found near Mount Altai, and infers thence that the Goths came originally from Tartary.

Lord; and, emigrating northwards, to have succeeded in making himself master of a great part of Scandinavia, introducing a new worship, of which he and his principal companions were the chief divinities. He is said to have established himself for a time on the banks of the Duna, where he built a new Asgard.

About forty years before the birth of Christ, on the overthrow of Mithridates, a third Odin, or, as some pretend, Sigge, a Scythian prince, being forced to quit his country, fled to Scandinavia, where he found the religion of Odin already established, and by his superior talents, instruction, skill in arts reputed magical, viz. medicine, astronomy, writing; and in war, not only assumed the priesthood and with it the supreme authority for himself and his descendants, but obtained also divine honours.[3]

He first introduced into the north the custom of burning the dead, and taught that the deceased would have the benefit of all that was buried with him, as also of the treasures which he himself concealed in the earth during his life. The ashes of deceased persons were to be thrown into the sea, or deposited under ground, and Barrows were to be

---

[3] Suhm cites instances of men deified in the north so late as the ninth century.

raised over men of consideration; Bauta or monumental stones over brave warriors.

Finding his end approaching, he caused himself to be transfixed with spears, saying that he was about to repair to Godheim, or Asgard, where he would be ready to receive his friends.

One celebrated Danish antiquarian, Skule Thorlacius, sets the duration of Odin's religion between the last century previous to the birth of our Saviour, and the end of the tenth of the Christian era. He is of opinion also, that the gods worshipped in the north previously to the introduction of this religion were not deified mortals, but elementary deities.

Suhm is of opinion that a communication was kept up, from the time of the second Odin, between the north and the countries of the east; and we know that there was a commerce between the northern part of Russia, where he is supposed to have long resided, and the Black sea. He seeks thence to explain why all the barbarians from the shores of the Baltic, who overran the Roman Empire, took this course.[4]

Having thus briefly spoken of Odin as a historical personage, we will proceed to the Odin of the Edda.

---

[4] Om Odin.

According to the Eddas, Odin was the first and most powerful of the Aser; the father of Thor, Baldur, &c. the creator of the world and of the human race; the god of war, of poetry, and of eloquence.

He was made acquainted with everything that happened on earth through the agency of two Ravens called Huggin and Mummin (observation and memory,) which had been given to him by the enchantress Hulda. They flew daily round the world, and returning about the time that he sate down to table in Valhalla, perched on each side of his throne, and whispered in his ear all that they had seen. Hence he was called the raven-god.

He used always to speak in rhyme, and with such eloquence, that every one believed whatever he said. He was master of the art of effecting wonders, by means of Runes, and could change his form at will, and wander about the world in the shape of birds, beasts, fishes, or reptiles, his own body remaining in the mean time, to all appearance, in a profound sleep.

He was lord of the elements. In fight he could blind the eyes of his enemies, and blunt their swords. But his most important art was the secret of mixing together various ingredients into a magic ointment, by means of which he could work all kinds of enchantments, and force the dead to rise from their graves.[5] This art was called Seid, and hence one of his names was Seidmadr, or the sorcerer.

Odin had several wives: First, Frea, or Frigga; mother to Thor, Baldur, Bragi, Hermodur, and Tyr. Second, Skada; mother to Semming. Third, Grydur, by whom he had Vidar, and fourth, Rinda, by whom he had Vale or Bo.

Besides these he had several other children by different women, and indeed from the dissoluteness of his habits, and some actions which were considered disgraceful, the gods were induced to depose him for a time, although afterwards he was held in greater esteem than ever.

He was in the habit of wandering about in disguise, and often went to the land of the giants, in order to get at the secrets which they possessed respecting the events which had come to pass before the creation of the gods.

---

[5] The ancient Scandinavians, like most of the people of antiquity, believed that by certain arts men could waken up the dead, and compel them to reveal the future. This power was peculiarly attributed to Odin. His evocation of the dead prophetess in the Vegtam's-quide or Song of the Wanderer, is well known to the English reader through Gray's spirited imitation. Snorro relates of his mortal Odin, that he would sit under the corpses of hanging men to obtain from them information respecting the other world.

54   SCANDINAVIAN MYTHOLOGY.

The following story from the Braga-rædur, in the prose Edda, is an entertaining specimen of the adventures in which he was sometimes engaged, and not an unfavourable one of Scandinavian wit.

THE ORIGIN OF POETRY.

"Ægir or Hler, the god of the sea, who was not originally one of the Aser, made a journey to Asgard, where he was received with great distinction, and a banquet given in his honour. Bragi, the god of eloquence, was placed next to him at table, and whilst they were drinking, related many of the ancient adventures of the Aser.

"Ægir having asked what was the origin of the art called poetry! Bragi answered as follows.

"The Gods were at war with a nation called the Vaner. Both parties having at length agreed to conclude a peace, sent negociators to an appointed place, each of whom, previously to his departure from the place of meeting, spate[6] in a vessel which

---

[6] Pliny tells us that spitting was had recourse to to avert witchcraft, or to give force to a blow to an enemy. Hence the author of the Popular Antiquities derives the custom of spitting in the hand previous to boxing, amongst the lower orders. A more curious coincidence exists between the ceremony here described and the custom on which he remarks,

had been placed for that purpose. The Aser afterwards formed its contents into a man, whom they named Quaser, and who was so wise that no one could question him on any subject with which he was not already acquainted.

"He travelled far and wide to instruct men, and one day fell in with the dwarfs, Fjalar and Gelar, who slew him and let his blood run into two vessels, called Son and Bodn, and into a kettle called Odrær. Having mixed this with honey, the produce was mead of so rare a quality, that whoever drank of it became a poet and a wise man. They made the gods believe that Quaser had been suffocated with wisdom, because no one could be found capable of asking him sufficient questions.

"Some time after this the two dwarfs invited a giant, whose name was Gilling, to visit them, and soon after his arrival proposed to him to row out with them on the sea. When they had rowed

---

amongst boys when asseverating in a matter of consequence, "*of spitting their faith.*" He tells us, moreover, that it is usual in the north, in combination amongst the colliers, &c. for the purpose of raising wages, to spit upon a stone together, by way of cementing their confederacy, and that there is a popular saying when persons agree in one manner of thinking, or are of the same party, that " *they spit upon the same stone.*"

some distance from the land, they ran the boat on a ridge of rocks and upset it. Gilling, who could not swim, was drowned, and the dwarfs then righted the boat and rowed back to shore.

"The wife on learning the accident took it much to heart, and began to lament loudly. Fjalar asked her whether it would ease her mind to look out on the spot where her husband had been drowned. She said it would; upon which he told his brother to go over the door-way and let a millstone fall on her head as she went out, for that he could not endure her noise. Gelar did as he was desired.

"Suttung, Gilling's son, to revenge the murder of his parents, seized the dwarfs, and set them on a bare rock surrounded by the sea. They bewailed their lot bitterly, and offered the incomparable mead in ransom for their lives. Suttung accepted it, and, taking it home with him, set his daughter Gunlöde to watch it.

"It is from these circumstances, added Bragi, that poetry received the epithets of ' Quaser's blood,' the Dwarf's drink or quit-money, Odrær's, or Son's, or Bodn's mead,[7] &c. Ægir remarked that these seemed to him strange appellations for

---

[7] Appellations constantly made use of in the Songs of the Scalds.

poetry. But how did the Aser get possession of Suttung's mead? Bragi continued.

" Odin set out from Asgard, and arrived at a place where nine thralls were cutting hay. He offered to whet their scythes, and as they thankfully accepted his offer, he took a whetstone from his belt and made the scythes so sharp, that the thralls all became desirous of obtaining possession of the stone. He said that he had no objection to part with it, upon which they fell a-quarrelling who should have it, and a contest ensued in which they slew each other.

" Odin now went to seek lodging for the night with Bauge, a giant, brother to Suttung; Bauge lamented his ill-luck in having lost his nine thralls, and said that he did not know where to obtain other labourers, to get in the harvest. Odin, who called himself Bölwerk, offered to undertake the work of the nine men, on condition that Bauge should obtain for him a draught of Suttung's mead.

" Bauge replied that this did not rest with him, since Suttung kept it entirely for himself; but that he would conduct him to the place where it was kept, and aid him in obtaining possession of it. During the summer Bölwerk performed the work of the nine men, and when winter came demanded of Bauge the performance of his promise.

" Both accordingly set out for Suttung's residence, and Bauge informed his brother of what he had promised Bölwerk, but Suttung, very peremptorily, refused their request. Bölwerk then called upon Bauge to aid him in getting possession of the mead by artifice, to which Bauge consented.

"Bölwerk took an auger and desired Bauge to bore through the mountain in which the mead was kept under the care of Gunnlaug. Bauge set about boring, and after a time said that he had bored through. But Bölwerk blew into the hole, and, as the dust flew outwards, he discovered that Bauge wished to deceive him, and insisted that he should bore it through completely. Bauge, therefore, having set to work afresh, Bölwerk blew into the hole a second time, and the dust flew out on the other side.

"He then changed himself into a worm and crept through the hole. Bauge thrust after him with the auger but without reaching him.

"Bölwerk remained with Gunnlaug three nights, and so ingratiated himself that she allowed him to take three draughts of the mead. In the first he drank out Odreirr, in the second, Son, in the third, Bodn, and thus secured the whole. He then transformed himself into an eagle, and flew away in great haste to Asgard.

"When Suttung saw the flight of the eagle, he guessed what had happened, and taking his eagle's dress also flew after him. The Aser, perceiving the approach of Odin, set out vessels to catch the mead, which Odin poured into them.

"But in his extreme anxiety, when Suttung was close upon him, some of the liquor escaped,[8] and it is this which ever since has inspired bad poets."

The above is nearly a literal translation of the story as given in the Prose Edda. It will not be here out of place to give, as a specimen of the *poetry* of the Edda, a literal translation of the fragment in the Hava-mal, alluding to the same adventure. It is Odin himself who speaks:—

> "I sought the home of the old giant,
> And I am now returned.
> Silence availed me little there;
> It was only by many words
> That I attained my end
>   In Suttung's hall.
>
> "Gunnlaug gave me,
> From her golden seat,
> A draught of the lordly mead,
> An evil return,

---

[8] Verum quoniam Suttungus eum insequendo adeo propinquus urgeret, partem mulsi retrorsum e tergo emixit. —*Edda Sæmundar. Hafn.* 1817.

She had from me,
For her fond love
For her burning passion.

I bade Răte's tooth[9]
Force a passage
And gnaw thro' the rock:
Above and below me
Were the haunts of the giants.
   Thus put I my head in peril.

Well purchased beauty
I have well enjoyed—
Few things are wanting to the wise:
For Odreirer
Is now come up
   To man's earthly abode.

Great is my doubt
That I had e'er escaped
From the home of the giants,
Had not Gunnlaug aided,
The kind-souled maiden,
   Whom I held in my embrace.

The next day
Hied the Giants of the Frost
To enquire the fate of the high-one.
They enquired of Bölwerk,
In the high-one's hall;

---

[9] Rate was the name of the auger with which Bauge bored.

If he had reached the Gods
Or if Suttung had destroyed him.

An oath on the ring[10]
I trow Odin hath sworn.
How shall we believe his vows!
From Suttung
He hath stol'n his mead
And brought Gunnlaug to woe.[11]

The principal titles of Odin were :—1. Alfadur (the father of all things). 2. The lord of the dead. 3. Har, Jafuhar, and Thridi, (the exalted, the equal to the exalted, and the third[12]) 4. The lord of life and death. 5. The Raven-

---

[10] It was the custom with the Scandinavians, on solemn occasions, to swear on a sacred ring, preserved in their temples.

[11] Finn Magnussen declares the whole fable to be allegorical, and explains it as follows :—Odin, the god of heaven or the sun, descends into the earth to fructify it, and give birth to the productions from which man derives his nourishment, and from which also are extracted the exhilarating liquors, (mead, ale, wine), which strengthen him, and produce poetic inspirations. Suttung is the spirit of darkness, with whom at the winter-solstice, many of the ancient heathens believed that the sun had to undergo a severe struggle for the mastery.

[12] These names are given to him in the Grimnismal, and are also those applied to the three persons to whom Gylfe addresses his questions in the Prose Edda.

god. 6. The Wise-one. 7. Val-fader, (or the father of the slain).[13] 8. The chooser of the slain, &c.

But great as was Odin's power he was not omnipotent. He had, as we have seen, but a narrow escape from the Giant Suttung, and on another occasion, could only obtain a draught from Mimer's well, on condition of leaving one of his eyes in pawn. On this account he was often represented as an old man with one eye, and was called the one-eyed.

Thor was a greater favourite with many of the Scandinavians, and indeed his worship seems to have prevailed in the North previously to that of Odin. Some are of opinion that Odin finding it impossible wholly to eradicate the ancient religion, had the art to engraft it on his own, rendering Thor a subordinate divinity. Odin was *principally* worshipped in Denmark, Freyr in Sweden, and Thor in Norway and Iceland: but the religion of Odin prevailed in a greater or less degree throughout Denmark, Sweden, Norway, Iceland, and was received by the Saxons, Anglo-Saxons, Suevi, Frisians, Germans, Goths, the inhabitants of Biar-

---

[13] Val signifies the slain in battle—hence Val-fader, the father of the slain; Val-halla, the hall of the slain; Valkyrier, the choosers of the slain.

meland, (Russia), the Russians of Holmgaard, (Novogorod), Circassians, Alani or Aser, Hunns, &c.[14]

Wednesday (Danice Onsdag) is named after Odin. The hawk was sacred to him, and every ninth year, ninety-nine of these birds or, in place of them, an equal number of cocks were sacrificed to him at Ledrun, Leira, or Lethra, in the island of Zealand.[15]

Odin had three peculiar residences in Asgard. 1. Gladsheim, a vast hall where he presided over the twelve Diar or Judges, whom he had appointed to regulate the affairs of Asgard. 2. Valaskialf, built of solid silver, in which there was an elevated place, Hlidskialf, from his throne on which he could perceive all that passed throughout the whole earth. 3. Valhalla.

Of this last and most celebrated of his palaces we shall now speak. The word, literally interpreted, signifies the hall of the slain. The Edda tells us, that it was the place in which he received

---

[14] Suhm, and Schöning, pretend that besides the three Odins, already mentioned, there was another worshipped by the Saxons, who came originally from Scania, and was a descendant of the third Odin. He was a valiant warrior, and reigned over Sleswic, and the Anglo-Saxons.

[15] Bones of hawks and falcons are often found in the tombs of Scandinavian warriors.

the souls of warriors killed in battle,[16] who were called Einheriar. It had five hundred and forty gates, and a vast hall of gold, hung around with golden shields, and spears, and coats of mail.

These Einheriar were in great number, and were entertained by Odin, in order that they in return might combat for him at Ragnarokur, against the giants and spirits of fire. They passed their day as follows:—In the morning they were awakened by the crowing of a cock with a golden comb, whose cries are to be the first signal of the approach of the evil genii at the last day. Having apparelled themselves they sallied out, eight hundred at each of the gates of Valhalla, and spent the forenoon in tilting, after which they returned to the banqueting hall, where each one had a place assigned to him according to his exploits.

Notwithstanding their great number, the flesh of one boar was sufficient for them all. The name of this boar was Sehrimner, and although eaten every day, he was whole again in the evening. His lard and fat prepared by the cook Andrimner surpassed in flavour every thing in the world. The goat Heidrun which derived its nourishment from the leaves of the tree Leradur, furnished in

---

[16] The old Persians, and Parthians believed that those who fell in battle would be eternally happy.

place of milk mead enough to intoxicate all the guests.

A certain number of Einheriar resided in that part of Vingolf which belonged to the goddess Freya, called Folkvangur, she, according to the Grimners-maal, having a right to the souls of half of those who fall in battle. No women were admitted into Valhalla. The only females there were the Valkyrs, whose office it was to wait on the Einheriar and to pour out their mead.[17]

---

[17] It will not be out of place here to remark, that the accusation under which the ancient Scandinavians so long laboured, that one of the pleasures of their deceased heroes in Valhalla was to drink out of the sculls of their enemies, has been shewn to be wholly without foundation. The passage which has so generally given rise to this mistake is in the well-known death-song of Regner Lodbrog, and runs as follows:—

" Drecksom bjor at bragdi
Ur bjug vidom hausa."

literally translated:—" Soon shall we drink out of the curved trees of the head," which, in the figurative language of the Scalds, signifies no more than horns, the usual drinking utensil. Olaus Wormius, the first who translated the song, rendered the passage, " *ex concavis crateribus craniorum,*" a forced and incorrect interpretation, in which he was followed by later translators, and by all the historians; and Bartholin, whose authority was of great weight, has it " *ex concavis craniorum poculis.*" So also Berntzön and Sandtvig,

The Valkyrs belong exclusively to the Northern Mythology, and, as Gräter justly observes, are in the highest degree poetical creations. They were females and the messengers and followers of Odin in his quality of god of battles.

Sometimes they were to be seen riding through the air and over the sea on shadowy horses, from

---

in Danish, Gräter in German, Mallet in French, his translator Dr. Percy, and Johnstone in English.

The discovery of the mistake is not however of very late date. Svend Sölvesen, in 1769, using the metaphor *bjugvið hausa*, explains it, *drinking horns*. John Olassen, in his " *Essai sur la musique ancienne et moderne. Paris*, 1780," renders the very same passage, " *Bientôt j'y boirai de la cervoise dans de cornes recourbées.*" About the same time, 1780, Gunnar Paulsen, in some remarks on Egil's Saga, says " that *hausa bjugvið* in Kraku-mal signifies the crooked trees of the head, and this again horns. Lastly Professor Finn Magnussen, the translator of the Elder Edda, and author of " the doctrine of the Edda," in an essay on certain passages of Ossian, 1813, and Professor Rafn, the translator of the Icelandic Sagas, (from whom this note is taken), have shewn that the whole fiction has no other foundation than the above mistake. The former of these two writers has further remarked, that the death-song of Regner Lodbrok, properly called Kraku-mal, is by no means a fair sample of the spirit of the old Scandinavian poetry. According to Suhm, it was written by Brage the elder, at the desire of Aslaug or Kraka, the widow of Regner, to excite her sons to avenge their father's death. Not to speak of others, the erotic songs in Viglund's Saga are of a very different character.

whose manes fell hail on the mountains and dew in the valleys. At others, cleaving the clouds in the forms of wild swans. Again, surrounded with fiery lances in the Aurora Borealis, which was under the immediate control of Odin.

It was the province of Gudr and Rota with Skulda, the youngest of the nornies, to lead on the van of the battle, exciting the combatants, and marking out those who were to remain on the field. Others with helmets on their heads, and flaming swords and bloody harness, surrounded with lightnings and meteors, hovered above the conflict, mounted, directing the warriors as they fell on their way to Valhalla.

In a song of great poetical merit, still extant, and which Gray's imitation has rendered familiar to all lovers of English poetry, they are represented as weaving the web of the fate of warriors about to fall in an impending fight. It was stretched on spears; the threads were human entrails; skulls were the weights; the shuttles, arrows; the treadle, spears; the loom, iron. They chanted the song of death with naked swords.

At other times, however, they are represented under softer colours; as virgins clothed in white, with flowing ringlets, performing the office of Hebe at the table of the Einheriar.

"There, poured by blue-eyed girls,
The clear Metheglin flows,
Light float their wanton curls,
Their breath outscents the rose."

Oehlenschläger.

Nor is there much inconsistency in this, seeing that to fall in battle was an object of desire rather than of terror.

They watched with intense interest over their favourite warriors, and sometimes even lent an ear to their love; but were punished by Odin when they ventured to decide the victory contrary to his instructions.

They were called the sisters of war, and in the field were always in complete armour. The chief of them were Hilda,[18] also called the goddess of war, the Bellona of the north, and Rist and Mist, whose privilege it was to pour out wine for Odin.[19]

---

[18] The Valkyrs were known to the Anglo-Saxons under the names of Valcyrge, Valcyrian.

[19] Hilda, or Hildur, seems to have been worshipped as the goddess of war by the Anglo-Saxons. She was said to be always on the watch when a battle was about to begin. War was termed "*Hilda's sport.*" She is often confounded with a Danish princess of the same name, who was the cause of a bloody fight between her father Högne and her ravisher,

Odin always sate alone at a separate table. His sole nourishment was wine. With the meat placed before him he fed two wolves, called Geri and Freki.

The poor were not welcome to Valhalla, and for this reason, money, bracelets, and costly ornaments were often buried with the dead, as also weapons, to be employed at Ragnarokur. In many barrows whetstones have been found, placed, probably, for the purpose of sharpening the weapons of the deceased. It was thought a good thing when many were slain together, in order to go in a large company to Odin.

Many of the old Scandinavians believed that, after a life spent in warfare and perils, any violent death, although not in actual combat, would entitle them to a place in Valhalla; and instances where not unfrequent where warriors, feeling their end approach, caused themselves to be dispatched. In Nial's Saga, Hagen Jarl tells one who had burned a temple, " that the gods avenged slowly, but that he would never go to Valhalla."

Hedin, in Höy, one of the Orkneys. Each successive night the slain were restored to life and the battle renewed.

Many northern names have been derived from this goddess, such as Brynhilde, the helmed Hilda; Hildebrand, the sword of Hilda, &c.—*Magnussen.*

It was a general belief amongst the heathen Danes, that the Einheriar often descended from Valhalla to visit their barrows, and, in an old poem about king Helge Hundingsbane, the hero is described as riding nightly from Odin's hall through the air to his barrow, to console his young and sorrowing widow, leaving her again at the dawn of day.

Odin was in possession of several rarities, the celebrated spear Gungnir, and the magic ring Draupnir, made by the Dwarfs, &c. but the most precious was his eight legged horse, Sleipner, which the Edda informs us he obtained in the following manner:—

ODIN'S HORSE, SLEIPNER.

"Notwithstanding the constant enmity between the Aser and the Giants, there had been several instances of matrimonial alliances between them, and the Giants in particular were continually forming plans to get into their power the fair daughters of Asgard.

"One day a Giant, who gave himself out for a builder, came to the Aser, and offered to build them a castle so constructed, that it would set at defiance all the efforts of their mortal enemies, the

Frost-Giants and Evil Spirits, even though they should have obtained possession of Midgard.[20] In recompense for his labour he demanded the goddess Freya, and the sun and moon.

"The Aser were in a great dilemma at this proposal. They were aware that they were not wholly immortal, and also that their destruction could only be effected by the Frost-Giants and the Genii of Fire. It was, therefore, of the utmost importance to secure themselves against attacks from this quarter. At the same time how could they exist without Freya and the sun and moon.

" Being desirous of profiting by the skill of the architect, without loss to themselves, they employed Loke to arrange the matter for them, and it was at length agreed that the builder should receive the required reward, provided he accomplished his work within a single winter, without the aid of any being excepting his stallion, who was called Svadilfare.

---

[20] Midgard, or the middle court, was so called from being in the centre of the Scandinavian system, the fifth of the nine worlds of which the universe was composed. It was also called Mannheim, because Odin had given it as a place of residence to Askur and Embla and their progeny. The term Midgard was sometimes applied to the atmosphere, and, in this sense, Thor, the thunder-god, is called the defender of Midgard.

"The Giant set to work lustily; by day he never for a moment ceased, and at night he rode his horse to the mountains and brought back stones of unequalled size. The Aser were in utter astonishment to see Svadilfare dragging with the greatest ease entire rocks. The work advanced rapidly, and when there were yet three days of winter remaining, nothing but the gate was wanting to complete it.

" The gods, who had considered the enterprize as impossible, now began to be alarmed, and Odin summoned a council to deliberate on what course they should pursue. As it appeared that it was at the suggestion of Loke that the bargain had been made, they seized upon him and threatened him with instant death unless he would pledge himself to extricate them from their engagement.

" Loke who in his heart hated the whole race of Aser, and would have gladly witnessed their destruction, was now caught in his own trap, and was compelled to enter into a solemn engagement to baffle the Giant.

" The latter, as usual, towards night-fall, rode out to fetch the last stones for the completion of the building. He had scarcely dismounted from his stallion, to select what was wanting, when Loke, in the shape of a beautiful mare, came gamboling towards them. The stallion immediately broke loose and followed her far away. The Giant having in vain sought to recover him, found that there was no means of accomplishing his enterprize but by resuming his proper shape.

"When the Aser, however, found that it was with a Giant that their engagement had been made, they had no hesitation in not adhering to their oath, and called Thor, who dispatched the mock-builder with one blow of his hammer. Loke soon after produced a horse, which had eight feet, and excelled all others in the world, and this horse was called Sleipner."

Frea or Frigga (often confounded with Freyr and Freya) was the wife of Odin and the queen and mother of the gods. She knew beforehand all that was to come to pass, but never revealed it. She wept over the fall of Odin and foresaw the fate of her beloved son, Baldur, which she endeavoured, in vain, to avert. She understood the language of animals and plants, and was invoked by women in child-birth.

Her attendants were, Fulla, who had the charge of her jewels, and was her chief confidante: Fulla used to wear her hair loose, with a gold band round her head; Hlyn, whom she employs to save her favourites from danger; and Gna, her messenger, the Scandinavian Iris.

Frigga's palace was called Fensale, but she used

frequently to sit with Odin in Hlidskialf, and thence contemplate all that passed in Midgard.

By some Frigga is supposed to have been the same with Hertha, and a personification of the earth, but there seems great reason to doubt whether the old Scandinavians ever paid divine honours to the earth.

According to Tacitus, " Hertha, or Herthus, was a goddess worshipped by the inhabitants of northern Germany, whose chief sanctuary was an island in the Ocean, in which there was a grove so holy, that none but her priest ever ventured to enter it.

" Her temple was a covered waggon, in which, on particular festivals, she was drawn along by milch-kine to visit the people, followed by her priest. Wherever she came there was rejoicing and holiday, and all wars were suspended, and arms laid aside during her sojourn.

" When the goddess was weary of the society of men, she used to return in like manner to her holy solitude. The waggon, her garments, and the goddess herself were washed in a secret lake, into which the slaves who performed this duty were afterwards precipitated. Hence arose the secret awe and mysterious ignorance concerning what those only ever witnessed who were about to perish."

Bishop Münter, Anchersen, and others are of

opinion that the holy island, thus described, was Zealand, in Denmark, and that the grove sacred to her was that which still bears the name of Hertha-dal (Hertha's dale), not far distant from the site of the ancient capital of Denmark, Leira, or Lethra. Nor is this improbable, for the fertility and extent of Zealand render it likely that the principal fane of the goddess should have been placed here, and the localities of the spot, which retains her name, the secret lake, and the surrounding wood agree well enough with the description of Tacitus.

Others again with good grounds have placed Hertha's sanctuary in the island of Rügen, others in Heligoland, and some in a small island near Wolgast. The celebrated Northern Antiquarian, Suhm, argues with ingenuity against all these, and assigns this honour to the island of Femern.

If, however, the worship of Hertha was general in the north, it is not probable that she should have been restricted to one fane. A great many villages in the country of Angeln, near Sleswic, still bear her name.

CHAPTER III.

ASA-LOKE—HIS OFFSPRING, HELA, THE QUEEN OF DEATH, THE GREAT SERPENT, JORMUNGANDUR, THE WOLF FENRIS—HIS ADVENTURE WITH TYR—BRAGI AND IDUNA—IDUNA'S RAPE AND RECOVERY—THE GIANT THIASSE.

ALTHOUGH Loke, in power and dignity had no pretension to rank next to Odin, nor, in fact, had any place amongst the Aser, except by sufferance, still he plays so prominent a part in all their adventures, and he and his offspring are so continually alluded to, that for the clear understanding of what is to follow, it is essential to make the reader at once well acquainted with them. Some account of Loke has already been given in the first chapter, as well as of his kinsman and namesake, the demon-king of the Giants. These two important personages were, probably, originally one and the same, but in the Eddas very different parts have been assigned to them. They were distinguished by the titles of Utgard's Loke and Asa-Loke, and it is of the latter that the present chapter treats.

Asa-Loke is a creation which has no parallel in

any other Mythology. We learn from the Edda that he was the son of Farbaute, a giant, by the witch Laufeya. Although sprung from a race the mortal enemies of the Aser, he was, in some manner not explained, mysteriously associated with Odin in the infancy of creation. At that time they swore brotherhood together, and Loke was in consequence admitted to Valhalla, where a seat was allotted to him on the same bench with Thor. He had many good natural gifts, was tall, slight, well formed, of good address, and eloquent; but, on the other hand, he was fickle, sarcastic, malicious, cruel, a lover of evil, and exceeded every one in cunning. He was, moreover, a coward, and the first inventor of deceit and dishonour, vain, much given to boasting and always desirous of being seen in the society of the principal Aser, especially of Thor. His natural perversity and hatred of the Aser led him, notwithstanding, on many occasions to conspire with the Giants against them, and it will be seen that on more than one occasion they were brought into extreme difficulties in consequence. Still his subtlety usually enabled him to evade the punishment which his crimes so richly merited. Besides his name of Loke, he was sometimes called Loptur and Lopta.

> Amongst bright Asgard's lords
> Is one, As-Loptur hight:

Like honey are his words,
His heart is foul with spite,
His form is passing fair,
And winning is his mien,
But, still, his guileful leer
Shews all is false within.

Though, oft, his traitorous wiles
The Asers' ire provoke,
His smooth tongue, still, beguiles,
And stops th' impending stroke:
Oft, cited to appear,
He cowers the Ash before,[1]
At Odin's table near
His place to Asa-Thor.
Oehlenschläger.

Loke had a wife whose name was Signi, and who, notwithstanding all his defects, shewed her devotion to him in a remarkable manner. By her he had two sons, Nari and Vali, whose terrible fate will appear in the sequel. His more celebrated offspring, however, sprang from an amour with a giant woman, whose name was Augerbode, or the messenger of evil. These were Fenris, the wolf; Jormungandur, the great serpent; and Hela, the queen of death. The Edda accounts for the production of these horrible monsters by telling

---

[1] The great Ash, Ygg-drasill, under which Odin and the twelve Aser used to administer justice.

us that they were begotten after Loke's nature had become depraved, in consequence of his eating the half-roasted heart of a witch which he had found.

The gods having been forewarned that this progeny of Loke would one day cause much evil to Asgard, sent to the land of Giants to secure them. Odin cast Jormungandur, or, as it was also called, the great Midgard's serpent or worm,[2] into the ocean where it grew to such a prodigious size, that it girt round the whole world. There it was to lie with its tail in its jowl, in sullen expectation of revenge at Ragnarokur.

> —— Midgard's giant snake,
> Which in the ocean hurled,
> His tale in jowl doth take,
> And girdeth round the world.
> *Oehlenschläger.*

Jormungandur was the chief object of fear and hatred to gods and men.[3]

---

[2] The bold promontory which terminates the neck of land, at the mouth of the river Conway, in Denbighshire, is still called the great Orm's, or Worm's head. Orm being the Danish for worm. So also the remarkable point at the western extremity of the district of Gower, in Glamorganshire, at the entrance of the Bristol channel, is called " *the Worm's head.*"

[3] Magnussen considers the great serpent to be a symbol of the raging sea.

Hela was thrust down to Niffl-heim, where she received the sovereignty over nine worlds, and ruled over all who died by any other than a violent death. Hence her title of queen of the dead. Her palace was called from her Hel-heim, and was very spacious, but cold and gloomy, and filled with shivering, shadowy spectres. It was surrounded by a lofty fence, with huge grated gates. " Hela's hall," says the Prose Edda, " is affliction; her table, famine; her knife, hunger; her valet, delay; her handmaid, slowness; her threshold, a drawbridge, her bed, lingering sickness; her tent, cursing."[4] Her attendants, the evil Nornies, used to appear to dying persons, by night, to call them away, and she herself was supposed at times to make herself visible to those

---

[4] Ibant obscuri sola sub nocte per umbram,
Perque domos Ditis vacuas, et inania regna;
. . . .

Vestibulum ante ipsum, primisque in faucibus Orci
Luctus et ultrices posuere cubilia curæ,
Pallentesque habitant morbi, tristisque Senectus,
Et metus et *malesuada Fames,* ac turpis Egestas,
Terribiles visu formæ, letumque labosque;
Tum consanguineus leti sopor, et mala mentis
Gaudia, mortiferumque adverso in limine bellum,
Ferreique Eumenidum thalami et Discordia demens.
        Æneid, lib. vi. l. 268 to 280.

about to die. She was hideous to look upon, one half of her body being blue, the other of the natural colour. It is not said who was her husband, but her sons are mentioned as the followers of Loke at Ragnarokur.

Her palace is thus described by Oehlenschläger:

> Close crowded, side by side,
> Cold Helheim's shadowy folk,
> Aghast, the strangers eyed,
> With glazed and fearful look:
> And still, as Thor drew near,
> Shuddering, his path they fled,
> Their shivering forms were bare,
> Snakes o'er them venom shed.
>
> Between two rocks enclosed,
> At th' end stood Hela's throne:
> Of heap'd up skulls composed,
> And many a mouldering bone:
> There sate the spectre queen,
> A monster, dire to view,
> Her body wither'd, lean,
> Distort, half white, half blue.
>
> A naked bone she held
> In her lank, clammy hand,
> 'Fore which the pale ghosts quail'd;
> On the lone ocean strand,
> In the moon's magic light,
> Long, bleaching, it had lain;
> Now serves the queen of night
> T' assert her silent reign.

Save hollow, deep-drawn sighs
No sound the cavern gave;
All round damp fogs arise,
Th' air smelt as fresh-stirr'd grave.
For light of cheerful sun,
Three funeral tapers glared,
By each a skeleton
Its fleshless form uprear'd.
                    Oehlenschläger.

Hela had a cock of a dusky red colour, and a spectre horse, which is called by the peasants Hel's horse, to this day.

With Fenris the wolf,[5] the Aser had somewhat

---

[5] The superstition respecting men-wolves which prevailed so widely during the middle ages was probably derived from Fenris. Boissardius, in his posthumous work on magic, declares that two shepherds in the archbishopric in which he was born were publicly burned, having confessed that by means of an ointment given to them by the devil, they were frequently in the habit of changing themselves into wolves, and of committing in this shape great ravages amongst the neighbouring flocks. He adds that these transformations had become very common in his time, especially in Prussia, Livonia and Lithuania, and adduces testimonies to this effect from various writers, and amongst others from Herodotus. The father of history, however, only states that it had been asserted that certain men amongst the Scythians once in the year became wolves, and after some days resumed their proper form, but at the same time intimates his disbelief of the fact. One story is gravely told on the authority of Garzonus—

more trouble than with the other two. When they had got him into their power, they sought to secure him with bonds, but none could be found sufficiently strong for the purpose. They constructed, therefore, a massive chain, and begged Fenris to try his strength upon it, which he consented to do, and broke it with the greatest ease. They exerted

---

"That a man-wolf who had caused much destruction amongst the flocks in Russia, having been at length captured by the peasants, was taken before the prince of the country, and being closely questioned, acknowledged that he did frequently assume the form of a wolf. The prince offered him pardon on condition of his doing so before those who were assembled. He consented, and having withdrawn to a little distance and performed the magic ceremonies taught him by the devil, on a sudden he stood before them a gaunt wolf, with bent neck, bristles erect, and glaring eyes, but bound in chains as before. The prince caused two fierce Molossian dogs which he had provided to be let loose upon the wolf, who tore him to pieces before he could resume his natural shape." Olaus Magnus, Archbishop of Upsala, in his work de Gentibus Septentrionalibus, writes, " De animalibus sylvestribus luporum genus ex hominibus conversum, quod Plinius lib. viii. c. 22. fabulosum et falsum confidenter existimandum esse affirmat, tales in terris ad Septentrionem maximè vergentibus etiamnum magnâ in copiâ reperiri adjicerem, l. xxviii. c. 15. So in Ovid's Metamorphoses, lib. i. speaking of Lycaon.

> Fit lupus, et veteris servat vestigia formæ;
> Canities eadem est, eadem violentia vultûs;
> Iidem oculi lucent: eadem feritatis imago.

their utmost art to make a second of double the strength of the former, but by a slight effort he brake this also. They now sent Skirnir to the black elves, or dwarfs, to procure a chain capable of resisting any force that could be exerted against it, and he brought back one, called Gleipnir, which to all appearance was no stronger than a silken thread, but which, notwithstanding, was so skilfully composed, that no force was sufficient to break it.

Thus provided, the Aser repaired with Fenris to a solitary island, and there proposed to him to allow himself to be bound with Gleipnir. The wolf replied that it would reflect but little honour on his strength to break a small silken cord, but that, on the other hand, slight as it appeared, art and magic might have given it extraordinary powers, and he therefore refused to suffer himself to be bound. On this the Aser began to taunt him, and observed that if he had not strength to break such a cord they would themselves set him at liberty, as too weak to be an object of terror to any. The wolf, who was not so easily to be deceived, replied, I know well that if I cannot help myself, I have but little favour to expect from you; but, lest any one should reproach me with cowardice, I am willing to suffer myself to be bound, on condition, as a pledge that you mean honestly, that one of your number will consent in the mean while to lay his hand in my mouth. The Aser were now put to silence, for no one amongst them seemed disposed to place himself in the power of Fenris. At length the undaunted Tyr,[6] the son of Odin by a giant woman, advanced boldly and laid his hand in the wolf's jaw, who then allowed himself to be bound with the cord, one end of which was dragged through a massive rock, and made fast in the centre of the earth. When this was done, he began to exert his utmost strength, but the more he struggled to free himself, the more closely did Gleipnir encircle him, and he was at length forced to abandon the attempt. The gods rejoiced to find their most dreaded enemy thus secured, but Fenris in revenge bit off Tyr's right hand. Since this, he has been one-handed, but wields his sword in his left hand as effectively as he did before in the right. So little was he terrified by this adventure, that he alone has the courage to give Fenris his daily food, for the wolf would suffer no one to

---

[6] Tyr was one of the chief of the Aser, and a great favourite with Thor, on account of his courage, for which reason also he was worshipped by warriors, and when any one distinguished himself in battle he was said to be as brave as Tyr. He was as prudent as he was brave. The planet Mars was sacred to Tyr, and the third day of the week (Danicé Tirsdag) was named after him as also the Runic letter ↑ (T) Tir.

approach him, and howled so fearfully, that the gods were obliged to thrust a sword through his jaws, and in this state he is to remain until Ragnarokur.

The chain with which Fenris was bound was composed, as the Edda informs us, of six things, viz. the noise made by cats' feet, the beard of a woman, the roots of rocks, the nerves of bears, the breath of fishes, the spittle of birds.

When, in Thor's journey to Jotunheim, he and his companions arrive suddenly before the gate of Helheim, and Loke, unwilling to meet his daughter, is about to return in anger, Oehlenschläger puts the following words into the mouth of Thor:

> But Thor, with warning voice,
> Cried out; " Laufeya's son
> Beware! bethink thee twice,
> Nor on destruction run:
> What boots it to repine
> At that the fates decree!
> Befits it Loke to whine,
> And yield so womanly?
>
> The tall maid, Angerbode,
> Thou tookest to thy bed:
> All know, of giant blood
> No produce ever sped.
> What then—thine amorous fit,
> No doubt, in Skulda's[7] book

---

[7] Skulda the norny or fate who presided over the future.

E'en from the first was writ;
Then why this angry look!

Horror thy race inspire,
But who contempt can feign?
Fate doom'd their birth, in ire,
To scourge both gods and men.
From thy loins sprang the plague,
E'en Odin's self can fill
With trouble. Panics vague,
Which oft the boldest chill,

Arise strange god from thee.
In Asgard's realm of joy,
'Midst banqueting and glee,
Dire thoughts our mirth alloy.
When Fenris shakes his chain;
In Valhal's festive hall
Silence and terror reign,
No god but feels appal.

On Earth's fair bosom look,
Smiling with flower-deck'd field,
Hill, dale, lake, rippling brook,
Doth scarce to Asgard yield:—
Were't not, that pain and death
Her sons in bondage hold,[8]
And the fell serpent's wreath
Her prison'd shores enfold.

Hela thy blood to call
Well proud thou mightest be

---

[8] All pestilential diseases were supposed to proceed from the serpent.

Of craven cowards all
Unpitying scourger, she.
Avenger of my might
The brave her name esteem,
Then think not, Loke, of flight,
Nor thy race luckless deem.
Oehlenschläger.

It has been already said that Loke was fond of being seen in the society of the great, and on this account he often contrived to accompany Odin and Thor on their excursions. In one of these with Odin, an adventure befel him which led to important consequences, and had nearly been fatal to the whole race of the Aser.

IDUNA'S RAPE AND RECOVERY.

" Three Aser, Odin, Loke, and Hænir, quitted Asgard to travel. They had to traverse vast mountains and wildernesses, where no food could be obtained, but at length they came to a dell where a herd of oxen were feeding, one of which they seized and killed for their supper.

" Odin and Hænir strolled about in the neigbourhood, whilst Loke was employed in preparing the meal. After a time, when he imagined that the ox must have been sufficiently roasted, he took it from the fire, but was much surprised to find it still raw. He tried it again, but do what he would it remained in the same state.

"Whilst he was endeavouring to explain to himself how this could be, he heard a noise in the tree above him, and, looking up, perceived an enormous eagle on one of the branches. Loke, said the eagle, it is I who have prevented the ox from being roasted, but if you promise to give me a share, you will find that it will be cooked quickly enough. Loke agreed, and the eagle flew down from the tree, and seating himself by the spit, seized hold on both the shoulders of the ox.

"Upon this Loke got angry, and taking hold of a billet of wood which was near at hand, struck at the eagle with all his might, who instantly flew upwards, and one end of the billet stuck fast to his back whilst the other adhered to Loke's hand. Away he flew over wood, rock, and river, dragging Loke after him at such a rate that the luckless Aser thought his arm must have been pulled off, at the same time that his feet were trailed along over the stones and tops of the trees.[9]

"Loke now changed his tone and bewailing his ill luck, called upon Odin and Thor for help, but

---

[9] The curious reader may here trace the prototype of Daniel O'Rourke's eagle, so humorously described in the Fairy Legends of Ireland.

the eagle, who was the Giant Thiasse in disguise, told him that he might spare his cries, for that he should never get loose unless he would bind himself by an oath to bring Bragi's wife, Iduna, and her apples out of Asgard.

"Bragi was the god of eloquence and poetry, and so good a Scald that Runes were said to be upon his tongue.[10] He was rather given to strong drinks, and, if Loke may be credited, not very celebrated for courage. His wife, Iduna,[11] was the daughter of the dwarf Ivalldr, and had in her charge certain apples, of which the gods used to eat when they found themselves growing old, and were thereby immediately restored to youth and vigour.

"It was these apples which Thiasse was desirous of getting into his possession, and Loke, who hated the Aser in his heart, made no difficulty in taking the oath, and being released from his unpleasant situation, returned to his companions.

---

[10] It was a custom with the Scandinavians that at the burial feast of a king or Jarl, his heir should sit upon a bench before the throne until a health was drunk, sacred to the god Bragi, upon which he rose up and swore that he would perform some signal feat, and then drank out the cup.

[11] Some have seen in the union of Iduna with the god of poetry and eloquence, an allusion to the power of those arts to confer immortality.

Nothing else particularly worthy of notice occurred on this expedition.

"At the appointed time Loke persuaded Iduna to leave Asgard, pretending that in a certain wood, at a short distance, he had discovered apples more beautiful, and of a more excellent quality than her own, which he recommended her to take with her in order to make the comparison.

"They had scarcely left the boundary, when Thiasse came flying rapidly towards them, in his old shape of an eagle, and catching up Iduna carried her off.

"The Aser were in the greatest consternation at this loss. They became wrinkled and grey-haired, and subject to all kinds of diseases; the trees and flowers all withered, and spring was turned to autumn. A council of the gods was held to endeavour to discover how Iduna had disappeared, but all that they could learn was that she had been last seen going out of Asgard with Loke. He was accordingly brought before the assembly and threatened with a painful death. Thor, who was present, seized him and threw him several times so high up in the air, that his heels touched, alternately, the moon and the sea, telling him that this was a sample of what he would get unless he brought back Iduna.

"Loke, almost frightened to death, engaged to

search the goddess out in Giant-land, provided that Freya would lend him her hawk's dress (Falke-ham). Having obtained this he flew away, northwards, and fortunately reached Thiasse's residence just as the Giant had rowed out to sea, so that Iduna was at home, alone. He changed her into a swallow, and taking her in his claws lost no time to fly off with her.

"As soon as Thiasse returned and missed Iduna, he put on his eagle's dress (Orne-ham), flew after Loke, and by the rapidity of his flight was gaining fast on him.

"When the Aser saw the hawk coming with the swallow in his claws, and the eagle close after him, they went out to the walls of Asgard, where they heaped up a vast pile of chips. As the hawk approached the town, he descended towards the walls. The Aser now set fire to the chips, and, as the eagle could not at once check his course, the ascending flames burned up his wings so that he could fly no farther, and fell to the ground The Aser, who were standing around prepared for the event, immediately slew him, and in this manner the gods were saved from destruction, and Thiasse lost his life within the walls of Asgard. This event is very celebrated."

The foregoing tale may serve as a specimen of one of Loke's numerous adventures. How, when

Thor's hammer had been stolen by the Giant Thrym, he discovered the theft and gave information of it; how he contrived to recover it by making Thor dress himself like Freya; how he made love to Sif, Thor's wife, and when Sif repulsed him with scorn, in revenge, cut off her matchless hair; how he procured, for the gods, incomparable rarities from his kinsmen the dwarfs; and how at length he brought on his own cruel punishment, and hastened the destruction of the gods by maliciously procuring the death of the gentle Baldur, whom all things in nature loved; will be told in the sequel.

He was enabled to escape many dangers by means of his power to assume various shapes, and by the aid of certain shoes, which gave him the power to traverse land and sea with the utmost speed. The word Loke or Loge signifies a flame, and Magnussen suggests that Loke is a personification of fire, which in its nature partakes of good and evil, and was found in earth and heaven, with the gods and the giants.

In Jutland rank weeds are still termed Loke's corn, and the peasants in Norway, Iceland, and some parts of Denmark, call the devil Loke to this day.

CHAPTER IV.

THOR — MIÖLNER — THRUDVANGER — SIF — GIANTS — ULLER-UTGARDELOK — MIMER — THOR'S VISIT TO GEYRUTH — THOR AND THE DWARF ALVES.

THOR was the eldest son of Odin and Frigga, the strongest and, next to Odin, the first in rank amongst the Aser. His stature was so lofty that no horse could bear him, and for this reason he always travelled in a chariot drawn by two he-goats.

He was the implacable and most dreaded enemy of the giants, in his combats with whom he always took care to be provided with three things, which he had obtained from the dwarfs, and on which he set the highest value; namely, 1st, his celebrated hammer, Miölner,[1] whose force no giant or sorcerer could withstand. Although thrown to ever so great a distance it never failed to return into his

---

[1] The word "*miölner*" signifies the bruiser or pounder, being derived from the old verb "*myl*" to pound. The word "*mill*" has the same root, and in old Danish was "*mylna*." Miölner was a symbol of the thunderbolt.

hand, and at the same time it was so small that he could carry it in his pocket; 2nd, his belt, Meigingardur, which had this virtue, that whenever he girt it up, his strength was doubled; 3rd, a pair of steel gauntlets with which he held Miölner.

His residence was called Thrudheim or Thrudvanger, after his daughter Thrude,[2] and his palace, Bilskirner, was the largest building in the world, containing 540 halls.

> In wide Thrudvanger's land
> (So ancient Scalds indite)
> A palace vast doth stand:
> Unmatch'd in breadth and height.
> Its halls with burnish'd gold
> Are richly fretted o'er;
> Their number, rightly told,
> Five hundred and two score.
>
> Blue lakes and verdant fields
> Smiling around are spread,
> Studded with copper shields
> The palace glows in red.
> From distant earth its walls
> Some radiant meteor seem;
> Far off the warrior halls
> In purple splendour gleam.
>
> There sits on golden throne
> Aloft the god of war,

---

[2] Thrudr, in Icelandic, signifies strength, and Thrudheimar the home of the strong one.

Save Odin, yields to none
'Mongst gods great Aser-Thor.
He gives what warriors feel
When first the battle joins;
His gauntlets are of steel,
A belt binds up his loins.

His hammer, Miölner hight,
All weapons far exceeds;
Where falls its massive weight
No leeches fee there needs.
And when his strength 'gins melt,
When hot the battle burns,
He girds him up his belt
And two-fold it returns.
Oehlenschläger.

Thor had two sons, Magne and Mode, who, with the aid of Miölner, were to avenge his death at Ragnarokur, and two daughters, Thrude and Lora. As chief defender of the boundary of Asgard, he was continually on the watch in Midgard, or the atmosphere, to repel intruding giants and evil spirits.

Lightning flashed from his eyes and from his chariot wheels, as they rolled along, and from his hammer also, and this was why he was obliged to have on his steel gloves when he grasped it.

From out some murky cloud,
Pendent in middle air,

His wheels oft creak aloud—
Then mortals thunder hear.
Oehlenschläger.

In many parts of the north, but more especially in Norway and Iceland, Thor was more highly honoured than Odin himself, and, as has been before remarked, there seems good ground for the belief that the worship of Thor, as the god of thunder, was established there from the remotest antiquity. Suhm is of opinion that Thor, at first, was a personification of thunder. In the Scandinavian dialects, Tor-dön signifies a dull, rolling noise, and we find that thunder is rendered in Danish, Torden; in Swedish, Thordôn; in German, Donner; in Latin, Tonitru; in British, Taran; Phœnician, Thorom; Highland Scotch, Toron. Lucan calls Thor Taranis, which still, in Welsh, signifies thunder.[3]

The Elder Edda itself in one place expressly calls Auka, or Oka-Thor, the first and most powerful of the gods, and the name or worship of Odin is never once alluded to in the remains of the ancient Celts or Sclavonians, whilst that of Thor is frequently mentioned.

As all warriors of high birth were received after their death into Valhalla, the palace of Odin; so

---

[3] Suhm om Odin.

those of inferior rank, and slaves, were to repair to Bilskirner.

> "Odin à jarla
> Tha er i val falla
> En Thor à thrælakyn."

"Odin owns the Jarls (Earls) who have fallen in battle, but Thor owns the race of slaves (thralls)."

Magnussen suggests that Odin having foisted his son or follower, Asa-Thor, into the place of the old divinity, Auka-Thor, left to the conquered Finns and Celts their ancient paradise. But there were also two Scandinavian sects attributing respectively the highest place to Thor and Odin, and these two deities are sometimes introduced in the Eddas as reviling each other.

Thor's name was given to the fifth day of the week, which was kept holy from noon by many of the heathen Scandinavians, as well as by the Finns and Finnlaps, and with which the Scandinavian summer always commenced. Sunday, on the other hand, was considered an unlucky day, and children born thereon were thought never to live long. Even to the present time, in many parts of Norway and Sweden, a belief in the superior sanctity of Thursday over other week-days may be traced. In some parts of England Thursday is still considered as unpropitious for weddings, a superstition which originated, probably, in the fears of the first half converts to Christianity. In the same manner as in the north at the first introduction of the new belief, when the day sacred to the deserted deity returned, it was the custom to pray.

" Gud tal for os: det er Tors-dag over hele Verden."
" God speak for us: it is Thor's-day (Thursday) over all the world."

During the feast of Juul, the oldest and most solemn of all the religious festivals of the inhabitants of the north, and which was held at the winter solstice, about the time of our Christmas, oxen and fatted horses were sacrificed to Thor. The Runic letter P (Th) was also sacred to him.[4]

Thor's wife was Sif, the chastest of the goddesses; she had been married before Thor took her to wife, and had Oller or Uller by her first

---

[4] In the Eyrbiggia Saga there is a description of the temple erected by Thorolf on his first landing in Iceland, about the year 883 A.D. to the god Thor. On the altar was placed a silver ring weighing two ounces, which was worn by the priest on solemn occasions, and on which oaths were sworn. On this altar human sacrifices were frequently offered up, and the mode of destroying the victims was by crushing the spine. The holy mount (Helga-fels) was so sacred that no one might even look upon it until after his morning ablutions, and to enter within its limits was punishable by death.

husband.　Her hair is celebrated in the Edda for its extraordinary beauty.

>Sif, tall and fair with native grace,
>To none in beauty need give place
>Save her whom Odin called to light
>To make the erst dull world more bright.
>Fair tho' she be, to Freya ne'er
>Can stately Sif in form compare.
>　Not hers the clear eye's speaking glance,
>Age-frozen blood might make to dance:
>Or heart which passion ne'er had felt
>Like snow 'neath mid-day sun to melt.
>
>　.　　.　　.　　.　　.
>　　.　　.　　.　　.　　.
>
>Sif seems some Amazon to be,
>Her look replete with dignity,
>Her eye beams no impassion'd glance,
>But rests in cold indifference.
>Her round arms, form'd alike to prove
>The contests or of war or love;
>Her swan-like bosom's faultless curve
>Would Bragi's golden lyre deserve.
>Smaller tho' Freya's hand, not snow
>Than Sif's, fresh fallen on mountain brow,
>More white, nor softer virgin down
>Of Eyder-fowl, nor breast of swan.
>Two pencill'd brows of darkest brown
>Meet on her front, and seem to frown:
>What gentler beauty would deface
>To hers but adds another grace;
>Her pearly teeth, of dazzling white,
>With ruby lips form contrast bright;

> But her first charm, past all compare,
> Is her long, silken, amber hair.
> *Oehlenschläger.*

Sif was worshipped in the heathen temples in Norway, and by the Vendish and other nations; by the latter as a fair-haired goddess, dispensing flowers and fruits; and is considered as a personification of the earth in summer. She was said to have the gift of prophecy.

Sif's son by her first husband was called Uller. He was handsome, and had the appearance and manners of a warrior, an excellent archer, and unrivalled in the art of running on skees or snow-shoes. It was usual to invoke his name in duels, and he protected those who were exposed to danger from fire. He was entitled the hunting god, and his residence was called Ydale, or the dewy valley.

The remains of the worship of Thor lingered longer in the north than those of any of the other Scandinavian deities. In Nial's Saga, a female Scald says to a Christian—" Do you not know that Thor has challenged your Christ to single combat, and that he dares not fight him."

The planet Jupiter was sacred to him. He was represented with a great red beard, and his symbols upon monuments were a wheel, a glove or a cross, the latter denoting either his hammer or two crossed thunderbolts. Hence we have an easy explanation of the crosses on Rune-stones, older than the introduction of Christianity into Scandinavia, which have so greatly puzzled antiquarians.[5]

As Thor's principal occupation consisted in repelling the attacks of the giants on Asgard, or at times in seeking them in their own gloomy abodes, this is perhaps the proper place to condense the information contained in the Eddas respecting these eternal foes to gods and men.

After that the primitive race of the giants, with the exception of Bergelmer (the old dweller on the mountains) and his wife, had been submerged in the blood of their parent Ymer; a new progeny sprang up from these two, who were condemned by Odin to inhabit the dark barren rocks which encircled the earth, and were separated from it by a trackless waste and by the stormy ocean, in which lay imprisoned the great serpent, Jormungandur.

This gloomy region, chilled by ice and eternal snows, and into which the sun's light never penetrated, was ruled by their king Utgardelok, a mighty magician, who within the limits of his realm exercised an uncontrolled power, so that no

---

[5] Magnussen.

Aser ever ventured to cross them unless in disguise. The giants who conceived that they had a prior right to the Aser to the sovereignty of the universe, looked upon the latter as usurpers, and hence bore a deadly hatred to them and to their creation, the sons of Askur; and although there were some instances of intermarriages between the inhabitants of Asgard and of Utgard, these ill-assorted unions never caused any long suspension of hostility.

The giants never ventured to quit Jotunheim, or Giant-land, unless by night, when their influence predominated. They were well skilled in magic, of great sagacity, and possessed secrets relating to the origin of things, unknown to Odin himself. The great prophetess, Vola, and the three nornies or fates, were brought up amongst them, and from them derived their knowledge of the past. They possessed inexhaustible subterranean treasures, were cruel and treacherous, but had one good quality, viz. that they were religious observers of their promises.

In Thor's journey to Jotunheim, he thus addresses the giant Skrymner, who was seeking to deter him by enchantments from proceeding further:

>The great Alfader set
>Midst thickest gloom your home,

Treasures ye're skill'd to get
From out the mountain's womb.
When o'er the silent earth
Night spreads her sable veil,
Ye rush, blood-thirsting, forth.
Her helpless sons t' assail.

Then, at the midnight hour,
When spirits of light retire,
Then rules with hellish pow'r
Dark Utgard's demon sire.
Whate'er is good or fair
To harass, all your joy;
Like rav'nous wolf or bear,
Ye live but to destroy.

In th' Empyrean heaven
Who sits with sleepless eye,[6]
To th' Aser pow'r hath given,
Wisdom and courage high.
By us your felon race
And Loke[7] himself, your king
Must perish, nor your trace
Be left,—so nornies sing.
Oehlenschläger.

The most celebrated of the giants was Mimer, who does not appear, however, to have partaken of the evil nature of his brethren. He possessed a well, situated under that one of the three roots of the

---

[6] The omnipotent being, Alfader.
[7] Utgardelok, not Asa-Loke.

great Ash, which stretched out to the land of the giants. Wisdom was said to be hidden in it, and Mimer was the wisest of all beings because he drank daily of its water. One day Odin went there, and begged permission to quench his thirst, but Mimer would not allow him to do so until he had left one of his eyes in pawn. Afterwards he was in the habit of repairing thither every morning to drink.

Mimer having been left by Odin as hostage with the Vaner, they cut off his head, and sent it back to the Asgard. Odin, by means of his magic art, Seid, embalmed it, and, having pronounced Runes over it, consulted it ever after in all difficult cases.[8]

THOR'S VISIT TO THE GIANT GEYRUTH.

Geyruth or Geirraudr was a powerful giant, and one of the most inveterate enemies of the Aser.

---

[8] Magnussen thus interprets the allegory of Mimer:—His well is the great ocean, Odin's eye is the sun, which in the northernmost latitudes disappears during one portion of the year, Odin's daily drink, the alternation of day and night. He suggests that Mimer is only a corruption of Ymer, the name of the great Cosmogonic giant, and that in the lapse of time two divinities have arisen from one.

He ruled over a country which was dark and rainy, and inhabited by hateful spectres; it was surrounded with palisades on which were placed men's heads, and large fierce dogs guarded the entrance. His own residence was a dark cavern full of noisome stenches, the walls of which were covered with filth, and the floor with adders and other venomous reptiles.

Opposite to the entrance of the cavern, on a rock, sat an old grey-headed giant, with an iron wedge through his breast, and close to him three withered old women, with broken back-bones. These were Geyruth and his three daughters, and the cause of their deplorable state is thus related in the Edda:

" Loke ventured once in the shape of a hawk, into Geyruth's territory, and had the ill luck to fall into his power. The giant suspected that he was an Aser in disguise, and bade him speak, but Loke remaining silent, he was shut up during three months in a chest. At length his courage failed him, and he confessed who he was. Geyruth then let him out on condition that he would bring Thor to his residence without belt or hammer. Thor had no objection to undertake the adventure.

" There was in Utgard an enchanted forest, called Jernvidi or Jarnvidr, where dwelt certain giant witches, who had power to raise terrible storms, and used to entice travellers into their power in order to destroy them. The trees of this forest were of iron,[9] and it was ruled by an old giant who used to sit immoveably in a bending position. From these witches descended sorcerers, male and female, who had the power of assuming at will the forms of wolves.

"On his way, Thor fell in with one of these old witches, who put him on his guard against the arts of Geyruth, and gave him a pair of iron gloves, a girdle, and a staff. When he arrived at the river Vimur, the largest in the world, he perceived Gialp, one of the giant's daughters, standing astride across the river, with one foot on each bank, ready to oppose his passage, and causing the waters to rise. Thor drove her away with a large stone, and waded across to Geyruth's hall. A lodging was assigned to him in a separate house, on entering which he sate down upon a stool placed at one end. Perceiving that the stool under him began suddenly to rise from the ground, he struck the witch's staff violently against the top of the cavern and at the same moment heard a crack and a loud scream beneath him. On searching for the cause of these noises, he discovered that Geyruth's

---

[9] In the Indian Mythology there is mention of similar wood, where the trees bear swords and spears instead of leaves. (*Magnussen.*)

three daughters had placed themselves there with the design to crush him, and that he had broken their backs.

"After this Geyruth invited Thor to come into his drinking chamber. There was a large fire in the midst of it, on one side of which sat the giant, and Thor over against him. On a sudden, Geyruth seized a wedge of red-hot iron, which was glowing in the fire and threw it at Thor, who, however, caught it with his iron gloves, and sent it back with such force that, although the giant crept behind a pillar to avoid it, it passed through the pillar, the giant, and the wall, and he has remained in the same position ever since."

THOR AND THE DWARF ALVIS.

A dwarf whose name was Alvis, had contrived by cunning to obtain from Thor's foster-daughter a promise that she would marry him. He went secretly to her bower when he imagined that Thor was absent, but whilst he was endeavouring to persuade her to accompany him to his home in the mountains, the god suddenly returned, and surprised him in the midst of his courtship.

The dwarf's alarm was not lessened, when Thor addressed him in the following manner:

"A pretty kind of a fellow you are to come here a wooing with that white nose of yours; you seem to me to have a strong resemblance to the Thurser,[10] you were never born for a bride like this."

Alvis, finding that this was no time for deceit, acknowledged that he was a dwarf, and lived beneath the rocks, and at the same time boldly claimed the maiden, on the ground that a solemn promise ought never to be broken.

Thor replied, that he would break the promise, that he who stood in the place of the maiden's father had made no promise, and that no one else had a right to give her away.

The dwarf, in despair at the prospect of losing his bride, began to question the right of the intruder to interfere, and asked him who he was.

Thor told him: and said that neither he nor any one else should have the maid without his, Thor's, consent; but that if his wisdom was so great as his name indicated,[11] and he could answer all that was asked him respecting each of the worlds, her love should not be denied him.

Alvis answered: "O Thor! you know well how to draw out the wisdom of the dwarfs. I

---

[10] The Thurser, a name for evil spirits generally.
[11] Al-vis, or All-wise.

have travelled through each of the nine worlds and am acquainted with all that they contain."

Thor then began to question him on a variety of subjects, respecting the names which they bore in the different worlds, and the dwarf's answers showed that each class of beings, the Aser, the Genii of fire, the Vaner, the Giants, the Elves, the Dwarfs, Men, and the spirits of the dead, had their particular language; a superstition, remarks Magnussen, which prevailed amongst many heathen nations, and particularly with the ancient Greeks and the Hindoos.

Thor's questions related to the earth, heaven, the moon, the sun, the clouds, wind, calms, the sea, fire, forests, night, grain, ale, &c.

The dwarf, carried away by his wisdom, dwelt so long on these subjects, that he did not perceive the approach of day until the sun fell on him, and he was turned at once to a stone.[12]

Thor remarked that he had never found so much wisdom in any breast, but that the dwarf had suffered himself to be taken in like a fool.

The above tale is taken from the Alvis-maal, in the poetic Edda. Like many other of the poems

---

[12] No dwarf or evil spirit of any kind could endure the light of the sun, but if surprised by it was instantly converted to stone.

of the same collection, it is in the form of a dialogue, and the tale seems designed merely as an attractive mode of conveying the mythological and other information which it contains.

The most celebrated, however, of Thor's adventures, was his journey to Giant-land, to which, on account of its length, we shall devote the ensuing chapter, following Oehlenschläger's poetical paraphrase of the account given in the prose Edda.

CHAPTER V.

THOR'S JOURNEY TO JOTUNHEIM, OR GIANT-LAND.

I. THOR SETS OUT ON ADVENTURES WITH LOKE.

THERE was at Upsala, in Sweden, a temple sacred to Odin, which exceeded all others in magnificence. Kings and Jarls and distinguished warriors from every part of the world frequented it, and no place in Midgard was more especially under the protection of Odin. Thor and Frigga were also worshipped there, and the priestesses of Frigga were king's daughters.

Utgardelok, the prince of darkness and king of the giants, blinded by his rancorous hatred to the Aser, and desirous of putting a mortal affront on their chief, repaired to this temple, put out the sacred fire, and laid the whole edifice in ruins.

When Odin learned this he lost no time to summon the Aser to council, and declared to them, in full assembly, what had happened. The Aser were filled with indignation, and called loudly for vengeance on the dark king.

When they had sate down to table, Thor's anger was so great that he spake not a word, but struck his brow with his clenched hand, revolving in his mind how he might best chastise the insolence of Utgardelok. As soon as the repast was ended, and the Valkyrs had filled horns of mead for each of the guests, Thor announced his intention to drive his car, and, having harnessed his goats, and nailed on their golden shoes, and called to Asa-Loke, who always sat next to him at Odin's table, to accompany him, he wound the leathern reins round his waist, and taking Miölner in his hand, drove towards the bridge Bifrost.[1]

> Adown the painted way
> As drove th' impetuous god,
> The red flames, lambent, play
> Along the wheel-tracks broad.
> Heimdall his horn blew loud,
> The god with sleepless eye,
> Seven maids submissive bow'd
> As the gold car flew by.
>
> On earth some meteor dire
> Men thought then to behold;

---

[1] The bridge Bifrost, or the rainbow, was the bridge over which the gods passed on their way from heaven to earth. Heimdall was the warder of the gods and had his station on its summit. The seven maids were the seven colours of the rainbow.

> The heavens were fraught with fire,
> In peals the thunder roll'd:
> Swift as enamour'd swan,
> Passed on the Aser's car,
> With Thor, the Giant-Bane,[2]
> And Loptur thro' the air.
>
> *Oehlenschläger.*

Asa-Loke, who, although the Thunderer had said nothing, suspected his purpose, and who, notwithstanding repeated chastisements, could never be taught to hold his tongue, began now tauntingly to propose a journey to Utgard,[3] remarking that although the trip might be attended with some hazard, the giant king was well worth the seeing. Thor answered him shortly that he cared very little for Utgardelok, and that he had only to fling his hammer to crush him and his whole train of trolds and dwarfs.

> So spake the god of war
> And fearlessly drove on,
> With Loptur in his car,
> To earth's green regions down:
> The little birds sang sweet,
> The trees, in reverence, bow'd,

---

[2] One of the epithets applied to Thor.

[3] Utgard, literally the outermost dwelling, was the frozen circle of rocks which was supposed to surround the universe, the residence of giants and evil spirits.

All nature seem'd to greet
Valhalla's warrior god.[4]

The rose and violet blue
Wither'd afore his look:
Their tender forms to view
Such radiance could not brook:
Closed was each honied cup,
As their great lord drew nigh;
The gentle flow'rets droop,
Breathe on their god and die.

It was now getting towards night-fall:

The sun had sunk to rest
In purple green and gold;[5]
In simple yellow drest
The moon rose o'er the wold.
Great Aüka-Thor drove fast
Two warrior barrows[6] by,
As the dark tombs they pass'd
Bright flash'd the Aser's eye.

---

[4] There is much poetical propriety in the respect thus paid to Thor, the personification of thunder, the refreshing rains accompanying which, so powerfully affect vegetation.

[5] Those who have never visited Norway during the autumn, can scarcely form an idea of the splendour of its setting sun, at that season of the year.

[6] Odin is supposed to have introduced into the north the custom of burying the dead under eminences or mounds of earth from Scythia, where it appears to have existed from the remotest times. These mounds or barrows are very numerous in Denmark and in the west of England. They are found

At length they arrived at a lonely peasant's hut, and Thor called out to ask for a night's lodging. The peasant readily granted it, and the travellers

---

also on the banks of the Black Sea, in the Crimea, and may be traced from the Steppes of Great Tartary throughout Europe, (particularly in Bohemia, Normandy, and the Low Countries) to the ocean. They were generally thrown up near some public road, fountain, or frequented spot, and often, still, bear the name of the warrior or prince over whose bones they were raised. The old Scandinavians had three kinds of burial places, called—" *haugr*," " *kuml*," and " *dys*." The " *Haugr*," the latest in date, were raised to the greatest height, and constructed with the most care. They were turfed on the outside, and the interior was composed of well beaten earth, in the centre of which was an oblong chamber of stone, called a giant-chamber (Jætte-stue), from the enormous size of the stones of which it was usually composed. In these the body was laid, sometimes in a sitting posture, sometimes stretched out, or when it had been burned the ashes were sometimes placed in an urn, sometimes scattered about. In latter times the entrance to these chambers was secured by beams of timber.—The " *Kuml*," of older date than the haugr, was lower and less considerable, but in these also, the body was above ground, being covered with earth loosely thrown together.—The " *Dys*" was destined for slaves, criminals, or prisoners, offered to the gods. The bodies were cast into a hole, under a hedge or into a wood, and earth or rubbish thrown over them. These were never covered with green turf, nor marked by monumental stones. The summits of barrows are often encircled with stones, and those were the most complete which consisted of three eminences, with a stone altar (Cromlech) on the centre one.

alighting entered the cabin, which was so low that they were obliged to bend nearly double. The peasant's family consisted of himself and his old wife, and of a son and a daughter, Tialf and Roska. The old woman lamented to Thor, that she had nothing to offer him for supper but some roots. Thor answered that he would provide food, and bade her prepare the table. He then took Miölner, his hammer, and slew his two he-goats, and having stripped them of their skins, put them into the boiler. The skins were spread out carefully before the hearth, and Thor desired the peasant to be sure to put all the bones into them. When the meat was cooked, they all sat down to supper:

> The peasant's meagre store
> Not ev'n a dish could yield:
> It matter'd not to Thor,
> Who ate from off his shield.
> The goats were soon devour'd,
> A part was left to bleed,
> The blood in jugs they pour'd,
> And straight 'twas sparkling mead.

During the supper, however, Tialf, the boy, had contrived to get a thigh-bone of one of the goats, which he brake for the sake of the marrow. Thor staid over the night in the cottage. The next morning, before dawn, he rose, and taking Miölner in his hand he swang it in the air over the goat-skins and bones.[7] The goats immediately sprang up in life and spirits, but one of them was lame in the hind leg. Thor's anger on this was kindled. He said that the peasant or his people must have been careless with the bones, seeing that a thigh-bone had been broken. It would be in vain to seek to describe the terror of the whole family, when they saw how Thor's forehead became wrinkled, and his eye-balls nearly turned round with fury. He grasped his hammer-haft so hard, that his knuckles became white. They all fell on their knees and begged for mercy, offering as compensation all that they possessed. When Thor saw their terror he took pity on them, and his anger completely disappeared. He demanded, however, that Tialf and Roska should forthwith enter into his service, to which the peasant gladly consented. The goats and car were now left at the cottage, and the two Aser with their attendants set out on foot for Jotunheim.

> Of Tialf it should be told,
> Right well the lad turn'd out:
> He proved a warrior bold,
> His heart and arm were stout.

---

[7] The heathen Finn-lapps still take care not to break the bones of the animals which they sacrifice, saying, that the gods may put flesh and skin on them again.—*F. Magnussen.*

This came of hearty food,
To eat he ne'er was slack;
In favour high he stood
With Thor, and bare the pack.

A form as Freya's bright
Had Roska, blue-eyed maid;
Her bosom round and white
In glittering steel array'd.
Proud smiled the maiden fair,
Pleased with her waving crest,
Her yellow, silken hair,
A golden morion prest.

Miölner o'er shoulder thrown,
Resolve mark'd in his look,
As Thor strode stoutly on
His rattling[8] copper shook.
With arms less cumbrous dight,
Loke, lightly tripp'd along,
From casque with silver white
His dark locks loosely hung.

They travelled on with such speed that they soon arrived at the sea, which it was necessary to pass.

---

[8] The Scandinavians had made considerable progress in the art of working copper, whilst yet ignorant how to separate iron from the ore. In the interesting collection of Northern Antiquities at Copenhagen, there are some swords of copper, the edges of which are sheathed with thin plates of iron (probably meteoric), for the sake of its superior hardness.

The storm was raging with great fury, and Ran's[9] voice might very easily be distinguished in the midst of it. It was now evident to Thor that Loke's heart began already to fail, and turning to him he told him that it was of no avail to be alarmed, that he himself had first proposed the adventure, and that it should never be said that Thor turned back from any undertaking for fear of danger.

> Then like some ponderous rock
> He plunged into the wave:
> Ran, frighten'd at the shock,
> Slunk to her inmost cave.
> With courage fill'd, the rest
> Follow'd their fearless lord;
> The sea their mail'd sides press'd,
> And round them, threat'ning, roar'd.
>
> For many a league they toil'd,
> With desperate strength, along:
> Hark! o'er the billows, wild,
> And clear mermaid's[10] song.
> Hid by some sea-worn cliff
> She chants ill-omen'd dirge:
> I trow, with sinews stiff
> They buffet now the surge.

---

[9] Ran, the wife of the sea-god, Ægir, was cruel and avaricious, and caused all shipwrecks.

[10] The belief in mermen and mermaids is still common in Norway and Denmark. Their appearance portends a storm.

The storm increased in violence, but Thor continued to encourage his companions, and to help them when their strength was failing, and at length, in spite of all difficulties, they reached the opposite shore. They were however still in a lamentable plight, hungry and dripping with wet. The moon which gleamed for a moment from out the dark clouds, showed all around a wild, trackless desert, overgrown with dwarf birch. Thor said that no time was to be lost, but that they should proceed at once up into the country.

> With many a weary step,
> Through fen and bog they wend,
> Now on the smooth ice slip,
> Now sink into the sand.
> The labouring sky was black
> As raven's glossy plume,
> Save where with vivid streak
> Blue lightnings mock'd the gloom.
>
> Comets with fiery tails
> Shot swift the heaven athwart,
> The hail fell thick, huge whales
> Bellow'd in monstrous sport;
> Bitter the keen wind blew,
> Young Roska swoon'd for fear,
> Loke quick to aid her flew,
> He ever loved the fair.

Thor at length began to lose his temper, which Utgardelok had tried to the utmost. He muttered:

the giant thinks to bring me to shame, but I will tame his insolence. At length in the midst of the desert, they espied a kind of hut, which they entered, in order to obtain shelter against the pelting of the storm. It consisted of one vast room, of an extraordinary shape, being neither round nor square, and one entire side was occupied by the entrance. They were too wearied, however, to trouble themselves much about this, and having devoured the contents of Tialf's pack, they all lay down to sleep except Thor, who placed himself to watch at the entrance of the hut in a sitting posture. His eye-balls glared dreadfully out on the waste, with one hand he grasped Miölner, the other was placed beneath his chin. He did not stir once during the whole night.

II. ENCHANTMENT ON THE HEATH.

Whilst Thor was thus on the watch, he heard suddenly, towards morning, a noise which seemed to issue from beneath his feet, and so loud that it could not have been caused by anything mortal. Thor called out angrily to know who dared to disturb the rest of those within the hut, and receiving no answer, his ire got up, and he sprang upon his feet, resolved to punish the intruder. By the aid of the fiery meteors which were playing about, he perceived, stretched out at length, a huge giant asleep, whose bulk was so great that it covered several acres of ground. Thor did not hesitate long as to the course he should pursue, but swinging Miölner around was about to put an effectual stop to the insolent snoring of the giant, when suddenly as if aware of the stroke, he rose up lightly, and then first Thor became fully aware of his prodigious size. He had a long spear or spud in his hand. Thor could not help being a little amazed at so unexpected an apparition, but after a slight pause, demanded of the giant who he was, and whence he came? He replied that his name was Skrymner, and that he came from Jotunheim, where he served the king Utgardelok. He added that he had no need to ask who Thor was as he knew very well that he was no friend to giants. He had heard, he said, a great deal of Thor's feats, but that after all the god seemed to him nothing very wonderful, and that it would be no hard matter to place him, armour and all, on one hand. He remarked at the same time that he himself was held in but little esteem in Jotunheim. Soon after, turning round, he called out that he had lost his gauntlet, and kneeling down groped about in search of it, when at length, laying hold of the hut in which they had been passing the night, he lifted it up with the greatest ease.

> Now morn the heaven had clear'd,
> And plainly all descried,
> What erst a hut appeared,
> Was but a gauntlet wide.
> Muttering betwixt his teeth
> The giant drew it on,
> Thor's comrades held their breath,
> Their courage was nigh gone.

Thor, however, was not in any degree daunted, but told his companions not to be down-cast; that he had never yet heard that size was a proof of courage, and that a wolf would have no difficulty in overcoming an ox. He added, that the foul giant was much mistaken if he thought to intimidate him, or to weaken his trust in Miölner. After a short silence, Skrymner observed, that it was a very strange taste to journey so far to see a barren waste of sand, and asked Thor why he came to Jotunheim?

> Him answer'd haughtily,
> The god to warriors dear;
> It pleased me here to be,
> And therefore am I here.

He added, that having heard much in Asgard of Utgardelok, he was resolved to see him face to face, and that as for his magic and his frozen mountains, he only laughed at them.

All Niffelheim seem'd loose,
So loud the giant roar'd:
" Thy neck into a noose
Thou runn'st:" such was his word :
" Take warning ere too late,
Tall ramparts gird about
Our realm, from which ne'er yet
Unscourged came Aser out.

" Turn back, thou warrior true,
Nor madly further roam,
Too late, the hour thou'lt rue,
Thou sought'st the giant's home.
With no benign intent
Thou com'st our monarch near:
On strife and war thou'rt bent,
Be warn'd, 'twill cost thee dear.

" Turn back, thou Aser bright,
Back from this hostile soil;
Turn to thy realms of light,
What boots it here to while!
A wild, which foot ne'er paced;
A sea, where tempests roar;
Thy sires as barriers placed
'Twixt us and Asgard's shore.

" There joys which never cloy,
The feast, the fight, the dance,
By turns your days employ,

Gilt by Soel's[11] ceaseless glance.
To ye fond nornies shared
A lordly destiny;
On earth, adored, and fear'd,
Blissful in heaven to be.

" But Ymer's banish'd race
Far other lot obtain'd:
Bare rocks our dwelling-place,
To hard deeds we are train'd.
For us no flame ascends,
Mortals no altars raise;
Terror our steps attends,
Cunning and strength our praise.

" Our halls, caves dark and low!
Torch-lit, our rocks beneath:
As th' Aser life bestow,
We bring disease and death;
Earth hides us in her womb,
Thick, knotted clubs we wield,
Within our cavern's gloom
E'en gods with fear are chill'd."

An instant Thor held back,
He struck his shield with force,
" Enchanter foul," he spake,
In voice with passion hoarse:
" 'Tis well thy stature tall
Saves thee from Miölner's swing:

---

[11] Soel was a goddess who directed the course of the sun; her brother, Mone, governed in like manner the moon.

Were we in Thrudheim's [12] hall,
Mine arm should lightnings fling.

" Of Utgard, a vile slave,
Bid Thor to change intent!
A peasant, arm'd with stave,
Question my hardiment!
What, tho' thy misshaped head
Thou lift'st on high, so proud,
Think'st thou to strike with dread
Valhalla's warrior god!"

The god with rage flow'd o'er,
He clench'd his mail-clad hand:
" Were there of giants more
Than grains of ocean sand,
Or snakes on Nastrond's [13] wall
Me little 'twould import,
To earth I'd fell them all,
Nor ask more welcome sport.

" Thou swoln and turgid sponge,
Spite of thy brittle spear,
I'd slay thee with one lunge
Of my good falchion here:
Let earth's weak children cow'r
Before thine aspect grim,
To crush thee, Thor hath pow'r
With but his buckler's rim."

---

[12] Thor's residence.
[13] Nastrond, the Scandinavian hell, was built of snakes.

Thor ended by upbraiding the giant with the treachery and cruelty of his race, and by reminding him of the Nornies' decree, that the whole of them and Utgardelok himself were one day to perish by the hands of the Aser. Skrymner was now in great alarm, and seeing that Thor was preparing in earnest for combat, he sought to pacify him, and said, that since the god was resolved to go to Utgard, he himself would be the guide, and would find provision on the way, of which they would stand much in need. He added, that he had no doubt, that his monarch would be well pleased to see so distinguished a warrior at his court. Accordingly they proceeded onwards, Skrymner with a wallet on his back leading the way. The road led along a wide lake, and as they advanced began to assume a more smiling appearance. Roska, who had been much alarmed, resumed her courage, and Loke beguiled the time by his pleasant jests.

> They quicken'd now their pace,
> For th' evening star 'gan peer,
> Skrymner, with smiling face,
> Show'd where a grove was near.

> This reach'd, his wallet down
> The weary giant laid,
> And, in a friendly tone,
> Thus to the wanderers said:

> "Beneath this leafy shade
> We'll lay us down to sleep,
> Till o'er the dewy glade
> The grey morn 'gins to peep."

He gave Thor the wallet, which was fastened in a curious manner, saying, that it contained as good a supper as Sif[14] herself could have prepared, at the same time he begged the god be careful in untying the strings, as he did not wish them to be broken. He then retired into the wood and lay down to sleep.

> Under the grove's warm lee,
> Shelter'd from rain and blast,
> Stretch'd 'neath a greenwood tree,
> He soon in sleep was fast.
>
> Upon the velvet lawn
> God Thor, and Roska fair,
> And Loke, and Tialf, sate down
> To breathe the ev'ning air.
> The elves, with flow'rs who deck
> The meads, their strength renew.
> Being hungry, Skrymner's pack
> The thund'rer near him drew.
>
> To Roska then he spake:
> "Let's to our host be true:—

---

[14] Sif was Thor's wife.

> The supper out to take,
> Sweet maid, must fall to you.
> The giant charged enow
> To spare his paltry bands:
> His wallet scarce, I trow,
> Could fall to gentler hands."
>
> With ready smile the maid
> Sank on her knee, so round,
> T' unloose, as Thor had bid,
> The strings the pack that bound.

This, however, she found no easy matter, and having tried in vain for some time, she was obliged to give up the attempt. Thor now called to Tialf to take the job in hand, observing that he had not the appearance of one who would like to go to bed supperless. Tialf sate down on his hams, and putting the wallet betwixt his knees thought to have opened it presently, but he found that the more he picked at the knot, the tighter it became, so he abandoned the task also, and said that were he master, he would cut it at once. Thor, however, would keep his word and bade Loke try, remarking that it would be a cunning wight who could puzzle him. Loke did so, but could not succeed. Thor laughed heartily to see how Loke was vexed at his ill success, and at last set about untying the wallet himself; he pulled and twisted the knot with his brawny hands, but it foiled him as well as the others. His wrath now began to rise, and drawing his sword, he sought to cut the strings, but although he hewed with all his might, he could not sever one. By this time he had become quite furious, and seizing Miölner, cried out, the churl would be merry at our expence, but unless my hammer fail, he shall rue his joke.

> The God with fell intent,
> Now gather'd all his strength,
> And to the giant went,
> Who lay stretch'd out at length.
> A well-aim'd blow he struck
> Just where the brows unite,
> With force might cleave a rock,
> Truth, 'twas a fearful sight.

> Scarce roused, his heavy eyes
> The giant open'd, half;
> At his side Thor espies
> All arm'd, and with him Tialf—
> " What could have made me wake,"
> Quoth he; " 'twas sure a leaf—
> Well Thor, what news o' th' pack?
> Hast eaten all the beef?"

> With rage Thor near had burst,
> Fiercely his lips he bit:
> He mutter'd: " Slave accurst!
> Thou shalt not 'scape me yet."
> The giant gave no heed,
> But slowly turn'd him o'er,

And soon the woody glade
Re-echo'd with his snore.

Thor, bent on deadly harm,
Frowning again drew near,
Miölner with out-stretch'd arm
Three times he swang in air.
The stroke was levell'd well,—
Swift as the meteor shaft
Full on his front it fell,
And sank up to the haft.

This Skrymner seem'd to move;
With force he struck his head.
" A murrain on the grove,"
In grumbling tone he said :
" In peace one cannot rest,
Some berry's bruised my crown,
What, Thor! still up! 'twere best
Till morn to lay you down."

Low murm'ring 'twixt his teeth,
He soon resank to sleep.
Awhile Thôr held his breath;
He groan'd in spirit, deep;
To Odin, his great sire,
He raised his voice on high,
The little feather'd quire
The grove, in terror, fly.

His eyes like lightnings flash'd,
He drew his girdle tight,
On Skrymner's temple crash'd
The steel with awful might.

> It made the giant start:
> He roar'd aloud: " How now!
> What makes my forehead smart?
> There must have fall'n a bough."

But the morning sun having now appeared above the trees, he rose up, and saying that it was time to proceed on their journey, he took up the unopened wallet and led the way to Utgard. In a short time they came in sight of the town, and Skrymner having pointed it out to Thor, told him he must now leave him. He showed him, however, the way he was to take, and gave him his spud, by placing which against lock or bar, they would immediately open or fly back. He then bade the travellers farewell, wishing them luck, and telling them they would have need of their courage, and striding straight over rock and river he was soon out of sight.

III. THOR IN HELHEIM.

The facts which we have now to relate are of so extraordinary a nature, that they almost exceed belief. The way of the travellers lay across a wide plain covered with ice, and for every step that Thor and his companions took it seemed as if they slipped back two. At length, when nearly exhausted, they reached a point from whence a pathway led through the rocks, down towards the gates of the town.

> The night-owl mournful scream'd,
> The heav'ns as pitch were black;
> Half crazed poor Roska seem'd,
> Kept close to God Thor's back.
>
> For many a weary hour,
> Still deeper down they went,
> Heard chafing torrents roar,
> In rocky prisons pent:
> Pale spectres flitted past;
> The god, with lengthen'd stride,
> Adown the steep way fast,
> In silence, onwards hied.

On a sudden on turning the point of a rock, they perceived what through the thick darkness seemed to be a taper's light, but as they advanced they found it was the glare of a fire-brand. At the same moment the moon gleamed faintly on the bare rocks near them, and they saw a large cavern which yawned across the path-way. Entering it, they arrived at a wicket before which sate two tall ghastly spectres.

> Both hasten'd up to rise
> As Asa-Thor drew near,
> And with dull, stony eyes
> Return'd the war-god's stare.

A woman one appear'd,
The other was a man:
No mortal eye had dared
Their hideous forms to scan.
Rattled their leaden teeth,
They shook with icy pain,
Theirs was the chill of death,
May ne'er know warmth again.

A plume of raven hue
Shadow'd each bloodless head:
Over their armour blue
White winding-sheets were spread.
Their maces, strange to tell,
Of dead men's bones were made.
Heavy to earth they fell,
Might stout heart have dismay'd.

In deep, sepulchral tone,
The spectres slowly spake,
'Twas like a half-check'd groan,
Made Tialf and Roska quake.
" What hath your footsteps here,
Ye rash intruders, sent?
Your blood runs warm and clear,
Your days not yet are spent.

" Ye yet may fall in fight,[15]
What come ye here to seek

---

[15] Those who were slain in battle passed at once to Valhalla, and were not subjected to Hela, who had sway over those only who died peacefully in their beds.

> Within these realms of night?
> Turn back, insane, turn back!
> Here an enchantress dread
> Governs with iron sway,
> All who on peaceful bed,
> Inglorious, quit the day."

Thor, upon this, turned to his companions and said, that from what they had just heard it was evident that they had been misled, and that this must be the gate of Helheim. He added, jeeringly, to Loke, that the prospect of seeing his daughter Hela must be highly gratifying to him.

> Loke felt the bitter taunt,
> Was white with ire his cheek;
> Sudden he turn'd askant
> As if retreat to seek.
> " I'll stay not here, my race,"
> He cried: " in plight forlorn
> To view—this hateful place,
> I'll quit and back return."

But Thor told him to beware how he took a step which might bring him to destruction, and reproached him for repining like a woman at what the decree of the nornies had rendered inevitable. He added, that although no one could think on his offspring without shuddering, even Odin himself could not pretend to despise them, and that he for his own part and all good warriors held Hela in high esteem, as the scourger of cowards. This discourse of Thor succeeded in bringing back Loke to a better way of thinking, and the god now lifting up Skrymner's spear struck it against the gate, which immediately flew open with a noise like a gust of wind.

> The way Thor foremost led,
> He fear'd nor foe nor spell;
> Heavy and dull their tread
> In the dead silence fell.
> Roska, the fearful maid,
> Her cheeks as lilies white,
> To Thor close ever stay'd,
> And his rough hand held tight.

The travellers were now completely shut out from the light of day, and the road, which wound through fractured rocks of granite, was so narrow that it was with difficulty that two could go abreast. At length they arrived at a lofty vaulted cavern, along the walls of which were ranged side by side a countless multitude of pale shivering ghosts, who gazed timidly on the strangers as they passed, and as Thor drew near, fled from him in great terror.

At the end of the cavern stood a throne composed of skulls and human bones, on which sate Hela, the queen of death, she was hideous to look upon, half of her body being white and half blue. Instead of a sceptre she held in her hand a dead man's bone, which had been bleached in the moonlight. No sound was to be heard but hollow sighs, damp fogs rose from the earth, and the air smelt like a newly stirred grave. The only light proceeded from three funeral tapers, which were held by the same number of skeletons.

  Reck'd not the Aser proud,
  With fierce disdain he burn'd,
  And to the trembling crowd
  Contemptuously turn'd:
  " So be it with those," he cried:
  " Who fear like men to die,
  Who, living, Thor denied,
  Dead, let them wail and sigh.

  " Ye woman-hearted fools,
  Who shrank from wounds and strife,
  What boots, where Hela rules,
  Your soft inglorious life?
  Your souls the battle-horn
  Ne'er fill'd with warlike glee:
  To cower were ye born,
  Cower to eternity!"

  Then straight to Hela's throne
  Advanced the warrior stern,
  And spake in gentler tone:
  " Well pleased am I to learn
  That in thy realms, gaunt queen!
  Cowards find fitting doom,
  But do not falsely ween
  That willing, here we come.

" Tow'rds Jotunheim to hie,
To Utgard's king, we thought;
'Twas Skrymner's ready lie
Our footsteps hither brought.
I trow the way we've lost:
To the dark monarch's home,
Then say, if that thou know'st,
How we may readiest come."

Hela to Miölner's lord,
With grating voice, replied;
(Such noise gives edge of sword
On steel-proof helmet tried).
" Leave quick my cavern's gloom!
Your way is straight, begone!
Your full cheek's healthful bloom
I dare not look upon."

Thor now made a sign to his companions to move on quickly. As Loke passed his daughter he turned away his head, and seemed choked with grief. A mournful sigh escaped Hela, which was re-echoed heavily through the cavern. They all made the best of their way out of the kingdom of the grisly queen, and passing through the bowels of the earth, at length reached the northern side of the icy mountain.

IV. THOR ARRIVES AT UTGARD.

After all his adventures, Thor was not sorry at length to have reached Utgard, although it had but a gloomy appearance, being surrounded with black rocks and yawning chasms, and the neighbourhood covered with ice and eternal snows. Before the gates, which were secured by massive chains and bolts, there were huge giants keeping watch. Their spears were tall pines, and their shields were made of granite.

When the strangers first drew near, they rose up as if to oppose their progress, but looking a second time they sate down in scorn, and bade them pass on. They were much amused with Thor's hammer.

Thor for the present took no notice of them, but striking his spear against the gate the bolts flew back and it swang open. They entered a hall of a wondrous size and height, lit up by torches, and it soon appeared that they had forced the palace of Utgardelok himself, for in the centre they beheld the monarch seated on a lofty throne, surrounded by a triple ring of giants in complete armour.

Thor, nothing daunted, advanced towards them with a firm step. No one was stout enough to attempt to bar his way, but yielding place he reached the foot of the throne, and cast so fierce a look upon the king that he could not endure it, but turned away trembling.

The king now, on his side, in the hope of terrifying Thor, struck thrice on his shield with his steel mace, and immediately the hall began to shake, the walls and roof laboured and split, flames burst from out the ground, and vast heaps of treasure were exposed to view. Thor himself could scarcely keep his legs. Utgardelok called out to him that he had better be gone, or that the roof would fall upon him. The god, looking upwards, perceived a huge rocky fragment just tottering over his head. He had scarcely time to say, that " what could not be cured must be endured," and that " whatever happened to him he should not ask for his enemy's pity," when down fell the mass, with a tremendous noise, and strewed the whole ground with its fragments. This only caused Thor to smile. At the same moment a dense, white vapour, with a suffocating smell, issued from two clefts in the rock, and creeping onwards, completely enveloped and threatened to overwhelm them.

> On grim Utgardelok
> Thor scowl'd with vengeful eye:
> " Innocuous fell thy rock,
> Thy poison I defy.
> Cease from thy malice vain,
> Thou'st now to deal with one
> Scorns thee and all thy train;
> Thou strivest 'gainst Odin's son."
>
> The demon quick replied:
> " Thou thund'ring god, full well

I know thee—wrath and pride
The Aser's race reveal;
Usurping race, which now
Reigns in the realms of light;
Nay, boots not knit thy brow,
And Miölner grasp so tight.

" Thy pow'r to work us ill
Thou'st learn'd too high to rate;
Giants are giants still!
And that from ancient date:
Our race to light was brought
Full many an age before
Aser were known, or thought
Of Miölner was or Thor."

He then proceeded at length to give an account of the first creation of the earth, &c. which, as our readers have nothing to learn on that point, we shall not repeat here. Thor, on his side, showed that he was not a whit behind him in his cosmogony, and maintained stoutly that there were no grounds for the vain boast that the giants were of a loftier descent, and that if Bergelmer and his wife had not been by chance at sea, fishing, when Ymer was killed, there would have been an end to the whole race.

" But as the noxious weed,
Tho' ne'er so oft destroy'd,
Still, from some hidden seed,
Is ever fresh supplied :

So ye, infernal brood,
To earth oft howling cast,
Still thirst for strife and blood,
Unmindful of the past.

" But know 'twill work ye ill,
On evil ever bent,
The world with crimes to fill,
And sorrows not content,
Your sacrilegious ire
Not Odin's self e'en spared.
His fane and sacred fire
To desecrate you dared:

" 'Tis therefore I am come
Here, to these regions low,
To tell thee, in thine home,
Thy treasons foul I know:
That thee and all thy brood,
For these thy felon deeds,
T' extirpate, but the nod
Of Bore's great son[16] there needs."

'Twas a fair sight to see
The lofty warrior god,
As in his majesty
And conscious might he stood.
Bright on his godlike breast
His golden cuirass shone,
The trembling giants prest
Close to their monarch's throne.

---

[16] Odin.

Utgardelok was evidently much alarmed, but, pretending that what had been done was only to try Thor's courage, he said that he could not suffer him to depart in anger, and invited him to a feast, after which, they might prove their skill in such sports as warriors delight in.

> God Thor a prompt assent
> To Lok's proposal gave:
> To banquet then they went
> Into an inner cave.
> Of porphyr rimm'd with gold,
> A slab with meats was spread;
> From cups, the warriors bold,
> Of amber, drank their mead.
>
> For musick, rippling streams
> And moaning winds made chime;
> A concert strange, me-seems,
> But suiting place and time.
> With Roska by his side,
> The mead Thor deep 'gan quaff,
> Loke Tialf with bumpers plied,
> And loud went round the laugh.

V. ENCHANTMENTS IN UTGARD.

Whilst they were thus feasting and making wassail, Asa-Loke, who could never remain long quiet, said to Utgardelok: you talked of trials of strength; for my part there is one feat to which I challenge the best amongst you. The king asked him what it was; and Loke answered that he never yet met with any one who could equal him in eating, that what he had already had was scarcely enough to whet his appetite, and that unless he obtained more he certainly should not desire to visit Utgard a second time

Utgardelok calmly said that he would pledge himself to find one who should be more than his match, and making a signal there issued from one side of the hall a giant, whose appearance might have alarmed the boldest.

> He gazed around with ire,
> All o'er his armour play'd
> Fork'd, hissing tongues of fire,
> Most white, some blue, some red.
>
> His long jagg'd iron teeth
> Were set in double rows.
> His mouth—of monstrous width—
> His nails—like vulture's claws—
> His body—meagre, gaunt—
> His eyes two live coals seem'd—
> His cheeks—of ashy tint—
> Fire from his nostrils gleam'd.

Loke was a little astonished at this apparition, but relying on his powers, declared himself confident of the victory. A trencher was now laid across the table, and meats of every kind were heaped upon it until it could hold no more. Loge, which was the name of the giant, was placed at one end, Loke at the other. At a given signal they commenced like two famished wolves, but were soon forced to desist, having met just mid-way.

> The umpires then drew near,
> Loke had not striv'n in vain;
> His bones of flesh were bare,
> No jot was to be seen:
> But when the giant's place,
> In turn they came to view;
> He'd swallow'd all his mess,
> And bones, and trencher too.
>
> I trow there then was mirth,
> Thor's sides were near to split,
> Tialf rolled upon the earth,
> Roska was in a fit.
> Loke, crest-fall'n, left the hall,
> And all, with one accord,
> Unto the giant tall
> The victory award.

The monarch then turned to Thor, and said that it would be a reproach to him if by some feat he could not make up for Loke's discomfiture, and asked what the stripling could do. Tialf sprang up and said: that he saw no great reason to be proud of eating bones like a dog, but that he would challenge any of the dark king's court to run with him upon skees or snow-shoes.

Utgardelok remarked that the choice was a good one, and that swiftness of foot had often stood the bravest in stead.

> Then loud the king 'gan call,
> And forth a dwarf there came,
> Pliant as yew, but small
> Of limb, *Hugo* his name.
> His semblance vague and strange,
> None captive him could make,
> Still, restless, he would range
> Nor e'er repose would take.
>
> A veil was o'er him thrown.

Tialf owned that he had never before seen any one so supple. They repaired to a vast plain covered with snow, and began the race, but Hugo had by far the advantage, and met Tialf face to face, returning from the goal. Utgardelok said that they had better try again, and that Tialf might speed better. They did so, but Tialf, although he never once drew breath, still lagged behind a whole bow-shot. He begged for one more trial which was granted, but Hugo again reached the goal before Tialf had gone half way.

On this the judges declared that Hugo was the conqueror, who straight vanished away like a dream. Utgardelok said: that as far as he had witnessed he held the expertness of his guests in but light esteem, but that Thor had yet to choose what feat he would attempt, and might perhaps redeem their credit.

> The god replied: " 'tis well,
> Let straight be brought me here
> A horn of Hydromel,
> The draught I love, or beer;
> Though Asa-Loke with shame
> Was foil'd, he deep must drink
> Who Thor to treat the same,
> In emptying cups, doth think."
>
> The king a signal gave,
> And, on his shoulders borne,
> Straightways a brawny slave
> Dragg'd in a monstrous horn—
> Right ancient did it seem,
> 'Twas form'd of wroughten gold,
> And, all around the rim,
> Were graven letters old.

They had now returned to the hall. Thor could not help looking with astonishment on the horn, which was so large that one end remained on the outside of the cavern. The king said, sneeringly, that he would not be very thirsty when he had drunk that out, adding that there were but few in Utgard who could empty it at a draught, and that it required good wind to do so in two, but that none ever failed in three.

Quoth Loke to Utgard's king:
" With Asa-Thor to drink
No god in Valhal's ring,
But with despair would shrink—
When the brisk mead goes round,
By blue-ey'd Valkyrs pour'd,
His potent draughts astound
The thirstiest at the board.

" It may have reach'd your ear
How that to Mimer's fount,
Each morning, to repair
Odin to drink is wont:
The horn in which the sage
The gifted liquor pours,
The one-eyed's [17] thirst t' assuage,
In size far passeth yours.

" It chanced, when Odin once
From Asgard was away,
Thor thought him, for the nonce,
The magic well to see;
The horn, fill'd to the brim,
The thirsty thunderer quaff'd,
Light emprize seem'd it him
To drink it at a draught.

" Of th' hardy deed the fame
Was in each Aser's mouth,
When t' Odin's ears it came,
The raven-god was wroth;

---

[17] An epithet of Odin, vid. c. 2.

> It grieves me of my son,
> Quoth he: that men should tell
> Such freaks, I trow that soon
> He'll drink e'en Urda's well.[18]
>
> " Thus, by a lucky theft,
> Did Thor his wit obtain,
> He'd, else, been quite bereft,
> Nor great e'en now the gain:
> But if that Mimer's cup
> To clear, so little cost,
> Be sure your lesser stoup
> Will off with ease be tost."

Loke, thus as usual, vented his spleen against Thor in an under voice to Utgardelok, who told him to be under no apprehension as to the result of the undertaking. But they now ceased their conversation, for Thor taking up the huge cup in both his hands began to drink, and at the same moment a hollow noise, like the rushing of waters, was heard.

> Not thirstier the parch'd sand
> Drinks up the thunder shower,
> When on th' exhausted land
> Its quickening waters pour;
> Than Thor the liquor plied;
> When now he'd quench'd his thirst,
> Into the horn he spied,
> But lo! as at the first,

---

[18] Urda, the Norny of the past, v. ch. viii.

'Twas full up to the brim.
He stood not long in doubt,
Though strange it seem'd to him;
Resolved to drink it out,
He lean'd on Miölner's haft,
And quaff'd the mead again,
Which down his weason chafed,
Like torrent down ravine.

So lustily he swill'd,
Might turn e'en Glommen[19] dry;
"I trow it now will yield,"
Quoth he: and turn'd his eye
To see how far 't had sunk,
But still, e'en as before,
'Twas full—in vain he'd drunk—
Furious he stamp'd the floor.

The lord of Thrudheim shook
With baffled pride and wrath:
The horn he fiercely took
And lifted to his mouth;
He drank, as when of yore
Th' abyss drank Ymer's blood,
The dark king's brow 'gan lour,
Trembling the giants stood.

---

[19] The Glommen is the largest river in Norway, clear and rapid. It rises in the mountains above Roraas, and, after a course of near three hundred English miles, entirely through Norway, falls into the North Sea near Friedrichsstadt. In its course it forms from fifteen to twenty considerable waterfalls, of which the principal are the Sarpen-foss, near its mouth, the Mörch-foss, and the Vammen's-foss.

Thor was not one to flinch,
But all the god could do,
The drink scarce sank an inch,
The horn to earth he threw,
And cried: " More and I burst,
Boots not to strive at odds,
The fever's burning thirst
Consumes not Valhal's gods.

" With revelry and laugh
In the bright face of day,
To glad our hearts we quaff,
Not parching heat t' allay."
Quoth Lok: " We giants think
Deep drinking proof of might,
That those at board who shrink
Are like to shrink in fight."

He added, however, as there was time enow left, that if Thor was disposed they might try some other feat, and proposed to lift weights from the ground. Thor had no objection, and the king defied him to lift up his cat. Upon this a strange dingy looking cat appeared with scales like a serpent, and fixed its fiery eyes upon the god. Thor, bending down, placed his hand under the belly, and summoning his strength, sought to raise it from the ground,

But still, the more he strove
The cat the higher stretch'd,

Until the very roof
O' th' cave at length it reach'd :
Thor struck it with such might
A fragment vast flew out;
But, all his force despite,
He could but raise one foot.

Now, when all vain he found,
With rage his teeth he gnash'd,
And, furious, to the ground
The struggling monster dash'd.
Quoth Lok : " My cat, no doubt,
Is large as here are all,
But though he think him stout,
The Thund'rer is but small."

Thor replied, that he hated all vain boasters, and since Utgardelok had dared to mock him to his face, he challenged him to come down from his throne, and that they two should fairly try their strength. The king said that there was no need for such heat, seeing that they had only met for sport, and that if Thor was anxious to wrestle he'd call in his old nurse to try a fall with him.

On this, with wonted sneer,
Dark Loke of Asgard spake :
" The crone had best beware,
Nor, rash, her credit stake :
Perchance she ne'er hath heard
Thor's deeds on Geyruth's rock,[20]

---

[20] Vid. ch. iv.

How of the giant lord
The daughters' backs he broke:

" Passing a river, one
Well-nigh the god had drown'd,
But with a pebble stone
He drove her from the ground;
Sure, of the mighty Thor
Well worthy was the feat,
In fight, three virgins fair
And an old man to beat."

Thus th' Aser false 'gan rail,
But Thor, who ill could brook
His taunts, with glove of mail
To earth the caitiff struck.
His anger fiercely burn'd—
" What now, thou prating fool,"
He cried: " not yet hast learn'd
Thy venom'd tongue to rule?

" Thou shuffling weathercock,
Which each breeze turneth round!
Seed thrown upon a rock!
Echo to every sound!
Well doth it thee befit
The heavenly gods to jeer,
Whom, bounteous, they permit
At Valhal's board t' appear!

" But, by great Odin's throne
Forbearance may be tried
O'er much"—with alter'd tone,
The prostrate recreant cried:

" What have I done, great lord,
To rouse thy fearful ire?
Can then an idle word
Set Auka-Thor on fire?

" Who'd e'er believed a jest,
In sportive humour spoke,
Had in the thunderer's breast
Such angry feelings 'woke?
The hags, to all 'tis known,
Who fell beneath thy stroke,
Did nought in common own,
Save sex, with Embla's stock.

" They were not maids who feel
And cherish Freya's pow'r;
Their rugged breasts with steel
Were arm'd, and clubs they bore.
When that the sorcerer talk'd
Of the foul witch, his nurse,
Methought how they were baulk'd,
With her 'twill sure fare worse."

Quoth Thor: " To Loke ne'er yet
Did specious reason lack,
But what is past forget,
And learn thy tongue to check."
And now, a wither'd hag
Hobbled into the hall,
Like to a leathern bag
Her breasts, all shrivell'd, fall.

Upon a knotted crutch
Her feeble steps she stay'd;

Her eyes which rheumed much,
Were deep sunk in her head;
Like saffron was her cheek;
Her back as bow was bent;
Her foul hair matted thick;
She still cough'd as she went.

Quick from the witch unclean
The pure god, loathing, turn'd:
" What doth the sorcerer mean!
Is Thor the thunderer scorn'd!
Does the dark monarch trow
I'll stoop to prove my strength
With one, who's scarce enow
To walk the cavern's length?"

But soon the god's disgust
Did to compassion yield;
In haste his hand he thrust
Into his copper shield,
And, from a hollow, out
Two fragrant apples took;
" Eat, mother, of the fruit,"
Quoth he: " fair hands did pluck

" From Bragi's golden tree:
Such is their magic pow'r
To th' oldest, presently,
They vigorous youth restore."
Oppress'd with age, the crone—
To see her, aye! 'twas ruth—
Upon a stool sate down—
" I'm old," quoth she; " but youth

" Eternal I enjoy—
Your needful apples keep—
Though all things I destroy,
I need nor food nor sleep."
With wonder Thor was struck
At such discourse obscure;
The god would fain have spoke;
But, sudden, from the floor

She leap'd, and round him tight,
Her long, lean arms she wound;
And strove, with all her might,
To cast him to the ground.
Like raging tigress, wild
Upon her prey she sprung,
And, though full long she toil'd,—
At length on one knee flung.

When, that a toothless crone
Valhalla's pride could worst,
The Áser saw, a groan
Forth from their bosoms burst.
Thor, wrathful, turn'd about
Unto the giant foul—
" Straight, traitor, lead me out,"
He cried; " this witchcraft's hole.

" Unknown to my great sire,
I left the realms above
To Utgard to repair,
Thy hellish power to prove;
Hence is it that thy spells
O'er all my strength prevail,

He, who presumption quells,
Has doom'd it, here, to fail.

" But let not triumph vain
Move thee to ill-timed glee!
Soon shall these rocks again
My weighty hammer see;
Then shall appear who shuns
The strife, and if thy power
Thor's sword and Odin's Runes,
Combined, can triumph o'er."

This said, the god in wroth
Hied tow'rds the gate with speed,
The way the monarch forth
From out the cave must lead:
In haste, Loke and the rest
Their lord to follow rose,
The gates, when scarce they'd past,
With a harsh grating close.

VI. ENCHANTMENTS EXPLAINED.

When Thor and his companions found that they were clear out of the region of night, their blood, which had been half frozen, began once more to flow freely through their veins. The sun shone brightly on the green fields and flowers, but it was evident that Thor could not chase from his mind the galling thought of his defeat. Utgardelok remarked the dark cloud on his brow, which boded him no good.

>Deceived by magic art,
>Though Thor had left his reign,
>And burn'd but to depart
>For Asgard's realms again;
>He knew that the deceit
>To Hlidskialf's lord [21] was known,
>And fear'd, when th' Aser's feet
>Stood before Odin's throne,
>
>Th' all-knowing might reveal
>His arts, and both unite
>To make the giants feel
>Their then resistless might.

He resolved, therefore, to put on the appearance of candour, and to confess to Thor the imposture which had been played upon him:

>And so, in candid guise,
>Though his false heart did quake
>Within, the sire of lies
>Thus to the thunderer spake:
>" At length my fear's at end,
>Thy foot my threshold's past,
>And Skulda [22] dire forefend
>It there again should rest.

---

[21] Odin.
[22] One of the three Nornies or fates, who presided over the future.

" But since concealment now
No peril would avert,
And that, e'en in a foe,
I honour high desert;
Those feats, which e'en the best
Of Utgard glazed with fear,
And with alarm my breast
O'er-whelm'd, I'll now declare.

The rattling of thy car
On Bifrost,[23] when I heard,
Nought good I hoped, O Thor!
From thy trip netherward:
But when that thine intent
I learn'd, t' Utgard to hie,
Each art thee to prevent
I straight resolved to try.

" I knew that, for defence,
'Twas vain to arms to flee
'Gainst Miölner's lord, and hence
Call'd to aid sorcery.
'Twas I the furious storm
Stirr'd up, thy course t' oppose;
In vain—thy bosom, firm,
Still o'er the wild waves rose.

" Here foil'd, quick out I drew
My form to monstrous height,
And, where thy course I knew,
As 'twere by chance, did wait:

---

[23] The bridge of the Gods, the rainbow.

I thought thee thus t' affright,
And back thy footsteps turn;
But I had yet thy might,
And courage high to learn.

" If with a magic knot
I knew thy pack to bind,
To mock thee, Thor, the thought
Ne'er came within my mind;
That freak nigh cost me dear,
The truth to tell, e'en now
My blood runs cold with fear,
To think how thy first blow,

" To th' other twain though light,
Close to my temples fell;—
Perdy, an 't had me hit
I'd not been here to tell
The tale. But if, in doubt,
Thy mind still proof doth need,
Turn but thine eyes about,
Thy prowess thou may'st read."

Thor turn'd to where the plain
A rocky barrier crost,
Wherein three dells were seen,
One deeper than the rest.
" Each time that Miölner fell,"
Quoth Lok, " the mighty stroke
Caused, as thou see'st, a dell,
I lay behind the rock,

" From thee, by magic, hid:
Trow me, I'll ne'er deny

That when, O Thor! there's need,
Thy blows fall heavily—
I led thee next astray
To Hela's shadowy reign,
But here thy course to stay
My hopes, as erst, were vain.

" And now, in turn, to speak
Of all that late befel,
Need was by charms to seek
Your prowess to repel.
Thou, Loke, in eating, first
The palm did'st well contest;
E'en hunger's self might burst
To swallow such repast.

" But, though you quickly clear'd
The trencher, piled on high,
Your tooth, it soon appear'd,
With Lōgĕ's could not vie:—
Still, need not thence be lower'd
Your pride, the Giant dire,
Who bones and flesh devour'd,
Know, was ' *incarnate fire.*'

" In running, Tialf, your meed
In question none will call;
To say the truth, your speed
With wonder fill'd us all.
The dwarf, so quick of limb,
Whom to out-run you sought,
No shame his victory deem—
That dwarf, Tialf, was my ' *thought.*'"

Utgardelok then turning to Thor, said: "Your achievements here, Thor, will be talked of in Utgard for ages to come, and, indeed, exceed belief. And first, with respect to the horn; you must have perceived that one end of it was on the outside of the hall, but it never struck you that it communicated with the sea. I shall not speedily forget our alarm when the liquor began to sink in it. If, however, you have any doubt of the truth of what I say, you have only to appeal to the evidence of your senses."

Thor raised his eyes, and saw in fact that the ocean, as far as they could reach, was dry. Upon this his anger was kindled afresh to find how he had been taken in, but the dark king would not give him time to brood upon it, saying that he would surely find no difficulty in pardoning a deceit which had set the greatness of his power in so clear a light, that he would soon reach Asgard, and there—

> The magic horn would find,
> And, when in sportive mood,
> Might cause, if so inclined,
> The ocean's ebb and flood.

This last gibe made Thor quite lose his patience, and he lifted up Miölner to fell his enemy to the earth, who now, pale with fear, said that it would be little worthy of the Thunderer to slay one in no respect his equal, and that the feats which he had still to explain were even more worthy of admiration than the rest.

The beast, which he had taken for a cat, and had nearly strangled, was in fact Jormungandur, or the great serpent, and the height to which he had raised it would appear from the circumstance that it was only its tail that remained on earth.

The ancient, wrinkled crone,
'Gainst whom your strength was staked;
Who seem'd with age fordone,
Who e'en your pity waked—
So feeble deem'd to be—
Who foil'd your manhood's prime,
And forced you bend the knee,
That hag despised was *Time*.

" Time, who eternal youth,
Though old, doth still enjoy;
Whose ever-gnawing tooth
Must all at length destroy.
She leaneth on a crutch,
And slow doth seem her pace,
But ne'er wight her may catch,
If once she by do pass.

" Her all-consuming might
Will lay us giants low;
Ay! and the spirits of light
Must fall before her too.

To earth on one knee thrown,
The aged beldame's power
Already once thou'st known,
Learn, hence, thy pride to lower."

Thor's patience now was spent,
Miölner with glove of steel
He grasp'd in firm intent
The king to earth to fell—
But king and rocks were gone,
The Thunderer's wrath was vain;
The Aser stood, alone,
In a wide silent plain.

VII. RETURN HOME.

At first Thor and his companions were much perplexed to know exactly where they were, but after journeying for a time they perceived a wood at a distance, and proceeding towards it, at length distinguished plainly a cottage in the midst of the trees, which Tialf first recognized to be that of his old parents. He set off at full speed towards it, and Roska after him, striving which could arrive the first.

A pollard lime, near bare
With age, stood nigh the cot,
'Neath which the ancient pair,
In the warm sun-shine, sat:

When the twain breathless came,
Th' old folks, leaped up for joy;
My Roska! cried the dame—
The gaffer—Tialf! my boy!

Th' old mother wept out-right—
Close to her aged breast
Her pride, her eyes' delight,
Her darling girl, she prest;
As the pure morning dew
Doth on the violet lie;
So the full tear the blue
Scarce dimm'd of Roska's eye.

Such scenes and horrors past,
When least she'd hoped again
In mother's arms to rest!
Sure 'twas some phantasm vain—
Not less the dame's surprize,
Ah! threefold happy day,
And can I trust mine eyes!
Can these my children be!

The aged sire, whose hair
Was white and eyes were dull,
Had well nigh dropp'd a tear:
On his son gazing full,
He cried: " Why, Tialf, my lad!
I scarce my son had known;
Thou'rt taller by a head,
And Roska, too, is grown.

" One moon has scarce grown old
Since, clown, thou left'st this place,

And, now, thy portaunce bold
No warrior would disgrace.
With ease thou wield'st thy lance—
And little Roska's mien
How changed! her blue eye's glance
Less downcast now I ween."

Tialf said that if any change had taken place in them it was all owing to Thor, and the God then coming up, the old peasants fell prostrate before him, and by their simple expressions of gratitude, soon dissipated the ill humour which Utgardelok's treachery had caused in him. Having visited his goats and car, and prepared a supper as before, they retired to rest after their fatigue.

Not yet the lark had sung
Her earliest matin lay,
When up from couch they sprung,
And, e'er that dawn'd the day,
Nail'd on the shoes of gold,
The harness'd goats led out;
Then up the warriors bold
Into the chariot got.

I trow o' th' aged pair
Not little the surprise,
When, sudden, in the air
Aloft the car 'gan rise;
At first, young Roska's head
Was dizzy with the height;
But soon the maiden's dread
Was changed t' unmix'd delight.

From Bifrost's lofty bow
With wond'ring eye she gazed
On the wide scene below—
Quoth Thor: " Thou'lt sure be pleased,
Dear maid, all dangers o'er
To learn,—henceforth a home
Thou'lt find in Freya's bower—
In Thrudheim's hall may come

" No woman."———

He then gave her a long description of Folkvangur, which was the name of the residence of Freya, for which, on account of the length of this chapter, we must refer the reader to another place.

Thor here, in Freya's train
The maid would place, for shield
And spear he well had seen
Were not for her to wield.
" Give back the arms," he said:
'Twas plain regrettingly:
" Such gear, thou gentle maid,
Is all too rude for thee.

" To fair Folkvangur's queen
And nymphs I'll thee present—
More fit for Freya's train
Than deeds of hardiment.
No terror there thou'lt feel,
Pleasures thou'lt have enow,
To bear the warrior's steel
Needs sterner stuff, I trow.

Without any more delay, as Roska was content, Thor repaired to the palace of the goddess, who received her into her bower, where she has remained ever since.

>Thor to Valhalla hied
>With Tialf, and took his place;
>His son when Odin spied,
>Could scarce a smile suppress.
>The Valkyrs, clothed in white,
>Fill'd him a welcome cup;
>Then out they went to fight,
>And hew'd till time to sup.

CHAPTER VI.

THOR'S VISIT TO THE GIANT HYMIR.

HYMIR, whom the reader must take care not to confound with the Cosmogonic Ymer, was one of the most powerful giants in Utgard. The sea-god Ægir once gave a great entertainment to the Aser, at which there was abundance of game and fish, but a lack of drink. Ægir was highly gratified by the honour of receiving such distinguished guests, but his joy was somewhat diminished when Thor called sternly for more liquor. The cause of the deficiency appeared to be that Ægir had no cauldron of sufficient size to brew as much as was required, and he therefore humbly requested the God to procure him one against another occasion.

Tyr who, although an Aser, is represented in the Hymisquida as Hymir's son, told Thor that his father possessed a kettle large enough, which might be obtained by stratagem; and on this suggestion the two Aser set out without delay on the adventure.

On reaching Hymir's residence, near the ocean,

they were met by Tyr's grandmother, who had nine hundred heads, in company with whom was his beautiful, fair-haired mother, who offered to her son and to Thor a welcome cup.

She told them that Hymir was from home, and advised them to hide themselves under some kettles, for that he was at times inhospitable, and prone to sudden fits of anger.

Late in the evening he came back from hunting in bad humour; his wife received him with great gentleness, and informed him of the arrival of their son Tyr, whom they had so long expected, adding that Veor,[1] their enemy, and the friend of man was with him, and that they were both at that moment under the kettles, and had scarcely the courage to come forth.

Hymir, whose beard, covered with hoar-frost, resembled a frozen forest, cast such a fierce look at the kettles, that the beams and uprights on which they stood split before it, and eight kettles fell down, only one of which remained whole. Tyr and Thor upon this advanced towards their host, who did not seem very well pleased to see the latter.

He ordered, however, three oxen to be roasted

---

[1] The giants and gods spake different languages, in that of the giants, Veor was the name given to the Thunderer.

for their supper, of which Thor for his single share ate two, which made Hymir remark that the next evening they must sup on what they could catch for themselves. Thor proposed to go to fish, and asked for bait. Hymir told him he might go amongst the cattle and search for some. He accordingly went, and seizing a coal-black bull by the horns, tore off its head, they then rowed out to sea.

Hymir took on his hook two whales at once: Thor having baited his with the bull's head, hooked the great Midgard's serpent, and dragging its head to the edge of the boat, struck it with his hammer, when it sank again.

On their return home, Hymir told Thor that if he wished to give good proof of his strength, he might break a cup, which the giant put into his hands.

Thor dashed it against several stone pillars, but to no purpose. At length Hymir's wife whispered to him to throw it against her husband's head, which he did, and the cup split into pieces, and the giant bitterly deplored its loss.

At last, as a decisive proof of the strength of his guests, Hymir challenged them to lift his large kettle. Tyr endeavoured to do so in vain. Thor took it up with ease, placed it upon his head, and walked away with it. Hymir and a troop of giants followed in order to recover it by force, but Thor, as usual, slew them all, and carried off the kettle in triumph to the place where the gods were assembled, so that ever since Ægir, at the flax harvest, has been able to give them a good drinking bout.

Such is the account of Thor's visit to Hymir, as given in the " Hymis-quida,"[2] or " Song about Hymir," in the Elder Edda. The Prose Edda, which Oehlenschläger has chiefly followed, gives a different account both of its motives, and of its result.

Thor could not sit down patiently under the affront which had been put on him by Utgardelok, and fearing lest his reputation might suffer from the circumstance of his having been out-witted by the giants, he resolved to repair to Jotunheim a second time.

He presented himself therefore before Odin, and acquainting him with his purpose, begged his assistance. Odin told him that force would be of but little avail against the giants, unless it was joined with foresight, and by his magic art, Seid, he prepared an ointment by means of which Thor acquired the power of changing his form.

Having good reason to suspect Asa-Loke's ho-

---

[2] Hymisquida.

nesty, he resolved this time to undertake the adventure alone, and leaving behind him his car and goats, he proceeded on his journey on foot.

> O'er Dovre's ridge[3] he strode,
> For cliff nor torrent slack'd;
> The tall pines, where he trode,
> Like field of stubble crack'd.
>
> Sneehattan's peak of snow,
> And Jotunfieldt he past,
> Then sought the plains below,
> And the sea reach'd at last;
> He mark'd in curling wreath,
> The dull wave roll away,
> And saw where, far beneath,
> The serpent, brooding, lay.
>
> His heart with hope beat high,
> His voice shook as he spake,
> Turning to Heaven his eye,
> " No more, accursed snake,"
> Quoth he: " in giant bend
> Earth prison'd shalt thou keep,
> Nor struggling sea-man send
> To fell Ran's cavern deep."

But being now resolved to proceed with caution, he began by changing his form. Throwing his

---

[3] The Dovre-fieldt is one of the loftiest parts of the great Scandinavian chain of mountains, and Sneehattan its highest peak.

ponderous helmet on the ground, it became a rock covered with pines.

>Next, from his cloven chin,
>He tore the bushy beard;
>Which, cast in the ravine,
>A thorny copse appear'd.
>A smooth-faced peasant boy
>He stood, in wadmel[4] blue,
>White Heimdall[5] smiled for joy
>The cunning wile to view.
>
>Now straight to Hymir's grot
>He hies, a simple hind,
>His flaxen ringlets float
>Wild in the morning wind;
>His belt, by magic cheat,
>A woollen girdle seem'd,
>Art with like art to meet,
>No shame the Aser deem'd.
>
>Miölner, as woodman's axe,
>Athwart his arm he bare,
>His courage high 'gan wax
>At thought of vengeance near.
>In moss-lined cavern deep,
>Lull'd by a torrent's play,

---

[4] Wadmel is a kind of coarse cloth made in Iceland, and worn universally by the peasants in Norway and Denmark.

[5] Nothing that passed on earth could escape the watchful eye of Heimdall, the warder of the gods, who never quitted his post, on the summit of Bifrost.

> Taking his morning sleep,
> At length the giant lay.

The poet in describing Hymir's residence gives a vivid picture of Norwegian scenery, black rugged rocks crowned with pines, a waterfall, a river white with foam dashing through thick brushwood down the ravine, and hard by a verdant dell filled with cattle. On hearing a stranger's step, Hymir sprang up, and demanded of the stripling how he dared unbidden to venture into his wood. Thor replied that he felt no apprehension:

> " My pulse beats steadily,"
> The youth replied : " for ne'er
> Hath Nornies stern decree
> Been changed, I trow, by fear—
> One of a form so good,
> Of generous soul should be;
> My little drop of blood
> What would it profit thee ?"

He finishes a long speech by saying, that his object was to obtain the giant's permission to accompany him when he went out to fish.

> The grisly giant grinn'd
> So wide, that either ear
> His mouth appear'd behind,
> Ne'er yet was seen such leer;
> The earth shook all around,
> He laugh'd so heartily,

> " One with a heart so sound
> I'll never harm," quoth he.

He then granted the request, and invited Thor to take shelter in his cave from the keen morning wind, adding tauntingly,

> " When many a league from shore
> The kraken's[6] snort we hear,
> And whirling Maelström's roar,
> 'Tis then we'll talk of fear.

---

[6] In a work like the present, a description of this much celebrated monster ought not to be omitted, and we insert, therefore, the account given of it in the Natural History of Norway, by Bishop Pontoppidan, in his own words:—
" I now come to the third, and, without doubt, the greatest marine monster in the world, called the kraken or kraxen, or, as some have it, the crab, which name seems to answer best to the appearance of this round, flat animal, full of arms and branches. Our fishermen relate (all with one story and without the slightest contradiction), that when in warm summer days they have rowed out a number of leagues to sea, where usually there is a depth of from eighty to one hundred fathoms, they sometimes find only thirty, twenty, or less, and are then certain of taking fish in the greatest abundance. This is a sign that the kraken is under them, and they lose no time to profit by the circumstance, so that sometimes a score or more boats are assembled together, within a moderate circumference.

They have only to take the precaution of ascertaining, by means of their leads, whether the depth remains the same or diminishes. In the latter case not a moment must be lost.

Thor asked only to be put to the proof, and now begged to be allowed to take with him what he might want for his fishing. Hymir assented, telling him that for bait he would find a grub amongst the cows. Thor went into the field, and a wild bull rushing towards him, he seized it by the horns and brake off its head, and then throwing it over his shoulders leaped the enclosure, and hastened to Hymir, who was getting the boat ready.

They give over fishing, and row away with all their might, until they get into the usual depth. There, resting on their oars, in a short time they see this unparalleled monster rise to the surface, that is, not its whole body, (which probably no human eye ever yet beheld, except in its young,) but merely the upper portion of it which, according to eye-witnesses, is about a mile and a half in circumference, many say more, but I take the least for surety. This, at first, has the appearance of a reef of low rocks covered with something which resembles floating sea-weed. At length appear a number of shining points and jags, which are thicker the higher they are seen above the surface. Sometimes they are as high as a moderate ship's mast, but strong enough to drag down the largest ship of war. After a short time the kraken begins to sink, when the danger is as great as before, for the whirlpool caused by the descent of its body is so powerful that it draws in every thing near it, like the Maelström. From the long observation of fishermen, it appears that this animal feeds for several months together, and during the succeeding months evacuates its food in a substance resembling mud, which discolours the water, and attracts immense shoals of fish of every species, and when a sufficient number are assembled

When Hymir the bull's head
On the youth's shoulders saw,
He laugh'd, and own'd the deed
Was good for one so raw.
Then shoved the boat from shore,
Swift through the waves it flew,
Hymir plied well his oar,
And Thor row'd stoutly too.

The god now became elated at the near prospect

---

over him, he swallows up his thoughtless guests, who in their turn serve as a trap for others of a similar taste."—The Bishop continues :—" As it is not to be expected that an occasion should speedily occur of examining this terrible monster alive, it is the more to be regretted that no one profited by one rare opportunity. In the year 1684, a kraken (probably young and heedless) came into Ulvangen Fjord, in the province of Bergen, and stretching out its feelers, which it seems to employ as a snail does its horns, they got entangled in some trees near the Fjord, and in the crevices of the rocks, so that it could not get loose again but died and rotted, the stench arising from it being so great, that for a long time after a part of Ulvangen's Fjord could not be passed by persons of delicate smell." The fishermen in the north of Norway still believe in the existence of the kraken, and a story somewhat similar to the above was related to the author at Dronthem a few years ago. The Maelström is scarcely less celebrated than the kraken. It was a terrific whirlpool in the Lofodden islands, the noise of which was said to be heard at a great distance, and its strength so great as to engulph everything which approached it. It was supposed to be caused by a vast hole which went through the earth. Many of measuring himself with the serpent, and gave full liberty to his thoughts. If he could succeed in slaying it,

> " By Yggdrasill,[7] the feat
> Would glad me more, by far,
> In Valhall than to beat
> Ten score Einheriar.
>
> What fruitful seeds of ill
> To mar man's mortal state,

---

have denied the existence of any whirlpool at all in these islands, but Von Buch (no mean authority) maintains the affirmative, and explains the phenomenon as follows.—" In all the streights between the Lofodden islands, the current runs with great rapidity, on which account they bear for the most part such names as Grim-ström, Nass-ström, Sund-ström, &c. and in the long canals, where the influence of the tide reaches but partially, a bonâ fide waterfall is produced, similar to that under the old London bridge, only in a much greater degree. Such is the celebrated Maelström near the islands Moskoe and Veroe. These currents change their direction with the ebb and flow four times a day, but the Maelström is only dangerous when the north-west wind blows violently in a contrary direction to the ebb. Then the conflict of the meeting waters is truly terrific, whatever approaches the whirlpool, whether boat or fish, is engulphed, and its roar is heard at sea at a great distance. The expectation of mariners is almost always disappointed, for these violent winds are rare in summer, the only time at which they visit these seas."

[7] The name of the great Ash.

And earth with woes to fill,
From the worm emanate!
His pestilential breath
Fevers and plagues doth cause,
And each disease to death
Which man untimely draws.

When one in manhood's prime
Feels his approaching end
And ere yet lapsed his time,
To Hela's power must bend;
When his heart-broken spouse
Sees hope's last promise fail,
Then his fell might he'll rouse
To mock the widow's wail.

Her babe, which will not rest
When the pale mother clasps,
And gives in vain the breast,
Struggling for life it gasps.
Poor babe, as early rose
Late fresh—she sees its eye
In death for ever close—
Nor weeps for agony:

When one, who purely burns,
Absent for many a year,
To his true love returns
And finds her on her bier.
When from a mourning realm
Some virtuous prince is ta'en,
Or chief has bow'd his helm;
Then sure the foul snake's seen

Writhing for joy. Their birth
All serpents, which infest
Man's central spot of earth,
Draw from his nostril's blast.
The great snake, whose wide jowl,
(To th' southwards, far away)
Will gulp a raging bull,
Through him first saw the day.

Its tail wound round an oak
It watcheth long its prey,
Which from th' affrighted flock
Struggling it drags away.
Others, with diamond eyes,
To Askur's mortal race,
Death-doom'd! though less in size,
Alas! not fatal less.

Fair sight their forms to view
Basking in new-donn'd sheen,
To theirs the violet's blue
Must yield, or emerald's green:
They know, by wizard gaze,
Coil'd 'neath some leafy bower,
Their prey with fear to glaze,
And charm him to their power.

Gaunt Fenris, Loptur's son,
Who loves to prowl the night,
Bewilder'd travellers down
Hurling from rocky height:
When bloody treason's rife,
When for some murder foul

The bandit whets his knife,
The wolf for joy doth howl.

All who delight in blood
From him beginning have,
From him the tiger brood
Th' hyæna's traitor laugh;
The like each robber beast,
Which from the fair light shrinks,
Fitchet of plunderers least,
Marten, and fox, and lynx.

For nought hath Fenris ruth,
When midnight winds blow hoarse,
His sacrilegious tooth
Tears from its grave the corse—
Still 'twere my chiefest joy
The foul worm and his brood
Of reptiles to destroy.
Grieves me that man the food

Of crawling worms should be—
This slain his life should pass,
From loathsome sickness free,
In years of happiness.
And, when th' o'er-peopled earth
No more her sons could feed,
The bravest should stand forth,
And like good warriors bleed.

" Not hatred should unsheath
Their swords, nor lust of power,
But a soul-warming wrath
Gone, when the fight was o'er;

From some dark cloud the fray
I'd watch, my bolts in hand
The boldest on their way
To Odin's hall to send."

Thus mused the Aser Thor,
And pull'd with all his might,
Each time he struck his oar
The dark-green wave turn'd white.
The more his anger burn'd
The huge boat sped the more,
Seem'd as the waves it spurn'd
Skimming like Dolphin o'er—

So swiftly on it flew,
The sides began to split,
The sea so fast came through,
The twain in water sit.
Quick Hymir sprang to bale
It out, and loud to roar,
(His giant-heart 'gan fail)
" Avast there! back your oar.

" An you keep on this rate
We soon to Ran shall go"—
Quoth Thor: " Take heart, must yet
A score good leagues or so."
" Score leagues!" cried Hymir: " why,
Art mad! mark'st not the storm!
E'en now I can descry
Where lies fell Midgard's worm."

" And what care I for worm!"
Cried Thor, the fisher good:

"The bleak north's bitterest storm
But fans my heated blood—
I love the tempest's roar—
Ha! there the foul worm struck,
Now I'll take in mine oar,
And try with line my luck."

Then, rising to full height,
The iron kedge he took,
Which, though it seem'd him light,
Must serve him for a hook.
The gory bullock's head
He took him for a bait—
The giant, pale with dread,
In the stern, trembling, sate.

For line he next made loose
His belt, and one end pass'd
Twice round his waist, with noose
Well bound to th' other fast
The baited hook he tied,
And in the ocean threw :
O'er the boat's yielding side
The girdle, hissing, flew.
Oehlenschläger.

" It must be confessed," says the Prose Edda, " that Thor here made quite as great a fool of Jormungandur as Utgard's-Lok did of him, when the giant king caused him to lift up the worm believing it was a cat. The worm gulped down the ox's head so ravenously, that the hook stuck deep in his jaws. As soon as he perceived this, he plunged with such violence, that both Thor's fists struck against the sides of the boat, on which the god's anger got up and his strength at the same time, and he pulled so furiously against the snake, that both his legs went through the boat, and he remained standing on the bottom of the sea. He now pulled up the serpent to the edge of the boat, and, to say the truth, it was a terrible sight to see Thor look so grim at the serpent, and the serpent all the while gaping and spewing out poison against Thor. It is reported also that the giant Hymir changed colour, and became white with fear, when he saw the snake, and the dark blue sea breaking through the sides of the boat.

In the same moment Thor seized hold of his hammer and swung it round in the air, but the giant fumbled about for his knife, and scored Thor's knot over, by which means the snake got loose and sank down to the bottom of the sea. Thor threw his hammer after it, and it has been asserted that he thus knocked its head off against the breakers. But I think that it is pretty certain that the Midgard's worm still lives and lies in the sea. Thor then lifted his arm and gave Hymir such a cuff on the side of the head that he fell overboard, and the soles of his feet were turned up in the air, but Thor waded to shore.

THOR'S FISHING.

On the dark bottom of the great salt lake
Emprison'd lay the giant snake,
With nought his sullen sleep to break.

Huge whales disported amorous o'er his neck,
Little their sports the worm did reck,
Nor his dark, vengeful thoughts would check.

To move his iron fins he hath no power,
Nor yet to harm the trembling shore,
With scaly rings he's cover'd o'er.

His head he seeks mid coral rocks to hide,
Nor e'er hath man his eye espied,
Nor could its deadly glare abide.

His eye-lids half in drowsy stupor close,
But short and troubled his repose.
As his quick, heavy breathing shows:

Muscles and crabs, and all the shelly race,
In spacious banks still crowd for place,
A grisly beard, around his face.

When Midgard's worm his fetters strives to break,
Riseth the sea, the mountains quake;
The fiends in Nastrond [8] merry make.

Rejoicing flames from Hecla's cauldron flash,
Huge molten stones, with deafening crash
Fly out—its scathed sides fire-streams wash.

The affrighted sons of Askur feel the shock
As the worm doth lie and rock,
And, sullen, waiteth Ragnarok.

---

[8] Nastrond, the Scandinavian hell.

To his foul craving maw nought e'er came ill,
It never he doth cease to fill,
Nath'-more his hungry pain can still.

Upwards by chance he turns his sleepy eye,
And over him suspended, nigh,
The gory head he doth espy.

The serpent, taken with his own deceit,
Suspecting nought the daring cheat,
Ravenous, gulps down the bait.

His leathern jaws the barbed steel compress,
His pond'rous head must leave th' abyss,
Dire was Jormungandur's hiss.

In giant coils he writhes his length about,
Poisonous streams he speweth out,
But his struggles help him nought:

The mighty Thor knoweth no peer in fight:
The loathsome worm, his strength despite,
Now o'er-matched, must yield the fight.

His grisly head Thor heaveth o'er the tide,
No mortal eye the sight may bide,
The scared waves haste i' th' sands to hide.

As when accursed Nastrond yawns and burns,
His impious throat 'gainst heaven he turns,
And with his tail the ocean spurns.

The parched sky droops, darkness enwraps the sun,
Now the matchless strength is shown
Of the god whom warriors own.

Around his loins he draws his girdle tight,
His eye with triumph flashes bright,
The frail boat splits aneath his weight:

The frail boat splits—but on the ocean's ground
Thor again hath footing found;
Within his arms the worm is bound:—

Hymir, who in the strife no part had took,
But like a trembling aspen shook,
Rouseth him t' avert the stroke.

" In the last night, the Vala [9] hath decreed
Thor, in Odin's utmost need,
To the worm shall bow the head."

Thus in sunk voice the craven Giant spoke,
Whilst from his belt a knife he took,
Forged by dwarfs aneath the rock:

Upon the magic belt straight 'gan to file;
Thor in bitter scorn to smile;
Miölner swang in air the while.

In the worm's front full two-score leagues it fell,
From Gimle to the realms of hell,
Echoed Jormungandur's yell.

The ocean yawn'd, Thor's lightnings rent the sky,
Through the storm, the great Sun's eye,
Look'd out on the fight from high.

Bifrost [10] i' th' east shone forth in brightest green,
On its top, in snow-white sheen,
Heimdal, at his post, was seen.

---

[9] The Vala or prophetess, whose celebrated song, the Voluspa, is one of the most curious relics of Scandinavian Mythology.

[10] Bifrost, the rainbow, the bridge of the gods, the preponderance of the green indicated the hope of the Aser that their most formidable enemy was about to be overcome.

On the charm'd belt the dagger hath no power,
The star of Jotunheim 'gan lour;
But now in Asgard's evil hour,

When all his efforts foil'd tall Hymir saw,
Wading to the serpent's maw,
On the kedge he 'gan to saw.

The sun, dismay'd, hasten'd in clouds to hide,
Heimdall turn'd his head aside;
Thor was humbled in his pride.

The knife prevails, far down beneath the main
The serpent, spent with toil and pain,
To the bottom sank again.

The giant fled his head mid rocks to save,
Fearfully the God did rave,
With his lightnings tore the wave:

To madness stung to think his conquest vain,
His ire no longer could contain,
Dared the worm to rise again:

His radiant form to its full height he drew,
And Miölner through the billows blue
Swifter than the fire-bolt flew.

Hoped, yet, the worm had fallen beneath the stroke,
But the wily child of Loke
Waits her turn at Ragnarok.[11]

His hammer lost, back wends the giant-bane,
Wasted his strength, his prowess vain;
And Miölner must with Ran remain.

Oehlenschläger.

---

[11] At the great battle of Ragnarokur, Thor and the serpent destroy each other.

CHAPTER VII.

THE VANER—NJORD—SKADA—FREYR AND GERDA—SKIRNER—FREYA, HNOS AND GERSIME—ODDUR—SIOFNE—LOFNA—VAR—SIN—HEIMDALL—BIFROST.

THE Vaner are often mentioned in the Eddas as being of a different race from the Aser, and the epithet of wise is usually applied to them. They were said to have had much commerce with the Aser previously to the departure of the latter from the original Asgard, on the banks of the Tanais or Vanaquivl, and a long war was carried on between the two nations, which terminated in an exchange of hostages, the Aser giving Mimer and Hænir, and receiving Njord and Freyr in return. Njord obtained the sovereignty over the winds, and it was he who checked the fury of the sea, of storms, and of fire.

Vanaheim, or the region inhabited by the Vaner, represents the region of air, and is often called also Vindheim, or the home of the winds. Njord's peculiar residence was called Noatun. He was lord over all inland waters, and the protector of sea-faring men, and therefore to be invoked before setting out on any voyage or fishing expedition. He was the giver of fruitfulness, ease and wealth, and was himself exceedingly rich. As Vaner or spirit of air he watched over temples and places of worship, which in the beginning were without covering. Njord was often in league with Ægir, the god of the sea.

> Njord, who with ocean's god,[1]
> Full oft in league is found,
> Loves o'er the raging flood
> In swift career to bound.
> Skimming each billow's back,
> Loud neighs his coal-black steed,
> On the calm wave no track
> He leaves—so great his speed.
> *Oehlenschläger.*

It was a custom amongst the Vaner for brothers and sisters to marry, and, previously to his reception amongst the Aser, Njord had two children by his sister, namely, Freyr and Freya. He afterwards married Skada, the daughter of the Giant Thiasse, who was killed by Thor, and the occasion of their marriage was as follows:

When Skada heard how her father had been

---

[1] Vid. c. 2.

slain, she took her helmet and arms, and set out for Asgard to avenge him. The Aser offered her an amicable arrangement and atonement, and it was agreed that she should choose a husband from amongst them, but that, whilst making the choice, her eyes should be blinded. Perceiving, however, feet which were small and well shaped, she cried out: " I choose this one: Baldur is without blemish," but it was not Baldur, it was Njord from Noatun.

The new married pair could never agree about their place of residence, Njord desiring to live near the sea, and his bride amongst the rocks and mountains, where her father used to dwell. At length it was agreed that they should pass, alternately, nine days on the mountain at Thrymheim, and three days by the sea at Noatun. This arrangement, however, did not last long; they separated, and she was married to Odin, by whom she had several sons, of whom Seming was the most noted.

Since that time she has lived on the mountains, hunting and running on snow-shoes.[2] It was she

---

[2] For Magnussen's explanation of the fable of the marriage of Njord and Skada, see ch. 1. p. 39. He is of opinion that the spring or May-festival, which prevailed throughout the North, was originally in commemoration of this event. The

who hung the poisonous snake over Loke's head, in revenge for the abuse which he poured on her at Ægir's feast.

Njord was probably a deity of greater importance than would appear from the little said of him in the Prose Edda, witness the solemn oath of the old Scandinavians, *" So help me Freyr and Njord and the mighty Aser."*[3]

Freyr, Njord's son, although born in Vanaheim, was considered as one of the chief of the Aser. He was the lord of the sun and the rain, and dispensed fruitfulness over the earth. The gods gave him Alf-heim, or the kingdom of the Light Elves, as a present, on the occasion of his cutting his first teeth. He was to be invoked for peace and good times, and the first Runic letter ⚡ was called after him.

One day Freyr was tempted by curiosity to ascend to Odin's throne in Hlidskialf, and, looking

---

magpie (Danicé Skada) was sacred to this goddess, and is still held in superstitious reverence throughout Scandinavia.

[3] The person about to take the oath advanced towards the altar, and dipping a ring in the blood of the victim upon it, not unfrequently a human one, pronounced the above words. The mighty Aser might be Odin or Thor, most probably the latter, since that god is often represented sitting between two other figures, probably Njord and Freyr, the thunder god between the two Vaner, deities of the atmosphere.

over all the world, his eye at length rested on a large building in the north, from which there issued a maiden of such surpassing beauty that the splendour of it lighted up the whole country round. This maiden was Gerda, a daughter of Gymer, a giant.

As a punishment for his presumptuousness in having sat upon Odin's holy seat, Freyr was seized with a violent passion for this maiden, so that he would neither converse, sleep, nor drink, and no one ventured to speak to him.

At length Njord called Skirner, his armour-bearer and companion, the same who had been sent by Odin to the dwarfs to procure the chain with which Fenris was bound, and directed him to learn from his son the cause of his anger. Skirner, after some hesitation, ventured to address him.

SKIRNER.

[4] Tell me this, Freyr!
Prince amongst gods,
Which I desire to know—
Why dost thou sit alone
In the spacious hall—
Lord! the live-long day.

---

[4] The following is a literal translation from the Poetic Edda.

FREYR.

How shall I tell thee,
Thou young man!
My great sorrow of heart;
For the rays of the Elves[5]
Shine out every day,
But gladden not my soul.

SKIRNER.

Thy sorrow, I trow,
Is scarce so great
That thou may'st not tell it to me;
We have lived together
In the morning of childhood,
We two should trust each other.

FREYR.

In Gymer's court
I have seen a maiden
For whom I long.
Her arms shone
So that air and sea
Were brighten'd therewith.
I love the maid more ardently
Than e'er loved youth
In the spring of his days.
Yet of Aser or Elves[6]

---

[5] The Light Elves who lived in the region of the sun, of which Freyr was the symbol, were poetically supposed to be the dispensers of its rays.

[6] The Aser would be naturally averse to any alliance between their race and that of the giants.

> None will permit
> That we should live together.

Skirner then offered, if Freyr would give him his courser, to bear him through flames; and his sword, to wield against the giants; to undertake to woo the maiden for him. Having mounted, Skirner thus addressed his horse:

> It is murk without,
> It is time for us to hasten
> Over the misty mountains,
> Through the land of the Thurser.
> We will return together,
> Or we will both be taken
> By that powerful Giant.

He rode to Jotunheim to Gymer's house. There were savage hounds bound before the gate of the court. Seeing a herdsman sitting on a hillock, he rode towards him and said:

> Tell me, Herdsman!
> Who sittest on a hill,
> Watching the way;
> How shall I succeed
> To speak with the young maiden,
> For Gymer's hounds?

HERDSMAN.

> Art thou about to die,
> Or already one of the dead?

> Never shalt thou speak
> With Gymer's daughter.

SKIRNER.

> A better remedy
> Than lamentation, has he
> Who willingly confronts death.
> For but a day and a night
> Has mine age been doomed
> And my life destined by the fates.

Gerda hearing the noise without, sent one of her maidens to enquire the cause of it; who brought back word that a stranger had arrived and just dismounted from his horse. Gerda desired her to invite him in to drink mead. On his entrance she said:

> Who art thou of the Elves,
> Or the sons of the Aser,
> Or of the wise Vaner?
> Why comest thou hither, alone,
> Over raging flames,
> To visit our hall?

Skirner denied that he was one of the race of the Elves, or of the Aser, or of the Vaner; but, taking eleven golden apples from his breast, he offered them to her, if she would bestow her love on Freyr. Gerda refused the apples, and declared that she and Freyr should never live together. He next offered Odin's magic ring, which she rejected also. Skirner now drew Freyr's sword, and threatened to behead her if she did not accept Freyr as her husband; but Gerda was not to be intimidated, and merely said that she foresaw that if Skirner and her father met, there would be bloodshed between them. Seeing that she feared not death, Skirner told her that he would shut her up in a cavern where no eye should see her, that she should there lose her beauty, and when she was suffered to depart should have a form so hideous, as to fill all who saw her with horror, so that she should become a byword to gods and giants. He added, that she should be wedded, moreover, to a three-headed Trold, or remain for ever husbandless, a prey to fiery passion.

None of these threats, however, seeming to make any impression on Gerda, Skirner continued:

>I went to the mountain,
>To the dewy wood,
>To search out a magic wand;
>The magic wand I found.
>
>Odin is wroth with thee;
>The first of Aser is wroth with thee;
>Freyr shall shun thee,
>Thou maid of evil!

Nor shalt thou escape
The powerful vengeance of the gods.

Hear it, ye Giants!
Hear it, spirits of the frost,
Sons of Suttung!
And ye friends of the Aser,[7]
How I prohibit,
How I shut out the maid
From the converse of man.

I carve thee, Thurs![8]
And characters three,
Impotence, frenzy, and impatience.

Gerda's resolution could not hold out against this threat, and without giving Skirner time to finish his incantation, she held out to him a cup full of mead in token of her yielding; saying that she had not thought that she should have ever bestowed her love on one of the race of the Vaner. Before he would leave her, however, Skirner made her name the day on which she would be Freyr's bride, and she agreed to meet him after nine nights in the wood Barre.

---

[7] This evocation included Giants of every kind, Dwarfs, Aser, Vaner, and Elves.

[8] Thurs was the name of the Runic letter þ (th), and together with the other three characters would have completed the spell which Gerda so much dreaded.

Skirner now rode homewards, and found Freyr on the look out for him.

> Tell me, Skirner!
> Ere thou tak'st saddle from steed
> Or advancest a step,
> How hast thou sped
> In Jotunheim,
> To thy or my desire?

SKIRNER.

> Barre is the name
> Of the pleasant grove,
> Which we both know:
> There after nights nine
> Njord's son and Gerda
> Shall embrace with passion.

FREYR.

> One night is long,
> Two are long,
> How shall I hold out for three!
> Often hath a month
> Appeared to me shorter
> Than the half of the nights of desire.

Gerda kept her promise, and Freyr rewarded Skirner with his famous sword. This was the reason why he was weaponless in his contest with Bele, whom he slew with a hart's horn; but the time will come when he will have more reason to regret his loss, when the sons of Muspell issue out to fight the Aser.

Freyr's sister, Freya, was the goddess of love, and herself unrivalled in grace and beauty. She was the kindest of all goddesses, and fond of singing. Her residence in Vingolf was called Folkvangur, whither all maidens of birth, and those who killed themselves, hoped to come. Oehlenschläger has given a full description of the goddess and of her palace.

——— Freya's hall,
With precious gems o'erlaid,
Stands in a lonely vale,
Which rose-tree forests shade;
Swans, white as virgin snow,
There on the calm lakes sail,
Lovers, who ne'er brake vow,
Tell there their ardent tale.

But in Folkvangur's bower
Nought like its matchless queen;
Mid many a beauteous flower
No flower like her, I ween.
Her form so round and slight,
Her look which love doth beam,
Her step as Zephyr's light,
Exceeds e'en poet's dream.

Each small, white, taper hand
A blushing rose doth bear,
Which through her faery land

Breathe forth their fragrant air.
Their sweets no guardian thorn
From rude touch needs defend,
'Tis they to even and morn
The roseate tints which lend.

Like her no goddess kind,
She saves from wounds and death,
Her sigh—the sweet south wind
O'er the wild flowers doth breathe.[9]
Round tears for mortal woe
Each morn her blue eyes fill,
Which on the flowers below
In purest dew distill.

Her daughters Siofna[10] hight
And Hnos, with amber hair,
Not e'en the spirits of light
Can boast of aught so fair.
Whate'er is passing bright
On earth, from Hnos we call:
Siofna gives slumbers light,
The morn on pure souls fall.

Oehlenschläger.

Freya had an equal share with Odin in the spirits of those slain in fight; an allusion to the wars and bloodshed caused by the passion of love. Her

---

[9] O, it came o'er mine ear like the sweet south,
That breathes upon a bank of violets.
Twelfth Night, Act i. Sc. 2.

[10] Freya's daughters were Hnos and Gersime, Siofna was only one of her followers.

chariot was drawn by two cats or leopards, and, after Frigga, she was the most powerful of the goddesses. She had two beautiful daughters, Hnos and Gersime, by her husband Odr, or Oddur. They were so fair, says the Edda, that everything that was beautiful upon earth was called after them. Respecting Oddur the Edda only says that he travelled far away, and that Freya was so attached to him that she followed him over all the world, weeping tears of gold.

Notwithstanding this proof, however, of conjugal affection, she was by no means celebrated for her chastity, and amongst others she is accused of having bestowed her favours on four dwarfs in succession, as a price for her matchless gold chain, Brysing, their workmanship.

In her journey after Oddur through so many countries she received various names,—Marthaul, Forn, Hæn, Gafn, Syr, and Vana-dis, or the goddess of the Vaner. Her name was given to the sixth day of the week, and all women of distinction were called after her.[11] She was the goddess of the moon, and in the north the constellation, Orion's belt, still bears the name of Freya's spinning wheel.

---

[11] In Danish the word Frue, in German Frau, answers to our lady.

Oehlenschläger, in his poem of the Vaner, profiting by the obscurity of the Edda respecting Freya's husband Oddur, has converted him into Bacchus or Osiris, who in their Indian expeditions might have very well fallen in with the gods of Caucasian Asgard, themselves of Indian descent.[12] As the poem is not long, and there can be no more faithful or more agreeable interpreter of the Edda than Oehlenschläger, it can scarcely be deemed out of place.here.

THE VANER.

When the gods of wide Valhalla
Ruled of yore in eastern land,
Far away, mid Asia's mountains,
Near where Vana[13] rolls his sand;

---

[12] Speaking of the festival of Rama and Seeta, at Allahabad, Bishop Heber remarks: " I was never so forcibly struck with the identity of Rama and Bacchus. Here were Bacchus (Rama), his brother Ampelus (Luchmun), the Satyrs smeared with wine-lees commanded by Pan (the monkey army, their bodies died. with Indigo, led on by the divine monkey genéral Huniman). The fable, however, can hardly have originated in India, and has been imported, probably, both by Greeks and Brahmins, from Cashmire or some other central country of the grape."—*Heber's Journal.*

[13] Vana, or Vanaquivl, the Tanais or Don.

Ere they hither, northwards wended,
Where tall glaciers break the flood,
Ere they blended
Hostile dwarfs' and giants' blood;

Then were wont the skilful Vaner
Oft to Asgard to repair;
Vaner, famed for hidden wisdom,
Arts and manners debonair;
They the Aser first instructed
Flowers to plant, to till the earth,
There conducted,
Hostage, Njord, of noble birth.

When in sultry heat of summer,
Earth is parch'd and fevers rule:
If Njord mount his coal-black courser,
Air and earth once more are cool.
Njord the skies with rain-clouds covers,
Hides awhile, the fair blue sky;
Anxious hovers
O'er the murk storm passing by.

Njord was wed by law of Vaner:
Heeded nought blood's holy tie,
Children twain had of his sister,
Blue-eyed Freya, lofty Frey.
Fair as spring flowers earth which gladden,
All with joy their charms behold:
Swain and maiden
Own their beauty—young and old.

When Valhalla's mighty princes
From their native vales went forth,

Fire of southern clime to mingle
With the cold blood of the north;
Asgard's warriors nought contented,
Till Njord to their prayer they'd won;
Njord relented,
Follow'd too with maid and son.

Odin spake: "The north invites us
With its mountains, pine o'er-grown;
With its lakes, and falls, and rivers,
And dark woods to ocean down:
Spite of foe or hostile barrier,
Soon we'll reach the verdant shore,
Thor, the warrior,
There shall lead our chiefs to war.

"Soon its tyrant, giant rulers,
'Fore our conquering spears shall bow,
Soon shall rise a loftier Asgard,
Where clear mead in streams shall flow,
When with cold north's iron race
Fiery east shall mingle blood—
From the embrace
Think what matchless warrior brood!"

Njord in front, on winged charger,
Leads the sacred squadrons on;
Dries up marshes, levels mountains,
Beats the compact forests down;
Thick, opposing clouds doth sever,
Shows the winds the vessel's course
Restless ever,
Wearies ne'er his mettled horse.

'Twas a goodly sight to look on
Njord glide through the cloudy way,
With his dark steed's pinions waving,
Like a dream in morning grey;
Swift as light—o'er horse-neck pendent—
Past, e'er yet well seen from far—
Beams resplendent
On his helm the morning star.

And without benignant Vaner
What were th' Aser in the North?
What thy wisdom, mighty Odin?
What, great Thor! thy prowess worth?
Freyr calls forth the quickening waters,
Makes fair fruits in deserts grow;
On earth's daughters
Freya beauty doth bestow.

Freya once had husband, godlike,
He, in Asgard, Oddur hight,
Him she met beyond the Ganges,
Victor god, in morion bright.
Youths and maids, with flutes and cymbals,
Follow, shouting, joyous throng,
Ocean trembles,
Earth re-echoes with their song.

In his golden chariot seated,
See him in his proud career,
Tawny lions, mottled tigers,
Crouching at his feet for fear;
The forest's lords the car rolls after,
Maids with timbrels dance before,
Shouts and laughter
Drown e'en father ocean's roar.

Wondering at th' unwonted clamour,
Rugged men start from the glade,
Trembling, gazing, leaping, shouting,
Half enraptured, half afraid.
Oddur calm'd their groundless terror,
Charm'd them with his magic lay,
Held his mirror,
Shew'd to peace and wealth the way.

On south slope of sun-gilt mountain,
Near a river swift and clear,
First the stocks divine he planted,
Which the luscious berry bear;
Soon he taught the simple nation
Press the sugar'd purple blood,
Love's hot passion
From the nectar takes its food.

Freya, once bewilder'd roaming,
Chanced the treacherous drink to sip:
Oddur, drunk with wine and pleasure,
Watch'd the rich juice kiss her lip:
Oddur now in manhood's flower,
Grapes and vine-leaves wreathed his hair,
From his bower
Raptured view'd the goddess fair.

Oddur saw how Freya musing,
In a soft delirium lay;
At her feet his burning passion
Told, could Freya turn away?
Feather'd choir their pleasures vaunted,
Violets were their bridal bed,
Earth, enchanted,
Thousand sweets around them shed.

P

Freya thus was spouse to Oddur,
Still together were they seen,
And when th' Aser left their city,
Oddur follow'd too his queen.
In his gold car drawn by leopards,
Sate the warrior with his bride,
Maids and shepherds
Sorrowing paced the car beside.

True, his sunny land t' abandon,
And vine hills, the god did grieve;[14]
But the grape's more vapid pleasures
Who for beauty would not leave!
Piled on high, in osier waggons,
Choicest wine with care he stores,
Which in flagons
Rist each noon to Odin pours.[15]

For though all less noble Aser
Quaff but cider, ale and mead,
Still for Odin, raven-monarch,
Oddur's purple grape must bleed.
Freya's heart with grief corroding,
When he quitted Valhal's shore;
Left to Odin
Of the nectar, Oddur, store.

---

[14] M. de Chaptal considers Iberia (now Georgia) near Mount Ararat, as the original country of the vine, which still grows wild there in great luxuriancy.

[15] It was the privilege of Rist and Mist, two of the Valkyrs, to pour out daily to Odin his wine, the only nourishment he ever took.

So they lived, the joy of Asgard,
Brighter dawn'd each golden morn,
Secret prayer of love-sick maiden,
On soft sighs, to them was borne.
And could love so pure, so holy,
Like a vision melt away?
Like youth's folly,
Scarce outlive a summer's day.

Idun, stol'n by false Loke's treason,
Long Valhalla's gods had wept,
And old age, with withering wrinkles,[16]
O'er each late full cheek had crept.
When for Freya, blooming, youthful,
Radiant with celestial charms,
Sorceress loathful
Oddur found within his arms;

Starting from the couch with horror,
" Ha! and am I thus deceived?
Was't for this then, foul enchantress!
Fondly I thy tale believed?
Spells worn out the cheat discover,
Now in native form thou'rt seen;
The charm over,
Henceforth, witch! thine arts are vain."

Freya's weeping nought avail'd her;
From her arms in wrath he tore,
From those arms, now shrunk and feeble,
Where he'd found his joy before.

---

[16] Vide page 91.

Not e'en one last farewell taking,
Mounted quick his golden car,
With heart aching,
Freya follow'd him from far.

But when Asgard's chiefest treasure
Coward Loke again retrieved;
Beauty's queen a prey to sorrow,
Still to witness, Odin grieved;
Full of wrath 'gainst fickle Oddur,
Breach of vow to punish bent,
Swift Hermodur,[17]
Arm'd with Runic staff, he sent.

Spirits sunk, with dark forebodings
Oddur secret shades had sought;
On his once loved, blooming Freya,
And fond dream of joy he thought;
Nymphs with loose hair, ivy-woven,
Dancing, sought to soothe his pain,
With feet cloven,
Satyrs sang and piped in vain.

Sick at heart, the sun's light loathing,
In the dark grove's thickest gloom,
Oddur thought in bitter anguish
On his joys soon wither'd bloom:
Bow'd to earth—his aching forehead
'Twixt his burning palms he prest,

---

[17] Hermodur was the son and messenger of Odin, and resembled Mercury or Hermes in attributes as well as in name. Odin gave him a helmet.

Visions horrid
Rack'd his brain, sobs rent his breast.

Hermod through the leaves stole on him,
On his head the Rune-stock laid,
And the heart-blood's fervid current,
Chill'd in death, at once was staid,
Thus, long since, the poet found him,
Changed into a senseless stone,
All around him
Vines and ivy wild had grown!

Long the goddess sought her lover,
O'er parch'd sands and mountains cold;
From her eyes, all swoln with weeping,
Dropp'd round tears of purest gold.
All, who 'neath love's fever languish,
Hence derive their burning care;
Freya's anguish
Each true lover's breast must share.
Oehlenschläger.

Besides her two beautiful daughters, Hnos and Gersime, Freya had four nymphs, attendants, each of whom presided over a particular department of that complicated passion of which their mistress was the supreme chief. Siofna was the goddess of first love: "It was her business," says the Edda, "to dispose favourably the minds of young people, both men and women, towards each other."

Lofna, the second of these Diser or nymphs, was mild and propitious to all who called on her. She received from Odin and Frigga the power to unite hearts in the bonds of love, to remove all obstacles which might stand in the way of true lovers, and to reconcile those who had quarrelled. Magnussen derives her name from the old word "*leyfa,*" to love, as that of Siofna, from "*Sion,*" sight, and "*sia,*" to see, since it is sight which causes first love.

Var or Vör is the goddess of betrothal. She hears the oaths and solemn engagements which lovers make to each other. She is wise but severe, and punishes with the utmost rigour those who break their troth.

Lastly, Sin is the door-keeper of Freya's palace, which she keeps closed against those who are not worthy to enter it. It is she who persecutes unfortunate lovers, either because their motives are impure, or that the attainment of their wishes would bring misfortune on them.

Thus could the Scandinavian Mythology boast a more complete, more beautiful, and infinitely a purer system of love than that of the Greeks. " Freya," remarks Magnussen, " was the goddess of true love and of wedded faith, and although her name has not been free from reproach, yet that reproach proceeded only from the slanderer Loke, who spared none, and from the Sagas written after the introduction of Christianity."[18]

---

[18] Magnussen.

Before we terminate this chapter on the Vaner, it will be necessary to speak of Heimdall who is often said to be of their race. He was one of the twelve principal Aser, the son of nine virgins, called the white, or bright Aser, also the god with golden teeth, his teeth being of that metal.

He was the warder of Asgard, and lived on the celestial mount, at the entrance of heaven close to the bridge Bifrost, which he ascended every morning early to observe all that was passing throughout the universe.

Bifrost was the bridge which the gods had to traverse in passing from heaven to earth. It was extremely solid and built with great art: mortals call it the Rainbow, and the red colour which is seen in it is a flaming fire, to serve as a defence against the giants.

Heimdall needed less sleep than a bird, and could see a hundred miles round him, by night as well as by day. No sound could escape him: he heard the grass grow in the earth, and the wool on the sheep's back. He had a horse, Gullintop, with a golden mane, and a sword called Höffud, also a trumpet (Gjallar-horn), the sound of which, when blown by him, was heard in all the worlds. It was with this that he was to awake the gods to the great fight at Ragnarokur. He was said to be the progenitor of the inhabitants of the north.

CHAPTER VIII.

THE ASH—THE THREE NORNIES—ELVES—DWARFS.

THE Prose Edda gives the following description of the sacred Ash, Yggdrasill. " The principal and most sacred tree of the gods is the Ash-tree, Yggdrasill, which is the best and greatest of all trees. Its branches extend over the whole universe, reaching beyond the heavens; its stem bears up the earth; its three roots stretch themselves wide around; one is amongst the Gods; another with the Frost-Giants, where Ginnungagap was before; the third covers Niffl-heim. Under this root is the fountain Hvergelmer, from which flow the infernal rivers, and in which lies the serpent-king, Nydhoggur, who is continually gnawing at the root. Under that root which is situated in the land of the giants, there is a well, in which all wisdom and prudence are hidden, and which belongs to Mimer. Under the root of the Aser is the well of the Norny, Urda, and it is here that the gods sit in judgment.

Near Urda's well stands a fair building, from

whence issue the three maidens, Urda, Verdandi, and Skulda. These maidens appoint the time that all men have to live, and are called Nornies. They take water each day from the well and pour it upon the Ash, lest its branches should perish. This water has so great virtue that whatever comes within the well remains white as the membrane of an egg. The dew which falls from Yggdrasill's branches is called honey-dew, and on this bees love to feed.

Two birds, called swans, were born in Urda's well, and from them were produced all birds of that species.

> I know where stands an Ash,
> It is called Ygg-drasill,
> A lofty tree, moistened
> With white waters;
> Thence comes the dew,
> Which falls in the valleys,
> Ever green, it grows
> Over Urda's well.
>
> Thither come the maids
> Who know much,
> Three from the hall
> Which lies by the tree;
> Urda they called the first;
> Verdandi the second;
> They scored on the shield
> Skulda, the third:

> They gave laws,
> They decreed life,
> To the children of men
> They deal out fate. *Voluspa.*

On the branches of the Ash sits an eagle who knows many things, and between his eyes is a hawk called Vedurfolgner, or the storm-damper. A squirrel, Ratatöskur (rain and snow-shower), runs up and down the tree, sowing strife betwixt the eagle and the serpent Nyd-hoggur. Four stags are constantly devouring the branches and roots of the Ash.

The Ash Yggdrasill (which word has been interpreted the dew-dropper, or bearer, or from another root the bearer of the thoughtful, an epithet of Odin, here put for heaven) is evidently a symbol of the earth. "Its branches," remarks Magnussen, "which spread over the whole world, are the atmosphere. The eagle who sits upon them represents the storms. The hawk or falcon (storm-damper) was supposed to fly the highest of all birds, and was therefore the symbol of the calm æther. The four stags, according to Gräter, were Time. The squirrel, whose name shews that he was the emblem of rain and snow, which falls from the air on the earth and the deep, and is thence drawn up again, is in northern latitudes white in winter and grey in summer. The Nornies, Urda,

Verdandi, and Skulda (or the past, the present, and the future), are not unfitly represented as preserving by their care the Ash from destruction. It is the same as the sacred tree of the Saxons, Irmensul."[1]

Of the origin of the three Nornies nothing is told us; they appear to have sprung up with the tree itself. Their doom was irrevocable, their wrath announced death. Urda (or the past) was the chief amongst them, and her protection was very powerful. Besides her sacred well, she had the charge of Odreyrer, or the vessel of wisdom and poetry. Of Verdandi (the present) little is said in the Eddas. Skulda (the future) was the youngest of the three Nornies. In her book all events that were to take place were written, and she is represented as riding with two of the Valkyrs, Gudr and Rota, before the van of the battle, pointing out the warriors who were to be slain.

The Nornies were said to weep over the fall of their favourites. The Gods themselves, who had but a dark foreboding of their destiny, used often to consult them.

There were inferior Nornies, sprung some from the Aser, some from the Elves, some from the Dwarfs. It was the business of these to spin the

---

[1] Magnussen.

thread of fate for new-born children, to aid women in child-birth, and some of them were always present to determine the destiny of the infant. The name of Nornies was given also to witches and fortune-tellers, and a bier was called " the Nornies' stool."

It is now time to speak of the Alfer or Elves. They were of two kinds—the white, or Light Elves, who were immortal, very beautiful, and of a beneficent nature; the Black Elves, often confounded with the Dwarfs, and who were subject to death.

The Light Elves were under the sway of Freyr, the god of the sun, and were thought to give good crops, to preserve cattle from danger, or, if offended, to cause avalanches, conflagrations, &c. On this account sacrifices called Alfa-blot, were offered to them. They could assume all shapes, particularly those of four-footed beasts and birds, and used often to appear in dreams.

It was believed that every man had his Elf or Norny, whose business it was to forewarn him of impending dangers, and to help him out of them when they arrived. The Elves were of various ranks; those of the highest took charge of men of distinction, the inferior ones of the lower orders of the people. The ancient laws of Iceland commenced by recommending mariners, on approaching the shore, to remove from their vessels such figure-heads as represented dragons or other monsters, for fear of irritating or frightening away the good Elves. When a prince was unfortunate in war his Norny was said to have left him.

The peasants in Denmark and Norway still believe in the existence of Elves, and in fact these minor deities continue to this day to occupy no unimportant place in the superstitions of all the people of Gothic descent. The Swedes still class them into bad and good. The latter reside in the air, frolic on the sward, or sit on the leaves of trees: the former dwell under ground, and bring with them sickness and ill-luck.

As the Elves may be considered intermediate beings between the Aser and men, so the Dwarfs seem to occupy the same position between men and the Giants or evil spirits. These pigmy deities are often confounded in the Eddas, although their natures were essentially different. The Dwarfs were originally engendered, like maggots, in the dead body of the giant Ymer, but at the command of Odin received the human shape and reason. They are represented as deformed, little men, with huge oblong heads and flat noses. Their dwelling-places were in the earth and in stones, and four of them, whose names were East, West, North, and South, were placed by Odin at the four corners of heaven, where they rule over the four winds. They were a bustling industrious race, loving and highly skilled in all mechanical arts, particularly turning and smith's work. Odin's spear, Thor's hammer, Sif's hair, Freya's golden chain, the ring Drupner, the ship Skidbladner, and many other masterpieces, were the productions of their skill. They knew also how to cut and explain Runes, to interpret the dreams of the gods, and could render themselves invisible or appear as spirits to men.

> Full many a cunning work,
> In cavern smithy wrought,
> Gauntlet and helm and dirk,
> To Asgard's sons they've brought.
>
> A dwarf, was Brokur hight,
> Thor's matchless hammer gave,
> Breathes not, I trow, the wight
> Its desperate swing might brave;
> The like his girdle rare,
> And Odin's spear and ring,
> Freyr's ship, and Sif's gold hair,
> And many a costly thing.
> *Oehlenschläger.*

Like all other beings who dwell under the earth, they could not endure the light of the sun, but if surprised by it were immediately converted to stone. Two of them are called in the Edda Ny and Næ (the increase and wane of the moon), and the names given to them in the Voluspa are, for the most part, indicative of elementary qualities; for example—wind, blast, gleam, light, day-finder, frost-giver, sleep-giver, ice-berg, dropper, &c. Their chief was Modsognur, and Durinn the second.

At Ragnarokur the Dwarfs take no part in the contest, but are represented as standing at the entrance of their caves, weeping and wringing their hands. Their general character is, however, cruel and vindictive.

The belief in them still lingers in the North, especially amongst the Norwegians and Icelanders, with whom all rare natural productions are yet called " *Dverg-smidi*" (Dwarfs-smith's work), and the echo " *Dverg-mal*" (the Dwarfs' song), from the superstitious belief that they thus answered the questions of mortals.

It appears, in fact, that ancient Scandinavia was scarcely less thickly peopled with subordinate elementary deities than Greece herself. They had a great variety of names, and were believed to exist in the sea, waterfalls, rivers, fountains, woods, meadows, mountains, caverns, &c. To use the words of Finn Magnussen: " Millions of Light Elves await only a signal from Freyr to drive from the sleepy earth the dark genii of night; Odin's Valkyrs hover over the battle field, gleam in the

Aurora Borealis and in portentous meteors, or come to the aid of warriors in danger of shipwreck; Njord's daughters play on the billows, in the midst of tempests; mermaids and mermen and various kinds of water-spirits people the ocean; the Black Elves dwelt in trees and mountains; the taciturn Dwarfs with hammer and apron smelted gold and precious stones in the bowels of the earth." Every waterfall, spring and river had its presiding Norny, or spirit; some male some female.

One of the most skilful of the Dwarfs was Brokur or Brokkur, with whom Loke once wagered his head, that Brokkur and his brother Sindri could not produce three such masterpieces of art as Sif's golden hair, which grew on her head like natural hair :[2] the ship Skidbladner, which, whenever its sails were set, was sure of a fair wind, and at the same time that it was of sufficient size to hold all the gods with ease, might, if necessary, be taken to pieces and put in the pocket; and, lastly, Odin's famous sword Gugner, which had never been known to fail him who used it.

All these had been made by the sons of the Dwarf Ivallda, at the request of Lok, who having for a jest cut off Siff's hair, could only escape

---

[2] Vide page 228.

Thor's vengeance by promising to obtain for her new hair of gold.

Brokkur accepted the wager, and the two brothers set to work and made—first, the boar Gullinbörste; second, the ring Draupner, and lastly the hammer Miölner. The last had been nearly spoiled through Loke's malice, who changed himself into a wasp and set himself upon Brok's eye-brow whilst he was blowing the bellows, so that he was obliged to stop for the pain of the sting.

It was agreed that Odin, Thor and Freyr should be umpires. Loke gave Odin the sword Gungner; to Freyr Skidbladner; and to Thor the hair for Sif, explaining at the same time the virtues of these rarities. Then came Brok with those he had forged. He gave Odin the ring, and said that every ninth night eight other rings, equally costly, would drop from it. To Freyr he gave the boar, and explained that he might travel on it incessantly both through the air and over the sea, by day and by night, since it possessed greater strength than any horse, and that however thick or dark the weather might be, there would be always light enough from its bristles. To Thor he gave the hammer, and said that he might strike as vigorously with it as he chose, and whatever came in his way, without risking any hurt to it. To whatever distance or in whatever direction he should throw it, it could not be lost; for let it fly ever so far it would return again into his hand.[3] If he desired it, it would become so small as to enable him to put it in his pocket. The only blemish it had was that the haft was full short.

The Aser decided that the hammer was the best piece of workmanship of all, since in it they had a great defence against the frost-giants, (Hrimthurser) and that Brokkur had won the wager. Loke offered ransom for his head, but the Dwarf would on no account agree to it. "Then lay hold of me," said Loke: but so soon as he attempted to do so Loke was far away by means of his magic shoes. Brokkur then asked Thor to catch him, which he did.

Brok was proceeding to cut off Loke's head, when he called out to him to remember that only the head was his, and to take care not to touch the neck. We shall close this chapter with Oehlenschläger's version of this fable, in which he has described at large the habits and residence of the dwarfs.

---

[3] This appears rather at variance with the account in the preceding chapter of the loss of Thor's hammer in his fishing adventure, but in that instance it must be remembered that it was Ran's avidity which prevented the return of Miölner to its master, her net never failing to catch whatever fell into the sea.

ONE OF LOKE'S KNAVISH TRICKS, AND HIS PUNISHMENT.

When Loke found that Thor had set out on his second journey to Jotunheim without him, he was greatly mortified, for his vanity was gratified at being seen in company with the Thunderer. Being much addicted to roving about, he got weary of staying at home in Asgard, doing nothing, and lost his spirits and appetite. His chief amusement consisted in gibing and mocking the gods. At length for want of something better to do, and in order to be revenged on Thor for the slight he had put upon him, he resolved to make love to Sif, Thor's wife. He accordingly watched her one day as she returned from the bath, and followed her to her crystal grotto, under Dovre. He there with his smooth tongue endeavoured to win her favour, seeking to persuade her that Thor did not know how to appreciate her beauty, but amused himself with fighting giants and fishing for whales, whilst she was left in solitude. Sif, however, repulsed his addresses with the utmost contempt, threatening him with her husband's vengeance if he did not desist. Loke to be revenged on her took an opportunity, when she was asleep, to cut off her hair, which was celebrated for its beauty, and indeed had nothing to equal it in Asgard.

THE DWARFS.

Loke sat and thought till his dark eyes gleam
  With joy at the deed he'd done;
When Sif look'd into the crystal stream
  Her courage was well nigh gone.

For never again her soft amber hair
  Shall she braid with her hands of snow;
From the hateful image she turn'd in despair,
  And hot tears began to flow.

In a cavern's mouth, like a crafty fox,
  Loke sate, 'neath the tall pine's shade,
When sudden a thundering was heard in the rocks,
  And fearfully trembled the glade.

Then he knew that the noise good boded him nought,
  He knew that 'twas Thor who was coming,
He changed himself straight to a salmon trout,
  And leap'd in a fright in the Glommen.[4]

But Thor changed too to a huge sea-gull,
  And the salmon-trout seized in his beak:

---

[4] The Glommen is the largest river in Norway, clear and rapid. In its course of nearly three hundred English miles, from the mountains above Roraas, whence it springs to where it runs into the sea at Friedrichstadt, it forms from fifteen to twenty considerable waterfalls, of which the most remarkable are the Sarpen-Foss, near its mouth; the Mörch-Foss, and the Vammen-Foss.

He cried, " Thou traitor, I know thee well,
    And dear shalt thou pay thy freak.

" Thy caitiff bones to a meal I'll pound,
    As a mill-stone crusheth the grain."
When Loke that nought booted his magic found,
    He took straight his own form again.

" And what if thou scatter'st my limbs in air!"
    He spake : " will it mend thy case?
Will it gain back for Sif a single hair?
    Thou'lt still a bald spouse embrace.

" But if now thou'lt pardon my heedless joke,
    For malice sure meant I none,
I swear to thee here by root, billow, and rock,
    By the moss on the Bauta-stone.[5]

" By Mimer's well, and by Odin's eye,
    And by Miölner, greatest of all;
That straight to the secret caves I'll hie,
    To the Dwarfs, my kinsmen small:

" And thence for Sif new tresses I'll bring
    Of gold, ere the day-light's gone,
So that she shall liken a field in spring,
    With its yellow-flower'd garment on."

---

[5] Bauta-stones were the stones placed over the tombs of distinguished warriors, and were held in great reverence amongst the Scandinavians, the more so in proportion to their antiquity, of which the moss on them was a sure token.

Him answer'd Thor: " Why, thou brazen knave,
    To my face to mock me dost dare,
Thou know'st well that Miölner is now 'neath the wave
    With Ran,[6] and wilt still by it swear?"

" O! a better hammer for thee I'll obtain,"
    And he shook like an aspen-tree,
"'Fore whose stroke, shield, buckler, and greave shall be vain,
    And the Giants with terror shall flee."

" Not so," cried Thor: and his eyes flash'd fire,
    " Thy base treason calls loud for blood;
And hither I'm come, with my sworn brother Freyr,
    To make thee of ravens the food.

" I'll take hold of thine arms and thy coal-black hair,
    And Freyr of thy heels behind,
And thy lustful body to atoms we'll tear,
    And scatter thy limbs to the wind."

" O spare me, Freyr, thou great-souled king!"
    And, weeping, he kissed his feet.
" O mercy, and thee I'll a courser bring,
    No match in the wide world shall meet.

" Without whip or spur round the earth you shall ride;
    He'll ne'er weary by day nor by night;
He shall carry you safe o'er the raging tide,
    And his golden hair furnish you light."

---

[6] Every thing lost at sea was said to go to Ran, who was represented as being as avaricious as she was cruel.

Loke promised so well with his glozing tongue,
    That the Aser at length let him go,
And he sank in the earth, the dark rocks among,
    Near the cold fountain,[7] far below.

He crept on his belly, as supple as eel,
    The cracks in the hard granite through,
Till he came where the Dwarfs stood hammering steel,
    By the light of a furnace blue.

I trow 'twas a goodly sight to see,
    The Dwarfs with their aprons on,
A hammering and smelting so busily,
    Pure gold from the rough brown stone.

Rock crystals from sand and hard flint they made,
    Which, tinged with the rose-bud's dye,
They cast into rubies and carbuncles red,
    And hid them in cracks hard by.

They took them fresh violets all dripping with dew,
    Dwarf women had pluck'd them, the morn,
And stain'd with their juice the clear sapphires blue,
    King *Dan*[8] in his crown since hath worn.

---

[7] The cold fountain was Hvergemler, which existed before the creation.

[8] Dan, surnamed Mikillati, or the magnificent, is supposed to have reigned in Denmark towards the latter end of the third century, and to have given his name to the Danish islands, which before had been called Ey-Gothland. He is said also to have introduced into Denmark the custom of burying the bodies of the dead, which until then, since the time of Odin, had been burned.

Then for emeralds, they search'd out the brightest green,
　　Which the young spring meadow wears,
And dropp'd round pearls, without flaw or stain,
　　From widows' and maidens' tears.

And all round the cavern might plainly be shewn
　　Where Giants had once been at play;
For the ground was with heaps of huge muscle-shells strewn,
　　And strange fish were mark'd in the clay.

Here an Icthyosaurus stood out from the wall,
　　There monsters ne'er told of in story,
Whilst hard by the Nix in the waterfall,
　　Sang wildly the days of their glory.

Here bones of the Mammoth and Mastodon,
　　And serpents with wings and with claws;
The elephant's tusks from the burning zone
　　Are small to the teeth in their jaws.

When Loke to the Dwarfs had his errand made known,
　　In a trice for the work they were ready;
Quoth Dvalin:[9] "O, Loptur, it now shall be shown
　　That Dwarfs in their friendship are steady.

"We both trace our line from the self-same stock;
　　What you ask shall be furnish'd with speed,
For it ne'er shall be said, that the sons of the rock
　　Turn'd their backs on a kinsman in need."

Then they took them the skin of a large wild-boar,
　　The largest that they could find,

---

[9] One of the principal of the Dwarfs.

And the bellows they blew till the furnace 'gan roar,
    And the fire flamed on high for the wind.

And they struck with their sledge-hammers stroke on stroke,
    That the sparks from the skin flew on high;
But never a word good nor bad spake Loke,
    Though foul malice lurk'd in his eye.

The thunderer far distant, with sorrow he thought
    On all he'd engaged to obtain,
And, as summer-breeze fickle, now anxiously sought
    To render the Dwarf's labour vain.

Whilst the bellows plied Brokur, and Sindrig the hammer
    And Thror,[11] that the sparks flew on high,
And the sides of the vaulted cave rang with the clamour,
    Loke changed to a huge forest fly.

And he sate him, all swelling with venom and spite,
    On Brokur, the wrist just below;
But the Dwarf's skin was thick, and he reck'd not the bite,
    Nor once ceased the bellows to blow.

And now, strange to tell, from the roaring fire
    Came the golden-haired Gullinbörst,
To serve as a charger the sun-god Freyr,
    Sure of all wild boars this the first.[12]

---

[10] Inconsistency is the predominant feature in the complicated, but not unreal character of Loke.

[11] The names of Dwarfs.

[12] This was no light praise, inasmuch as the boar Sehrimner was with good ground in high favour in Valhalla.

They took them pure gold from their secret store,
   The piece 'twas but small in size,
But ere't had been long in the furnace roar,
   'Twas a jewel beyond all prize.

A broad red ring all of wroughten gold;
   As a snake with its tail in its head;
And a garland of gems did the rim enfold,
   Together with rare art laid.

'Twas solid and heavy, and wrought with care,
   Thrice it pass'd through the white flames' glow;
A ring to produce, fit for Odin to wear,
   No labour they spared I trow.

They work'd it and turn'd it with wondrous skill,
   Till they gave it the virtue rare,
That each thrice third night from its rim there fell
   Eight rings, as their parent fair.

'Twas the same with which Odin sanctified
   God Baldur's and Nanna's faith,[13]
On his gentle bosom was Draupner[14] laid,
   When their eyes were closed in death.

Next they laid on the anvil a steel-bar cold,
   They needed nor fire nor file,
But their sledge hammers following, like thunder roll'd,
   And Sindrig sang Runes the while.

When Loke now mark'd how the steel gat power,
   And how warily out 'twas beat,

---

[13] Vide Chapter x.
[14] Draupner was the name of Odin's famous ring.

('Twas to make a new hammer for Auka-Thor)
   He'd recourse once again to deceit.

In a trice, of a Hornet the semblance he took,
   Whilst in cadence fell blow on blow,
In the leading Dwarf's forehead his barbed sting he stuck,
   That the blood in a stream down did flow.

Then the Dwarf raised his hand to his brow, for the smart,
   Ere the iron well out was beat,
And they found that the haft by an inch was too short,
   But to alter it then 'twas too late.

Now a small elf came running with gold on his head,
   Which he gave a dwarf-woman to spin,
Who the metal like flax on her spinning-wheel laid,
   Nor tarried her task to begin.

So she span and span, and the gold thread ran
   Into hair, though Loke thought it a pity:
She span and sang to the sledge-hammer's clang,
   This strange, wild spinning-wheel ditty.

" Henceforward her hair shall the tall Sif wear,
   Hanging loose down her white neck behind;
By no envious braid shall it captive be made,
   But in native grace float in the wind.

" No swain shall it view in the clear heaven's blue,
   But his heart in its toils shall be lost;
No goddess, not e'en beauty's faultless queen,[15]
   Such long, glossy ringlets shall boast;

---

[15] Freya.

"Tho' they now seem dead, let them touch but her head,
 Each hair shall the life-moisture fill,
Nor shall malice nor spell henceforward prevail
 Sif's tresses to work aught of ill."

His object attain'd, Loke no longer remain'd
 'Neath the earth, but straight hied him to Thor,
Who own'd than the hair, ne'er, sure, aught more fair
 His eyes had e'er look'd on before.

The Boar Freyr bestrode, and away proudly rode,
 And Thor took the ringlets and hammer,
To Valhalla they hied, where the Aser reside,
 Mid of tilting and wassail the clamour.

At a full, solemn Thing[16]—Thor gave Odin the ring,
 And Loke his foul treachery pardon'd:
But the pardon was vain—for his crimes soon again
 Must do penance, the arch-sinner harden'd.
       Oehlenschläger.

---

[16] Thing—any public meeting. The present triennial parliament of Norway is called Stor-thing, the great meeting.

CHAPTER IX.

ÆGIR—RAN—ÆGIR'S FEAST—GEFRONE.

ÆGIR, who was also called Gymer and Hler, was the god of the ocean, and although not one of the Aser, being descended from the giants, was possessed of considerable power. His dominion did not interfere with that of Niord, who had sway over the inland waters only. By his wife Ran he had nine daughters, who became billows, currents, and storms.

Ran, the queen of the ocean, was of a cruel and avaricious disposition. It was she who caused all shipwrecks, and she was in possession of a net, in which she entangled and drew to her whatever fell into the sea. All who were drowned were believed to go to her, a belief which the Swedish peasants still hold of the mermaid.

Ægir was very rich, and was celebrated also for great prudence and wisdom. His chief residence was in the island of Hlesey or Lessöe, in the Cattegat.

In crystal halls his head
Rears Ægir, Ran's stern spouse;
A silver helmet red
With coral guards his brows;
His beard, of ocean weeds,
His spear with amber deck'd,
And pearls, but shew he needs,
And the proud waves are check'd.

The emblem of his sway
When lifts the watery god—
Quick sinks the raging sea,
Obedient to his rod;
His pearly muscle throne,
In Hlesey may be seen;
Has daughters nine by Ran,
Three are the billows green.
Oehlenschläger.

The description of Ægir's feast, as given in the Elder Edda, is one of the most curious and characteristic relics of Scandinavian antiquity, whether considered as illustrative of the religious belief, or of the manners of the time in which it was written, it could not therefore with propriety have been omitted in a work of this nature. The coarseness, however, of the original, has obliged the author at times to use a great latitude of translation, and, in some instances, where the grossness would not be veiled, to have recourse to the Latin version. With this caution we shall proceed to give an account of

ÆGIR'S FEAST.

Ægir once made a journey to Asgard, on which occasion the gods received him with great distinction, and gave a feast in his honour. Ægir in return invited them all to an entertainment, of which an account has been given in the sixth chapter. Having obtained through Thor's assistance, as there described, Hymir's great kettle, he brewed in it a sufficient quantity of ale, and again invited the gods to a feast. Odin and Frigga were there; Sif, Thor's wife (Thor himself was engaged otherwise); Bragi and Iduna; Tyr; Niord and Skada; Freyr and Freya; Vidar, Odin's son; Loke also was present, and Beygver and Beyla, Freyr's attendants, and a great many Elves and Aser.

The banquet was very brilliant, gold was made use of for lights, and the drink passed about of itself. The guests particularly praised the alertness of Ægir's two attendants, Fimaseng and Elder, which exciting Loke's spleen, he maliciously slew Fimaseng. The Aser, on this, rose with one accord, and drove him from the hall, but in a short time he returned, and meeting Elder addressed him as follows:

LOKE.

Tell me this, Elder!
Before you set your foot
A step farther—
Of what do the Aser
Converse within
Over their drink?

ELDER.

Of their weapons,
Of their warlike deeds,
Speak the holy Gods:—
Amongst the Aser and Elves
Who sit within,
No one is in speech your friend.

LOKE.

I will enter
Into Ægir's hall,
To hear their babble.
Hatred and scorn I bear
To the sons of the Aser,
And will mingle evil with their mead.

ELDER.

Know, that if thou enterest
The hall of Ægir
To see the feast,
And on the mild Gods
To pour abuse,
They will turn it on thy head.

LOKE.

Know thyself, Elder!
That if we two
Exchange sharp words,
I in answer
Shall have far the better,
If thou speakest too much.

On this Loke went into the hall, and when the guests saw who it was they remained silent. Loke said:

Thirsty cometh Loptur
From a long journey
To this hall;
To ask of the Aser
That they will give him a draught
Of the clear mead.
Why are ye silent, ye Gods!
So swoln out
That ye are not able to speak?
Either give me seat and place
In your company,
Or bid me go my way.

BRAGI.

Seat and place to thee
In their company
The Aser will never give;
For they know well
Whom they should bid
To the holy banquet.

LOKE.

Rememberest thou, Odin!
How, in the morning of time,
We mingled blood together?
Then didst thou promise that never
Thou wouldst taste of drink
Unless we both were bidden.

ODIN.

Stand up, Vidar!
And let the sire of the wolf
Take his place;
Lest Loke should fall on us,
With words of abuse,
Here in Ægir's hall.

Then Vidar rose up and poured out a cup for Loke, who before he drank of it thus spake:

Health to the Aser,
Health to the Asynier,
And to all the holy Gods,
One alone excepted,
Bragi, who sitteth
Upon the bench above.

BRAGI.

A horse and a sword
I give to thee—
Thus doth Bragi offer—
If only with the Aser
Thou stirrest not up strife:
Make not the Gods wroth with thee.

LOKE.

Horse and weapons
Both, O Bragi!
Thou canst well spare;
Of Aser and Elves,
Who are present here,
No one shunneth fight
And steel as thou.

BRAGI.

I know that if I were
Without Ægir's hall
As I am now within it—
In my hand
I would bear your head,
And so repay your lie.

LOKE.

Thou art bold on thy seat—
This becometh thee not—
Bragi! pride of the bench![1]
If thou art angry,
Go out to the fight,
A brave man doth not calculate.

---

[1] Loke here speaks ironically, and calls Bragi pride of the bench, either as a reproach for his sedentary life, or for his love of feasts and drinking-bouts, at which the Scalds had always the high place.

IDUNA.

Bragi! I conjure thee
For our parents' sake,
For our children's sake,
That thou wilt not exchange
Words of scorn with Loke
Here in Ægir's hall.

LOKE.

Hold thy peace, Iduna!
Thou of all women
Lustest the most after men—
Since the time when
Thou passionately didst embrace
Thy brother's murderer.[2]

IDUNA.

Loke, to thee
I speak not in scorn
Here in Ægir's hall;
I do but still Bragi,
Heated with drink,
I would not that ye two should strive.

GEFIONE.

What will ye here,
Ye Aser twain!

---

[2] The story to which this alludes is now lost. Iduna was the daughter of the dwarf Ivalldur, whose sons made Sif's hair, &c.

Exchange rancorous words?
Doth not Loptur know
That cunning hath ensnared him,
And that misfortune is at hand.[3]

Although the interference of Gefione, the virgin goddess, cold and severe, the Diana of the north, to whom all maids who had never known love on earth repaired after death, was natural and in place, since being possessed of the gift of prophecy she knew what must be the result if this indecent altercation was persevered in—the reply of Loke was an insult of the grossest nature, so outrageous as to call up Odin himself.

ODIN.

Thou art mad, Loke,
And without understanding,
That thou stirrest Gefione to wrath;
For I trow that she knoweth
The destinies of all
Even as I myself.

LOKE.

Keep silence, Odin!
Never didst thou fairly share
The fight with warriors;
Often hast thou given the victory

---

[3] Gefione had the gift of prophecy, and was said with eight magic oxen to have ploughed the island of Zealand out of Sweden.

> Where thou shouldst not,
> To the least valiant.

ODIN.

> How knowest thou if I gave
> To the least brave the victory!
> Eight winters wert thou
> Beneath the earth—
> A milch-cow and a woman—
> Engend'ring monsters—
> Such is the part of a vile fellow.

Loke's answer is unintelligible, being, like Odin's remark, in allusion to some circumstance, with which we are not now acquainted. Frigga interfered, to prevent the revealing of secrets unknown to the rest of the Aser.

FRIGGA.

> It becometh you not
> So to declare
> Your destinies;
> What ye two Aser did
> In the morning of time—
> What is pass'd should not be ripp'd up.

LOKE

> Tace tu, Frigga!
> Tu es Fiorgyni gnata;
> Et semper virosa fuisti.
> Quando Veum et Vilium,
> Tibi vidreris uxor!
> Ambos in sinum suscipiebas.
>
> *Edda Sæmundar.*

Loke's first reply to Frigga was little less insulting than that to Gesione, and so excited the indignation of the mother of the gods that she exclaimed,

FRIGGA.

O! that I had but here,
In Ægir's hall,
A son like to Baldur;[4]
Never shouldst thou depart
From amongst the Aser;
A sword should stop thy venom.

LOKE.

Will'st thou, Frigga,
That I should address thee
More bitter words;
I will procure
That thou shalt never again
See Baldur ride to hall.

FREYA.

Thou art mad, Loke!
Thus to give vent
To foul and false railing.
Frigga knoweth all things
Past and to come—
Though she revealeth nought.

LOKE.

Silence, Freya!
Right well I know thee,

---

[4] Baldur was Frigga's favourite son.

Thou art not free from spot.
Of the Aser and Elves
Who are here assembled,
Each has enjoy'd thy favours.

FREYA.

False is thy tongue,
The day will come
When it will cause thine own woe;
Aser and Asynier
Are wroth with thee,
Thou shalt depart hence with shame.

LOKE.

Hold thy peace, Freya!
Mingler of poisons,
Full of evil art thou;
By magic arts,
Lustful goddess,
Thou hast drawn thy brother to thy side.

This brings up Njord the father of Freyr; and Freya's imputation on Loke as well as Loke's retort are so gross, that we must refer those who desire to read them, to the Edda of Sæmund.

LOKE.

Keep silence, Njord!
From the east hither
Thou wert sent, a hostage, to the Gods.
Hymer's daughters employed
Thy mouth for a vile purpose.[5]

---

[5] The passage will not bear a literal translation.

NJORD.

It is my pride,
That long ere I came hither,
A hostage to the Gods,
I could boast a son
Whom none hate,
And who is held the prince of the Aser.[6]

LOKE.

Cease now, Njord!
Lower thine arrogance,
I will no longer deny
That with thy sister
Thou hast begotten a son
No better than thyself.

TYR.

Freyr is the noblest
Of all the Gods
In the kingdom of the Aser.
Never hath he caused sorrow
To woman or maiden,
But freeth us all from bonds.

LOKE.

Hold thy peace, Tyr!
In vain hast thou sought
To use both hands
Since the time that Fenris
Bit off thy left hand.

---

[6] Freyr.

TYR.

I lack a hand,
Thou, an honourable name;
Sorrow to him who hath lost such,
Nor has the wolf much to boast;
In bonds must he languish
Until the world passeth away.

In reply Loke as usual asserts that Tyr's wife was in love with him, and had given him substantial proofs of her love.

FREYR.

The wolf lieth howling
At the mouth of the river
Until the powers shall perish—
Thou causer of strife!
So shalt thou be bound,
Unless thou straight holdest thy peace.

LOKE.

For gold didst thou purchase
Gymer's daughter,
And so soldest thy sword—
But when Muspell's sons
Shall ride over the dark wood,
Know'st thou not how thou must fight

BEYGVER.

If I were as nobly born
As Ingun's Freyr,
And had so lordly a castle,

I would crush
That evil raven,
And pound his bones to marrow.

LOKE.

What little creature is that[7]
Whom I see wagging his tail,
And, like a spunger, snapping what he can?
Thou wilt still be hanging
At Freyr's ears
When thou art not labouring at the mill.

BEYGVER.

My name is Beygver,
Gods and men
Call me the rapid,
Here am I come with honour—
For the whole race of Odin
Assemble gladly to the feast.

LOKE.

Hold thy tongue, Beygver
Never hast thou succeeded properly
In serving men their meals;
Thou hiddest thyself
Under the straw beds
When warriors were fighting.

HEIMDALL.

Loke! thou art drunk,
And hast no longer any sense!

---

[7] Beygver was a Light-Elf and attendant on Freyr the god of the sun.

Wilt thou never be quieted!
He must be overcome
With drink continually,
Who himself remembers not what he sayeth.

LOKE.

Peace now, Heimdall!
In the morning of time to thee
Was destined a hateful lot—
With a wet back
Shalt thou ever remain,
And watch as the warder of the Gods.[8]

SKADA.

Thou amusest thyself, Loke!
But not long shalt thou be free
At will to indulge thy spleen:
On the sharp points of the rock
With the bowels of thy ice-cold son
Soon shall the gods bind thee.

LOKE.

Know thou, though the gods
With the bowels of my ice-cold son
Should bind me to the rocks;
Yet first and fiercest was I
To give Thiasse[9] his death wound
When we entrapp'd him.

---

[8] In allusion to Heimdall's post on the rainbow as warder of Asgard.

[9] Thiasse was Skada's father, vid. ch. 3.

SKADA.

Know—if thou first and fiercest wast
To give the death-wound
When Thiasse was entrapp'd,
From my mountains
And waters, in return
Thou shalt receive cold counsel.

LOKE.

Gentler were thy words
To Laufeya's son
When thou offeredst me thy love,
Such things should not be forgotten,
When we desire with exactness
To enumerate thy actions.

Sif now advanced, and pouring out mead to Loke in a crystal cup, said:

Hail to thee, Loke!
And take the crystal cup
Full of old mead.
So that Sif alone,
Amongst the Aser's faultless race,
Thou mayst suffer to sit in peace.

LOKE.

Thou alone art—
If indeed thou art—
Prudent and constant against men—
I know but one—
So far as I believe—

Who acts the gallant with Hlorida's[10] wife—
And that is the cunning Loke.

BEYLA.

The rocks all tremble;
I trow now Hlorida returns
Homewards from his journey.
He will teach silence
To the one, who here insults
All gods and men.

LOKE.

Keep still, Beyla!
Thou art Beygver's wife,
And full of malice.
A fouler monster
Ne'er came amongst the sons of the Aser
Than thou—filthy slut.

At this moment Thor entered—

THOR.

Peace, ribald knave!
My weighty hammer, Miölner,
Shall stop thy tongue;
The rock of thy shoulders
I will strike from thy neck,
And thus deprive thee of life.

LOKE.

The son of earth
Is now arrived—

---

[10] Hlorida, one of Thor's names.

Why dost thou rage so, Thor!
Thou wilt not be so daring
When thou shalt fight with the wolf,
And he shall swallow the Father of Victory.[11]

THOR.

Peace, ribald knave!
Miölner, my weighty hammer,
Shall stop thy tongue;
I will fling thee up
To the eastern corner,
So that none again shall see thee.

LOKE.

Of thy journeys eastwards
Never, if thou art wise,
Shouldst thou talk to others.
Since the time, Einheriar!
That thou satest in the thumb of a glove,[12]
And scarce trow'd, thyself, that thou wert Thor.

THOR.

Peace, ribald knave!
Miölner, my weighty hammer,
Shall stop thy tongue;
Soon shall my right hand
Strike thee with Hrungner's bane,[13]
So that every bone shall be broken.

LOKE.

A long time yet
I hope to live,

---

[11] Odin.
[12] See Thor's journey to Jotunheim.
[13] Hrungner was a giant whom Thor had killed.

Altho' thou threatenest me with thy hammer.
The thongs of the wallet
Seemed hard to thee
When thou couldst not get to Skrymer's meat,
And wert near dead with hunger.

THOR.

Peace, ribald knave!
Miölner, my trusty hammer,
Shall stop thy tongue,
Hrungner's bane
Shall send thee to Hel—
And to the pit of the dead.

LOKE.

I sang for the Aser,
I sang for the sons of the Aser,
What my fancy bade me;
But, for thee alone
Will I depart,
For I know well that thou canst strike.
Ægir, thou hast brewed ale,
But never again
Shalt thou give a feast.
Over all thy possessions here
May the flame play joyfully,
And burn thee to the back.

On this Loke changed himself into an eel, leaped into Frananger's Foss, and escaped.

The following poem, translated from Oehlenschläger, is a paraphrase of the Thrymisquida of the Elder Edda.

LOKE'S CUNNING.

A slimy eel Loke cut through the wave,
From the Thunderer's vengeance his neck to save;
The peasants, for many a league, could see
How he glided and bent him so pliantly.
He pass'd thro' the monsters and wealth of the deep,
Saw whales a-sporting, the kraken asleep;
He swam straight to Norway, to Lindesnæss,
There hid him awhile in the mud and the grass,
Then, resuming his form, he sate on a rock,
Like a peasant boy watching a porpus flock.
"So at Odin's board my place I've lost,
Nor know if a Jotun[14] or Aser most:
Valhalla's pleasures for me are at end,
My days with demons I now must spend:
Midst thick-skull'd giants, shut out from light,
Who doze like bears through their endless night,
Where no sun e'er warms, no stars are seen;
No spring e'er gladdens the earth with green;
No music sounds through the torch-lit hall,
Save the mournful splash of the waterfall.
There love ne'er enters, Trolds[15] know no joy
But the good to harass, the fair to destroy;
They dream but of treason, and strife, and blood,
For a blockhead, all know, may be warrior good.
"Ne'er again As-Bragi's song shall I hear,
Nor scoff when his harp clangs false on mine ear,

---

[14] Jotun, a giant.
[15] Trolds, one of the names given to the evil spirits.

Nor with Diser[16] talk, till their necks of snow
With blushes, like heaven at evening, glow;
Nor sneer at As-Odin's silent state,
Till the Aser doubt if his wit be so great.
No more with gibes shall I tease As-Thor,
That the God gets wrath, and the hall's in a roar.
But by Farbaut, my sire, Thor has merit yet:
An he had but the tithe part of Loptur's wit
Might laugh at Odin—he wearies me least,
Though he chafes sometimes at my biting jest.
When aloft in his car we cut through the air,
I forget all envy, and malice, and care:
When Hlorida's[17] thunder shook earth and sky,
I thought me as great as the God, well-nigh.

" How I loved with the Diser of nothings to talk,
Or with dove-eyed Fulla by moonlight to walk.
Poor Fulla—I fear that her soft heart's gone;
But which of the Diser hath Loke not won.

" Sehrimner[18] I've lost, and the mead, and the beer,
And the tilting and sports of the Einheriar.
Those were jovial days, 'twere vain to deny:
The time fled quickly, the spirits were high;
Though an Aser but half, more wise than the rest,
I tasted all, knew all, and mock'd all that past.

" Their loss is greater than mine by half,
From Valhalla is banish'd the mirthful laugh.
The gods now yawn through the tedious day,
And regret, too late, that Loptur's away:

---

[16] The goddesses were termed Diser.

[17] A name for Thor.

[18] The boar on which the Aser and Einheriar made their daily repast.

They'll soon discover how little worth
Is pomp unlightened by wit or mirth.
Who'd bear long to feed on th' insipid dough,
Did none therein the sour leaven throw:
Did the rose-stock shoot smooth as stalk of corn,
'Twere a sorry rose with nor moss nor thorn!
What's the mid-day splendour, or court's parade,
Without humbler joys, without soothing shade!
"Let them sit with their closed hands their chins beneath,
Excitement ended, their rest is death."
Loke thus gave vent to his fever'd thought,
And to hide his grief from himself e'en sought;
But he could not reason away the smart,
And he writhed as he spake like a wounded hart.
He thought: "Could I pardon of Thor obtain,
All hope of Asgard were yet not vain."
Thus, racking his brain, he paced the rock,
When sudden, pausing, his brow he struck,
And cried—"Thor's hammer! 'tis done—by my life,
To gain back Miölner he'd yield his wife."
Then light as a falcon away he flew
To Jernvidi forest, nor once breath drew;
There he found King Thrymer,[19] who sate on a hill,
A feathering his arrows with eagle's quill;
By his side was a quiver of sea-calf's skin,
And the moon-beam play'd on his bushy chin.
Thrym lift up his eyes and, of Loke aware,
Cried, "Valhal's jester! what, thou come here!
Doth Loke the Aser thus condescend,
In his greatness, to think upon Giant-land!

---

[19] Thrymer or Thrym, a powerful giant, who stole Thor's hammer whilst the God was asleep, and refused to restore it until Freya was brought to him.

Hast fallen in disgrace? have the gods turn'd thee out?
Hard treatment this for their jester and scout!
What brings thee here like a skulking fox,
Do the Aser begrudge us our barren rocks?"
With a cringing boldness, Loke sate him down
By the Giant's side, on a moss-grown stone:
"The joys of Asgard are dearly bought,
And were 't not thy good, more than mine I sought,
Its hated frontier, long since, I'd crost,
And a spy in the Aser's camp you'd lost;
Who knows to cover his hate with smiles,
And to turn on his foes their rancorous wiles.

"That my friends suspect me, I deeply feel;
But offer myself for my kinsmen's weal.
Long, much, I've suffer'd, in body and mind,
But in conscience clear my reward I find."

Thus, weeping, the arch dissembler spoke:
Then Thrym loud laugh'd, and, with scoffing look,
He cried—" Wilt giants with tears ensnare,
As boys catch blackbirds with berries and hair?
Thou weep'st, like the monster of Egypt's flood,
When he's plotting murder and thirsts for blood:
What wilt thou here? weathercock, out with the lie,
Or, by Utgard, thou'lt rue thou cam'st hither to spy."

"Ay! he well may threaten," Loke fawning spake;
"At whose name e'en th' Aser in Valhal quake.
Whilst Thor was sleeping, his hammer you've ta'en,
And hid it deep down in the ocean with Ran:
Though none but the Thunderer can Miölner wield,
'Tis a noble prize, and good ransom will yield."

"What ransom?" cried Thrymer, with louring brow;
"Can Thor boast treasures like mine, I trow?
What need I of jewels, or gold or gear?
True; of Diser Freya much praise I hear:

Of her dark blue eyes, and her golden hair,
Coral lips, and skin as the lily fair;
Her mouth like rose-bud, its silvery sound
The flute's soft music; arms white and round:
Such ransom might tempt me—complexions brown,
And hair like the raven, I love not, I own,
Nor the swarthy beauties our mountains afford.
Bring hither the daughter of wealthy Njord,
And the self same day I'll give back to Thor
His trusty Miölner, as Freya's dower.

" Did not Freyr tall Gerda take to his bed?
Then why should not Thrym Freyr's sister wed?

" With this my resolve to your master hie.
Twelve leagues 'neath the ocean doth Miölner lie,
Nor ever shall Thor his hammer see,
Unless Njord's daughter its ransom be."

This said—he stamp'd, and there straight appear'd
A short, thick dwarf, who on Loptur leer'd,
And closed with a loud laugh the mountain's cleft,
That Loke in darkness alone was left.

Then Loke laugh'd too—that the mountains rang—
So laughs the hyæna, and whets his fang;
Huge owls fell down from the trees for fear,
And Ran look'd out o'er the deep to hear?
The serpent writhed, and the affrighted flood
High over the mountains in white foam stood:
The wolf bark'd hoarse, and his chain 'gan shake,
When, with ire concentred, thus Loptur spake:
" I hate ye all!—men, giants, and Gods!
I hate and defy ye! nor fear your odds.
Ye reject me, idiots! but soon shall learn
The power of him whom ye madly spurn.
I'll find me a way to vengeance yet,
Though the world once more into chaos split.

And the time will come, ye shall weep too late
The hour ye waken'd Loke's deadly hate.

" But I know your power, proud spirits of air,
And the giants' strength, and will act with care;
If but once my cunning great Thor can lead
To act like a Nidding[20]—nought else I need."

But, spite of his hatred, Loke did not dare,
Unbidden, to Asgard at once to repair:
So he stole through the woods, to the beech-hill's brow,
At even, as the boor drove homeward his plow;
'Twas where a spring, through the white sand prest,
Sprang, bubbling, from Hertha's parent breast;
Near where Leira stood, and where since King Ro
Built a spacious palace, as legends show.[21]

---

[20] Nidding, a term of contempt implying cowardice, falsehood and baseness of every kind,—in like manner remarks Dr. Percy, as the lye in modern days. He quotes a passage from Matthew Paris, shewing that W. Rufus, having occasion to draw together a sudden body of forces, sent word to such as held of him in fee that those who did not repair to his standard should be deemed Nithing, upon which, esteeming nothing more disgraceful than this ignominious epithet, they thronged to him in great numbers. Dr. Percy shews that the term continued long in use in England, but in a less contumelious sense, and cites the following lines from an old MS. poem between the reigns of Edward III. and Edward IV.

> Looke thou be kind and curteous aye
> Of meate and drinke be never Nithing.

[21] Where still stands the town of Roskilde, or Ro's-spring. The spring exists still in all its purity. Leira was the ancient capital of Denmark.

There small elves and faines were wont to play
Whilst the dew was falling, but fled the day.
Once a thorn pierced Freya, a drop from the wound
A small fay caught, ere it fell to ground,
And shed o'er the sward—ere the morning's dawn
Thousand purple flowers breathed sweets o'er the lawn.
'Tis the elves paint the redbreast and goldfinch's wing,
And teach the thrush, blackbird, and linnet to sing.
Erst the nightingale sang not, till once, in a freak,
The fairy queen caught it, and, kissing its beak,
E'er since with love-ditties it wearies the grove,
And melts maids to love who by moonlight rove.

Freya's ringlets are wash'd with a perfume rare,
Her nymphs in Folkvangur's bowers prepare:
Once a butter-cup full was stolen by a fay,
Who flew with the prize to the forest away,
And pour'd it by night on the violet.
But he found the fragrance for earth too great,
So he took fresh dew-drops, and mix'd them up
With the perfume was left in the buttercup,
And scented the wild-thyme and daffodil,
And cowslip, and woodbine and, loving the rill,
Forget me not, floweret which maids know well,
But 'twere vain all their frolics to seek to tell.

They pinch the dull shepherd, when wolves threat the flock,
And wake in the morning the farmer's cock:
Hodge turns him round, with a lingering yawn,
And ere the morn breaks brushes dew from the lawn.
They whisper the youth where his true love's gone,
And shew the green path which she haunts alone,
Or put on her form, in light dreams, the morn;
But from faithless lovers they turn with scorn.

They now danced merrily round the spring,
To the water-elf's song, hand in hand, in a ring,

When Loke, in the form of a fire-king, stepp'd
From a hollow ash tree, where to hide him he'd crept:
On his black shaggy locks was a bramble crown,
And his tail 'neath his blood-red robe hung down.
In a trice they all vanish'd, for strife they flee,
And they thought that the black elves lay hid in the tree:
But when they discover'd 'twas nought but Loke,
They leap'd for joy, and laugh'd loud at the joke:
All fairies love Loke for his tricks and his wiles,
They know not the malice that lurks 'neath his smiles.
They cried—" Welcome, Loptur, it long doth seem
Since together we danced in the full-moon's beam."
Quoth Loke—" Dear children, you know I love
To sport with you here in your leafy grove:
What hath kept me from you you soon shall learn,
But, first, on the greensward let's dance a turn."
   Then merrily round in a circle they danced,
Whilst Loke's tail, like a snake, through the long grass glanced.
The spring ceased to bubble, the small birds fled,
Bloated toads croak'd hoarse in their festering bed:
Thrice started the elves at the death-watch's cry:
Still nought suspected of treachery.
   When the youth at the feet of his true-love lies,
Whilst poisonous damps from earth's bosom rise;
In each other wrapt, nought the danger they heed:
Then Loke, from a dark thicket, laughs at the deed,
And the pitying moon, who attests their vows,
Nor t'avert his devilish malice knows;
Its deadly fruits ere he wanes doth mourn,
A bier with white flowers to the cold grave borne.
   Now, with dancing wearied, they press'd round Loke,
Who, stretch'd 'neath a huge beech, thus artful spoke:
" Last-born of Asgard, of gods beloved,

Whom Odin, at prayer of Freya moved,
Of purest æther from Muspel made,
Much your friendship, now, might poor Loptur aid.
By passion blinded in evil hour,
Unmindful of all I to Odin's power
And th' Aser's bounty, ungrateful, owe;
To my tongue's keen venom I gave full flow.
With tears of blood I have wept my fault;
But 'twas Ægir's liquor the madness wrought:
His mead is potent, his horns are deep,
When the cup quick passes the wit's asleep;
Nor God nor Diser my gall would spare,
Nor fear'd e'en Alfadur himself to dare.
But if Odin, moved by your prayer, relent,
And Thor, with unfeign'd remorse content,
Once more admit me to Asgard's reign,
I pledge me his hammer to bring again.
Dire Miölner, badge of the Thunderer's power,
By dark Thrymer stolen in unguarded hour."

The fairies promised all they could do,
And on gossamer wings to Valhalla flew:
There, with folded hands, and with eyes cast down,
Two by two they knelt before Odin's throne.
Alfader must yield to their artless prayer,
Freyr smiled, Freya's eye was dimm'd with a tear.

Then Loke from his covert all pale they led,
Who knelt, fawn'd, promised, and big tears shed,
And to kiss the dust from Thor's feet was fain,
But th' indignant god, fill'd with fierce disdain,
Struck the grov'ling suppliant with force to earth,
That the blood from his mouth in a stream gush'd forth.
" Hence, shame on thy dastard tears," he cried:
" I can better thy crimes than thy sorrow abide."
Loke raised him up with a vengeful scowl,

His heart was bursting with malice foul.
The blow he thought shall be dearly paid,
But he hid his ire, and thus smiling said:
" Not hope of pardon, though great my fault
My footsteps hither alone have brought.
Herald I come of love and peace,
'Tis time the rancorous wars should cease,
Which gods and giants so long divide:
Thrymer the tall, dark Utgard's pride,
For whom its maidens still sigh in vain,
In his turn hath felt the amorous pain.
Foul crimes and treasons he plots no more,
But sits alone on the bleak sea-shore,
Freya's spindle,[22] a-watching the live-long night,
As o'er the murk waters it twinkles bright.
All her beauty know—and poor Thrymer trows,
Such symbol a thrifty housewife shows.
He's heard too for Oddur she sorrow'd long,
And thinks this of truth a presumption strong.
Who for spouse departed such love can feel,
Must believe that a spouse may love as well.
Else what the reward for a faith so rare,
And most in Freya so passing fair.
  The nightingale coldly the thistle woos,
But with song of fire plies the blooming rose."
  Freya smiled, and said, " This at least is plain,
That Loke to himself e'er will true remain:
But your errand from Thrymer we fain would hear,
Your opinions on truth till a fitter time spare."
  Quoth Loke: " Fair goddess, not mine the praise,

---

[22] With the Scandinavians Freya's spindle was the name for the constellation called Orion's belt.

'Tis your matchless beauty Thrym's soul can raise
From its native dulness, and wit inspire
Unwonted. He loves thee with manhood's fire,
And Utgard's king, by his ardour won,
Hath granted the prayer of his darling son;
He hath sent me the raven-god to greet,
And of Freya's marriage at large to treat.
If to Thrym's suit Odin an ear will lend,
'Twixt evil and good all distinctions will end,
All nature will blend in chaotic love:
The screech-owl will pair with the turtle-dove,
The cavern's gloom with the great sun's light,
Men will talk no longer of day nor night,
But a dusky twilight o'er all shall reign,
Mouldy damps the bright walls of Asgard stain:
Blue violets spring from the carcass foul,
Warriors wield distaffs—wives empires rule;
Spear-staves bear blossoms, white lilies thorns,
Men lack beards, soft maidens boast beards and horns.[23]
What a glorious chaos—the live-long day
In cavern, stuccoed with moistening clay,

---

[23] The poet appears to have had here in view a similar passage in Shakspeare's Midsummer Night's Dream, where the consequence of the quarrel of Oberon and Titania are thus described:

> "The ox hath therefore stretch'd his yoke in vain,
> The plowman lost his sweat, and the green corn
> Hath rotted ere his youth attain'd a beard.
> . . . .
> . . . .
> The seasons alter, hoary headed frosts
> Fall in the fresh lap of the crimson rose,

Fair Freya shall sit on her rocky throne
To solace her Thrym in his grandeur lone.
Then all love shall end—but what need of love
When no hate shall exist baneful passions to move!
All extremes then shall vanish—the red, yellow, blue,
Men no longer in Bifrost's arch shall view,
But all hues shall blend in fraternal grey,
And the frog for the nightingale carol his lay."

Then to Freya's cheek rush'd the indignant blood,
And the big round tear in her blue eye stood,
Which flash'd on Loptur in fierce disdain,
Like a bright setting sun thro' a summer-eve's rain;
She turn'd tow'rds Odin a suppliant look,
But her heart was so full, that no word she spoke.

Then Odin rose and declared his will,
That a Thing straight should meet beneath Yggdrasill;
But Loke was not bidden, his tongue they fear'd,
So to Heimdall, on Bifrost, he quick repair'd,
And looking around that no god was near,
Thus his counsel whisper'd in th' Aser's ear.
I complain not that Odin suspects my zeal,
But the affair touches nearly high Asgard's weal:
You are wise—for myself I have nought at stake,
Tis for you of my hints the fit use to make;
But whatever is done must be done with speed,
Of decision the gods ne'er stood more in need.

And on old Hyems' chin and icy crown
An odorous chaplet of sweet summer buds,
Is, as in mockery, set: the spring, the summer,
The chilling autumn, angry winter, change
Their wonted liveries; and the 'maz'd world
By their increase now knows not which is which.
Act ii. scene 2.

White Heimdall who, seated on Bifrost's bow,
Knows all that passes its arch below,
And can hear the herb grow in the earth—each word
'Twixt Loptur and Thrym on the mount had heard;
He knew that for once the false god did not jest,
So thank'd him coldly and joined the rest,
'Neath the sacred Ash, where the gods in a ring
Were seated on stones round the raven-king.

Spake Heimdall: O, Aser, 'tis time to lower
These giants' pride, which all bounds runs o'er;
Of our power no longer they stand in awe,
But presume e'en to Odin to dictate law.
Dark Thrymer burns with unhallow'd fire,
And to Freya's hand e'en presumes t' aspire.
" True—Skada's fervour Njord knows t' assuage,
And of cruel Ran Ægir checks the rage.
Tall Gerda is gentle and loves As-Freyr,
And illumines the pole with her sparkling fire.
(From Gerda descend all dark-hair'd dames,
In whose bosoms a fiercer ardour flames).[24]
But follows it thence that our loveliest rose,
The pride of Valhalla, we tamely must lose!
If the apples of Ydun our vigour bestow,
'Tis from Freya love's softest endearments flow:
O'er her small mouth of coral when plays the arch smile,
Its spell e'en the woe-stricken heart can beguile;
To behold it each Aser's pulse thrills with delight,
Without her not Asgard's blue arch would be bright.
And shall we then—(may Skulda avert the disgrace)

---

[24] All these were instances of a union between the races of the Aser and of the Giants. Gerda was a personification of the aurora borealis.

Thus poorly resign her to Thrymer's embrace!
Shall that form which e'en but to look on is bliss,
Be polluted at will by a foul giant's kiss;
Those eyes which with love and expression late beam'd,
In despair coldly fix'd, or with bitter tears dimm'd!

" No—rather let radiant Bifrost's bow
Into ocean sink or dissolve in dew;
And the od'rous summit of Yggdrasill,
With its leaves and blossoms dark Nastrond fill.

" On the utmost verge of Heaven I watch,
And but transient glimpse of her charms may catch,
As she's daily wont o'er my bridge to pass,
All be-deck'd with flowers, earth's sons to bless;
When she smiles, in transport I seize my horn,
And wind a strain that wakes up the morn.
At the sound thousand feather'd songsters spring
From their dewy lair, and on buoyant wing
Proclaim to the earth that the blue-eyed queen,
White Heimdall on Bifrost's arch hath seen."

All th' Aser approved what the wise god said,
And Freya his speech with a look repaid,
Went straight to his heart, that the blood out-rush'd,
And his cheeks like an untaught youth's were flush'd.
Continuing, the counsel of wily Loke
And Thrym's demand in review he took:
" Thor's hammer," quoth he, " Ran ne'er will leave,
Unless by some wile we may Thrym deceive.
He seeks for a bride of a snowy hue,
With golden ringlets and eyes of blue.
Such beauties in Utgard 'tis hard to find,
But we still may send him a bride to his mind:
If only Thor to my plan will yield,
And to gain back Miölner, the distaff wield.
'Tis he shall be bride, one whose stern embrace

Shall make Thrym long for a swarthier face.
  We'll deck him out with the costliest gear,
A wimple and coif on his head he shall wear,
The polish'd keys from his belt shall pend,
And Freya t' adorn him her jewels lend:
Great Odin a magic salve shall make,
Unseemly scars from his front to take,
His skin shall turn white, his beard disappear,
Nor loss of courage thence need he fear;
To Utgard with unshorn strength shall he wend,
And Loke to dull Thrym that he's Freya pretend.
  Two shields on his breast we will fasten well,
Which like Freya's bosom twin globes shall swell.
We'll hang fair Brysing [25] around his neck,
Thus the Thunderer his hammer may get him back.
Loke shall serve the goddess as guard and guide,
And conduct to Thrymer his gentle bride.
  "When the bridal cup passeth round the board,
And the dwarfs bring Miölner from Ran's dark hoard;
When Thrymer with liquor and rapture drunk,
In an amorous stupor on Thor hath sunk:—
But why tell the Thunderer what part to choose,
He will scarce learn from Heimdall how Miölner to use."
  The Diser loud laugh'd, and the counsel applaud,
And clapp'd their white hands, and will dress out the god.
E'en Odin himself could not help but laugh,
To think of his son in a kirtle and coif.
  Then a sighing was heard from out Urda's well,
And thrice waved the summit of Yggdrasill.

---

[25] Brysing was Freya's famous necklace, which caused the scandal of her adventure with the four dwarfs, whose workmanship it was.

Great Odin's finger thrice Drupner[26] press'd,
And raised some doubts in the *wise-one's*[27] breast.
But intent on the Diser, their mirth and their smiles,
He forgat his wisdom and Loptur's wiles;
Baldur, Mimer, and Forsete,[28] all were away,
And Loke to his malice had now full play.

But Auka-Thor nought approved the joke,
The hardy warrior but ill could brook,
To a dark adventure to lend his name,
And risk a blot on his well-earn'd fame.
" What! Thor like a puling maiden drest!
Thor stoop to a paltry cheat at best!
I will hear no more of the dastard freak"—
But Freya drew near, and with dimpled cheek,
Her taper hand on his broad front placed,
" And is mighty Thor then so soon disgraced!
Earth's sons who live in suspense and fear,
Each doubtful emprize should shun with care;
For envy and malice are still awake,
Foul vantage of each false step to take,
And with devilish rancour the brightest fame
To sully, and cover with endless shame.
But Thor is an Aser, his deeds of light
Not the tongue of slander herself could blight.
'Twould scarce dim his glory to hear the prayer
Of an injured goddess he once thought fair."

The prayer of beauty doth seldom fail,
And tears o'er reason will still prevail.
A robe of scarlet arch Fulla brought,

---

[26] Drupner, Odin's magic ring.
[27] Odin.
[28] These were the wisest of the Aser.

Which Odin by magic must widen out.
In a leathern boddice they laced him tight,
But nought could induce him his hauberk to quit.
Two shields of copper, well smoothed and round,
On the Aser's bosom Hermodur bound,
Whilst the Valkyrs'[29] cheeks like a furnace burn'd
To see great Thor to a mummer turn'd.
Brysing, all sparkling with gems, hung down
On his tawny breast with black hair o'ergrown;
But Odin his skin with an ointment smear'd,
And white as a maiden's it straight appear'd.
No fitting coif for the god could be found,
So his copper helmet, with wadmel bound,
With flaunting ribbons and plumes they deck,
But his gloves of steel Thor will with him take,
And his magic belt—last with blood of bear
And wild boar's suet his cheeks they smear.

His dress now complete, Hnos a nosegay took
Of peony, sunflower, and hollyhock,
And stuck in his breast and said, Thor, farewell,
Such charms sure before ne'er graced Thrymer's cell.

Then Tialf the gold shoes on the goats made fast,
Thor wound the reins round his lusty waist,
He long'd for his hammer—bade Loke ascend,
But no flames stream'd forth as the clouds they fend;
The seven maids[30] bow'd, Heimdall blew a blast,
As with Loptur and Tialf the giant-bane pass'd.

---

[29] The Valkyrs, whose business it was to protect and reward warriors, are fitly represented as blushing at this degradation of their pride.

[30] The seven colours of the rainbow thus personified.

THOR RECOVERS THE HAMMER.

> Now Auka-Thor
> In golden car
> Cleaves the thick clouds
> With dark-hair'd Loke;
> And Loke the while,
> In's heart doth smile,
> And trolds and gods
> Alike doth mock.

On reaching Utgard they were met by Thrym and the officers of his court.

> There, waiting, stood
> The giant brood,
> An escort grim
> To greet the bride;
> And at their head,
> In flames array'd,
> The monarch Thrym
> In all his pride.

At the gate, as yeomen, the metal-kings stood,
The gold-king all radiant, the tin-king in white,
The dark sullen lead-king, the copper, like blood,
The stern king of iron, the silver-king bright.

> To Thor they bow'd,
> The warrior-god,
> Who sprang in haste
> Upon his feet,

And hasten'd on
Tow'rds Utgard's son,
Whose am'rous breast
With passion beat.

The nymphs of the gems, each in brightest attire,
The gay laughing emerald without thought or care;
The ruby still burning with amorous fire,
The vain sapphire and proud stately diamond were there.
Oehlenschläger.

The bride was conducted through dark, subterranean passages to the banquetting hall, where a great feast had been prepared. Thrym was at first a little surprized at the appetite of the goddess, who in a short time, as we are informed in the Thrymis-quida, had devoured an ox and eight salmon, and emptied three huge measures of mead; and he remarked to Loke,

" Never did I see a bride [31]
Take her meal better;
Never did I see a maiden
Drink more mead."

Loke soon explained the matter by saying,

" Freya nought hath eaten
For four days,
So great was her longing
For the journey hither."

---

[31] From the Thrym's-quida, or song about Thrym in the Elder Edda.

Thrym now got impatient to salute his fair one, and for this purpose ventured to lift up her veil, but was deterred by the fierce looks of Thor, and again applied for explanation to Loke.

> "How is it that Freya's
> Looks are so cutting,
> Fire seems to me
> To flash from her eyes."

Loke answered that her desire for the journey had deprived her of sleep for four nights. Thrym's sister now came in, and told the bride that if she wished for her friendship, she must give her money, and the ring from her hand. At length Thrym ordered the hammer to be brought in, to consecrate the marriage. A troop of dwarfs came puffing and blowing and bending under its weight, and laid it in the bride's lap.

> "Hlorida's heart
> Laugh'd in his bosom
> When he recognized
> His trusty hammer."

He lost no time to make use of it, but, beginning with Thrym and his loathsome sister, he slew the whole party.

CHAPTER X.

BALDUR—HIS DEATH—NANNA—HERMODUR—HÖDUR—FORSETE—VALE—RAGNAROKKUR.

BALDUR or Balldr was the second son of Odin and Frigga, and the noblest and gentlest of the Aser, insomuch that he was beloved of everything in nature. He exceeded all beings not only in gentleness, but in prudence and eloquence also, and was so fair and graceful that light was said to emanate from him. His palace was called Breidablik, or the wide-shining, in which nothing impure could exist.

Baldur had once a mysterious dream, wherein it was revealed to him that his life was in danger, and this weighed so heavily upon his spirits that he shunned the society of the Gods. His mother, Frigga, having at length drawn from him the cause of his melancholy, the Aser assembled in council upon it, and were filled with sad forebodings, for they knew that the death of Baldur was to be the forerunner of their own downfal, the first victory of the Giants.

Odin cut Runes, but could not succeed in his endeavours to obtain an insight into the future. Odreyr, the vessel of wisdom which might have served the Aser in their need, was in the keeping of the norny Urda, and the Aser were obliged to apply to two dwarfs, Thrain and Dain, who exceeded all others in Runic wisdom. Thrain said: " That the dream was heavy," Dain " that it was dark," and both agreed that it foreboded the destruction of the universe, but could give no information respecting the quarter from whence the evil was to proceed.

The goddess Iduna, by some misfortune, had fallen into the power of the giants, and, accustomed to the joys of Asgard, she pined away in the realms of night. The gods unable to rescue her had sent her in pity the skin of a wolf, by clothing herself in which her form and nature were entirely changed, and the past was thus forgotten. Odin, in the present emergency, instructed Heimdall, Loke, and Bragi to seek her out in her captivity, and to endeavour to learn from her the designs of the giants. The three Aser rode on monsters to the gloomy pit, singing magic songs as they went, and Odin, in the mean time, ascended to Hlidskialf, to observe their progress.

Heimdall endeavoured in vain to obtain from Iduna any information respecting the events which were about to happen. The goddess remained in mournful silence, answering only with tears. Heimdall and Loke returned on the wings of the winds to Vingolf, where the gods and goddesses were assembled together in anxious expectation. Bragi remained in Jotunheim to watch over his unfortunate spouse.

Many questions were put to Heimdall and Loke respecting their journey, and the Aser remained conversing upon its result until night was far advanced.

> Odin then spake,
> And all listened:
> "Night should be chosen
> For deep thought.
> Till morning cometh
> Let each one reflect
> What best can be done
> To aid the Aser."

On this the assembly broke up, and the Aser separated.

In the ancient poem from which the foregoing extract is taken, there follows a description of daybreak, of which we give a literal translation, as a characteristic specimen of the metaphorical poetry of the Scalds.

ODIN'S RAVEN SONG.

The son of Delling[1]
Drove out his horse,
Gloriously deck'd
With glittering stones:
Wide o'er Mann-heim[2] shone
The mane of the steed:
The Bewitcher[3] of the Dwarfs
Ascended his car.

Towards the earth's
Northern-most gate,
Under Ygg-drasill's
Outermost root,
Witches and giants
Went to rest,
Spectres, dwarfs,
And the black-Elves.[4]

Warriors roused themselves
As the sun stood up:
Northwards, towards Niffl-heim,
Night fled away;
The bridge, which shines early,
Ulvrune's son ascended;

---

[1] The son of Delling is the dawn.

[2] Mann-heim, the earth.

[3] The Bewitcher of the Dwarfs, the sun; a single ray of which transformed the dwarfs to stone.

[4] All the evil-spirits are represented as retiring to rest on the appearance of the sun. Ygg-drasill's outermost root, says the Edda, was amongst the giants.

> Whose horn's loud sound
> Echoes from Himmelbierg.[5]

The Aser were now again assembled, the oracles being consulted, left no doubt that Baldur's life was in peril, and it was determined, therefore, at Frigga's prayer, that all the elements and every thing in nature should be bound by an oath not to harm the gentle God. Nothing was omitted, except one insignificant plant which grew westwards of Asgard, and which, on account of its youth, Frigga thought was innocuous.

Odin's mind misgave him that still all was not right, and, to use the words of the original, that the nornies of good-fortune had flown away. To clear up his doubts, he resolved to visit the tomb of a celebrated Vala, or prophetess, and to learn from her the secrets of the dead. Grey's beautiful version of his journey is well known, but as it was taken from Bartholin's Latin translation, and as no literal one has ever been published in English, the following may not be deemed superfluous.

> Up rose Odin,
> The watcher of time,
> And upon Sleipner[6]

---

[5] Ulvrune's son, Heimdall, who lived on the celestial mount (Himmelbjerg), and every morning early ascended the bridge Bifrost (the rainbow).

[6] Odin's celebrated horse.

Laid the saddle:
Downwards he rode
To death's spectre-realm;
He met a hound
Coming from Hela.

Clotted blood
Was on its breast,
Round its savage fangs,
And its jowl beneath.
Against the father of song
It bayed fearfully,
Opened wide its jaws,
And howled aloud.

On rode Odin,
The earth shook,
He came to Hela's
Drear abode:
Then he rode
Eastwards before the gate,
Where a Vala
Lay interred.

He sang for the wise-one
Dead-men's songs;
Then, towards north
Laid the magic letters,[7]
Muttered incantations,
Summoned wizard words,
Till he forced the dead
To rise and speak.

---

[7] Runes.

VALA.

Who is the man
Unknown to me,
Who disturbs
My spirit's rest?
Enwrapp'd in snow,
Drench'd with rain,
Moisten'd by dew,
Long have I lain in death.

WANDERER.

Wanderer is my name,
Valtam's son am I;
Tell me of Hela's realm,
I will tell thee of earth:
For whom are prepared
The decorated seats,
The lordly couch
Radiant with gold?[8]

VALA.

Here standeth mead,
For Baldur brewed;
A shield covers
The clear liquor;
The race of Aser
Yield to despair—
Force hath made me speak,
Now will I be silent.

---

[8] These unusual preparations in the regions of death denoted the expectation of some distinguished guest.

WANDERER.

Be not silent, Vala!
I will question thee
Until I have learn'd all.
More I must know—
Who shall compass
Baldur's death?
Who Odin's son
Deprive of life?

VALA.

Hödur beareth
The fated plant,[9]
He shall be cause
Of Baldur's death,
And Odin's son
Deprive of life—
Force hath made me speak,
Now will I be silent.

---

[9] The plant here alluded to, is declared in the Voluspa to be the Misletoe. The reverence in which it was held by the Druids is well known, but it does not appear that the Scandinavians attributed to it any particular virtue, nor is it mentioned in any of their remains but as an instrument in the hands of the evil principle to destroy their favourite god.

It is not easy to understand, therefore, how the ingenious author of the Northern Antiquities should consider the mention of this plant in this place as nearly decisive of the identity of the Celts and Scandinavians, an opinion most satisfactorily refuted by his English translator, Dr. Percy.

WANDERER.

Be not silent, Vala!
I will question thee
Until I learn all.
More I must know—
Who shall on Hödur
Pour out vengeance?
And Baldur's bane
Lay on the bier?

VALA.

Rinda bears a son
In the western halls.
On the day of his birth
He shall lay low the son of Odin:
His hand he shall not lave
Nor comb his hair,
Ere that he placeth on the bier
The adversary of Baldur—
Force hath made me speak,
Now will I be silent.

WANDERER.

Be not silent, Vala,
I will question thee.
Who are the maids[10]
Who will not weep?
But suffer their veils
To float towards heaven?
Tell me this only,
Thou sleepest not before.

---

[10] This stanza will be explained by the sequel.

VALA.

Thou art no wanderer
As I believed;
Surely art thou Odin,[11]
The watcher of time.

ODIN.

Thou art not a Vala,
Nor a wise woman;
But rather the mother
Of three giants.

VALA.

Ride home, Odin,
And boast of thy journey:
For never again
Shall another disturb me,
Until Loke shall break
Loose from his chains,
And the last twilight
Fall on the gods.

Having said this the prophetess sank again into her tomb, and Odin was obliged to return to Asgard with his doubts confirmed as to the inefficiency of the precautions taken by the Aser, to

---

[11] It was an ancient and general superstition that when a dying person cursed one in life under his real name, the curse would be terribly fulfilled. As the prophetess might be said to die now a second death, it was fatal to Odin to have his name discovered.—*Magnussen.*

avert the misfortune they apprehended; and with the consciousness of having lost, through his imprudent questions, the only opportunity of ascertaining by what means if by any the impending evil might yet be averted.

Oehlenschläger, in his drama entitled Baldur's Death, has spiritedly filled up the outline furnished by the Eddas. Asa-Loke having retired from the society of the Aser to indulge the malignant humour which often came on him, whilst venting his malice against the gods and the demons, and at the same time deploring his fate in being distrusted and despised by both parties, on a sudden, a dense fog began to rise from the ocean, and after a time the dark figure of the demon-king, Utgardelok, issued from it, Loke, in some terror, demanded what brought him thither, on which the monarch began to reproach him with the contemptible part, he a demon by birth, was acting in consenting to be the buffoon of the Aser, and their auxiliary against the giants, to whom he owed his origin. It was out of no affection to himself that he was admitted to the society of the gods, but because Odin knew well the ruin which he and his offspring were destined to bring upon them, and sought, by thus cajoling him, to defer the evil day. He who from his power and cunning might have been a leader w h either party, was now rejected by all. The giant-king further reproached him with having already frequently saved the Aser from ruin, and with furnishing them even with weapons against the giants, and ended by appealing to the hatred which rankled in his bosom against Odin and his whole race, as a proof that his natural place was with the giants.

Asa-Loke acknowledged the truth of all this, and professed his readiness to aid his brethren by any means in his power. Utgardelok told him that the moment was now at hand when he might seal the fate of the Aser. That if Baldur was slain their destruction must sooner or later follow, and that the gentle god's life was at that time threatened by some as yet undiscovered danger. Loke replied, that the anxiety of the gods was already at an end, for that Frigga had bound every thing in nature by an oath not to injure her son. The dark monarch said that one thing only had been omitted, but what that was lay concealed in the breast of the goddess, and was known to no other. The day now being about to dawn, Utgardelok sank down again to his dark rocks, and left Loke to his darker thoughts.

To return to the Edda, Loke having assumed the figure of an old woman, repaired to Frigga, and by his artifice drew from her the fatal secret, that presuming on the insignificance of the Misletoe, she had omitted to include it in the conjuration by which she had bound everything else. Loke lost no time to repair to the place where the Misletoe grew, and tearing it up by the roots, gave it to the Dwarfs to form into a spear. Oehlenschläger describes their incantations; when the spear is completed, one calls for water to temper it, and a child free from all taint is brought in. The dwarf plunges the spear into its breast and sings,

> The death-gasp hear!
> Ho! ho!—now its o'er—
> Soon hardens the spear
> In the babe's pure gore—
> Now the barbed head feel,
> Whilst the veins yet bleed—
> Such a deed—such a deed—
> Might harden e'en steel.

In the mean time the gods, as usual, and the Einheriar had assembled together to tilt, and as Baldur's life was now deemed to be charmed, in order to convince him how groundless were his apprehensions, they made him the butt of all their weapons. Loke repaired thither also with the fatal spear, and seeing the blind and strong god Hödur, standing apart from the rest, asked him why he did not honour his brother Baldur by tilting with him also. Hödur excused himself on account of his blindness and because he had no weapon. Loke put the enchanted spear into his hand, and Hödur, unsuspicious of his malice, pierced Baldur with it through the breast, so that he fell lifeless to the ground.

The Aser were in unspeakable grief, and would have instantly avenged his death on Hödur but for the holiness of the place; Odin's grief, however, was the greatest, for he best knew the extent of the loss they had incurred. This in fact is the greatest misfortune that ever happened to gods or men. Since this event, the Aser never willingly hear mention of the name of Hödur.

The gods now bare the body of Baldur to the sea-shore, and endeavoured to launch his ship Hringhaune, that it might serve as a funeral pile, but so great was its size that they could not move it. They sent messengers therefore to Jotunheim, to a giant-woman, Hirrokin, who came riding on a wolf with adders for a bridle. When she dismounted, Odin gave the wolf in charge to four Berserkir,[12] who had enough to do to keep it quiet.

---

[12] The Berserkir were men of extraordinary strength, who, previous to a battle or any arduous undertaking, worked themselves into a kind of delirium (aided perhaps by spirituous drink), biting their shields and abandoning themselves entirely to the impulse of their frenzied imagination. In this state of temporary madness they committed every kind of excess. It seems to have been the fashion with great men to have a certain number of these Berserkir in their train. In

Hirrokin launched the ship with such force that flames burned up from beneath it, and there was an earthquake. Thor, who was standing by, would have slain her with his hammer had not the rest prevented him.

When Baldur's body was placed on the ship, his wife Nanna wept so bitterly that her heart brake, and the gods laid her beside him and set the pile on fire. His horse and harness were also burned with him; and Odin placed the ring Draupner on his breast, and whispered some words in his ear.

There were a great many present at Baldur's funeral. Odin and Frigga, with the Valkyrs; Freyr with his car, drawn by the boar Gullinborste; Heimdall, on his horse Gull-topp; Freya drove her cats. There were also a great many giants, and Thor, standing over the blazing pyre,

---

Viga Styr's Saga it is related that an Icelandic nobleman having rendered Hacon Jarl some services, the latter bade him name his reward, whereupon he begged two Berserkir who were in the Jarl's service. Hacon represented to him that he would have much trouble with such ungovernable spirits, but at length granted his request. He soon found, however, that although ever ready to fight, they could not be brought to work, and prevailed on his warlike brother, Viga Styr, to take them off his hands, but he also soon repented, and could only get rid of them by treacherously slaying them.

consecrated it with his hammer. The dwarf Litur happening, at that moment, to run before his feet, he kicked him into the flames, so that he was burnt also.

Frigga could not reconcile herself to the loss of her favourite son, and to pacify her Hermodur consented to ride to Helheim, to offer Hela a ransom for Baldur. Odin lent him his horse, Sleipner, for the journey, and the gods again breathed for awhile. But the sons of Askur,[13] better acquainted with death, were not so easily elated. Oehlenschläger puts the following words in the mouth of his chorus:

> But cold is my hope!
> Light my consolation.
> Whosoe'er pale Hela, queen of death,
> Once circleth with her arms,
> Returneth no more from Niffl-heim.
> As famished wolf in winter's night
> Drinketh the warm heart's blood—
> So doth she gloat—so her cold, clammy lips
> Press upon gentle Baldur's.
> Sooner shall the lynx
> Resign the prostrate roe,
> Than Baldur 'scape from Niffl-heim.
>   Yet shall not the worm of despair
> Gnaw on my heart, so long
> As hope but glimmereth—
> Time enow to yield to pale despair

---

[13] The human race.

When inexorable destiny
Shall extinguish its last expiring spark.
Oehlenschläger.

Hermodur rode nine days and nine nights, deeper and deeper amid impenetrable darkness, until he reached the river Giallar, over which is the bridge of death. Here he was stopped by Modgudur, the maiden who kept the gate, and questioned as to his name and descent.

She added that he had not the appearance of a deceased person, that the noise of his horse's feet exceeded that which had been caused the day before by the arrival of three legions of dead, and that the bridge shook under him.

Hermodur declared his mission and who he was, and Modgudur then directed him on his way to Hela. On reaching the iron grating which surrounds the spectre queen's palace, he descended from Sleipner to girth up his saddle, and then remounting, spurred him over the fence and alighted in the hall, where he found his brother Baldur sitting in the high seat.

He now laid his errand before Hela, and in order to move her pity, told her how the loss of Baldur had afflicted everything on earth and in heaven. The goddess after a time consented that he should quit her realm, provided that everything on earth would weep for him.

The Aser sent this intelligence over all the world, and there was an universal mourning. Men, beasts, trees, metals, and the stones themselves wept, like as when the sun causes a thaw in spring. The messengers, on their return, found an old, withered giant-woman, whose name was Thök, sitting in a cavern. They entreated her to weep also, but she answered: " That her téars were dry, and that Hela might keep her prey."

It is generally believed that it was Loke who had taken the form of this old woman.

Hermodur brought back from Helheim Odin's ring, which he had placed on Baldur's bosom, and Nanna sent back to Frigga a rich garment, and to Fulla a gold ring.

But now the cup of Loke's crimes was full to the brim, and the fearful vengeance of the gods at length overtook him. It first fell upon his sons, Nari and Vali, the latter of whom they changed into a wolf, in which shape he devoured his brother. After many attempts to escape Loke himself was taken by Thor, who bound him down on three sharp stones with the intestines of his son. Skada, Njord's wife, in revenge for his revilings at Ægir's feast, hung a serpent over his head, whose burning venom fell drop by drop upon his face. In this terrible situation there was one who did not abandon him. His wife Signi sate near his head with a bowl in which she caught the poison as it fell, nor did she ever quit him unless from time to time to empty the bowl, and then the drops which fell upon him caused such torture, that with his writhing and howling earthquakes were produced. Here he must lie bound down until Ragnarokkur comes, the twilight of the gods.

Baldur was to remain with Hela until the destruction of the world, and afterwards to dwell in the new Asgard where no evil will be known. His memory is still preserved in Denmark in the names of springs and particular places. A plant *Baldur's braa"* (Anthemis cotula, Lin.) says the Edda, resembles his eye-brows, and is the fairest of plants. In Icelandic an excellent man is still called *Mann-Balldur* (a Baldur amongst men).

Baldur and Nanna had one son, Forsete, who was one of the twelve principal Aser, and was considered the justest of judges. All who appealed to his decision in quarrels, whether gods or men, always departed from his tribunal reconciled.

Forsete is supposed to have been worshiped by the ancient Saxons, and in Heligoland formerly called Forsete's land, there was a temple to his honour.

Vale, who avenged Baldur's death by killing Hodur, was a son of Odin and Rinda, and lord of the celestial palace, Valaskialf. He was a bold warrior, with golden arrows, and a lover of the chase.

A feast was celebrated in his honour towards the end of January or the beginning of February, in which torches were lighted and bonfires made. On the introduction of Christianity, this feast was replaced by Candlemas.

Having thus completed this imperfect sketch of the principal divinities and leading features of the Scandinavian Mythology, and endeavoured to convey to the reader a general and connected picture of the superstitions of our heathen ancestors, it remains only to give some account of the great catastrophe which was at length to sweep away these transitory deities and the whole fabric of the universe, in order to make way for a more perfect system.

The Prose Edda gives us the following account of Ragnarok, or the twilight of the gods. "There will first come a winter which shall be called Fimbulveter; snow will fall from every quarter, and hard frost and cutting winds have sway, so that the heat of the sun will have no influence. Three such winters unalleviated by any summer, will follow each other. Previously to this the whole world will be scourged, during three winters also, by wars and blood-shed. Brothers will kill each other through avarice, and there will be no mercy, even from parents to their children.

"And now, to the great affliction of mankind, one wolf will devour the sun, another the moon, the stars will disappear from the firmament, the earth quake violently, trees be torn up by their roots, mountains fall together, all chains and bonds be burst asunder, and the wolf Fenris will break loose. Then will the ocean rise above its shores, for the great Midgard's-serpent will recover its giant strength, and struggle to gain the land.

"At length he will succeed, the ship Nagelfare will be set afloat, and the giant Hymir take the helm. Nagelfare is built of the nails[14] of dead men, and it should be remarked that when a person dies and his nails are not cut, materials are furnished towards the building of a vessel, whose completion both gods and men should seek to delay as long as possible.

"Fenris now rushes onwards open mouthed; fire streams from his eyes and nostrils; his under jaw touches the earth, the upper heaven, and he would open them still wider if there were space. Jormungandur vomits out poison, which renders

---

[14] This superstition respecting nails was not confined to the Scandinavians, some of the ancients feared to cut their nails on certain days of the week. According to Ausonius,
"Ungues Mercurio, barbam Jovi, Cypridi crines."
Magnussen.

the air and the waters deadly. He is the most terrible of all, and fights by the side of the wolf.

"In the midst of the confusion the heavens are rent asunder, and the sons of Muspell (the genii of fire) ride forth, led on by Surtur, who is clothed in flame, and whose unrivalled sword surpasses in brightness the sun itself. The bridge Bifrost gives way beneath their weight. The sons of Muspell press onwards to the plain Vigrid, which extends five hundred miles every way, and where they meet Fenris and Jormungandur. Asa-Loke also has repaired thither, and at the same time appears Hymir with the Giants of the Frost. All the sons of Hela follow Loke.

"But now, on the other side, Heimdall rouses himself, and blowing with all his might on his Gjallar-horn, wakes up the Aser who hold council as to what is to be done. Odin rides to Mimer's well to ascertain what is best; the Ash Yggdrasill is shaken, and all earth and heaven are in dismay.

"The Aser and Einheirar march to the plain Vigrid, with Odin at their head. Armed with his golden helm, his glittering mail and his spear, Gungnir, he encounters Fenris who swallows him up.

> Then is accomplished
> The goddess' second-heart's grief[15]

---

[15] The first was the death of Baldur.

> Then falls the god
> Best beloved of Frigga.
> *Voluspa.*

"At the same moment his son Vidar advances to avenge his father; he presses down with his foot the wolf's lower jaw, and raising the other with his hand, rends him till he dies. Thor fights with the serpent, and acquires great fame by slaying him, but overpowered by the poison which he spews forth, recoils back nine paces and falls dead to earth.

"Freyr is opposed to Surtur, but now misses his good sword which he had given to Skirner and is slain. The dog, Garmer, who had hitherto been bound in a cavern, escapes and rushes upon Asa-Tyr, and both fall. In like manner Loke and Heimdall slay each other. After all this Surtur pours out fire upon the earth, and the whole world is consumed. The great Ash, however, outlives this general ruin.

> ' Ygg-drasill's Ash
> Totters, but stands.'
> *Voluspa.*

"Good and just men will now be transported to Gimle, which is built of red gold, and where there are various splendid and delightful habitations. Bad men, perjurers, murderers, and the seducers of other men's wives, will go to Nastrond, a vast, hideous dwelling, whose gates face northwards. It is built of adders, whose heads are turned inwards, and are continually spewing out poisons which form a large lake or river, where its inmates are to swim eternally, suffering horrible tortures.[16]

"A new earth, fairer and more verdant than the other, will arise out of the sea; from which the grain will shoot forth of itself. Vidar and Vale will survive the general destruction and dwell upon the plain Ida, where Asgard lay before. Thither also will repair Magne and Mode, the sons of Thor, taking Miolner with them. Baldur and Hodur will return from Hela, and these gods will sit together, and talk over the events of past times.

> The Aser will meet
> On Ida's plain,
> And talk of the mighty
> Earth-surrounder:[17]
> There they will call to mind
> Great deeds of olden-time,
> And the lofty gods'
> Ancient learning.[18]   *Voluspa.*

"During the conflagration caused by Surtur, a

---

[16] In another place, a ravenous wolf tormented the souls of the damned.

[17] The great serpent.

[18] Runes.

man and a woman, Lif and Livthraser, will lie concealed in a place called Homimer's Holt, and there nourish themselves with the morning-dew. From them is to spring the second race of men."

The Voluspa,[19] or song of the prophetess in the Elder Edda, a production which, as Grundtvig has remarked, bears incontrovertible marks of having originated in the remotest ages of heathenism, gives nearly the same account of this famous catastrophe. It terminates with the following stanzas:

> A hall I see
> More brilliant than the sun,
> Roofed with gold,
> On the summit of Gimle;
> There shall dwell
> A virtuous race,
> And enjoy blessedness
> To time eternal.
>
> Thither cometh the mighty one
> To the council of the gods,
> In his strength from above;
> He who thinketh for all.[20]
> He issueth judgments,

---

[19] The Voluspa has been three times translated into English, by the Rev. J. Prowett, 1816; by Mr. Herbert freely, in his poem of Helge; and by Dr. Henderson in the appendix to his Journey through Iceland.

[20] The mighty one can allude to none other than the supreme being, the true Al-fadur.

He causeth strife to cease,
And establisheth peace
To endure for ever.

[21] But lo! the dark dragon
Cometh, flying,
Spotted like a snake,
From the caverns of darkness;
Nyd-hoggur, on his wings
Bearing corpses,
Soars over the plain:
—Now must I sink.   *Volupsa.*

---

[21] The prophetess here seems to close her song, on the approach of night, which she likens to Nyd-hoggur, the great dragon or serpent king.

APPENDIX.

APPENDIX.

SOME ACCOUNT OF THE SCALDS AND SAGAS, AND OF THE PRINCIPAL SUPERSTITIONS OF THE ANCIENT SCANDINAVIANS.

The Scalds of Scandinavia differed essentially from the Bards and Druids of the Celts. They were invested with no priestly authority, nor had they, in virtue of their office, any political influence other than that which they might derive from their superior attainments or from the favour of the prince or chief by whom they were protected. They were for the most part mere adventurers, although often of high birth, who derived their subsistence partly from the art of making verses, and partly from their swords. If in the earlier periods of Scandinavian history we find them filling, not unfrequently, the most important offices of the state, it was because they were more intelligent and eloquent than their fellow-courtiers. Nor did this intellectual superiority imply any deficiency in the more essential qualities of strength and courage, but usually the reverse. In the Scaldatal, an old Icelandic manuscript, there is a list of all who had distinguished themselves as Scalds from the time of Regner Lodbroc to that of Waldemar II. from the latter end of the eighth to the beginning of the thirteenth century, in which are to be found the names of several crowned heads. Regner Lodbroc himself was an accomplished Scald, and Rognvald, Count of the Orcades, has also obtained great celebrity for his readiness in making verses. Eigil Skalagrimson, Eyvind Skaldaspiller, Gunlaug, and many others were as distinguished for their warlike achievements as for their skill in poetry. One warrior in recommending himself to his mistress boasts that he is master of nine accomplishments. " I play well at chess; I know how to cut Runes; I am apt at reading; and can handle the tools of a smith; I can pass over the snow on skees; I excel in shooting with the bow and in managing the car; I sing to the harp and compose verses." Another declares that he knows the names of all the stars, an attainment not without use to men who passed so great a portion of their lives upon the ocean.

The Scald at one time was an invariable appendage to the court of a powerful prince or jarl, but even though a stranger he needed no introduction. It was not unusual during a banquet or festal meeting, for Scalds[1] to enter the king's hall, and demand

---

[1] Alfred the Great took advantage of this privilege to explore the Danish camp, A.D. 878, in the character of a Scald or Minstrel.

permission to sing a *Drapa* in praise of the monarch, and on these occasions they were usually liberally rewarded. Canute the Great gave the Scald, Berse Torveson, two gold rings, each half a mark in weight, and a gold-hilted sword, and to another fifty marks of silver for a song. Hacon Jarl gave Halfred Vanrode a silver-hafted axe and a good suit. Gunlaug the Icelander received rich presents from King Ethelred, of England, King Sigtryk Silk-beard, in Iceland, the Sweedish King Oluf, the Earl of the Orkneys, &c. and so many others.

The Scalda or Kenningar, which has already been mentioned as forming a portion of the Prose Edda, is a kind of poetical dictionary which contains the rules of their art, but Arngrim is of opinion that it was not compiled before the thirteenth century. According to Wormius the Scalds had 136 metres, without reckoning rhyme.[2] The melody of their verses, like that of the Anglo-Saxons, consisted in alliteration, or a fixed recurrence of certain vowels and consonants. This method of versification was also in use with the Welsh bards, and the oldest Irish poems are alliterative. Another characteristic of their poetry is the frequency of their metaphoric expressions, which, however, are not always without force, and the reader may be amused with the following selection of them:

---

[2] The well known ode, entitled the Ransom of Eigil, is in rhyme.

Ice	The greatest of bridges.
Gold	The tears of Freya. (v. ch. vii.)
The Sea . . .	The girdle of the Earth—the plain of Waterfowl.
A Ship . . .	The horse of the Waves—The Skate of Pirates—Horse of Heffler (a famous sea-king)—Asses of Ægir. (v. ch. vi.)
A Shield . .	The moon of the battle—The tent of Hlaka (a Valkyr).
Arrows . . .	The sorceress virgins of the String—Hailstones of Helmets—Daughters of misfortune.
A Battle . . .	A bath of blood—Hail of Odin—Shock of Bucklers—Storm of Gondol (a Valkyr).
The flashing of a sword .	The mortal gleam.
Wine	Blood.
The Tongue .	The sword of words.
Rivers	Sweat of the Earth—Blood of the Valleys.
Odin	The Sire of Ages—The God of swords—The supercilious—The incendiary—The Sire of Verses—The Whirlwind—The Eagle, &c.
The Bow . .	The Worm.
Swords	Herrings of Death—Cleavers of Helmets.
Death	The long wandering.
Lances	Cutting Rays—Rods of Odin.
Battle-Axe . .	The hand of the Slayer.
The Eye . . .	The torch of the face—The diamond of the Head.
Hair	Forest of the head—(if white) Snow of the Brain.
Cuirass . . .	The Bark of Hilda (goddess of war).
Shirt of Mail .	Hillock of Skogul (a Valkyr).
Wolf	Brother of the Vulture.

Warrior	Shaker of Helmets.
Sailors	Sons of Endil (a sea-king).
Grass	The hair, the fleece of the Earth.
Earth	The vessel which floats on ages—The daughter of the Night—Foundation of the air.
Night	The veil of cares.
Rocks	Bones of the Earth.
Poetry	The drink of Odin—Suttung's mead. (v. ch. i.)
Loke	The Adversary—The Accuser—The deceiver of the Gods.
Giants	Sons of the Frost.
Birds of prey	Birds with yellow legs.
Horns	Curved branches of the Skull.
The Raven	The Swan of Blood.
Blood	The rain of Wounds, &c.

None of the northern monarchs held the Scalds in higher esteem than the powerful Harald Haarfager, and at his table they had always the second seat of honour. In his Saga there is a story of his being on a visit to his fair kinswoman, Ingebiorg, whose charms had such an effect on three of his Scalds, that each separately had the audacity to make a declaration of love to the princess, and to entreat her pity. Ingebiorg suppressing her indignation, pretended to yield, and made an assignation with each for that very night. It was in the month of December, in Norway, she contrived to lock them up in separate rooms, where they had to remain in the lightest possible attire until morning. When, on rising, the king enquired for his Scalds, Ingebiorg led him to the shivering lovers, half dead with cold and fear, and it was with much difficulty that they escaped with their lives from the effects of his anger."[3]

Sometimes, to aid their memory, the Scalds were accustomed to cut Runes or letters upon their staves, but for the most part their songs were either extemporaneous or learned by rote. It is related of one Scald, that in a single evening he sang sixty songs to Harald Haardraade, and knew four times as many. Müller asserts, and not without reason, " that no nation ever possessed a poetry more strictly national than the Scandinavians." Although the fact of their having any at all has been roundly denied, and he adds, " that Snorro Sturtesen could not (as has been pretended) have invented the verses inserted in his history, since he appeals to them in his preface as authorities well known to his countrymen." The songs of the Scalds were chiefly in praise of the living, but they were rarely guilty of flattery, at least not during that which has been designated the heroic age of the north.

The following sketch of the history of the art of the Scalds in Norway from Professor Müller's Saga Bibliothek, during a period of about two hundred years, from the middle of the ninth to the middle of the eleventh century, will not be without interest, nor

---

[3] Om Kong Harald Haarfager's Skalde.—*Müller Saga Bibl.*

foreign to our subject, to those at all conversant in Norwegian history.

"Harald Haarfager's reign was the augustan age of the Scalds. Ambitious and warlike, he kept a splendid court, to which he sought to draw all the distinguished men of his country. The Scald, Thiodolf Hvine, was his bosom friend, and there are extant many fragments of songs in his honour.

"Eric Blodoxe (who figures in English history), although a lawless sanguinary prince, proved the estimation in which he held Scalds by granting Eigil his life, on account of the beauty of an ode, although he had slain his son.[4] His death, which took place during a piratical expedition to England about the middle of the tenth century, was sung in a celebrated Drapa which still exists.

"Hacon Adelsteen, or Athelstan (the god-son of Athelstan of England, in whose court he had been brought up) was, at least in heart, a Christian, and therefore gave but little encouragement to the Scalds, whose art was so entirely identified with the religion of Odin, which it tended much to keep alive. His praises, notwithstanding, were sung by three famous Scalds, the most celebrated of whom or indeed of any of the Scalds, Eyvind Scalda-spiller, was present when he was killed.[5]

---

[4] Vide page 321.

[5] The death-song of King Hakon Adelsteen has been translated into English by Dr. Percy, in a work entitled,

"The sons of Eric Blodoxe, although reproached with parsimony, kept up ancient usages at their court, and there was no lack of Scalds during their reign.

"Hacon Jarl troubled himself but little about the art of the Scalds, but this able and ambitious prince was a zealous adherent to the old faith, and the Scalds, therefore, were ever welcome to his board. One of the most famous amongst them, Einar Skaaleglam, was truly devoted to him, and his Drapa to his patron was held a model for after-Scalds.

"Olaf Tryggesen's zeal for Christianity caused him rather to discourage than to favour the Scalds; but one of them, indignant at seeing his art slighted, forced the king to listen to his song, by declaring that if he did not, he would immediately abjure Christianity, which Oluf, with much trouble, had induced him to embrace.

"The sons of Hacon Jarl retained their father's religion and principles without his cruelty. They were great encouragers of the Scalds, and favourites with all ranks.

"Olaf was, at first, as little inclined to the Scalds as his namesake Olaf Tryggesen, but he afterwards encouraged them; finding, probably, how much they added to his popularity and to the splendour with which he loved to surround his throne. On his

---

" *Five pieces of Runic Poetry*," amongst which will be found also " *The Ransom of Eigil.*"

last expedition, undertaken with a view to recover his kingdom, he was accompanied by several." Previous to the battle of Stickelstadt, 1030, famous in the history of Norway, the king after watching all night having fallen asleep towards dawn, suddenly waked, and calling for the Scald Tormod, bade him sing a *vise*.

Then Tormod stood up and sang the whole Biarkemaal[6] with so loud a voice, that the whole army heard it. The following is a free translation of the first two stanzas of this spirited battle-song.

> The bird of morn has risen,
> The rosy dawn 'gins break,
> 'Tis time from sleepy prison
> [7] Vil's sons to toil should wake.
> Wake, from inglorious slumber!
> The warrior's rest is short—
> Wake! whom our chiefs we number—
> The lords of Adil's court.
>
> Har, strong of arm, come forth,
> Rolf, matchless for the bow,
> Both Northmen, of good birth,[8]

---

[6] Biarke was a celebrated Scald, and it was usual to sing some stanzas of his ode previous to a battle.

[7] Men in general—Vil was the brother of Odin, and aided him in the creation of Askur and Embla, the first man and woman.

[8] The Scandinavians attached great importance to pedigree.

Who ne'er turn'd face from foe,
Wake not for foaming cup,
Wake not for maiden's smile,
Men of the North! wake up,
For iron Hilda's[9] toil!

This waked up the army, and caused a great enthusiasm amongst them. And Olaf thanked Tormod and gave him a gold ring for his song, who replied that he hoped the king and he would never be separated, either in life or death; remarking that Sigvald, Scald, was now far away with the gold-hilted sword the king had given him. Olaf said that he would not quit the field so long as one man remained by his side.[10] The day before having called his Scalds within the circle formed by the bravest men of the army, he said, " It is well that you are here to witness what is about to take place, and not to be obliged to have recourse to others when called on, hereafter, to sing the events of this day." Then the Scalds, having conversed together, said, that it was fitting that a song should be sung in honour of what was about to happen, on which each extemporized a strophe, which many of the army learned upon the spot. It was in the same spirit and in pursuance of the same custom that Taillefer at the battle of Hastings obtained the permission of Duke William to sing the song of Roland before the onslaught, and

---

[9] Hilda, the goddess of war.
[10] Heimskringla.

having done so he was the first to ride into the ranks of the English, where he was immediately slain.

But to return to Müller. " The belief in Olaf's sanctity, he continues, made Christianity national in Norway; and the heathen songs soon ceased to be dreaded. Scalds were well received at the court of the Christian king, Magnus the good, who used himself to extemporize verses. Harald Sigurdsen was a still greater friend to the Scalds, poetry being his favourite recreation; and it was probably this taste which caused him to shew such favour to all Icelanders: whilst on their part the Scalds vied with each other in singing his praises. King Harald with the flower of his army perished in England, A. D. 1066, and from this time the art languished and gradually died away. The universal establishment of Christianity, and consequent oblivion of the old religion, rendered the Scalds' favourite figures of speech daily less intelligible, and classical learning introduced by the priests, took the place of the old poetry. Towards the end of the thirteenth century this taste had so much gained ground, that it is related in the Saga of Bishop Laurentius, that a Norwegian noble, being desirous of paying his court to a young lady, a kinswoman of King Eric, the priest-hater, applied to Brother Laurence to help him with a Latin verse. When a Norwegian disdained to write to his mistress in his native tongue, it was time, remarks Müller, for the Scald with his antiquated phraseology to quit the field. About this time, also, the ballads and romances of the south of Europe began to be introduced into the North."[11]

Although from the circumstances which have been noticed in the introduction, Iceland became the classic land of the Scalds, it is not to be supposed that the three great Scandinavian kingdoms could not boast of their peculiar poets, Eyvind Skalda-spiller, the most celebrated of them all who was termed " the Cross of Poets," was a Norwegian, and so were many others. No one amongst them, however, seems to have played a more important part than the Icelander Eigil Skalagrimsen, a distinguished Scald, and one of the most undaunted warriors and formidable pirates of his day. It was he who with his brother Thorolf contributed so materially to the important victory gained by Athelstan at Brunanburh, A.D. 934, which annihilated the Anglo-Danish power in the North of England, and first, strictly speaking, brought the whole of South Britain under one sceptre.[12] His History, or Saga, written towards the middle of the twelfth century, is still extant, and as the simple narrative of the adventures of this extraordinary character and of his family, throw a strong light on the manners of the age in which they lived (from the middle of the ninth to the end of the tenth century), and will convey to the reader a better idea of the na-

---

[11] Prof. P. E. Müller Saga-bibliothek, 3rd vol. Introd.

[12] Sharon Turner's *Hist. of the Anglo Saxons.* Edit. 1823. vol. ii. p. 181. Book vi. chap. ii.

ture of the Sagas, generally, than any laboured essay, we shall here extract from Müller's *Saga Bibliothek* an abridged account of them.

" Eigil's grandfather, Queldulf, was a powerful man in Heligoland, who died about the commencement of Harald Haarfager's wars. Foreseeing that the different princes or petty-kings of Norway must at length be overwhelmed by that able monarch, he would never be persuaded to take any part against him, but neither would he consent to enter into his service. His brother-in-law, however, who was the third of Harald's chief Scalds, obtained his reluctant permission that his eldest son Thorolf should repair to Harald's court, lest the king might take offence. Harald received Thorolf well and took him into his service. He soon distinguished himself, and, through the king's influence, married a rich widow in Heligoland. He was now named king's tenant, and was sent to levy tribute from the Finns, with the exclusive privilege of trading with them on his own account. He became by degrees rich and powerful, and used to go to Finland with a suite of a hundred men; whereas none of his predecessors had ever taken more than thirty. King Harald once paid him a visit with three hundred followers, and Thorolf went out to meet him with five hundred, and had prepared an enormous wooden house in which he feasted the whole. His ostentation of power excited the jealousy of Harold, and Thorolf found it prudent to appease it by a present of a ship of war, fully equipped. His enemies, however, contrived to awaken the king's suspicions a second time, and Thorolf received orders to repair to court. This he refused to do, but resigned his fiefs. He still retained, however, a hundred freed men, whom he employed in the herring and cod fisheries, and made an expedition to the east of the Gulf of Finland, where he gained much booty. He loaded a ship thence for England with dried fish, oil, costly furs, hides, &c. taking in return wheat, honey, wine, and clothes.[13] This was about the year of our Lord 870. His enemies having accused him to the king of having unlawfully exacted taxes from the Finns, Harald caused his ship with its valuable cargo to be seized. Thorolf went the next year on another piratical expedition up the Baltic, and returning through the Sound, where some Norwegian vessels happened to be lying at the time, he revenged himself by capturing one laden with malt, wheat, and honey, for the king's housekeeping.

He was, in consequence, declared an out-law;

---

[13] To form a just estimate of the character of the Scandinavian Pirates, the Danes or Normans of the middle-ages, we must view them in their double capacity of Merchant and Rover. "The Danish merchants of this period," says Müller, were the choice spirits of the age, navigating their own ships, and having no security but in their strength, tried warriors of high birth, and minds not wholly uncultivated, who went out on their expeditions equally prepared to trade or to plunder."

and, as in the ensuing spring he was about to leave the country, Harald fell on him by surprise, and he was slain after a vigorous defence.

Aulver Hnussen, the king's Scald before alluded to, became mediator between his kinsmen and the king; and as Harald promised to give considerable compensation,[14] Thorolf's brother Grim, called from his scald head Skala-grim, repaired to the king's court. Harald also insisted that Grim should enter into his service, and, when Grim hesitated, was so enraged, that Aulver advised him to make his escape as speedily as possible.

There was now nothing left for Queldulf's family but to repair to the new land which Ingulf had lately discovered (Iceland), and they accordingly set sail thither; but not until they had taken a bloody revenge on the king's servants and kinsmen. Old Queldulf died on the voyage, but Grim arrived with two ships in Borg-fiord; and on landing, finding the neighbouring district unoccupied, he divided it amongst his followers. He was an able man, and, above all, a skilful smith. He had two sons, Thorolf and Eigil. The latter, when only three years old,

---

[14] By the Saxon laws every man's life was valued at a certain sum, which was called his *were*, and was paid to his relations in compensation for its loss. In Scandinavia the payment of a sum of money on a like occasion implied not merely a compensation, but in some respect also an apology and submission to the next of kin to the deceased.

began to make verses, and at the age of seven, killed a child who had irritated him at play. When only twelve years of age his strength was remarkably great, and, his father having vexed him, in revenge he stabbed one of his favourite servants, so that he died. His brother Thorolf entered the service of King Eric, of Norway, and returning, after a time, to Iceland to visit his father, Eigil accompanied him back to Norway.

Whilst there, in a quarrel he killed one of the king's bailiffs, and it was with great difficulty that he was allowed to quit the country, one of his friends having paid compensation-money for him. He next went with his brother on a piratical expedition to Courland, where he was taken prisoner by peasants; but escaping, returned, set fire to the house where they were drinking, and burned them all alive. He was afterwards engaged in various adventures, and repairing to England, was present with his brother, as before related, at the battle of Brunanburgh, where Thorolf was killed. King Athelstan for his services gave him two chests full of silver, and made him great offers to induce him to remain with him. Eigil, notwithstanding, returned to Norway for the purpose of espousing his brother's widow; and then sailed for Iceland with the English money. Soon after his wife's father died in Norway, and her brother, Bergaumund, having seized the whole inheritance, Eigil again repaired thither, and cited Bergaumund, who was protected by King Eric Blodoxe, to the *Gule-*

thing. Eigil's friend, Arinbiorn, accompanied him thither with a great body of men. In the midst of a wide plain, hazel-rods were placed in a circle, on which were fastened the sacred strings, called *Vebond.* Within the circle sate the judges (*Dommer*), twelve being from Fjordefylke; twelve from Sognefylke; and twelve from Hördafylke, for every cause was to be judged by three *Fylks.* Bergaumund asserted that Eigil's wife being born of a slave, could not inherit, but Arinbiorn proved by twelve witnesses that her birth was legitimate; and when the time was come for the judges to pronounce sentence, Queen Gunhild, being apprehensive of the result, procured one of her kinsmen to cut in twain the holy strings, by which means the *Thing* was suddenly broken up. Then Eigil challenged Bergaumund to the *Holmgang*, to decide there to whom the inheritance should belong; and declared feud and enmity against any who should dare to meddle with it. King Eric was highly irritated, but at the *Thing* all were weaponless. Eric sent men to take Eigil, who, however, effected his escape in a small vessel, and even succeeded in killing a man on board the king's own ship. He was immediately declared an outlaw throughout the whole country; and, having been furnished by Arinbiorn with a vessel with thirty men, he sailed away. Returning, however, suddenly in the night, he unexpectedly fell upon Bergaumund, and slew him, together with Rognvald, King Eric's son, a child of eleven years of age, who was then staying with him. Before he sailed away he cut a stake, and setting a horse's head upon it said, as he raised it up, " I raise up this *Nid-stang*, and turn this curse against King Eric and Queen Gunhild." Then, turning the horse's head towards the land, said, " I turn this curse against the spirits which dwell in this land (Landvætterne), that they may wander about bewildered and no one find his home until they have driven Eric and Gunhild from the land." He then stuck the pole in a cleft of the rock and went his way.[15]

Eigil reached Iceland A.D. 934, where, soon after, his father died. That summer, on account of the civil dissensions in Norway, no intelligence came thence to Iceland, an embargo having been laid on all vessels; and Eigil, weary of a peaceful life, determined to repair to the court of King Athelstan. In his voyage thither he was shipwrecked on the north

---

[15] Similar ceremonies were by no means unusual. The stakes (*Nidstange*) thus consecrated, were supposed not only to bring the wrath and vengeance of the gods upon the guilty, but were often used also to brand an adversary with contempt as a coward or *Nidding*. In the *Vatnsdæla Saga*, Finboge the strong, and his brother-in-law, Berg, having challenged the two brothers, Jokul and Thorstein, to a combat; it happened that on the day appointed there was so violent a storm, that Finboge and Berg thought themselves exempted from coming. Jokul in consequence raised a *Nidstang* against them (a horse's head upon the end of a pole), and the end of it was that Finboge was forced to leave the country.

coast of England; and learned to his sorrow that Eric Blodoxe, his mortal enemy, who had been driven from Norway, had received the kingdom of Northumberland as a fief from the English king on condition of defending it from the Scots, and that he had his residence in the neighbourhood. Eigil reflected that he could scarcely hope to escape undiscovered, and, not caring to be taken in flight, he resolved to ride at once to the royal residence, where, by good fortune, he fell upon Arinbiorn, who had given up everything in Norway to follow the banished king. He followed Arinbiorn's advice, went into the king's hall as he sat at table in the evening, and embracing his feet, declared in verse, that he had set danger at nought in order to seek a reconciliation with him. Eric replied that he might prepare himself for death; and Gunhild would have had him executed at once, but Arinbiorn represented to the king that it would be murder to slay any one by night, and obtained that Eigil's fate should be deferred until the next day, and that in the mean time he should remain in his (Arinbiorn's) custody. Arinbiorn advised Eigil, in the mean time, to compose a *Drapa* to the king's honour, sent him food and ale, and then, assembling his men, sate and drank with them until midnight. When morning came Eigil had finished his *Drapa*, and the two friends went with a large troop of armed men to the king's court. On their arrival there, Arinbiorn again entreated Eric, for his sake, to let Eigil go in peace; but when

Gunhild still urged the king to destroy him. Arinbiorn declared that he would defend him to his uttermost with his men. This made the king more tractable, and Eigil now recited his famous song, which has been preserved to the present day under the title of " The Ransom of Eigil." Eric was much struck with the beauty of the song, and said that since Eigil, of his own accord, had surrendered himself into his power he might depart; but warned him and his children never again to come before his eyes.

After this Eigil repaired to King Athelstan, and on his recommendation returned once more to Norway, with the view under Hagen Athelstan's just government to demand his wife's inheritance, now held by Bergaunund's brother, Atle. Hagen or Haeon forbad Eigil to remain in Norway, but allowed him to bring his cause before the *Gule-thing*. On the way he visited Arinbiorn's sister, whose young son, Fridgeir, had been challenged to the *Holm-gang* by a powerful champion, Liotr the pale, a Swede, who had paid court to his sister and having been rejected, took this method to revenge the affront. Eigil fought the duel in Fridgeir's place, and slew Liotr. After having delivered the summons to Atle in his own house, Eigil repaired to the *Thing* and demanded his property. Atle declared on the oath of twelve men, that he had no property of Eigil's, on which Eigil challenged him to the *Holm-gang*. He who conquered was to have the property, and after the fight was to slay a votive ox, which was led to the place of combat. After hewing at each other for some time, Eigil rushed in upon Atle and threw him.

Eigil now returned to Iceland, where he remained until the news came that Eric Blodoxe was slain, and Arinbiorn returned to Norway. He went thither to spend a winter with him, and took him a long-ship's sail richly worked, and other good presents. Arinbiorn as a julegift presented him with a silk upper-garment embroidered with gold, with gold buttons in front, as also an entire new suit of English cloth much embroidered, on which Eigil composed a verse.

After Juul Eigil got out of spirits, because he had inherited nothing from Liotr the pale. It was the law that whoever slew another in a duel should be his heir, but it was the law also that the king should inherit the property of all foreigners who died within his dominions; and therefore the king's bailiffs immediately took possession of Liotr's property. Eigil entreated the aid of Arinbiorn to make good his right, but he shewed him how difficult it would be to carry the matter through, for, said he, " the entrance to the king's court is wide, but the outlet is narrow." As Eigil, however, still persisted, Arinbiorn repaired for him to Hacon, by whom he was received harshly, as one who sought to serve a foreigner rather than his own sovereign, and who, moreover, secretly favoured Eric Blodoxe's sons. Arinbiorn would make no excuse, but returned straight home, and, opening a chest, took from it forty marks of silver, which he gave to Eigil for

Liotr's land, because Eigil, by taking on him the duel, had saved the life of his sister's son. Eigil took the money and again recovered his spirits.

Towards the spring, Arinbiorn went on a Viking's expedition with three long ships, having an hundred men in each, the greater number of whom were of his own household. Eigil took the command of one of these vessels manned by some of his own men, and the remainder he sent with a merchant ship to South Norway. After they had plundered Sax-land and Friis-land, they separated at the Liim-fjord, in the North of Jutland. Arinbiorn repaired to Eric's sons, and Eigil to Norway, to spend the winter with Thorstein, who was of kin both to him and Arinbiorn. King Hacon having learned the defection of the latter, seized his property and persecuted his kinsmen. He ordered Thorstein, amongst the rest, either to leave the country immediately, or to go and levy the taxes which Jarl Arnvid held back. This was a perilous errand, for none of those who had hitherto undertaken it had ever returned. Eigil, however, took upon him the adventure, and, after many perils, brought back the tribute, on which Thorstein was reconciled to the king, and Eigil sailed back to Iceland.

Soon after his return he lost a son, and a short time after his eldest son, Baudvar, was drowned in the Borgfjord. When Eigil found his son's body on the beach, he took it in his arms and rode with it to Skalagrim, his father's barrow, which he caused to be opened, and laid the corpse in it. Whilst thus occupied, his emotion was so violent that his vest burst. He afterwards went straight home, entered the recess where he was wont to sleep, threw himself down and drew the curtain. No one dared to speak to him, and he lay there three days without touching meat or drink. On the third morning his wife, Asgarde, sent one of the men to Hiardarholt, where his favourite daughter, Thorgerde, lived, who was married to Oluf Paa. Thorgerde arrived the same evening. When Asgarde asked her if she had supped, she replied with a loud voice that she had not eaten nor would again taste food until she ate with Freya. She then went to the recess and called to her father to open, saying that she was come to travel the same journey with him. Eigil opened, and Thorgerde laid herself down on the second bed. You do well, my daughter, said Eigil, to follow your father; much affection have you ever shewn me. How, replied she, could I desire to outlive this calamity? After this they were both silent for an hour, when Eigil said, Are you chewing anything, my daughter? I am chewing *Sol*,[16] for I think that it will thus be sooner over with me, and I fear to live too long. Is *Sol* hurtful then to men—very hurtful, said Thorgerde, will you eat of it?—Why should I not? replied Eigil. Soon after Thorgerde called for drink, and they brought her water. This comes of eating

---

[16] An esculent sea-weed.

sea-weed, said Eigil, one is devoured by thirst. Drink then, father, said she. They took him a horn, and he swallowed the liquid greedily. We have been deceived, cried Thorgerde, the drink was milk. On this Eigil, in vexation, bit a piece out of the horn, and threw it violently to the ground. What are we to do now, said the daughter, for our project is thwarted. Should we not do well, father, to prolong our lives until you shall have composed a song for Bodvar, and I have carved it on a stave. Eigil said that he was in no state to write verses, but that notwithstanding, he would try. He then composed the song, called the loss of a son (*Sonar Torrek*), in twenty-four strophes, and as he proceeded his spirits rose, and when it was complete he took it to his family, and having seated himself in the high-seat, according to ancient custom, he caused the funeral-ale to be drunk for the dead. When Thorgerde departed home he made her rich presents.

After this Eigil lived peacefully for many years in Iceland; and learning that Eric's sons had returned to Norway, and that Arinbiorn had again become a powerful man there, he composed a song in his honour, of which a fragment remains, and afterwards a funeral song over him. Eric's sons were soon again driven out of their possessions by Hacon Jarl, in whose praise the Scald Einar Skaaleglam composed a *Drapa*, and received from the Jarl in reward a shield on which were figured old legends, and between the figures were plates of gold enriched with precious stones. When Einar returned to Iceland he went to visit Eigil, who, however, at the time was from home; but having waited for him three days, as it was not the custom to remain longer in a strange place, he hung the costly shield on the wall and departed, saying to the men about that he made an offer of it to Eigil. When Eigil returned, this was told to him. The pitiful fellow! he exclaimed, does he expect that I will spend the night in making verses about his shield! Bring me my horse, I will ride after him and slay him. When they told him that Einar was already far away, he was pacified, and composed an ode on the occasion, and afterwards he and Einar were friends. Eigil's youngest son, Thorstein, was a handsome and a powerful man, but not so strong as his father, who never had great affection to him. When Asgerde died he gave up his Gaard to him, and went to live with one Grim who had married his sister's daughter, whom he loved much. He would never visit his son, but when Thorstein had to carry a dangerous affair at the *Thing*, Eigil now old rode thither with eighty armed men and obtained a decision for his son. Eigil attained the age of ninety years, and lost his sight and hearing; but was still strong, and in two stanzas bewailed the infirmities of his old age. He had determined to ride to the *Althing*, and there on the mount of justice to scatter about his English money, in order to make the whole assembly fight for it. When Grim would not allow this, he went out one morning with his two chests and two slaves, and no one ever saw slaves or chests after. Soon after, he died.[17]

The word *Saga* means, literally, a tale or narrative, and is used in Icelandic to denote every species of tradition, whether fabulous or true. In fact the variety of those which are still extant is nearly equal to their number, and upwards of two hundred are preserved in the libraries of Copenhagen, Stockholm, and Upsala. They are biographical narratives of greater or less length, totally independant of each other, describing events which have taken place, for the most part, from the ninth to the thirteenth century, and end with the *Sturlunga Saga*. Some of these have already been published with Latin translations, and the remainder are in the course of publication. In 1817, Professor P. Erasmus Müller, of Copenhagen, published his *Saga Bibliothek* in three volumes, in which he has given an abridgment of all the Sagas extant, fixing with great ingenuity their probable dates, and strictly examining their claims to authenticity. His interesting researches have opened the way to much valuable information respecting the civilization and domestic habits of Northern Europe during the period in question, and to him the author of these pages is chiefly indebted for the information he has sought to communicate in this appendix. The Professor has shewn that the greater portion of the early Sagas may be depended upon as faithful

---

[17] Eigil's Saga. Müller, *Saga Bibliothek*. vol. i.

historical narratives. It was not until the middle of the eighth century that historical romance was introduced into the North, chiefly from Spain. In the Sagas written subsequently to that period, truth and fiction are so blended as to render them historically useless. The Sagas usually begin in the simplest manner, " There was a man whose name was, &c. the son of," &c. The narrator seldom intrudes his own opinions, but contents himself with remarking that such or such an event encreased the person's reputation, or that men generally condemned such another.

We shall make no apology for here inserting the abridgments of two Sagas, each widely differing from the other in character, but both giving a lively picture of the manners of the times. The chief actors in the first were well known historical characters, and men of great influence, and there is very little doubt that everything therein described actually took place, and pretty nearly as it is told.

ABOUT ENDRID'S WEDDING.

" Endrid, a son of Einar Tambeskiælvar, was the boldest youth in Norway. One day whilst on a cruise southward, he landed on the island Kormt. A maiden came down to the vessel and begged to be taken on board. Her name was Siegrid, a daughter of the powerful Erling Skialgsen, of Jedderen. She had accompanied her foster-father to this distant isle, and was now longing to return once again to her kinsmen. Endrid, who was occupied in lading the vessel, had not given much heed to her, and she was allowed to go on board. When the vessel was well under sail, he began to enquire who she was, and having learned, he said to her, There is danger in having you here, but now there is no remedy and so must it be. After a short time the wind got up, and they were driven by a gale out to sea, and at length were glad to find anchorage under the lee of a small rocky island, where there was no cover but a deserted fisher's hut. 'Where will you lie to-night?' said Endrid to the maiden. 'I will lie next the wall, and you the nearest to me,' she replied. They did so, and he placed his sword between them. The storm continued for three days, and, when the weather cleared, they sailed to Drontheim. Einar received them coldly, and said to Endrid, 'You have become choice in your mistresses, seeing that no less than Erling's daughter will content you.' Endrid replied warmly, 'I did not expect such a remark from you, father, because I consented to take back the maiden to her home. It is no fault of mine that the weather prevented me from choosing the shortest course.' 'It matters but little, my son,' said Einar, 'what I may remark, but the maiden's father and kinsfolk will not pass this matter over lightly, and I am not desirous that she should tarry here.' Upon this Endrid got angry, prepared without delay a small vessel, and, despite of his father's warning, conducted her himself to Erling's Gaard. On their arrival, they found no one without, the whole household being at table. They entered the drinking chamber, and meat was served up, but no one addressed them a word. Erling's hall was not decked out with tapestry, but, over every man's head hung a breast-plate, a head-piece, and a sword. When it was time to retire, Endrid was conducted to a well-furnished chamber, where he found Sigrid lying in a bed, who commanded him, instantly, to retire. He did so at once, but had scarce turned his back on the door when he met Erling with a number of armed followers. 'Why do you not lay yourself in the bed:' said he sternly, 'is it less befitting to lie with my daughter here than in a fisher's hut?' Erling replied, 'I lay with your daughter in a fisher's hut, but so as to bring no dishonour on her nor on her kin.' Erling said, 'That talking would not serve him there,' and challenged him to submit to the ordeal of fire. Endrid declared himself willing to do so, in order to free the maiden and himself from dishonour, and then recited a verse. Endrid now fasted, as was the custom, and bare the iron. Three days after his hands were unbound and found whole. Erling praised him highly, and pressed him to remain with him as his guest, but Endrid angrily refused, and straightways departed.

"Skialg Erlingsen advised his father to lose no time to seek to pacify Endrid, for that otherwise the feud might prove many a man's bane, and obtained from him full authority, not only to consent to his daughter's marriage with Endrid, but even to offer her to him.

"When Skialg came up with Endrid, he told him that his father had given consent to his marriage with Sigrid. Endrid replied that he would own that he preferred Sigrid to any other maiden, but that after what had passed he could not pay court to her. But when Skialg added that her father himself offered her to him, Endrid agreed that this was sufficient compensation for his affront, and returning asked Erling if such was, in truth, his intention. Erling said that it was, and Endrid accepted the proposition with joy, and a great feast was held.

"Endrid now prepared to return to his father, and whilst on his way fell in with him in a ship of war (Drage-skib), accompanied by twenty smaller ones. Einar asked his son why his head was shaved round like a clerk's: Endrid answered, that he had borne the iron. Since you have borne hot iron, said Einar, and burned your skin, I will take care that many a Jedderlander shall feel cold iron in his. You resemble but little your grandsire, Hacon Jarl, or your father's kinsmen, Kætil Hæng and Queldulf. Endrid explained that he had been reconciled with Erling, adding that he had received money from him. All this Einar heard with impatience and scorn. Erling then said that he was to marry Sigrid. Einar said that she was purchased at far too high a price, that all this was no compensation for the affront offered to his blood, nor should stop his journey to Jedderland. At least, Endrid said, that Erling himself had offered his daughter to him. 'Is it so!' said Einar, 'then Erling was afraid, and this honour to us is a counterpoise to your disgrace; but we will continue our voyage to Jedderland that they may behold our force.' They were received in the most distinguished manner, and Endrid drank the marriage cup with Sigrid."

The next extract which we shall insert is chiefly of value as shewing the domestic manners of persons of the highest rank in Scandinavia.

CONCERNING RAUDULF.

"Once when St. Olaf, King of Norway, was making a progress through Upland, and had come to Oesterdal, his bailiff, Biorn, complained to him that of late great robberies had been made among the cattle in the neighbourhood, and that some rich landholders, who lived in a lone Gaard, hard by, were suspected as the plunderers. This landholder was named Raudulf, and his sons, Sigurd and Dag. Soon after these men themselves came to make their duty to the king, whom they invited to their Gaard, three days after. The king accordingly repaired thither with three hundred men. On arriving, he saw a high and massive palisade with a strong portcullis. The owner was at the gate with many followers to receive the king. Straight before them was a fair building, which Olaf took for a church, but it was a sleeping house roofed with wood. The whole room was well floored, and there were a great many other houses within the enclosure, great and small, and all well built. There was no church, for no bishop had ever been there. The king caused his travelling tent to be set up, in which evening prayers were said, and he went afterwards into the eating room, and lights were borne before him. He sate himself in the high seat, which had been well adorned; on his right was the bishop, on his left the queen, and the chief men were ranged on both sides. Next the bishop sate Finn Arnesen, then Kalf Arnesen, Thornberg, and the sons of Arne, Arnbiorn, Kolbein, and Arne. The king's followers occupied all the upper part of the chamber, in the lower part sate the household and the guests whom Raudulf had invited.

"The feast was excellent, and there was a variety of good drinks. Raudulf's sons went round and saw that the guests were attended to. The king conversed much with Raudulf, whom he found an intelligent man, and who talked of the future. Are you a soothsayer, then? said Olaf. No, replied he; but I am able to come to certain conclusions from the course of the sun, moon, and stars, and especially from dreams, for which latter purpose I always put on new garments, and lie down in a new bed, placed in a new spot. The king asked the sons whether they had profited by their father's wisdom: Sigurd said that he had learned from the course of the heavens to know the time, whether by day or by night. The younger son said that he could divine the character of men from their eyes, and any man's defects, or excellencies, from his countenance. King Olaf was in high spirits, and asked the bishop upon what quality he prided himself? The bishop said that he could sing twelve masses without book, and in return put the like question to the king, who replied, that having once set eyes upon a man he never forgot him, a very important quality, but, continued he, every man in his turn. What do you pique yourself on, Kalf Arnesen? That I never suffer my wrath to diminish, said Kalf, how long soever it be suspended. Finn Arnesen said, that no danger could ever make him desert his feudal lord. Thorberg, that he would never break an oath made to his lord. Arnbiorn said, that the bow did not exist which he could not bend. Kolbein had three qualities, skill in the bow, in running on skees, and in swimming. Arne in managing a boat. Biorn Stallar prided himself, that at the Thing he delivered the king's message in such a manner that he heeded not whether his speech pleased any great man or not; and so on with the remainder, which caused much amusement. When the king rose from table, Randulf conducted him to the new sleeping house with lights burning. It was built of a circular shape, with balconies all round it. Within these was a wall covered with shields, having four doors, equally distant from each other; the beds were ranged along the walls. In the middle of the house were twenty thick and lofty pillars, supporting a painted dome or canopy. The pillars were connected by cloth, and within this enclosure were the beds of the principal persons. In this twenty might sleep, and in the outer chamber forty. In the centre was an elevated platform, on which was a large bed adorned with great skill. The wood was covered with iron and copper, painted, and in parts, inlaid with gold. On the corner pillars were large gilded bosses of copper, from which issued iron bars with branches, each having three lights. Randulf said to the king that if he desired to have significant dreams, he should sleep in that new bed. Olaf was content and lay himself down. On the canopy above was painted God and his angels, the upper heaven, below this the stars, then the clouds and winds, the fowls, and lowest of all the earth with plants, trees, &c. On the tapestry between the pillars were heathen figures, and traditions concerning celebrated kings. The queen and her women lay on the king's left, the bishop and priests on his right. Arnbiorn and Kolbein lay near the head of the bed with their men. Finn and Thorberg at the feet. Olaf, after having sung his evening prayer, lay awake longer than usual, gazing on the canopy, which at length seemed to him to turn round, and he fell asleep. The next morning he related his dream to Randulf, and bade him interpret it after high mass, which he did.

" He put to the test also the gifts of the two sons.

The weather turned out as Sigurd had predicted, and although the morning was thick and dark, he told at once the hour. Olaf bade Dag tell him from his appearance what was his constitutional weakness. After some hesitation, Dag said that the king was fond of women, and Olaf acknowledged that he was right. At Dag's suggestion the stolen cattle were sought for in the house of the bailiff himself, and there found, and Biorn was dismissed from his office."

It will not be here out of place, before quitting the subject entirely, to speak shortly of the favourite pursuits and amusements of these Northern warriors, so often alluded to in the Sagas.

It has been shewn that a particular constellation was consecrated to each of the twelve principal deities, and that the Scandinavians had their solar houses answering to the signs of the Greek zodiac. The frequent maritime expeditions of their chiefs, in fact, rendered a knowledge of the stars absolutely necessary; and this knowledge led naturally to a belief in astrology; a superstition from which scarcely any nation has been entirely exempt, and which has often enchained even the strongest minds. The Finlapps, to this day, are in the habit of predicting the fate of a new-born child from the position of the stars. Meteors, or shooting-stars, were supposed to be the horses of the Valkyrs; Ursa Major, they called the Great Dog; Ursa Minor, Charles' Wain; the three stars in Orion's belt, Freya's distaff; the

Swan, the Cross; the milky-way, the winter-road; and the dog-star, *Loka-brenna*, or Loke's burning. They had also stars called the wolf, the eagle, and the raven; and when Thor slew Thrym, he cast his eyes up to heaven, where they became stars, or, according to another passage, it was Odin who placed them there to console Skada.

Another accomplishment to which great importance was attached, was the art of cutting Runes. The old northern word *Run* (plural *Runar*) originally signified a word or discourse, more particularly in secret; and, on the introduction of writing, was naturally enough applied to those mysterious characters which could convey secretly, and at any distance, the thoughts of one person to another. Odin was considered as their inventor, and they were supposed to possess supernatural powers in the hands of those who had the secret of arranging them. In a little poem, called the Runic Chapter, or the magic of Odin, which forms a portion of the Edda, the father of the gods boasts, at length, of the wonders he could perform with their aid; such for example, as to render harmless the weapons of an enemy, to still the raging of the storm, to arrest sorcerers in their flight through the air, to gain the love of women, to restore the dead to life, &c. Runes cut on the rim of a drinking-horn, and sprinkled with blood from the hands, were considered a preservative against poison in the liquor. Great caution, however, was to be observed in the employment of them. A lover, once, desiring to awake love in the bosom of his mistress by cutting Runes, made a mistake in their position, and brought on her a lingering illness. The Runic staffs, also called *Riim-stocks*, and *Prim-staffs*, were smooth, flat pieces of wood, of a foot and upwards in length, and two or three inches in breadth. On these were scored marks denoting the principal fasts and holidays of the year, and they are still used as almanacks in Norway. The antiquity of the Runic characters has been denied, and their invention attributed to the Gothic Bishop, Ulphilas, who lived in the reign of the Emperor Valens; but it has been proved that his alphabet is wholly different. Runestones, older than the introduction of Christianity, are, however, of rare occurrence.

A third accomplishment was the art of running upon *Skees* or Snow-shoes (*Skieloben*, *Skidfæri*). This was of great antiquity amongst the Norwegians, and still greater amongst the Finns. The *Skees* are long flat pieces of wood, sometimes six feet in length, by means of which, and aided by a long pole held in both hands, a person expert in the use of them will pass over the deepest snow with great rapidity. It was one of the accomplishments on which warriors prided themselves the most. Einar Tambeskielvar, mentioned in the Saga concerning Endrid, Harald Hardraade, and Harald Blaatand, kings of Denmark and Norway, were celebrated for their skill in this exercise. It is still a common amusement in winter in Drontheim, and with them the Finns and Lapps will beat a man with skates on clear ice. When Norway belonged to Denmark, previous to 1814, it had two regiments of *Skee-runners*, each consisting of 480 men, whose services in a winter campaign might have been turned to excellent account. One Arnliot Gellina is said to have been so expert that he would let two others stand on his skees and yet run as fast as an ordinary person alone. In short the ancient Scandinavians were skilful in almost all athletic exercises. In foot-races, in which men of the first rank and kings themselves were wont to take part. Olaf Tryggesen, and King Harald Gille, an Irishman, were particularly celebrated in this and all similar feats, as well as in skaiting and leaping. The *Nials Saga* speaks of one Icelander who, in complete armour, could leap higher than he stood, of another who sprang twenty-four feet over a river, although the banks on both sides were frozen and slippery. Dances too were frequent with the Northmen, and amongst others a sword-dance, which required considerable dexterity. Wrestling was also common in all its branches, exactly as it still exists with us. Bowls, and a kind of hockey, were played on a plain, or, in winter, on the ice, and rowing was a favourite exercise, but the art of riding gracefully was introduced later from the south, with tournaments. The ancient Scandinavians, whose warlike expeditions were chiefly by sea, knew nothing of cavalry. They prided themselves much on their skill with the bow, particularly the inhabitants of Tel-

APPENDIX.

lemark: Einar Tambeskielvar was one of the most celebrated for this exercise. They excelled also in throwing the spear, in slinging, and in the use of the broad-sword. But of none of these exercises is such frequent mention made in the Sagas as of that of swimming, which was the favourite recreation of Olaf Tryggesen, who excelled in all these athletic sports. The following extract from the Saga of that monarch is too characteristic to be here omitted.

"About this time King Olaf was engaged in a great work, having commenced building the new town of Nidaros,[18] together with a palace and a church. A great quantity of building timber had been conveyed by his orders to the shore, which he gave to any who chose to build. Hacon Jarl was lately dead, and all the people had acknowledged Olaf as king, but many were unwilling to embrace the new faith which he was so anxious to introduce. There happened to be three Iceland ships lying at anchor at the bridge, on board of which were several Icelanders of distinction, who had come to a resolution to refuse adherence to the new faith. Kiartan, the son of Oluf Paa, a rich Icelander, arrived a few days after in a vessel which he had fitted out on an adventure. He was the handsomest and tallest man in Iceland, with fair silken hair which fell in ringlets, and large blue eyes, and was distinguished beyond others in all manly exercises, particularly in swim-

[18] Now Trondhjem or Drontheim.

APPENDIX.

courageous and promising as you appear should not return to his comrades without a cloak. I give you mine, and desire you to consider what has passed between us to-day as mere sport, for I think that your reputation as a swimmer will fall in the eyes of but few, even though it get abroad that I measured myself with you in that exercise.' Kjartan thanked the king for his cloak, which was of great value, but his countrymen were not well pleased that he had accepted it, since the fact might be construed as implying that he had submitted himself to the king."[19]

Lastly, skill in smith's work was an accomplishment held by the Northmen in the highest esteem. The most distinguished of northern smiths was the far famed Velent, or Vaulund, the nearly forgotten tradition concerning whom has of late been rendered popular in England, by the author of Kenilworth, in the person of Wayland Smith. About a mile from the White Horse Hill, near Ashdown, where the great battle took place in A. D. 871, between King Alfred and the Danes, there is a rude Bauta or monumental stone similar to those so frequent in Denmark and Norway. There was a tradition amongst the peasants in the vicinity, that an invisible smith lived there formerly; who, if any traveller's horse dropped a shoe on the road, would put it on again, and that this mysterious farrier was named Wayland Smith. There was a well known Norman or Danish

[19] Olaf Tryggesan's Saga.

ming. He was welcomed by his countrymen, who asked him what he intended to do concerning the new faith. He said that he cared but little about the matter, but was willing to abide by the decision they had already come to. It was a fine hot day in autumn, and several of the townspeople were amusing themselves with swimming in the river Nid. Kjartan proposed to his countrymen to go to see how the strangers acquitted themselves, and accordingly they went. One man evidently far outdid the rest in all feats in the water, and Kjartan, turning to Halfred Ottarsen, proposed to him to try his skill with this man. 'Far be it from me,' said Halfred, 'he is one with whom I have no desire to come in collision.' Kjartan then asked his friend Bolle if he would not swim with the townsman. 'I do not consider myself equal to it,' said Bolle. 'I know not what has become of your spirit,' said Kjartan, 'but I am resolved to try his force, though neither of you have the courage to do so.' Saying this, he went straight to the point opposite, to the place where the townsmen were swimming, and throwing off the scarlet short coat in which he was clad, sprang into the water, and swimming straight to the man, seized and dived with him, keeping him under for a time. When they came up the townsman, after a very short interval, took Kjartan down in his turn, and remained under the water longer than his adversary desired. They came to the surface a second time, spake not a word to each other, but, after a few moments, went

down together again, and remained under st[ ] than before. Kjartan now began to have s[ ] prehension as to how this sport might e[ ] thought that he, never before, had been in so [ ] ous a position. At last the man let him u[ ] they swam together to shore and began to [ ] when Kjartan first was fully aware how muscul[ ] large a man he had been struggling with. A[ ] time the stranger asked Kjartan who he was[ ] Kjartan told him his name and birth-place. '[ ] swim well, Icelander,' said the townsman, ' are[ ] as skilful in other accomplishments as in this?' [ ] have not acquired much honour by my swimmi[ ] returned Kjartan, ' and may probably succeed[ ] better with the others, although in my native la[ ] they have been called accomplishments.' ' The [ ] nour you may gain from them,' said the townsma[ ] ' will depend much on those with whom you t[ ] them. But why do not you ask me who I am[ ] Kjartan said, ' That he had no desire, whatever, t[ ] know.' ' To do you justice,' said the townsman[ ] ' you are a manly fellow, but you seem somewhat haughty also. You shall know, however, with whom you have been trying your skill in swimming, my name is Olaf Tryggesen, and here men call me the king.' Kjartan made no reply, but was going away without his cloak. The king called him back, and bade him not be in such haste. Kjartan returned, although very slowly, and the king, taking his own cloak from his shoulders, said, ' A young man so leader of the name of Veland, who desolated France about the years 861-62, and was supposed to have been killed in a duel there in 863; but, as Müller remarks, it is not improbable that a Norman leader of the name of Veland may have fallen on this spot, and in the course of time, been confounded by the people with the fabulous Velent, or Wayland, whose legend was current with all nations of Gothic descent. King Alfred, in his translation of Boethius, p. 43 and 162, asks, " Where are now the bones of the wise and famous Goldsmith Velent! who knows his barrow!" In Professor Thorkelin's translation of the Anglo-Saxon Scyldinger, p. 36. Biovulf prays that his good arms, the work of Veland, may be laid with him in his grave.[20] In Ritson's *Ancient Metririeal Romances*, Lond. 1802. vol. iii. p. 382. 32mo. there is mention of a sword made by Weland,[21] and the same name is often introduced in the old German legends. In a Latin poem, " *de primâ expeditione*

---

[20] Mitte Higelaci
Si me bellum auferat
Apparatum Martium optimum,
Quod pectus meum gerit
Gestamen præstantissimis
Id est spoliis conversatum
Welandi opus.

[21] It is the make of Mining,
Of all swerdes it is king,
And Weland it wrought
Bitterfer it hight.

Altilæ regis Hunnorum in Gallias," Walther of Vaskastein is said to bear weapons of Veland's make, and an anonymous French author of the twelfth century relates of William the Iron-cleaver, son of Aldrim, Duke in Angoulesme, that he derived that surname from the excellence of his sword, made by the Smith Valandus.[22] In pursuance of the plan adopted throughout this work, we shall here give an abridgment of the history of this mysterious personage from the Vilkina Saga, as a curious specimen of the fabulous Sagas generally.[23] It is of the most remote antiquity, and is remarkable, amongst other things, as containing, probably, the original of the fable of which in modern times William Tell has become the hero. The feat of shooting an apple from a boy's head was a favourite one with the Icelandic story tellers; and is to be found in more than one of the Sagas. The celebrated historian, Saxo the Grammarian, tells it of a famous chief, Palnatoke, who was cotemporary with the father of Canute the Great. Saxo himself lived about the end of the twelfth century.[24]

---

[22] P. E. Muller's Saga Bibliothek. vol. iii. p. 161. 162.

[23] Allusion is made also to Weland's misfortunes in the Anglo-Saxon poem from the Exeter manuscript, given in Conybeare's Anglo-Saxon Poetry, p. 238.

[24] Muller considers that the story told of William Tell is more probably derived from this tale, deemed by many originally German, than from Saxo. Some have declared the whole tale of Eastern origin.

VELENT'S SAGA.

" Velent's father, Vade, was the son of King Vilkinus, and a Mermaid whom he met in a wood near the sea-shore, as he was returning from a cruize in the Baltic. His father never took to him, but gave him twelve castles in Zealand. At the age of nine years Velent was sent to learn smith's work in the land of the Huns,[25] where he suffered much ill treatment from Sigurd Svend, who was under the same master, Mimer Smith. His father, therefore, removed him thence, and placed him with two skilful dwarfs, who lived in the mountain Kullen. After remaining with them more than two years, they became envious of his skill, and sought to take his life, but he slew them both, and having set himself with his tools in a hollow tree, with a glass window in front, he committed himself to the mercy of the waves, and was drifted to Thy, in Jutland, where he was well received by King Nidung. His father, sometime before had been killed by an avalanche. He soon found an

---

[25] The Huns are frequently alluded to in the songs of the Edda, and in the old fabulous Sagas. Magnussen is of opinion that these Huns were the subjects of Attila, who is himself often brought on the stage under the name of Atle, and also that the name of Huns is often applied to people of the Slavic or Vandal family.—*Magnussen Den Ældre Ædda*, v. iv. p. 312.

opportunity to shew how far he surpassed the king's smith, Æmilius, in his own craft. The king once set out on a warlike expedition with 30,000 knights, and after five days march having discovered that he had left behind the stone which always brought him victory, he offered his daughter and half his kingdom to any one who would bring it to him in one day. Velent did so, but the king evaded his promise, and banished Velent for having killed one of his men. To revenge himself Velent disguised himself as a cook, and put some magic herbs in a soup prepared for the princess. The plot was discovered in time, and Velent having been seized, the king ordered the sinews of his feet to be cut, and he was forced to sit in the king's court and to employ himself in forging jewels for his enemies. About this time Egil, Velent's younger brother, who was a celebrated archer, came also to King Nidung's court. The king had him seized also, and to prove his skill, forced him to shoot an apple placed on the head of his son, a child of three years old. Egil took three arrows from his quiver, and then shot the apple from the lad's head, which feat was much celebrated. The king asked him what he had intended to do with the other arrows. He answered boldly, that he had meant them for him had the arrow struck his boy, and the king approved the answer. Velent still meditated revenge, and, one day, when the king's daughter came into his workshop to have a ring repaired, he violated her, and soon after having enticed away her two youngest brothers, he killed them both, and inserted their bones in a costly vessel of gold which he had been forced to make for the king's table. He had made himself wings from the feathers of birds, shot by his brother Eigil, and by means of these flew up to the highest tower of the king's palace, from whence, with a loud voice, he declared to the king what he had done. The king caused Egil to be brought, and threatened him with instant death unless he killed his brother with an arrow. Egil shot, and the arrow struck Velent under the left arm, from which the blood flowed copiously, and although Velent flew away towards Zealand, the king was satisfied that he could not survive. Egil, however, had only struck a bladder filled with red liquor, which Velent, foreseeing what would happen, had placed under his arm. The king, soon after, died, and Velent effected a reconciliation with his son, and married the sister, who had already produced him a son, named Vidga."

We shall close this Appendix with a few remarks on the belief in magic and witchcraft amongst the ancient Scandinavians.

They believed in two species of sorcery, one of which was named *Galldur*, and was to be effected chiefly by means of songs and runes engraved upon the bark of trees: and it was in this art that Odin was so great a proficient. The second kind was called *Seid*, which the Aser learned of the Vaner. *Seid* was a kind of soup or ointment, the ingredients of which seem to have varied according to the effects to be produced. They consisted in part of the hearts and blood of serpents and wolves, of dew of boiled swine's liver, of various herbs, &c. and at last Runes were generally thrown into the cauldron. The preparation of *Seid* was said to be so loathsome that men became blind with it, and it was at last abandoned to women.

It was a very general superstition in the north, that by eating of the hearts of particular animals, a person might acquire the properties peculiar to the animals themselves. It is related in the *Heimskringla Saga*, that Sigurd, by eating of the heart of the great serpent, Fröfner, became so wise as to understand the cry of birds. Every jule-evening, for three years successively, a terrible animal, or rather an enchanter with wings, whom no steel would touch, used to come to King Hrolfe's palace in Leira. Biarke slew him, and made his comrade (Stallbroder), Hodur, eat of its heart, so that from being timid, he became strong and valiant. Nor was this property confined to the hearts of animals alone, since Saxo tells us that Eric the Wise learned to understand the conversation of all animals, by eating a soup made of snake's flesh. Guttorm ate of a snake and a wolf cooked together, and became very cruel and daring. Biarke's brother, Elg Frode, having wounded himself in the leg, gave Biarke some of the blood to drink, telling him that he would thus become stronger than other men; Sigurd, by drinking a certain potion, forgat his love to Brynhilde; and Asa-Loke himself is said to have acquired a great portion of his evil qualities, from having eaten the heart of a witch.

We learn from Th. Bartholin, that there were certain sorceresses or fortune-tellers (*Valas*) in Scandinavia, who wandered about the country predicting future events, and the fortunes of young children of rank. The sorceress Heidr, a widow, had in her troop thirty young men and fifteen maidens, who were set on high places, and had under them cushions stuffed with cock's feathers. They wore Hunnish belts, and purses in which they kept all that they had need of for their magic. One of them ate a soup of goat's milk, and a dish of the hearts of all the animals which were served up to the others. They could prophesy of good and bad times, and used various instruments and large *Seid-staffs*. The enchantress Hulda, whose legend has been translated from the Icelandic, by the learned Captain Abrahamsen, was a renowned witch (*Seid-kona-volva*) in the north, and superstitions connected with her still linger amongst the rocks of Norway. The peasants there believe to this day that Hulla or Huldren, is the queen of subterranean beings, and wife to the elf-king, Thusselin, who is described as of diminutive stature, whilst, on the contrary, Hulla is said to be a tall old woman of a dark colour, who, seen from behind, resembles a trough. The *Elle-*

maids also were to be known, from being hollow behind, and the sign of the cross was sufficient to make them turn round; but this defect does not seem to have been attributed to them before the introduction of Christianity. Hulla is also to be seen in stormy weather, driving before her through the woods large herds of dark grey cattle and sheep. Cattle of this kind are hence called *Hulla-creatur*, and are highly prized. Some pretend to have even seen her residence, and peasants still living assert that at particular moments they have perceived farm-houses and cultivated fields, where were usually only vast woods. Both Hulla and Thusselin are accused of carrying off cattle, and even human beings, but are obliged to return them on hearing the sound of a church bell. They were particularly addicted to stealing unbaptized children, leaving their own deformed bantlings in their stead. On whipping, however, the young imp three Thursday evenings successively, Hulla is forced to restore the rightful progeny. This is evidently a superstition from the times of paganism, Thor being the great foe of giants and all spirits of darkness. Hulla, however, is best known by her song, (the *Huldre-slaat*), a subterranean musick or hollow mournful sound, often heard in the mountains.[26]

Indeed none of the superstitions of the Scandinavians seem to have been more universal than their

---

[26] Müller Saga-Bibliothek.

APPENDIX. 355

belief in the preternatural powers possessed by certain women whom they called *Valas* or witches, who previous to the introduction of Christianity, were held in high esteem and respect, as we may perceive from the account given of Thorbiorg, called the lesser Vala, in the Saga of Eric the red.[27] They used wands and magical incantations, were often attended by a numerous suite, and possessed great influence. As Christianity gained ground, they were represented in an odious light, as demons, or sold to the devil, instead of being simply exposed as impostors. But in heathen times also the people believed in malignant witches, who were represented as aged and deformed, residing in gloomy impenetrable forests, and riding by night through the air on wolves with snakes for bridles. They were supposed to have the power of assuming the form of wolves, and were called Wehrwolves (Varulve). The Mar or night-mare, the belief in which is very ancient, seems to have been some such demon or evil spirit.[28] There is mention of it in the Heimskringla, and Suhm remarks that the word has the same signification in Danish (Maren), English (Nightmare), French (Cauche-Mar), and German (Nacht Mar).

The old Scandinavians had also many superstitions respecting barrows and the spirits of deceased men. Before the introduction of the religion of Odin, they

---

[27] Eric Rödes' Saga.
[28] Magnussen.

believed that these spirits, called by them *Draugr*, remained with the bodies which they had once inhabited, and at times wandered about the earth. Hence the general prevalence of the belief in spectres in the north of Europe, a belief not yet eradicated. According to Suhm, Odin, finding it impossible to destroy this belief, although, in fact, inconsistent with his doctrine, attributed to himself power over these spirits, and hence he was called king of spectres and king of the barrows, by sitting upon which, and employing certain spells, he was able to call up the dead. We are told in one of the old Northern Kiœmpe-Viser, that Odin gave permission to King Helge Hundingsbane, a celebrated Danish hero, to visit nightly his barrow, in order to converse with his young and disconsolate widow, who used there to meet him. King Helge was seen one night by an attendant of his widowed bride entering into his barrow. She conveyed the intelligence to her mistress, who immediately hastened to seek him, and on perceiving that there was no illusion, but that the spirit of her lord was indeed there, addressed him as follows :

>Now am I more glad
>At this our meeting
>Than the rapacious
>Hawks of Odin
>When they devour
>Their daily meal,
>Or when they perceive
>The dewy dawn of morn.

I will kiss
My lifeless king
Ere he throws off
His bloody helm;
Helge, thine hair
Is wet with blood,
The dew of death hath bathed
My warrior's body,
Thy hands, my king,
Are icy cold,
O Helge, how shall I
Find cure for this!

HELGE'S SPIRIT.

'Tis thou, Sigruna,
Art cause, alone,
That Helge is bathed
With the dew of sorrow.
O, sunny daughter of the south
Decked out with gold!
Ere that thou goest to rest
Thou weepest bitter tears:
Each bloody tear
Falls on my breast,
Icy cold, and torn with grief.

It was a very old belief that deceased persons were sorely afflicted by the grief of those who lamented them.

The power to raise spirits from the dead was not confined to Odin. In Groa's magic song, one of the poems of the Elder Edda, a son summons his mother's spirit from her grave, in order to ask her counsel how to escape from dangers in which she, whilst living, had involved him. He thus begins his invocation:

SON.

Wake up, Groa,
Wake up, good mother,
At the door of death I wake thee;
Dost thou remember
That thou badest thy son
Come to thy grave?

MOTHER.

What desireth
Mine only son,
What peril threateneth thee now;
That thou callest up thy mother,
Who is turned to earth,
Removed from the world of man?

He asks her advice and protection in his perilous enterprize She gives him nine rules for his direction, and bids him proceed fearlessly wherever the danger was greatest. The Scandinavians, like the Greeks, Romans, and other ancient nations, attributed certain mystic properties to the number nine. One of their deities, Njord, had nine daughters, another, Heimdall, nine mothers. Odin lay nine nights on the tree of the universe. The number of worlds according to them was nine. At the great feat at Upsala, held every ninth year, ninety-nine hawks or cocks were sacrificed to Odin, &c.

ming. He was welcomed by his countrymen, who asked him what he intended to do concerning the new faith. He said that he cared but little about the matter, but was willing to abide by the decision they had already come to. It was a fine hot day in autumn, and several of the townspeople were amusing themselves with swimming in the river Nid. Kjartan proposed to his countrymen to go to see how the strangers acquitted themselves, and accordingly they went. One man evidently far outdid the rest in all feats in the water, and Kjartan, turning to Halfred Ottarsen, proposed to him to try his skill with this man. 'Far be it from me,' said Halfred, 'he is one with whom I have no desire to come in collision.' Kjartan then asked his friend Bolle if he would not swim with the townsman. 'I do not consider myself equal to it,' said Bolle. 'I know not what has become of your spirit,' said Kjartan, 'but I am resolved to try his force, though neither of you have the courage to do so.' Saying this, he went straight to the point opposite, to the place where the townsmen were swimming, and throwing off the scarlet short coat in which he was clad, sprang into the water, and swimming straight to the man, seized and dived with him, keeping him under for a time. When they came up the townsman, after a very short interval, took Kjartan down in his turn, and remained under the water longer than his adversary desired. They came to the surface a second time, spake not a word to each other, but, after a few moments, went lemark: Einar Tambeskielvar was one of the most celebrated for this exercise. They excelled also in throwing the spear, in slinging, and in the use of the broad-sword. But of none of these exercises is such frequent mention made in the Sagas as of that of swimming, which was the favourite recreation of Olaf Tryggesen, who excelled in all these athletic sports. The following extract from the Saga of that monarch is too characteristic to be here omitted.

" About this time King Olaf was engaged in a great work, having commenced building the new town of Nidaros,[18] together with a palace and a church. A great quantity of building timber had been conveyed by his orders to the shore, which he gave to any who chose to build. Hacon Jarl was lately dead, and all the people had acknowledged Olaf as king, but many were unwilling to embrace the new faith which he was so anxious to introduce. There happened to be three Iceland ships lying at anchor at the bridge, on board of which were several Icelanders of distinction, who had come to a resolution to refuse adherence to the new faith. Kiartan, the son of Oluf Paa, a rich Icelander, arrived a few days after in a vessel which he had fitted out on an adventure. He was the handsomest and tallest man in Iceland, with fair silken hair which fell in ringlets, and large blue eyes, and was distinguished beyond others in all manly exercises, particularly in swim-

---

[18] Now Trondhjem or Drontheim.

down together again, and remained under still longer than before. Kjartan now began to have some apprehension as to how this sport might end, and thought that he, never before, had been in so dangerous a position. At last the man let him up, and they swam together to shore and began to dress, when Kjartan first was fully aware how muscular and large a man he had been struggling with. After a time the stranger asked Kjartan who he was, and Kjartan told him his name and birth-place. 'You swim well, Icelander,' said the townsman, ' are you as skilful in other accomplishments as in this?' 'I have not acquired much honour by my swimming,' returned Kjartan, ' and may probably succeed no better with the others, although in my native land they have been called accomplishments.' 'The honour you may gain from them,' said the townsman, ' will depend much on those with whom you try them. But why do not you ask me who I am?' Kjartan said, ' That he had no desire, whatever, to know.' ' To do you justice,' said the townsman, ' you are a manly fellow, but you seem somewhat haughty also. You shall know, however, with whom you have been trying your skill in swimming, my name is Olaf Tryggesen, and here men call me the king.' Kjartan made no reply, but was going away without his cloak. The king called him back, and bade him not be in such haste. Kjartan returned, although very slowly, and the king, taking his own cloak from his shoulders, said, ' A young man so courageous and promising as you appear should not return to his comrades without a cloak. I give you mine, and desire you to consider what has passed between us to-day as mere sport, for I think that your reputation as a swimmer will fall in the eyes of but few, even though it get abroad that I measured myself with you in that exercise.' Kjartan thanked the king for his cloak, which was of great value, but his countrymen were not well pleased that he had accepted it, since the fact might be construed as implying that he had submitted himself to the king." [19]

Lastly, skill in smith's work was an accomplishment held by the Northmen in the highest esteem. The most distinguished of northern smiths was the far famed Velent, or Vaulund, the nearly forgotten tradition concerning whom has of late been rendered popular in England, by the author of Kenilworth, in the person of Wayland Smith. About a mile from the White Horse Hill, near Ashdown, where the great battle took place in A. D. 871, between King Alfred and the Danes, there is a rude Bauta or monumental stone similar to those so frequent in Denmark and Norway. There was a tradition amongst the peasants in the vicinity, that an invisible smith lived there formerly; who, if any traveller's horse dropped a shoe on the road, would put it on again, and that this mysterious farrier was named Wayland Smith. There was a well known Norman or Danish

---

[19] Olaf Tryggesan's Saga.

will beat a man with skates on clear ice. When Norway belonged to Denmark, previous to 1814, it had two regiments of *Skee-runners*, each consisting of 480 men, whose services in a winter campaign might have been turned to excellent account. One Arnliot Gellina is said to have been so expert that he would let two others stand on his skees and yet run as fast as an ordinary person alone. In short the ancient Scandinavians were skilful in almost all athletic exercises. In foot-races, in which men of the first rank and kings themselves were wont to take part. Olaf Tryggesen, and King Harald Gille, an Irishman, were particularly celebrated in this and all similar feats, as well as in skaiting and leaping. The *Nials Saga* speaks of one Icelander who, in complete armour, could leap higher than he stood, of another who sprang twenty-four feet over a river, although the banks on both sides were frozen and slippery. Dances too were frequent with the Northmen, and amongst others a sword-dance, which required considerable dexterity. Wrestling was also common in all its branches, exactly as it still exists with us. Bowls, and a kind of hockey, were played on a plain, or, in winter, on the ice, and rowing was a favourite exercise, but the art of riding gracefully was introduced later from the south, with tournaments. The ancient Scandinavians, whose warlike expeditions were chiefly by sea, knew nothing of cavalry. They prided themselves much on their skill with the bow, particularly the inhabitants of Telonce, desiring to awake love in the bosom of his mistress by cutting Runes, made a mistake in their position, and brought on her a lingering illness. The Runic staffs, also called *Riim-stocks*, and *Prim-staffs*, were smooth, flat pieces of wood, of a foot and upwards in length, and two or three inches in breadth. On these were scored marks denoting the principal fasts and holidays of the year, and they are still used as almanacks in Norway. The antiquity of the Runic characters has been denied, and their invention attributed to the Gothic Bishop, Ulphilas, who lived in the reign of the Emperor Valens; but it has been proved that his alphabet is wholly different. Runestones, older than the introduction of Christianity, are, however, of rare occurrence.

A third accomplishment was the art of running upon *Skees* or Snow-shoes (*Skieloben, Skidfæri*). This was of great antiquity amongst the Norwegians, and still greater amongst the Finns. The *Skees* are long flat pieces of wood, sometimes six feet in length, by means of which, and aided by a long pole held in both hands, a person expert in the use of them will pass over the deepest snow with great rapidity. It was one of the accomplishments on which warriors prided themselves the most. Einar Tambeskielvar, mentioned in the Saga concerning Endrid, Harald Hardraade, and Harald Blaatand, kings of Denmark and Norway, were celebrated for their skill in this exercise. It is still a common amusement in winter in Drontheim, and with them the Finns and Lapps

Swan, the Cross; the milky-way, the winter-road; and the dog-star, *Loka-brenna,* or Loke's burning. They had also stars called the wolf, the eagle, and the raven; and when Thor slew Thrym, he cast his eyes up to heaven, where they became stars, or, according to another passage, it was Odin who placed them there to console Skada.

Another accomplishment to which great importance was attached, was the art of cutting Runes. The old northern word *Run* (plural *Runar*) originally signified a word or discourse, more particularly in secret; and, on the introduction of writing, was naturally enough applied to those mysterious characters which could convey secretly, and at any distance, the thoughts of one person to another. Odin was considered as their inventor, and they were supposed to possess supernatural powers in the hands of those who had the secret of arranging them. In a little poem, called the Runic Chapter, or the magic of Odin, which forms a portion of the Edda, the father of the gods boasts, at length, of the wonders he could perform with their aid; such for example, as to render harmless the weapons of an enemy, to still the raging of the storm, to arrest sorcerers in their flight through the air, to gain the love of women, to restore the dead to life, &c. Runes cut on the rim of a drinking-horn, and sprinkled with blood from the hands, were considered a preservative against poison in the liquor. Great caution, however, was to be observed in the employment of them. A lover,

The weather turned out as Sigurd had predicted, and although the morning was thick and dark, he told at once the hour. Olaf bade Dag tell him from his appearance what was his constitutional weakness. After some hesitation, Dag said that the king was fond of women, and Olaf acknowledged that he was right. At Dag's suggestion the stolen cattle were sought for in the house of the bailiff himself, and there found, and Biorn was dismissed from his office."

It will not be here out of place, before quitting the subject entirely, to speak shortly of the favourite pursuits and amusements of these Northern warriors, so often alluded to in the Sagas.

It has been shewn that a particular constellation was consecrated to each of the twelve principal deities, and that the Scandinavians had their solar houses answering to the signs of the Greek zodiac. The frequent maritime expeditions of their chiefs, in fact, rendered a knowledge of the stars absolutely necessary; and this knowledge led naturally to a belief in astrology; a superstition from which scarcely any nation has been entirely exempt, and which has often enchained even the strongest minds. The Finlapps, to this day, are in the habit of predicting the fate of a new-born child from the position of the stars. Meteors, or shooting-stars, were supposed to be the horses of the Valkyrs; Ursa Major, they called the Great Dog; Ursa Minor, Charles' Wain; the three stars in Orion's belt, Freya's distaff; the

APPENDIX.

They believed also in the existence of tutelar divinities, whom they called Fylgiur or following spirits. These Fylgiur were always of the female sex, for the most part friendly, but sometimes hostile. Thus in the Volsunga Saga, Sigmund's Fylgia guided and defended him, until Odin himself deprived him of victory, whilst in another place one warrior says to another,

> " The danger is great
> If thy foot stumble
> When thou goest to battle,
> Traitorous nornies
> Encompass thee on each side,
> And will have thee slain."

These Fylgiur were supposed to have the power of assuming the shapes of different animals. Previous to the introduction of Christianity, festivals (Disablot) were held in honour of them. In revenge for the neglect of their accustomed offerings, nine Fylgiur, tutelary spirits, of Thidrand's race, procured his death.[29] Another warrior, Halfred Vandrædakald, after embracing the Christian religion, was overtaken with a dangerous sickness, and being, as he believed, about to die, he was anxious that his Fylgia should not accompany him to the realms of death. She could distinctly be seen following the ship in which he was sailing; her form was that of a comely mai-

---

[29] Olaf Tryggesen's Saga.

den, and she walked over the waves as though they had been dry land. She had a helmet on her head, Halfred gazed at her and said that she was his Fylgia, and addressing her, declared that they were divorced for ever.[30] Upon this she said to Thorold, will you take me? but he refused, and Hallfred the younger said, Maiden, I will take thee.[31]

A confused belief in the transmigration of souls seems also to have prevailed at an early period in the north.[32] In the poem which narrates the deeds of the family of Volsung, we are told that Svava, the daughter of a king, was born again in the person of Siguna, also the daughter of a king. The same is also said of two other distinguished persons, Helge and Sigruna. The following story relating to this subject is told in the Heimskringla Saga, at the time when St. Olaf's mother, Asta, the wife of Harald Grenske, king of a province in Norway, was in labour of him and could not come to the birth, a man came suddenly to the court with some jewels, of which he gave the following account: King Olaf Geirstade-Alf, a wise and good prince, who had reigned over the same province many years before, and was the direct ancestor of the then king, had appeared to him in a

---

[30] In like manner the Romans believed that every one had a genius or tutelary spirit assigned to him at his birth, males to men, females to women.

[31] Hallf. Vand. Saga.

[32] Quad om Helge Hundingsbane.

dream, and directed him to open the barrow in which his body lay, and having severed from it the head with a sword, to convey the jewels laid up in the barrow to the queen, whose pains would then cease. The jewels were taken into the queen's chamber, who soon after was delivered of a male child, whom they named Olaf, and it was the general belief that the spirit of Geirstade-Alf had passed into the body of the new-born prince, called after him. It happened long after, when he had attained manhood and was King of Norway, that he rode one day by chance near to the barrow of Olaf Geirstade-Alf, attended by one of his court, who said, " Is it true, my lord, that you once lay in this barrow?" " Never," replied the king, " has my spirit inhabited two bodies." " Yet," said the attendant, " it has been reported that you have been heard to say, on passing by this barrow, ' Here were we—here we lived.' " " I have never so said," returned the king, angrily, " and never will I say so." He was very wroth, and rode hastily away.

The old Scandinavians believed that the power of discerning the spirits of deceased men was possessed by certain individuals; they were to be seen, however, only at night, and their presence was sometimes to be detected by a lambent flame, which disappeared when real fire was kindled. These spirits could assume bodies of air, but could not divest themselves of an unearthly paleness. They had the power of defending the treasures buried with them by emitting fire, causing suffocating vapours, &c. To this day the peasants in Norway believe that the spirit of a dying man may be seen at the moment of its departure from the body, in the form of a long narrow white cloud. When a warrior died, his arms, at whatever distance from him, were tinged with blood.

INDEX.

Ægir, the god of the ocean, 23, 54, 170, 237
Agnar, the son of Geirröd, becomes king of Gothland, 32, 34, 44
Alfadur, a name applied to the supreme being, 8, 301 ; an epithet of Odin, 28, 61
Alfheim, the region of the Light Elves, 29, 35, 194 (vide Elves)
Alvis, a Dwarf, 18, 108—111
Andrimner, the cook of the Gods, 64
Aser, an appellation of the Gods, 16, 18, 21
Asgard, the residence of the Aser, 18, 19, 21, 22, 29
Askur, the name of the first man, 17, 18
Asynier, the Goddesses (vide Freya, Frigga, &c.) 22
Audumbla, the mythic cow, which fostered the giant Ymer, 5, 10
Augerbode, the giant-wife of Loke, and mother of Hela, Fenris, and Jormungandur, 24, 78
Aurgelmer, a name given to Ymer by the giants, 15
Baldur, the second son of Odin, the god of the summer sun, 22, 28, 29, 40, 53, 277—294
Bauge, a Giant, 57
Belsta, the wife of Börr, 5, 16
Bergelmer, the sire of the Giants, 6, 102
Berserkir described, 290 note.
Beygver, a Light Elf, follower of Freyr, 239, 251
Beyla, Beygver's wife, 239
Bifrost, the bridge between Earth and Heaven, the rainbow, 23, 113, 189, 215
Bilskirner, Thor's palace, 95
Bodn, one of the vessels of wisdom, 55
Bölwerk, a name assumed by Odin, 57, 58
Börr, the father of Odin, Vile, and Ve, 5, 10
Bragi, the god of poetry and eloquence, 22, 23, 53, 54, 90, 241, 242, 243
Breidablik, the palace of Baldur, answers to the sign of the twins, 29, 39
Brokkur, a Dwarf, 222, 224
Brysing, Freya's necklace, 204, 271
Bure, the father of Börr, 5, 10, 15
Calendar of the Scandinavians, 46 (vide Zodiac)

INDEX.

Day, the son of Night and of Delling (the Dawn), 26
Dain, a Dwarf, or Black Elf, one of the spirits of sleep and dreams, 278
Delling, father of the Day, the Dawn, 26
Diser, the Goddesses; female divinities generally; the guardian spirits of men, 258
Draupner, Odin's magic ring, 70, 234
Durinn, a celebrated Dwarf, 223
Dvalin, a chief of the Dwarfs, 232
Dwarfs, beings sprung from the dead body of the giant Ymer, 25, 221—223, 230
Earth, the mother of Thor, 254
Einheriar, deceased warriors received into Valhalla, 25, 64, 70
Elder, a servant of Ægir, 239, 240
Elivagar, the great chaotic river, 4
Elves, spirits betwixt the Gods and Men, 16, 25, 220
Elves. The world of the Black Elves, the seventh world, 19
Embla, the first woman, 17, 18
Farbaute, a Giant, Loke's father, 77
Fenris, the demon-wolf; Loke's son, 24, 28, 78, 82—87
Fensala, Frigga's palace, 45, 73
Fjalar, a Dwarf who slew the wise Quaser, 55
Fimaseng, a servant of Ægir, 239
Fimbulveter, the great winter to last three years, and to precede the destruction of the universe, 296
Fiorgyn and Fiorgyna, the father and mother of Frigga, 246
Folkvangur, Freya's palace; answering to the sign of the lion, 29, 41, 65
Forn, one of the names of Freya, 204
Forsete, the god of justice; son of Baldur and Nanna, 22, 23, 30, 41, 295
Freki, one of Odin's wolves, 69
Freya, the goddess of fruitfulness, love, and song; the queen of the night; daughter of Njord, 17 note, 23, 29, 36, 41, 65, 202—205
Freyr, the brother of Freya; the god of the sun, 22, 23, 29, 35, 36, 194
Frigga, Odin's wife, 22, 30, 53, 73
Frost Giants, the descendants of Ymer, 5
Fulla, Frigga's confidante and messenger, 33, 73
Gafn, one of the names of Freya, 204
Gangler, Gangraad, names of Odin, 17
Garmer, a demon hound, 299
Gefione, a maiden Goddess, to whom all who died maids repaired after death, 245
Geirröd, a king of Gothland; a Giant in Utgard, 32—34, 43, 105—108

INDEX. 365

Gelar, a Dwarf, 55
Gerda, daughter of the giant Gymer; beloved of Freyr, 195—201
Geri, one of Odin's wolves, 69
Gersime, one of Freya's daughters, 203, 204, 213
Geyruth, a giant, (vide Geirröd)
Giants, the foes of Gods and Men; born before the Gods, 102—105
Gjallar-bridge, the shining bridge over which the spirits of deceased mortals pass to the region of Hela, 293
Gjallar-horn, Heimdall's horn, 215, 298
Gialp, one of Heimdall's nine mothers; a daughter of the giant Geirröd, 107
Gilling, a Giant, 55, 56
Gimle, the highest heaven; the eternal abode of the blest, 19, 20, 29, 299
Ginnunga-gap, the chaotic abyss, 4, 216
Gjallar, a river of Helheim, crossed by the Gjallar-bridge, 293
Gladsheim, the palace of Odin, answers to the sign of the Ram, 29, 38, 63
Gleipnir, the chain with which Fenris was bound, 84, 86
Glitner, the palace of Forsete; answers to the sign of the Virgin, 30, 41
Gna, Frigga's messenger, 73
Godheim, a name for Asgard, 19
Grimner, a name assumed by Odin, 33
Groa, a Vala or Prophetess, 358
Grydur, the wife of Odin, 53
Gudr, a Valkyr, 67, 219
Gulltopp, Heimdall's horse, 215, 291
Gungner, the name of Odin's spear or sword, 70, 225
Gunlöde, or Gunnlaug, daughter of the giant Suttung, deceived by Odin, 56, 58
Gullinborste, Freyr's wild-boar with bristles of gold; the sun, 225, 233
Gymer, a Giant, king of the frozen Ocean, 195
Hæn, one of the names of Freya, 204
Har (the high one), one of Odin's names, 61
Haunner-swinger, a name of Thor, 15
Heidrun, the goat of Valhalla, whose milk is mead, the drink of the Einheriar, 64
Heimdall, the son of nine mothers, one of the twelve Aser; the warder of Valhalla, 22, 23, 29, 40, 175 note, 189, 215, 249, 281
Hela, daughter of Loke; the queen of death, 24, 78, 80, 82, 135
Helheim, the eighth of the nine worlds; the region of death, 19, 80, 81, 135—138

Hermodur, a son of Odin; his messenger, 53, 212, 292—294
Hertha, a goddess worshipped by the ancient Germans, 74
Hilda, one of the chief of the Valkyrs, 68
Himmel-bjeig, the heavenly mount; the palace of Heimdall; answers to the sign of the crab, 29, 40
Hirrokin, a giant woman, 290
Hler or Ægir, the god of the ocean, 237
Hlidskialf, Odin's high seat, from whence he sees over the whole earth, 33, 63, 74
Hlorida, a name of Thor, 254
Hlyn, a Goddess who guarded the favourites of Frigga from impending dangers, 73
Hnos, one of Freya's two daughters, 203, 204, 213
Hödur, a blind Aser; the destroyer of Baldur, 22, 23, 40, 289
Hœner, or Vile, brother of Odin; one of the three creative deities, 17
Hringhaune, Baldur's ship, 290
Hrodung, king of the Goths, 32
Hrsuelgur, the giant eagle; ruler of winter, 27
Hrymfaxe, the horse of night, 26
Huggin, one of Odin's two ravens, 52
Hugo, a Dwarf, 147
Hulda, a celebrated enchantress, 52, 353, 354
Hvergelmer, the lowest pit; the eternal spring, 4, 20, 216
Hymir, a renowned Giant of Utgard; the mountain torrents were his daughters, 170—173, 175—190
Iduna, the wife of Bragi; the guardian of the apples of youth, 23, 88—92, 244, 278
Jafuhar, an epithet of Odin, 61
Jernvidi, an iron forest in Utgard, 106
Jormungandur, the great serpent; son of Asa-Loke, 24, 78, 102, 180—190
Jotunheim, the land of the Giants, 19, 102, 103
Ivalldr, a Dwarf skilled in smith's work; father to Iduna, 90, 224
Kraken of Norway described, 177 note.
Lessöe, the residence of Hler or Ægir; the ruler of the ocean, 237
Landvide, the palace of Vidar; answers to the sign of the scorpion, 30, 42
Laufeya, Loke's mother, 77
Leradur, a tree in Valhalla, 64
Light Elves, spirits inhabiting Gimle, the region of light; followers of the sun-god Freyr, 19
Liosberi, the light-bringer, the third month in the Scandinavian year, 36, 37
Litur, a Dwarf slain by Thor, 292

INDEX. 367

Lif and Livthraser, the only human pair who survive the destruction of the world at Ragnarokkur, 301
Lofna, one of Freya's four handmaidens, whose province it was to bring together true lovers, 213, 214
Loge, the Giant of fire, 145
Loke (Utgard's), the king of Utgard and of darkness, and chief of the Giants and Evil Spirits, 24, 71, 112, 141
Loke (Asa), a kinsman of Utgard's Loke, being descended from the Giants, but an associate of the Aser, 22, 24, 71—73, 76—79, 86—93, 224—236, 240-295
Lopta or Loptur, a name of Asa-Loke, 77 [vide Loke (Asa)]
Lora, a daughter of Thor, 96
Maane, the moon; son of Mundilfaxe, 26
Maelström of Norway described, 180 note.
Magne, a son of Thor by a giant woman, 96, 300
Mannheim (see Midgard), 19
Marthaul, one of the names of Freya, 240
Meigingardur, Thor's belt, 95
Midgard, the fifth of the nine worlds; the abode of man, 17, 19, 71
Midgard's worm, 79 (see Jormungandur)
Mimer, a Giant who possessed a well in which wisdom was hidden, 104
Mist, a Valkyr, 68, 210 note.
Miölner, Thor's hammer, 94, 225, 226, 300; its loss, 186, 189, 190; its recovery, 257—276
Mode, a son of Thor; brother to Magne, 96, 300
Modgudur, the maiden who kept the gate of the bridge of death, 293
Modsognur, the chief of the Dwarfs, 223
Mummin, the second of Odin's two ravens, 52
Mundilfaxe, the father of the sun and moon, 26
Muspel, the second of the nine worlds, 4, 5, 19
Muspell's sons, spirits of fire, who under the command of Surtur destroy the world at Ragnarokkur, 298
Nagelfare, the ship in which the sons of Surtur embark to destroy the world ; the first husband of night, 297
Nanna, the wife of Baldur, 291
Nar, or Narfe, one of Loke's sons, 24, 78, 294
Nastrond, the place of punishment for evil men after the destruction of the world, 29, 300
Nifl-heim, the region of shadows; the ninth and lowest of the nine worlds, 19, 20
Night, daughter of the Giant Nörve, 26
Njord, one of the twelve Aser; the father of Freyr and Freya; the god of inland waters, and protector of sea-faring men, 22, 30, 35, 42, 191

Noatun, the palace of Njord; answers to the sign of the scales, 30, 36, 42, 191

Nornies, the three Goddesses of Fate who watch over Yggdrasill, the tree of the universe, 26; female subordinate deities who preside at the birth of mortals, 217—220

Nörve, a Giant, the father of night, 26

Nydhoggur, the serpent king who continually gnaws at the root of the Ash, Yggdrasill, 216, 302

Odin, the ruler and supreme god of Asgard, 16, 17, 28, 29, 32, 47—76, 107, 280

Odrær, the vessel in which the liquor was kept, a draught of which conferred wisdom and the gift of poetry, 55, 219

Oddur, Freya's husband, 204

Poetry; a Scandinavian story of the origin of poetry, 54—59

Quaser, a man of great wisdom, slain by Dwarfs, who made from his blood the celebrated liquor of poetry, 54

Ragnarokur, the twilight of the Gods; the period of the destruction of the universe, 20, 22, 28, 296

Ran, the wife of Ægir, 23, 120, 237

Ratatöskur, the squirrel on Yggdrasill, 218

Rinde, the wife of Odin and mother of Vale, 36, 53

Rist, a Valkyr, 68, 210 note.

Roska, a maiden follower of Thor, 117, 119

Rota, a Valkyr, 67, 219

Saga, the Goddess of history, 29, 37

Sehrimner, the boar which served the Einheriar for their nightly supper, 64

Seming, son of Odin and Skada, 53, 193

Sif, Thor's wife, 93, 99—101

Signi, Loke's wife, 24, 78, 294

Sin, one of Freya's four handmaidens, her door-keeper, 214

Sindri, a Dwarf skilled in smith's work, 224, 233

Siofna, one of Freya's four maidens, who causes first love, 203, 213

Skada, daughter of the Giant Thiasse; married to Njord, 23, 29, 33, 192; the wife of Odin, 53

Skinfaxe, the horse of day, 26

Skirner, Freyr's armour bearer and messenger, 84, 195

Skrymner, a name assumed by Utgard's Loke, 123

Skulda, the future; one of the three great Nornies, 26, 67, 217, 219

Skidbladner, Freyr's ship, made by the Dwarfs, 224

Sleipner, Odin's horse, the noblest of his race, 70—73

Soel, the Goddess who rules the sun, 26, 126

Soequabeck, the palace of Saga; answers to the sign of the fishes, 29, 37

Son, one of the vessels of wisdom, 55

INDEX. 369

Svadilfare, a demon-stallion, 72
Svosodur, the lord of summer, 27
Surtur, the ruler of Muspelheim, 28, 298
Suttung, a Giant from whom Odin stole the liquor of poetry, 58 —61
Syr, one of the names of Freya, 204
Tialf, a follower of Odin, 117, 118, 147, 162, 166
Thiasse, a Giant slain by Thor, 23, 39, 90—92
Thök, a giant woman, who would not weep at Baldur's death, 294
Thor, the son of Odin and Hlodgna or the earth; the God of thunder; the defender of Asgard and terror of the Giants, 22, 30, 94, 97—99, 101, 105; his visit to Geyruth, 105—108; his adventure with Alvis, 108—111; his journey to Giantland, 112—169; his visits to Hymir, 170—190; his recovery of Miölner, 257—276
Thrain, a Dwarf consulted by Odin, 278
Thridi, an epithet of Odin, 61
Thror, a Dwarf; a surname of Odin, 233
Thrude, the daughter of Thor and Sif; a Valkyr, 95, 96
Thrudheim, Thor's kingdom; the atmosphere, 30, 35, 95
Thrym, a Giant who stole Thor's hammer whilst he was asleep, 259, 274
Thrymheim, the palace of Skada; answering to the sign of the bull, 29, 38
Thurser, a species of Giants or Evil Spirits, 109
Trolds, a general designation for all Evil Spirits, 257
Tyr, one of the twelve Aser; the son of Odin, but descended by his mother from the Giants, 23, 53, 85
Utgard, the outermost circle of rocks surrounding the earth; the residence of the Giants, 18, 114, 139—141, 144—158
Utgard's-Loke, see Loke.
Uller, the God of warriors and of the chase, 22, 29, 35, 101
Ulvrune, the first of Heimdall's nine mothers, 281
Urda, the first of the three great Nornies; the past, 7, 26, 37, 217, 219
Urda's well, 26, 38, 216
Vafthrudner, a Giant whom Odin seeks on account of his wisdom, 18, 181
Vala, generally a Prophetess, 189, 353
Valaskialf, the palace of Vale; answering to the sign Aquarius, 29, 36, 37, 63
Vale, an Aser; son of Odin and Rinde, 29, 36, 37, 53, 295
Valfader, the sire of the slain; a title of Odin, 62
Valhalla, the palace of Odin, the Aser, and Einheriar, 38, 63, 65
Vali, a son of Loke and Signi, 78, 294

INDEX.

Valkyrs, female messengers of Odin, whose province it was to select those who were to be slain in battle, and to serve them at table in Valhalla, 25, 65, 66

Vanadis, a name of Freya, 204

Vanaheim, the abode of the Vaner; the fourth of the nine worlds, 19, 191

Vaner, the Gods of the atmosphere (see Njord, Freyr, &c.), 16, 22, 54, 191; poem of the Vaner, 205—213

Var, one of Freya's four attendants, who takes account of the vows of lovers, 214

Vé, one of Börr's three sons; brother of Odin and Vile, 5, 10, 16, 17

Vedurfolgner, the name of a hawk, 218

Vegtam, an epithet of Odin; the Wanderer, 53

Veor, Thor's name amongst the Giants, 171

Verdandi, the second of the three great Nornies; the present, 26, 217, 219

Vidar, son of Odin and Grydur; an Aser, 22, 23, 30, 42, 299

Vigrid, the name of the place on which the last battle between the Giants and the Aser is to be fought, 298

Vile, son of Börr (see Ve), 5, 10, 16, 17

Vingolf, the place of assemblage for the Goddesses in like manner as Valhalla for the Gods, 45

Winter, the giant of, 27

Wolves; the superstition of men-wolves, 82 note.

Ydale, the palace of Uller, answers to the sign of the archer, 29, 35

Yggdrasill, the tree of the universe; the great Ash, 25, 78, 216 —218, 299

Ygg, the terrible; a title of Odin, 43

Ymer, the first of all beings; the chaotic Giant, 5, 9, 15, 25

Yvaldr, a Dwarf (see Ivalldr).

Zodiac of the Scandinavians, 29—31, 35—46

FINIS.

C. Whittingham, Tooks Court, Chancery Lane.

MYTHOLOGY

An Arno Press Collection

Constant [de Rebecque, Henri] Benjamin. **DU POLYTHÉISME ROMAIN.** 1833

Creuzer, Georg Friedrich. **SYMBOLIK UND MYTHOLOGIE DER ALTEN VÖLKER BESONDERS DER GRIECHEN.** Six vols. 1819-1823

David-Neel, Alexandra and The Lama Yongden. **THE SUPERHUMAN LIFE OF GESAR OF LING.** 1934

Dumézil, Georges. **DÉESSES LATINES ET MYTHES VÉDIQUES.** 1956

Dumézil, Georges. **HORACE ET LES CURIACES.** 1942

Ehrenreich, Paul. **DIE ALLGEMEINE MYTHOLOGIE UND IHRE ETHNOLOGISCHEN GRUNDLAGEN** *and* **DIE SONNE IM MYTHOS.** Two vols. in one. 1910/1915

Görres, Joseph. **MYTHENGESCHICHTE DER ASIATISCHEN WELT.** 1810

Gubernatis, Angelo de. **LA MYTHOLOGIE DES PLANTES.** Two vols. in one. 1878-1882

Gubernatis, Angelo de. **ZOOLOGICAL MYTHOLOGY OR THE LEGENDS OF ANIMALS.** Two vols. in one. 1872

Jensen, Adolf [E.] **HAINUWELE.** 1939

Jensen, Adolf E., ed. **MYTH, MENSCH UND UMWELT.** 1950

Krappe, Alexandre Haggerty. **MYTHOLOGIE UNIVERSELLE.** 1930

Langer, Fritz. **INTELLEKTUALMYTHOLOGIE.** 1916

Leenhardt, Maurice. **DO KAMO.** 1971

Lessmann, Heinrich. **AUFGABEN UND ZIELE DER VERGLEICHENDEN MYTHENFORSCHUNG.** 1908

Liebert, Arthur. **MYTHUS UND KULTUR.** 1925

Lipps, G[ottlob] F[riedrich]. **MYTHENBILDUNG UND ERKENNTNIS.** 1907

Mannhardt, Wilhelm. **MYTHOLOGISCHE FORSCHUNGEN AUS DEM NACHLASSE** *and* **DIE KORNDÄMONEN.** Two vols. in one. 1884/1868

Meyer, Richard M. **ALTGERMANISCHE RELIGIONSGESCHICHTE.** 1910

Müller, [Karl Otfried]. **INTRODUCTION TO A SCIENTIFIC SYSTEM OF MYTHOLOGY.** 1844

Müller, F[riedrich] Max. **INTRODUCTION TO THE SCIENCE OF RELIGION.** 1873

Mus, Paul. **BARABUDUR.** Two vols. in one. 1935

Nestle, Wilhelm. **VOM MYTHOS ZUM LOGOS.** 1942

Oppert, Gustav. **ON THE ORIGINAL INHABITANTS OF BHARATAVARSA OR INDIA.** 1893

Otto, Walter F. **GESETZ URBILD UND MYTHOS.** 1951

Otto, Walter F. **THE HOMERIC GODS.** 1954

Pettazzoni, Raffaele. **THE ALL-KNOWING GOD.** 1956

Pettazzoni, Raffaele, ed. **MITI E LEGGENDE.** Four vols. in two. 1948-1959

Pigott, Grenville. **A MANUAL OF SCANDINAVIAN MYTHOLOGY.** 1839

Preller, L[udwig]. **GRIECHISCHE MYTHOLOGIE.** 1894

Preller, [Ludwig]. **RÖMISCHE MYTHOLOGIE.** 1865

READINGS IN MYTHOLOGY. 1978

Siecke, Ernst. **DRACHENKÄMPFE** *and* **MYTHUS, SAGE, MÄRCHEN IN IHREN BEZIEHUNGEN ZUR GEGENWART.** Two vols. in one. 1906/1907

Vignoli, Tito. **MYTH AND SCIENCE.** 1882

de Vries, Jan. **HEROIC SONG AND HEROIC LEGEND.** 1963

STUDIES OF A. J. WENSINCK. 1978

Wirz, P[aul]. **DIE MARIND-ANIM VON HOLLÄNDISCH SÜD-NEU-GUINEA.** Two vols. in one. 1922

Zeitlin, Ida. **GESSAR KHAN.** 1927

Ziegler, Leopold. **GESTALTWANDEL DER GÖTTER.** 1920

Kirtley Library
Columbia College
Columbia, Missouri 65216